OTHER BOOKS BY BEBE MOORE CAMPBELL

Sweet Summer, Growing Up With and Without My Dad

Your Blues Ain't Like Mine

Brothers and Sisters

Singing in the Comeback Choir

What You Owe Me

Sometimes My Mommy Gets Angry

72 HOUR HOLD

72 HOUR HOLD

A NOVEL BY

Bebe Moore Campbell

Alfred A. Knopf   New York   2005

THIS IS A BORZOI BOOK
PUBLISHED BY ALFRED A. KNOPF

www.aaknopf.com

Library of Congress Cataloging-in-Publication Data
Campbell, Bebe Moore, [date].
72 hour hold : a novel / by Bebe Moore Campbell.— 1st ed.
p.   cm.
ISBN 1-4000-4074-4
1. Mothers and daughters—Fiction.   2. Manic-depressive
persons—Fiction.   I. Title.

PS3553.A4395A613 2005
813'.54—dc22   2004057620

Manufactured in the United States of America
First Edition

To Nancy, Lynn, JoHelen, Bunny, Linda,
Judy, and mamacita Rosina.
Y'all some baaad sistuhs.
To Sharon Dunas for showing us the way.
And to all the members of NAMI–Inglewood:
Be blessed.

Ring the bells that still can ring.
Forget your perfect offering.
There is a crack in everything.
That's how the light gets in.

—Leonard Cohen, *Anthem*

72 HOUR HOLD

I

RIGHT BEFORE THE DEVASTATION, I HAD A GOOD DAY. GOD should have pulled my coattail then and there: "Enjoy this while you can, honey, because Satan beat me in a poker game last night, and he's claiming you and yours sometime soon." After all the praying and tithing I've done, I deserved a heads-up. Damn. Whatever happened to sending a sign? Lean cow, fat cow. Burning bush. Dove with an olive branch. Yoo-hoo! Something.

It was probably better that the events evolved with no foreshadowing. Preparation wasn't possible. And what difference would it have made anyhow? Knowing that the hounds are tracking you doesn't mean you won't get caught; it means you have to get to the swamp fast.

So there I was, clueless: lolling in the bed, stretching my legs and my toes—which needed a pedicure—ticking off a list of things to do in my head, I began to wake up. It was the second Saturday in April. Sunshine was making its way through a thick haze. Rising up, I stared out of my bedroom window, squinting a bit as I tried to discern the LA skyline, framed neatly between the two huge palm trees in my backyard. Thick pea soup almost obliterated the view, but I didn't look away until I sighted those buildings. Once I knew the city had survived the night, my shoulders came down. Anything can happen at any time in an earth-quake zone, and I've learned to take nothing for granted. I've gone to bed some evenings only to awaken at dawn to broken windows and cracked dishes. That the Bank of America and Wells Fargo headquarters hadn't been shaken and dashed into oblivion during the night meant I had survived as well. I'm always grateful for a morning with no tremors, no frantic dogs barking.

Trina was beside me, not a heartbeat away, her hip pressed into my thigh. She felt warm against me, the pressure of her body weight com-forting. The day after her eighteenth birthday, when most girls were declaring their independence, my daughter was still creeping into my bed. Even when she hated me, she wanted to be close. She was still fresh from last night's bath and smelled like Dove and that pale yellow lotion in the big plastic bottle. That staple of American vanities and kitchen counters promises to banish dry skin forever but can't even begin to han-dle seriously crusty feet. My grandmother's feet at the end of February would have had that lotion begging for mercy. But then, when you grow up plowing Georgia clay barefoot in the hard times, nothing on or in you remains soft. For Trina's smooth, buttery skin, that watery lotion worked just fine. The toes pressed against my calves were just as supple as the rest of her and just as lovely. Gazing at my sleeping daughter, I could take her in without annoying her. Such a pretty child, I thought. There wasn't a blemish on her honey-colored face. When she was a lit-tle girl, I was lulled by the well-wishing smiles of strangers who were bewitched by the dazzling enormity of her round eyes and endless smile, her marble-sized dimples and naturally sandy hair. Trina seemed to take the attention in stride, but it inflated me. My gingerbread-brown face was symmetrical, with two eyes placed where eyes should be, lips that weren't full or thin, a nose that would keep me alive, hair that was thick and strong but otherwise unremarkable. Nobody turned to stare at me when I walked down the street, not the way they did with Trina. I used to think of her beauty as an insurance policy that would guarantee her a perfect life. A lot of people who aren't beautiful think this way.

It was six o'clock, and I had a standing appointment with the tread-mill and some free weights. Trina stirred, then turned over and stared at me.

"Hey, grown woman," I said, teasing.

"My back hurts," she said, her voice still tinged with sleepiness. She yawned and arched her body, then settled herself beneath the covers.

This was a setup, and we both knew it. "Well, you should get on the floor and do those exercises I showed you. That will get the kinks out."

"Aww, Mommeee!" she wailed, fully awake.

"Aw, Mommy, what?"

"Can't you rub it just a little bit?"

I felt a twinge of annoyance. She knew I worked out every morning. "Turn over."

Her motion was languid, a movement befitting the idle rich.

I leaned over my daughter and began kneading her back and shoulders. There were no knots of tension anywhere. She became limp beneath my fingers. In a few minutes she was asleep again.

Downstairs in my kitchen, I stopped to get a bottle of water before going into the small gym located next to the garage. Thirty minutes on the treadmill at five miles per hour, followed by fifteen minutes of lifting free weights, then about twenty minutes of floor exercises—that was my routine. I've always been into fitness. I opened the windows, turned on loud salsa music, and began my workout. By the time I had finished running in place, my forehead was dripping and my clothes were damp. I reached for the free weights, lifting and lowering, extending and holding, until my biceps were ready to secede from the rest of my body. I forced myself to do two hundred sit-ups and fifty leg thrusts, panting and sweating like a beagle on crack. Forty push-ups to go. I counted from one to ten, then ten to one, then twenty to one. Shrink the challenge—my way of psyching myself out. All my muscles seemed to be bursting when I finally began stretching. Time for euphoria. I did it!

"Let's go somewhere, Mommee," Trina said when I returned to the bedroom. She hadn't moved from the spot where I'd left her.

"Like where?"

Trina paused for a moment, considering her options, confident—now that the morning had begun with her first request being granted—that her every bidding would be honored. "Let's go downtown and get some flowers."

Her voice was childlike, with a smooth, unperturbed lilt, a tone that made her sound so vulnerable. This eight-year-old voice gave me reason to pause, to ponder. She hadn't sounded like that in a long time.

Trina was incapable of moving fast in the morning. If prodded, she turned first irritable and then insufferable. I, on the other hand, dressed quickly. But then my uniform for Saturdays was easy: sweats and sneakers, no makeup, no hairdo, totally unlike my fashion-plate weekday attire. I glanced in the mirror in my bathroom; my mother stared back at me. Impossible to escape her: same eyes, same mouth and smile, same cheekbones. I closed my eyes and untied the silk scarf that held my short bob in place. Two strokes of the comb, a few little flips with my fingers, and I was done.

From the kitchen I could hear Trina thumping around inside her room, opening and slamming drawers. She was her own personal tornado; the mess she'd leave behind her when she finally descended would be a viable submission for a Guinness record. She had on both the television and the radio. Hoping she wouldn't take forever, I made breakfast, cleaning up and putting things away as I cooked. The birthday cake I'd baked was still on the counter, the eighteen candles intact. The stove, floor, and sink were spotless. If I couldn't control my child, at least I was in charge of my kitchen.

When she was finally dressed, Trina bounded down the stairs like an exuberant puppy. "You fixed breakfast. Yummy."

There it was again, the baby voice.

I made breakfast most days, not that I'm such a little Betty Crocker but because Trina had to eat well. We sat at the kitchen table and gobbled up the nonfat bran muffins, scrambled eggs, and oatmeal I'd prepared. I poured hot coffee for me and orange juice for Trina. Taking the plates to the sink to scrape them, I could see Trina from the corner of my eye, stealing a sip from my cup. My shoulders tightened, inched upward. Trina wasn't supposed to have caffeine. But then she reached for the small bottle of pink pills that was between the salt and pepper shakers. She shook out one, placed it carefully in her mouth, and swallowed it with the hot liquid. For the last three or four months I hadn't had to remind her. She took another sip of coffee and then several more. Maybe she was having trouble swallowing the pill.

"You don't have to keep staring at me," she said, when I sat back down.

"I can't look at my own gorgeous child?" I always tried to stop myself from watching Trina, or at least being caught at it.

"I know what I have to do. I want to go to school in September."

"I'm not worried, sweetie."

Some days that was true.

CRENSHAW BOULEVARD WAS JUST BEGINNING TO OPEN ITS eyes as we made our way down from the hills of View Park, the quiet neighborhood that looms above the usually bustling business district. It was just after eight o'clock and the mall was still closed, of course, as were most of the stores that lined the street. But the small army of hucksters whose domain was the block just north of Slauson Boulevard had already queued up.

Their wares were arranged neatly on tables near the backs of their vans or on portable shelves that were as close to the oncoming traffic as was legally possible. Or illegally possible. CDs, tapes, African garb, a few food items, some household products, and clothing were for sale, as well as the occasional bootlegged video. "Pssst. Got that new Chris Rock, right here. Gimme five." The most colorful items were the T-shirts and caps hanging from the chain-link fence that surrounded a vacant lot and served as a backdrop for the makeshift outdoor mall. There were no hordes walking along Crenshaw. Customers had to be hunted, then captured. Several salesmen waded into traffic, vigorously waving their goods.

I beeped my horn as I passed Fish Man, a portly gentleman who sold fresh salmon from the back of a white van at prices that were far lower than at the grocery store. A few feet away Mr. Bean Pie, representing the capitalistic interests of the Nation of Islam, clad in the requisite suit and bow tie, hawked newspapers and mouth-watering pies created from the lowly navy bean to drivers stopped at the red light. Beyond the bakery section, young men were approaching idling cars, holding up T-shirts, caps, and all manner of Lakers regalia, not to mention American flags in every size, for every conceivable place. I whizzed by them. I had a flag sticking in my lawn and one on my car and no longer braked for Old Glory.

The last enterprise zone belonged to Crenshaw's most ubiquitous sales force: the Incense People. Later in the day they would prop themselves in front of Laundromats and beauty parlors, slouch against the exterior walls of Krispy Kreme Doughnuts, Rite Aid, and Savon Drugs, waving their wares and chanting "Buy some incense" to anyone who ventured close enough to be considered a possible sale. Based on the sheer size of the IP workforce, it was a wonder that a mushroom cloud wasn't hovering over South Central at all times. Either we were the dope-smokingest folks in the city or we were meditating around the clock. Maybe both. Several young men were eyeing my car, their fists dangling the telltale plastic bags, but fortunately the light was green. Among the legions of hucksters, the IP were the risk takers and had been known to jump in front of moving vehicles, defying death and dismemberment for the sale of a one-dollar bag.

Half a block away, Crazy Man was standing near one of the IP. Some of my neighbors referred to him that way, and even though I, of all people, should have known better, I did too. Mumbling to the air around him, he appeared to have schizophrenia but seemed harmless. According to some neighbors, he had been normal until he came back from Vietnam. Others swore his troubles began during high school. Crazy Man trekked in and around the community all day long, returning at night to his mother's house. His hair was a matted clump that hadn't seen shampoo, comb, brush, or scissors in a decade. He was clad in ancient dirty pants and a ragged shirt. His feet were bare and filthy. It would take heavy-duty equipment to get him clean. That and a crew. If mania and hallucinations, delusions, and paranoia have an odor, then that's what was rising out of his pores. Maybe pain, loss, and fury too.

The light ahead of me flashed yellow, and I sped up to get across the street. Just as I pressed down on the gas, I heard "Trina! Keri!"—a loud, exuberant yell. Trina turned around, and I glanced in the rearview mirror. A teenage boy in the car next to us was waving and shouting.

"Mom, that's PJ. Yo, PJ, whazzup?" Trina screamed out the window. I waved. My ex-boyfriend's son was one of my favorite people, and I hadn't seen him in the months since I'd broken up with his dad.

"Thanks for the cash!" he yelled as his car sped away. When I caught a glimpse of him, he wasn't smiling. Sometimes he looked so sad to me.

"You're welcome!" I hollered back, then chuckled. Only two weeks earlier I'd stuck three twenties into a birthday card and mailed it to him.

I craned my neck to get a better look at PJ, and at that moment Crazy Man stepped off the sidewalk against the light, directly in my path. There was no time to stop. To my right was an SUV; a man was driving and there were children in the back. Another man stood on the median, holding a bag of incense in his hand. If I braked and then aimed toward the median, maybe the concrete riser would slow me down enough for him to get out of the way. It was my only option.

When my front tires hit the concrete, the huckster jumped back and his incense went flying into the air, along with some handpicked words for me. I froze momentarily, grateful that the move I'd executed had been successful, then caught my breath, put the car in reverse, and backed up into my lane. Around me horns blared as I put my car in drive and continued forward, feeling a surge of rage as I passed Crazy Man. His face was placid as he stared vacantly straight ahead, seemingly unaware that he'd ever been in any danger.

"What's up with that stupid fool?" Trina asked.

"Not thinking, I guess."

"Dag." She brightened. "Did you see PJ?" She started laughing. "He was trying to look all hard and everything. He has a mustache." She giggled again.

"Does he really?" I always thought of PJ as *my* little boy, which of course he wasn't.

Trina and I had been going to the flower district since we first moved to LA from Atlanta, nearly ten years earlier. Located downtown, only blocks away from the huge aquamarine convention center and the massive Staples Center, home court of the Los Angeles Lakers, the flower mart was part of a larger area that housed the city's garment, jewelry, and fabric districts. In cramped, airless buildings, immigrant women who couldn't say *union* in English bent over sewing machines, stitching the bodices of prom gowns and swimsuits. Koreans mostly sold not-so-well-known brands and designer knockoffs. Israeli wholesale jewelers played dialing for diamonds. And Iranian merchants offered fine silks, woolens, and blends for less than a third of the price of the city's retail fabric shops. It was Seoul meets Tel Aviv meets Tehran as borders blended.

The flowers were the province of the Latinos, and there was as much Spanish as English, not to mention Spanglish, in the air as Trina and I meandered from florist to florist. Sellers were set up in adjacent stalls under one gigantic roof. Prices and quality varied, and years of experience, as well as my southern-girl origins, had taught me that it paid to compare. Trina, on the other hand, was not the child of a grandmother who'd survived the Depression and had instilled in her the belief that frugality and deferred gratification were the only entrance fees for Baptist heaven. I had indulged my daughter when she was a child. I hadn't *overindulged* her, but I had wanted her to grow up feeling as entitled to lessons and trips as the white kids at her private schools. That Saturday morning, her sense of entitlement was in full display; she stopped at each flower stall and said, "Mommee, let's get some of these," with no regard for cost.

That baby voice again. My daughter acted more like a preadolescent than someone now legally entitled to do whatever she wanted without my permission. Watching her drift from flower to flower, I had the feeling that she would be a child for a while longer.

The birds-of-paradise caught my eye. They were huge and bright, and even though the same flowers dotted many of the lawns in my neighborhood, they didn't grow on mine. "How much?" I asked a stocky man who had just wrapped up flowers for another customer.

"They very beautiful now."

"Yes, they are. How much? *¿Cuanto cuesto?*"

As he added up numbers in his head, a young white couple behind me chatted animatedly. I heard the words *screenplay, producer,* and *green light* and turned to see the requisite bony blond girl and her handsome, scruffy boyfriend. They weren't much older than Trina. In Los Angeles, Hollywood hopefuls are as ubiquitous as the lattes grandes they slurp. There is no escaping their driving ambition. Irritation swept over me. Just looking at them, I wanted to slap both those faces, to knock away the self-assurance that was etched there. They were bubbling over with enthusiasm and confidence, so sure they were on their way. I didn't want their oh-so-important moneymaking dreams to come true. The last thing on this earth I wanted to see was more of their images on screen, more of them kissing, having fun, being dramatic, or saving the day. I gave them a surly glance, but they didn't even notice.

The florist whispered the amount. I countered. The seller narrowed his eyes, scrunched up his mouth, did the math in his head. It didn't matter to me that no one else seemed to bargain at the flower mart. I was a charter member of the Let's Make a Deal club. The man glanced from side to side to make sure no one heard, then nodded.

"Wrap them up," I told him. "Aren't they pretty?" I said, turning to Trina.

She was gone.

For months, Trina had been my constant shadow. If she wasn't with me, I knew exactly where to find her. Not seeing her evoked the same kind of adrenaline-fueled alarm I had experienced when she was four and broke away from me in the grocery store. *Ohmygodohmygodohmygod.*

Within ten minutes I had raced through the entire building, including the restroom, and that was when the bubble of panic that was welling up inside me began to burst. I wanted to go find a loudspeaker, get on it, and plead for my daughter's safe return. I combed through the place once more. All I could hear was the awful hammering in my chest. *She'sgone-she'sgone-she'sgone.*

"Keri?"

It took me a moment to focus, make the transition. "Marie. How are you?"

Kiss, kiss, hug, hug. Her spicy fragrance rubbed off. My eyes not meeting hers, my eyes looking up the street, down the street, peering into corners.

"Girl, where have you been?"

"Oh, hey. Just busy."

"I guess so. Brooke and Nichelle and I were out last night, and we got to talking about you. Nobody's seen you in so long. You just dumped us."

Brooke and Nichelle. Brooke and Nichelle. I couldn't make their faces appear inside the fog that was my mind. "Oh, no. Just busy at the shop."

"So we'll have to buy some more clothes if we want to see you. Well, it's overdue. I still get compliments on that green suit I got from you."

"The Armani. That was a really nice deal, and you looked great in it. Just got a new shipment. Lots of fabulous stuff in your size. Eight, right? You know, I have shoes now. Everything you want for a fraction. What are you, a seven? I have some *bad* Todd Oldhams, black suede, pointed toe. Fabulous. Five hundred dollars new. My price is seventy-five bucks. Worn maybe three times. They'll go with everything. You want me to hold them for you?"

I could sell in my sleep. I could sell and be going crazy at the same time.

"I'll come and see you," Marie said. I knew she would.

Nodding, smiling, I looked past her, around her. My eyes were on the sidewalk, the corner, the entrance to all the florists' shops up and down the block.

"How is Miss Trina? Is she loving Brown?"

"She decided to wait a year before starting. You know these kids, right?" The words came fast; there was no eye contact. Please, go away. But she wouldn't.

"Oh." Marie grew quiet for a moment. "Such a brilliant girl. Brett says she hasn't seen her in a while. They used to be so close. Brett is loving Howard. She's pledging AKA."

"That's—oh, that's really . . ." What was stabbing me in my chest? Where was that pain coming from? ". . . great." Great that your kid is succeeding in college and my kid is lost. I didn't want to feel the cold trickle of envy spilling down my spine, the steady drip of acidic resentment searing my bones. Brett had called me Mama Keri; she used to spend the night with Trina. When they were young girls I confused the sound of their laughter. Please, don't let me stand here resenting her and her smiling mother.

"Listen," I said, craning my neck, still looking, "I have to get going."

"Well, let's hook up sometime."

"Okay."

"Maybe we could go out to dinner or something this month." She pulled out her date book. "Wednesday, the twenty-sixth, around seven. That work for you?"

"I think that's good. Sure. I'd better go."

"Call me."

"I will."

"Okay, I'm going to call Nichelle and Brooke. Let's make this happen. And I'll come by for the shoes tomorrow. Put them away for me."

"I will," I said.

Outside the sun was glaring. I shielded my eyes with my hands as I trudged up and down the block. Hysteria was gripping me by the throat by the time I stopped to stare. Trina was at the end of the street, talking animatedly to a tall, dirty man who appeared to be part of the legions of the homeless who congregated not far from the commercial area. Leave it to LA to position the unwashed and addicted right next door to the flowers, as if the city planners were seeking some kind of humanistic and botanical symmetry.

"Trina!" I raced to the corner, my heart banging against my chest.

"See you later," she said to the man, and shoved her hand inside her pocket. It was a movement that didn't register until later, when every detail mattered.

"You shouldn't disappear like that," I said quietly, as we returned to the store. "I was worried."

"You don't have to worry anymore."

"What were you and that man talking about?"

She smiled. "Oh, nothing."

We strolled around the corner and looked at tulips and roses, then crossed the street to another small shop and purchased half a dozen sunflowers and two bunches of gladioli. Walking back to the car I glanced at my watch, then quickened my pace.

"I have to go to the shop," I told Trina.

Resale clothing stores are big in LA. I owned one of a handful of shops that offered designer resale exclusively. In the entertainment capital of the world, the hook was elementary: All you had to do was imply that some star had worn this or that, and the ladies who lunched were dying to buy it. I never identified the original owner by name; that was against the rules. But I could allude with the best of them. ("Did you watch the Golden Globe Awards? Recognize this dress?") The rich ladies — stars, wives of ballplayers, expensive mistresses, and call girls — who turned in their clothes on consignment were happy to get cash for something they could wear only once. The buyers were ecstatic to be swathed, for a fraction of retail, in high-end fabric that had clung to celebrity hips. Everybody was happy, and I was getting paid.

I'd been a publicist in a large public relations firm right before taking the plunge and opening up my clothing store. It was through my clients, mostly actors and actresses, occasionally news anchors and politicians, that I learned about resale clothing. The people I represented often sold their outfits to specialty shops, especially after a big industry event, a charity ball, or a single television appearance. When they told me what they had paid for the new clothes and how much the consignment-store owners had given them, I was intrigued.

Business at As Good as New had gone from steady to fantastic since I opened the doors eight years ago. Location, location, location. My place was in Culver City, minutes away from the Santa Monica Freeway and dying to serve every major ethnic group connected by that highway.

Very conscious choice. A black woman with a designer resale clothing store in LA had to be midway between the African Americans with disposable incomes who lived in Ladera Heights, Baldwin Hills, and View Park and the whites and Asians who couldn't afford Beverly Hills prices but still wanted to look good. Truth be told, more whites bought from me than blacks. Buying resale required a mental adjustment for black women; they equated *secondhand* with *poverty*. But word of mouth was working among the sisters, and gradually more and more of them were coming in.

Saturday morning, and my place was packed. Made me feel good walking in the door. Shoppers were browsing. Cash register was cha-chinging away. Behind the drawn curtains all the dressing rooms were full. Adriana, one of my two saleswomen, strolled casually between the showroom and the back, where people were stepping into this, stepping out of that. She was an innocent-looking young white woman with long brown hair and a willowy body. There was a sense of wonder in her glance, as though she were in a state of continuous amazement. Adriana had a sweet, helpful attitude; the customers loved her. Around her the air thrummed with zippers zipping, fabrics rustling, sounds of jubilation and dismay. Disappointment was addressed immediately. We had a no-pressure policy, and I instructed my people to be truthful with the clients. If something looked good, we said so. If something was unbecoming . . . "Well, how about *this*?" I'd never been guilty of turning out some clueless woman who thought she looked great in a dress that was riding her butt like a seesaw. Of course, as delusions go, that's not the worst one.

As Good as New wasn't a huge store, but it was beautifully decorated. My goal was for every shopper to feel wealthier and more elegant when she left than she had before she walked in. A living fantasy, that's what a woman wants when she shops. The carpet on the floor was a swirl of earth tones set in a paisley design. The walls had the obligatory faux finish required in the chichi zone, but one so charming and unique it was more art than decoration. Hanging on the walls were antique window frames, accented by purple sashes. Potted palms were placed in every corner. There wasn't a huge inventory, but that was by design. Once inside As Good as New, a customer felt she'd walked into a rich woman's personal closet and was free to roam around and pick out what she liked.

The first thing I did was to pull out the shoes that Marie wanted to try on.

Adriana rushed over and gave Trina a hug. "Hey, girl," she said. Her voice was whispery, baby-girl soft. She smiled at me. "Good morning, Keri." She seemed perkier than usual, and I was glad to see her so happy.

"Hello, Adriana. How's it going?"

"I sold the blue pantsuit that Beverly Drive brought in, and her tan suede jacket just went out the door."

I learned early on that people who sell their clothes usually don't want other people knowing what they're doing. In order to protect the privacy of the clients who contributed our stock, we called them by the streets where they lived.

Adriana's smile was a high-beam dance that made me grin right back. Easy to see the kind of little girl she'd been, how hard she'd tried to please. Sometimes there was heartbreak in her smile. Maybe I recognized it because I could still taste my own.

I handed her the shoes. "Put these away for my friend Marie. She's supposed to come in tomorrow. Put them back out on Monday if she doesn't show up."

Adriana nodded, her light brown hair bouncing off her shoulders. "Topanga Canyon's housekeeper brought over the two pantsuits."

"How are they?"

"Beautiful."

"Any damage?"

"The navy blue pinstripe is perfect. The pale green has a slight tear in one of the buttonholes and a stain in the front. Frances is fixing them now."

"What's the stain?"

Customers would accept small imperfections in previously worn clothing. I'd sold torn items, pants hemmed unevenly, and a blouse with all the buttons missing. But a stain, even a small one, was a major deterrent for most people. People saw stains and thought of dirt that couldn't be washed out. Stained garments didn't sell.

"I don't know."

Clothes had fascinated me since I was a little girl. Ma Missy, my grandmother, sewed for wealthy people. I remember one night watching her laying out a pattern on her table. The fabric was purple silk.

She'd just begun to cut when the front door flew open with such fury it hit the wall. I smelled my mother before I saw her. The thick odor of bourbon ascended the stairs before she did. By the time she reached Ma Missy's sewing room, she was staggering. She collapsed on the floor in front of us, but not before she threw up all over the purple silk. I cried when she wouldn't get up. Ma Missy left her there on the floor and threw away the soiled fabric.

Days later she made me a beautiful dress out of pale blue satin. I escaped from my yearning in that froufrou frock with its balloon skirt. I was someone else: my mother's beloved child. Dressing up on the outside always helped me feel less exposed on the inside. Maybe that's the psychology of clothes for most women. Otherwise, we'd all be wearing a uniform.

Frances was sitting in front of a sewing machine that was pushed up against the wall of the small area in the back that served as both my office and the alterations room. She held up a pair of pale green pants and a navy blue pinstripe jacket.

"Ooooh," I said. "What are they?"

"Prada and"—she fingered the label of the navy suit—"Gambe-lorino?"

The name on the label was important. There was a time when I cared about flesh beneath my fingertips, kneading it until sighs of gratitude floated up. Healing occupied space in my mind then. Now designers were my bread and butter, and my fingers were for counting money. I shrugged, then reached over and examined the suit: felt the fabric, checked the seams and the topstitching. "This is very expensive. That's what we'll tell the clients."

Frances nodded, her nimble fingers tugging at the thread as she deftly repaired a small tear in the buttonhole of the green suit jacket.

"Where's the stain?"

She pointed to a crusty pinkish circle the size of a dime over the left breast pocket. "It was red. Looked like lipstick or blood. I put some remover on it. Don't worry, I'll get it out. Topanga Canyon wants four hundred apiece," Frances said.

I rolled my eyes, and Frances laughed.

"How should we size them?" I asked.

"A very small six. Petite. You should call Downtown Girl. These would fit her. She's another scrawny one."

I gave her a sideward glance and rolled my eyes again. I was only slightly bigger than Topanga Canyon and Downtown Girl. Frances had never met a Big Mac she didn't like. Everything about her was large: her size, her smile, her spirit. She patted her long weave and grinned.

"That's all right. I could take all y'all scrawny women's men," she said with a laugh. "Did Adriana tell you that she met somebody nice? She's going to the movies with him tonight."

"No wonder she seemed so happy."

Our eyes met. Adriana's romances always started out on an upbeat note. Her stop-and-start love life was of great concern to Frances and me. Adriana had never been a winner in love lotto.

"If my fat ass can get a man," Frances said, " I know she can, pretty as that girl is."

Getting wasn't Adriana's problem. *Keeping* was the operative word. There was an elephant stampeding through her life that chased men away. Frances and I liked to pretend it wasn't there.

The phone rang. Frances answered, then handed it to me. Her eyes issued a warning.

"Be nice," she said.

Be nice, I repeated to myself, a question mark in my mind. That admonition fit two situations, two sets of hot words and no apologies, two men.

Love in the past tense is always tricky.

"Hello."

I knew it was Clyde by the way he cleared his throat. That was my ex-husband's way of steadying himself: He cleared his throat and then barreled in. For my part, I took deep relaxation breaths and kept my fists clenched. "I don't want to argue with you. I was calling to see how Trina is doing."

"Well, Clyde, that's your lot in life. You make women want to argue. You have to admit I'm not the only one."

"I could say the same thing about you."

It was true enough to make us both laugh.

"I guess we're just difficult people," Clyde said.

"I'm not difficult, I'm misunderstood," I said. Clyde cracked up once again. "Trina is fine."

Trina is here, Clyde, I'll get her for you. That's what I should have said, knowing that for Clyde and me civility is a rainbow that fades almost as soon as it appears. But I'd never learned to break away quickly from the man I'd promised to live with forever; that, of course, was my problem, not his.

Frances rose quietly and closed the door.

"Did she get the birthday check?" His volume went up; it always did when he spoke of money he was spending. He wanted anyone in earshot to know that he was capable of paying.

"Yes, Clyde. That check is already spent." I could feel a surge of familiar anger. Clyde wrote checks and left me to do the heavy lifting.

"That quick? She couldn't have gotten it more than two days ago. Damn."

"Like father, like daughter," I said.

I'd been Clyde's first wife. Not exactly a childhood sweetheart but close enough. After me came the trophy blonde, Miss Gone-in-a-Flash-with-the-Cash herself. I had tried to tell the fool that white women don't leave the way sisters do. None of that "all I want is my peace of mind." She did a strip club on his bank account, and my child support was shaky for about two years. Then he came all the way back, overcompensated for wife number two by marrying the Sapphire of all Sapphires. Miss Body was a brickhouse: double Ds, big behind, shapely legs. Clyde was totally sprung. Butter wouldn't melt in her mouth—at first. But the centerfold had a split personality. Evilene would go off in a New York minute. When she started acting like she was getting ready to put her hands on Trina, I knew her days with Clyde and maybe on this earth were numbered. Now there was Aurelia, an elegant beauty with enough street in her to keep Clyde in line. She treated Trina kindly. For the first time, I felt replaced.

Trina's here, Clyde. I'll get her for you. Why couldn't I just say that? But if I knew how to quit with Clyde while I was ahead, I'd probably die of boredom. He'd been the outlet for my aggressive tendencies for quite a while.

"Well, I want her to have nice things."

"The nicest thing you could give her is more time."

I could hear him bristling on the other end. Clyde always chose offense over defense.

"You still have her in that program?"

"Yes."

"There's nothing wrong with Trina's mind, Keri. She was smoking too much weed and she got paranoid; that's all that happened. Then you go and put her in a psychiatric hospital like she's some crazy person."

"Your daughter has been diagnosed with a mental illness."

Clyde sputtered and choked. "I don't believe that shit. Half these doctors don't know what the hell they're talking about."

The weariness in Clyde's voice dismayed me. I was used to his mouthing off, being opinionated. Our fights were legendary, hard, long, below the belt, and bloody. We thrived on hot words and slammed doors, at least I did. As long as we fought, a part of Clyde still belonged to me.

"Are you all right?"

"I'm okay." There was a long pause that he didn't fill in.

"Trina's here. I'll get her for you."

I heard Trina say "Daddy!"—the name a gleeful exclamation, a shriek of delight, in the manner of girls who worship their fathers as much as they love them. I'd never experienced that kind of idolatry. By the time I was two, my father was dead from a motorcycle accident. By three, my memories of him had faded, and by five he was no more to me than a smiling picture under glass. As I grew, my father's absence became normal, like church on Sunday. It was my mother's detachment that stung like acid flung against my skin.

Oh, those beautiful mommies, just out of reach, removed and aloof because they lack the maternal gene, because they love their jobs, some no-good man, their reflections in the mirror, or the afterglow from the bottle or the hallucination from the pipe more than they love their children. Daughters can worship their mothers too. When I was a child, my mother was in and out of my life and mostly drunk in both locations. I wanted to be important to her, only that. To matter more than the next drink. It's amazing what people squander in a lifetime, what they walk away from as though it's just so much detritus in the street. I remember trying to hold on to my last bit of hope, how it seeped out just before I gave up on my mother. I stored my pain and anger in a place that became molten. And now I had to live with heat that wouldn't stay contained.

Trina was giggling. Clyde used to make *me* laugh too. When we were newlyweds with brand-new dreams, we laughed all the time. Driving through Atlanta, where we started out, Clyde would point out the site of our first mansion, our second. Stick with me, baby, and you'll be farting in a Rolls. I don't need a mansion or a Rolls, I told him. But he did.

Trina caught my eye, gave me a look, and I got up and walked outside, closing the door behind me. Not all the way, though. I left it open a crack and stood right there. Trina's laughter wafted out. I heard her say she was fine.

I had to give the man some credit. Clyde showed up for the important occasions: the birthdays, the holidays. He called. He had never been late with child support, except after his second divorce. When we were together, he did almost as much child care as I did. In between chasing down dollar bills, Clyde was a real daddy. Trina caressed the word, cooed, and giggled some more after she said it. If anybody said my name that way, I'd never leave her. But then, he hadn't left Trina. He left me.

My inner mule made me marry Clyde. That was one time God warned me big time. Minutes before the ceremony began, while I was standing outside the church getting ready to march down the aisle and say I do, a pigeon flew over my head, veered dangerously close, and shit right on my veil. Ma Missy was next to me, her bright clairvoyant eyes fevered with insight garnered from one look in her personal crystal ball. Between clenched teeth she whispered, "Babygirl, that's Jesus talking to you. You need to put your ass right back in that limo and get the hell on away from here."

She read my glance.

"Okay, don't listen to me. I got to seventy-five with all my teeth and in my complete right mind being a fool. This is your world, squirrel; I'm just living in it." She shook her head. "So damn hardheaded."

It wasn't that my grandmother didn't like Clyde; she just realized early on that he was a man intent on moving up so fast he'd leave behind whoever didn't keep up.

When I peeked into the office, Frances was dabbing more spot remover on the stain. "Don't want to come out," she muttered. She put her hand to her face, partially covering a scar on her cheek that she tended to rub when she was troubled. It had become a keloid. That smooth raised skin stood out like a brand.

I returned to the showroom. Trina and Adriana were both helping customers. Adriana rang up hers first and then came over to me.

"So, I understand you have a movie date."

Adriana nodded.

"Who's the guy?"

"Some dude in my class."

"Do you like him?"

Adriana shrugged, her movement full of tough-girl bravado. She didn't want to care. Then, just as quickly as it had been erected, the wall came down. "It doesn't matter if I like him or not. You know that."

She was back to being sad girl again. I wrapped my arm around her shoulder and squeezed her tightly. "Just have a good time," I said.

Trina was helping several customers. As I watched her, I recalled how she used to work in the shop every day after high school. A bright, clear-eyed young girl, she had made the customers laugh with her wise-cracks and sheer ebullience. She's still got most of that, I told myself, and what's missing will return. She's not so far behind she can't catch up. She'll go to college in the fall, go on to graduate school, get a great job, and meet a nice guy, an understanding go-getter. Everything will work out fine.

"Ready to go?" I asked her when her customer went to the cash register.

"Where?"

"I was thinking home. We have to put the flowers in water."

"Aww."

I sighed. "Where do you want to go, Trina?"

"To the movies, to the mall, to eat."

When Trina was in her early teens, she would jump out of a moving car in order to avoid being seen going into a movie with me. That was when she had friends who called, who met her at the mall, who spent the night and filled her bedroom with whispers and laughter and boys' names. She had been robbed of that casual happiness. I wanted to make up for that void, to fill in the empty spaces until she recovered all she'd lost.

There were moments, right before my world began to tip over again, that I don't want to forget. Simple, normal minutes, the sun bright, the breeze drying the dampness between my breasts, the clock ticking, nothing special. We took the flowers home, and I put them into water. We drove to the marina and saw a movie, a comedy that made us grab each other as we convulsed, and then had an early dinner at a Thai restaurant before returning home. Trina took her evening pill, and we sat in the hot tub in our backyard and drank lemonade. It grew dark as our legs bumped against each other in the warm water. The stars, at least those that were visible, came out. In LA, it's easier to see planes than stars. When I'm missing Atlanta, a lot of times I'm thinking about cold winter nights, me scurrying home under a sky filled with stars. But even in LA, I could make out the North Star, with its steady glow. It's bright like a plane, only it never moves.

The last thing I did before I retired was to count Trina's pills and subtract the days that had passed from the original number. Counting pills had become a way of life. Even though she'd been well for five months, I took nothing for granted. My old instincts hadn't yet dulled. The old fears hadn't completely receded. One more week to go before a refill; there were twenty-one of the pink three-times-a-day pills and seven nighttime white ones. I counted once again, to make sure; then I put the cap back on the bottle and breathed.

During the night Trina climbed in the bed with me, and I pulled her close, wishing she could be a baby again in my arms. No, inside me. We would start over; even my milk would be new. If only I'd known then what I knew now: everything that could turn a gift from God into a tragedy. I knew where the road turned slippery and treacherous and the baby fell out of the car seat. Women would kill for what I know.

Babies should come with instructions taped to the soles of their little feet. A cheery note from God: *Be careful! This child is accident-prone.* Or: *Lucky you! This one goes straight to the top!* How about: *Congratulations! You have just given birth to a natural beauty, who will never know acne or need braces or diets. Your darling straight-A student will be a pleasure, an endless source of pride and joy right up to high school graduation, and then she'll hit a wall of craziness that may never end.* Take lots of *before* pictures. *After* will be unphotographable.

As I said, the end of that day was unremarkable. Nothing really stood out. Everything flowed, the kind of flow you take for granted when your shackles have been removed, the scars from the last beating have all faded, and it's Sunday on the plantation. But I did pray. I will always pray. This is what I prayed: *Mother Father God, let the healing continue.*

2

TRINA GAVE ME A KISS WHEN I DROPPED HER OFF AT THE
Weitz Center two weeks later, on a Wednesday morning. Watching her
as she ran up the stairway to the five-story building, I didn't drive off
until the thick glass door closed behind her. The Weitz Center was part
of Beth Israel Hospital, the Beverly Hills medical behemoth, renowned
for innovative patient care and VIP rooms. In another wing I'd had my
uterus and two useless ovaries removed when Trina was nine, which
didn't end my yearning to bear another child, only the possibility. An ER
doctor had stitched up Trina's bleeding foot after a bicycle accident
when she was fifteen. In that case, I'd passed by two other hospitals on
the way to Beth Israel, which was, in my estimation, one of the finest.

In those early years I'd thought of hospitals as places to mend bodies.
But that was before a broken mind had rampaged through my life. The
Weitz Center was a place to heal brains. From nine to three, Monday
through Friday, Trina had group sessions and individual counseling
on the first floor. She'd been attending the partial program, outpatient
therapy for people with psychiatric disorders, ever since her third hospitalization, almost six months ago. Her three hospitalizations had run
together during the previous summer and fall after Trina had graduated

from high school just after her seventeenth birthday. Graduation summer, her teenage rebellion had exploded into one manic episode after another, a nightmare summer of long nights, smashed glass, and broken dreams.

In the beginning, it was like being suspicious of a husband. Those little pinprick inklings tickled the inside of my skull. I explained everything away until I couldn't. The reason he was gone all the time was because he was working; the reason she talked so fast was because she was excitable, emotional. The reason he didn't reach for me at night was because he was tired from working so hard. The reason she couldn't sleep at night was because she was so wound up from studying. None of her old friends came around anymore because—well, people outgrow each other. The silence at the dinner table, the quiet in our bedroom— he was preoccupied with his work. All the speeding tickets? Didn't all young people speed? The spending sprees? That was my fault. I never should have let Trina have a credit card. But then she cursed at me. His silences grew deeper. How could she say those things? Baby, what's going on? Trina, what's wrong?

Years before, Clyde had told me, "There's nobody else; there's just no *us*."

With Trina I drew my own conclusions: *My child is sick.*

I waded through quicksand to get to those words. It was up to my neck when I finally spoke them aloud.

"Your daughter is bipolar, also known as manic-depressive," the doctor at the second hospital had told me. That was at UCLA last August, a week before she was scheduled to leave for Brown University. I had taken her there after Trina began telling me that I was a devil who had stolen her from her real mother. I sat with her in admittance and told the clerk that my child needed psychiatric care. I whispered the words, but they came out of my mouth all the same.

"Are you her mother?" the clerk asked.

"Yes."

"Is she under eighteen?"

"Yes."

She looked up from the paper she was filling out. "That's good."

The woman checked our insurance, and then she found a bed for Trina in the psychiatric ward on the nonacute side. When I returned the next day, I demanded a psychological evaluation. When she'd been sent to the Weitz Center for her first hospitalization in June, the psychiatrist had told me it was too early to tell what was wrong with her. But this was the second time. I had to know. The UCLA doctor was Russian, his accent thick. His words bewildered me. I asked him to repeat what he'd said.

"Ms. Whitmore, your daughter is bipolar."

That was the scariest part, the way he said it. She *is* bipolar, not she *has* bipolar *disorder*. You *are* cancer. You *are* AIDS. Nobody ever said that.

"How long before she gets better?"

"Woman," the doctor said, not unkindly, "don't set your clock."

I'd almost had her hospitalized during the Christmas break when she was in eleventh grade—but for drugs, not psychosis. My ex-boyfriend and I had returned from the movies. When we drove up to my house, every light was turned on and music was blaring. Inside I found Trina wearing one of my cocktail dresses. Her face was a garish rainbow: silver eye shadow, red lips, pink cheeks. She was heading for the door.

"Whoa," I said. "Where do you think you're going?"

"You can't stop me, Demon Queen."

She began screaming, and when I listened to what she was saying— calling me a devil, accusing me of killing her real mother, themes she would return to again and again—I became alarmed. My ex-boyfriend and I tried to settle her down.

"What are you on?" I asked her over and over. Her answer was more screaming and cursing.

Ex-boyfriend and I drove straight to the hospital, but when the attendant suggested that her problem might be mental, I balked.

"My daughter doesn't have a mental problem," I told him.

By that time, Trina had calmed down so much that when the emergency room physician said he didn't see anything wrong, I was ready to believe him. Keep an eye on her for the next forty-eight hours, he told me. On the way back, Trina apologized for her outburst, swore she hadn't taken anything, explained she hadn't been sleeping well because she was studying so hard for midterms. It was a plausible excuse; that's what I told myself.

This junior year holiday episode was but a shadow of the post–high school graduation episode that landed her in UCLA. That night in August she seemed to be floating on a jet stream of hallucinatory energy that punctuated her every word. Around four o'clock that morning I awoke to her footsteps, kitchen cabinet doors slamming shut, music playing in her room, television voices that were way too loud. She began calling people on the telephone and had dozens of disjointed conversations, one right after another, as though she were frightened of being without a connection. Later, there were soft thuds as she ran down the back stairs into the kitchen, then more slamming, shutting, opening of drawers, cabinets, the refrigerator. After a while I smelled food. When I came downstairs, I found ten cold pancakes, lopsided from syrup and butter, piled on a plate.

Days before, I'd pulled two joints from her purse. I had screamed at her then, a frantic tirade; she cursed me. By that time, most of our conversations had deteriorated into verbal beat-downs, Thrillas in Manilas, with Trina as Ali to my tongue-tied Frazier. So I already knew something was terribly wrong. For the rest of the day, she stayed in her room. For at least eight hours, the light on her phone didn't go out for more than two minutes. That light mesmerized and terrorized, like a whip dangling from ol' massa's hand.

I was in the kitchen with Ex-boyfriend when she came down the back stairs that evening. It was Saturday. I had called her father, but I couldn't locate him. So my ex-boyfriend came. We were sitting at my kitchen table, and I was describing Trina's behavior.

"Baby," he said, as gently as he could, "it sounds like crack or maybe meth."

Hearing my worst suspicions voiced by another, I began to cry. Then we heard the clicking of high heels on the stairs. Minutes before she appeared, the room became filled with the odor of way too much perfume. Not a good sign. Nine o'clock and she was going out. Not a good plan. It was Mom's job to try to stop her.

Trina had on a micromini red leather skirt, a transparent white blouse, and, underneath, a black bra I'd never seen before. But what really took my breath away was her war paint. Her pretty mouth was a slash of iridescent white. The lids of her large clear eyes were smeared with bright green. Brick-colored blush accented her high cheekbones. She had shaved off her eyebrows and penciled in two black half-moons.

There were splashes of pink spray paint in her hair. He's right, I thought. Ex-boyfriend took my hand.

"Give me your leather coat," she called from the steps..

Different strategies and ensuing scenarios collided in my mind. Casual: Let her go, don't make a fuss. Make an appointment with the rape counseling center now. Aggressive: Scream, *"You're not going anywhere!"* as loudly as possible. Block the door with my body. Bribery: "Trina, if you . . . I'll take you . . . I'll buy you. . . ." But all the well-planned words would result in yelling and screaming, and by that time I'd begun to be afraid of where arguing might lead. The thing was, I couldn't stop choking, couldn't get my breath back, couldn't speak.

"Let me have your leather coat," Trina repeated.

"No," I said weakly, managing to add, "Where do you think you're going looking like that?" I got up from the table and walked over to the bottom of the stairs.

"I'm going to meet some very important people. They're helping me get into medical school."

"What people?"

She ignored me.

"Trina, have you looked in the mirror?"

"Why don't *you* look in the fucking mirror sometime?"

"Hey, hey, hey," Ex-boyfriend said. "Watch your mouth."

"You're not my father."

"You don't have to use that kind of language. What's gotten into you?" I was trembling.

"Shut up!" She reached in her purse and pulled out a cigarette and held it between her fingers.

"Don't light that thing in here," I said, as sternly as I could.

She rushed down the last steps, and in an instant we were nose to nose on the bottom step. "You're such a bitch," she hissed.

"You need to chill, babygirl," Ex-boyfriend said.

"Fuck you."

Ex-boyfriend stood up.

"Maybe you'd better go," I said to him.

"No, she's on something. I'm not leaving you with her," he said.

"Just go. I'm all right."

"No."

He stood there at the table. I could feel her breath on my face, see the flames rioting in her eyes. That's when I knew she wanted to hurt me. I knew that what was wrong was soul deep and strong as chains. What was wrong wasn't drugs. What was wrong was why she needed them. *My baby is sick.*

"Trina, you need help."

I embarked on my own Middle Passage that night, marching backward, ankles shackled. I journeyed to a Charleston auction block, screaming as my child was torn from my arms, as I watched her being driven away. Trina didn't belong to me anymore. Something more powerful possessed her. I saw her hand moving swiftly toward me, the fingers tightening into a ball, then opening again. The first blow was a slap, the next a punch. I fell against the counter, raising my arms to shield myself. Below her peek a boo blouse, Trina's chest was swelling. Her green eye shadow glared under the bright kitchen light. She raised her hand a third time, but by then my ex-boyfriend was coming across the floor.

"Fucking bitch!" she screamed, and ran out the door.

I wasn't hurt, not really, wasn't even stunned. In a way, I'd been expecting the blows. I didn't want a witness. The assault was meant to be a secret that got locked up in the internal vault, along with Uncle-Danny-liked-to-play-peepee-games-with-me or Mommy-used-to-get-drunk-every-night-and-that's-how-come-I-stay-with-Ma-Missy. Your pedophile uncle and your alkie mama aren't your fault, of course. Your child, however, is always your fault. If she grows up to be president, you did a good job. If he wears a black trench coat to high school and starts shooting up the place with his buddies—well, I damn sure didn't want to see that particular judgment reflected in anybody's eyes.

"I'm all right," I said, and then cried in my ex-boyfriend's arms. Those arms promised to keep my secret, to hold me up. It took me a while to realize how strong they were.

I made my ex-boyfriend leave before Clyde arrived, thirty minutes later. He had on a tuxedo, and he was buzzed from two or three glasses of champagne. Clyde had been in a happy partying mood when he finally answered his cell, and the news of his daughter's rampage had brought him down.

"Look," he said when Trina didn't come home after two hours, "this is obviously some mother-daughter stuff."

"It's more than that. Something is seriously wrong with Trina."

He shook his head. "It's just a stage," he said. "This happens when kids are about to go off to school. They have some fears about leaving home and so do the parents, so everybody acts out and pisses each other off so it won't be so hard to separate. It will pass."

"She hit me, Clyde."

No amount of arguing could persuade my ex-husband that whatever was going on with Trina wasn't part of normal adolescence. But his logic didn't sway me. After he left, I called the police. When Trina finally returned home, they were waiting. They heard her hysterical threats at the door. I followed their car as they drove to the hospital. When I called Clyde from the psychiatric ward, he yelled at me that I was overreacting.

"I won't have anything to do with this!" he said, and then he hung up.

"Do not look for reasons, Mother," the Russian doctor told me. "This runs in families, like diabetes or high blood pressure. This is mostly genetic."

"Or bad parenting." I began weeping.

Dr. Ustinov leaned across his desk and brought his face close to mine. "This is not clear thinking, Mother. All parents make mistakes. My own father beat me with a broomstick for the slightest infraction. I am damaged, but I am not mentally ill because I'm not genetically predisposed to this sort of disease. Did you give her this illness? No. Be careful, Mother, you will make yourself depressed, even physically sick. Most likely you have bipolar in your family or in your husband's."

I wasn't ready to let myself off the hook. Guilt was easier to manage than futile rage.

"But if it's in the family, why don't I have it? Why doesn't my husband have it?"

He shrugged his shoulders. "There is no rhyme or reason. Sometimes there are triggers. Drugs. Alcohol. Traumatic events. Just because you or your husband don't have this doesn't mean there is no bipolar disorder among your relatives."

I sat there in his office, trying to connect all the dots, to look for signs I'd missed. My mind grew clogged, and there were blanks in my memory. When did she catch this brain flu? Was it in tenth grade, when her best friend moved away? Was it in eleventh grade, when her sweetie broke her heart? Earlier, when we uprooted her from Atlanta? When Clyde left? What was the trauma? Had someone's hands touched her in the wrong place? Was I too critical, too perfectionist, too busy selling to pay enough attention?

I began to cry, and Dr. Ustinov handed me a tissue. "Listen, Mother, don't blame yourself."

Ha! Isn't it always Mommy's fault? Mom didn't do this, she didn't do that. She nursed too long; she bottle-fed. She slapped the shit out of the kid; she raised a spoiled brat. She was too dumb and lazy to get a job; she worked full-time and never paid attention. She weighed 300 pounds and waddled into school for open house; she weighed 110 and showed too much cleavage. She got high; she was too uptight. She traded Dad in for a lesbian lover; she did everything her man told her to do. She stayed with a husband who beat her and set a poor example; she left the fool and broke up the family or, worse yet, she kicked his ass and started running things. She let her boyfriends spend the night; she didn't provide a male role model. She never cleaned; she screamed when the little ones tracked in mud. Lazy cow fed the kids McDonald's every night. Negligent slob didn't attend the PTA. Too trifling to help sell Girl Scout cookies. She let her children run wild and had herself a good ol' time. Her child was drowning, and she didn't save her.

"It's not about reasons anymore. It's about medication. Your daughter can have a good life, even with this," the doctor said.

He prescribed a mood stabilizer and an antipsychotic. Miracle drugs, he proclaimed. When I asked if there was an alternative to the medication, he shrugged and said, "Mania." When I asked, foolishly, desperately, if Trina could still go away to college, I could see the pity swimming in his eyes as he stared at me. So I called the university and asked for delayed admission, which it granted.

Trina took the pills while she was in the hospital. She slept around the clock and gained ten pounds in one week. When Clyde saw her, he told me, in front of Trina, that she didn't need to take any pills. She just needed to stop smoking weed. Once she got out, she took the tablets sporadically and then not at all. Late in October, she wound up back in the hospital a third time.

For that last episode I had to call the police again, and I didn't call Clyde. When the dispatcher asked me if she was a danger to herself or others, I screamed, "Yes!" I could hear the sound of glass breaking as I spoke. At that precise moment, Trina was playing demolition derby throughout the house. With a hammer in her hand, she was going after windows. She'd already shattered all the glass in my car and dented the hood and the top. I was cowering in my bedroom, behind a locked door, listening: *crash! boom! bang!* Like in the cartoons, only not funny.

"Fifty-one fifty," the dispatcher said.

"What?" I asked.

"Ma'am, I'm talking to our officers. We'll have a car there in a few minutes. Is she armed?"

Hard question. Not so much answering it but dealing with the implications: a black girl going crazy with a hammer in front of cops. Eula Love, I thought, conjuring up an image of the mentally ill black woman shot dead by the LAPD as she brandished a knife in her front yard. "No. No. *No!* She isn't armed. She doesn't have a weapon. She is a minor. Please, don't hurt her. Don't hurt her."

Trina put down the hammer as soon as the officers came. They were gentle with her. Two big officers who never touched their guns. The Latino one sat her down on the living room sofa. From time to time he patted her arm.

"Trina, dear, you've wrecked your mom's house. Something's going wrong in your mind. We're going to take you to the hospital so you can get some help. You'll be on a seventy-two-hour hold. You won't be able to leave. After the three days, there will be a hearing to decide if they need to keep you longer. All right? We want your cooperation, dear. All right?"

"She's not really my mother. She killed my real mother and stole me from her when I was a baby. We don't even look alike."

Officer Martinez had heard it all before; he silenced my protestations by arching his brow.

"Hon, after you get back from the hospital, you and your mom will have to talk. Maybe you both can get some counseling. But right now, we'd like you to come with us."

"She has bipolar disorder," I said after Trina was sitting in the car and I was standing on the sidewalk, looking at the back of my child's head, watching it bob up and down with each sob. Officer Martinez was next to me. "She refuses to take the medicine."

He gave me a sympathetic look. "Yeah, that's usual. It takes them a while before they accept the fact that they're sick."

"I don't know if I can last much longer."

Martinez smiled. "Sure you can. You're a strong woman."

Strong enough to plant a crop, pick cotton, birth a baby in the field, and keep on working.

The police took Trina to a county facility, Daniel Freeman Hospital in the Marina, which was owned and run by the Catholic Church. The vibe there was less formal than at Beth Israel, a little warmer, perhaps. Maybe it was the Virgin Mary; her replicas were everywhere. I'd be coming around the corner on my way to Trina's ward, and *bam!* there would be Mary, her arms outstretched, the sculpted billows of her garments frozen, that "everything's going to be all right" gleam in her eye. I didn't necessarily believe in her intercessory powers, but I found her presence comforting.

There were all kinds of people there, from the homeless to celebrities. One actor, as famous for his addiction as he was for his movies, sat next to Trina at smoke break. He looked so frail in real life, a small, dark, handsome white man. And so polite. When the gray-haired Latina nurse called his name, he said, "Ma'am?" automatically, just like the well-brought-up southern boy his mama had raised.

The window repair ended up taking ten days. My housekeeper didn't say anything, but she knew what was going on. My nosy gardener asked if somebody held a grudge against me, if I'd had a fight with my boyfriend. This man who mowed my lawn was hungry for gory details.

I avoided my neighbors, rushing in and out of my house. At the grocery store I ran into the woman who lived directly across from me. We barely said hello, but when she saw me, two or three days after Trina broke my windows, she stopped her cart in the middle of the cereal aisle, walked over to me, put her arms around my shoulders, and held me, which told me two things I didn't want to know. Number one: people were talking; number two: I had become someone to be pitied.

Motherless child; childless mother. God was doing his stand-up routine again.

When the glass man finally showed up, he let out a long whistle as he surveyed the damage.

"Don't ask," I said.

"No, ma'am, I never do."

His price was reasonable. I was grateful for that too.

I VISITED TRINA EVERY NIGHT AT SEVEN WHILE SHE WAS AT Daniel Freeman. On my first visit, she stumbled out of her room like a zombie with broken toes. I called the nurse.

"Oh, a little too much Haldol," she said. "It'll wear off." The woman disappeared before I could reply.

The next night Trina was better, just depressed. She cried and apologized. "You're the best mom," she told me.

"I don't want to be crazy anymore," she said when the hospital released her to me. "I'm tired of it. I'll take the medicine. I won't smoke dope or drink. They said there's a program at the Weitz Center. I'll go there."

Frances and Adriana had come with me the night I brought Trina home. Frances drove. "Some things people ain't supposed to go through alone" was how she put it as the light from the streetlamps glinted off the scar on her face.

"Trina," she said when we were all seated in the car and she was driving off, "you have to work at staying well like it's a nine-to-five job, girly. Your mother can only do so much. You can spend your life going in and out of hospitals, or you can do the things you need to do to take care of yourself. Do you hear me?"

"I said I'd go to the partial program," Trina said, her tone surly.

"Listen, don't get no attitude. You can go to as many programs as you like," Frances said, "but if you're not committed to doing the work, trust me, it's just a waste of time. Put your heart in it."

Trina didn't answer for a few minutes. "I'm going to do the work," she said.

"It's hard," Adriana said.

A REPRIEVE. MASSA HAD CHANGED HIS MIND, BROUGHT BACK the slave child, and placed her in her mother's arms along with manumission papers for both.

"It's not going to be that easy," Frances told me a few days later, when I was rhapsodizing about Trina's progress, the resumption of her old life, *our* old life. But I dismissed her caution. I had set my sights on the promised land, and that was the only place I wanted to live.

As Good as New was quiet that Wednesday morning, as it was on most weekdays. I worked in the office and caught up with paperwork. When I came out around lunchtime, I heard Frances laughing. I smelled the French fries before I saw him. We just stood there staring, neither one of us wanting to cross the threshold. Finally, Frances said, "Keri, look who's here," as though my ex-boyfriend's coming to my store were some kind of good news.

I didn't say anything. "Come on over here, baby," he said, holding a bag of fries. "Meet me halfway." Frances disappeared. I stayed right where I was standing.

"Oh, so it's like that," he said, and in five steps he was right next to me. He waved the bag in front of my nose. Fries were his addiction, and he was always trying to corrupt me.

"From Chuck E. Cheese," he said, grinning.

I took a handful and stuffed them in my mouth. Chuck E. Cheese fries were the gold standard as far as fast food was concerned.

"Three preschoolers tried to jack me for these, but I fought them off just so I could bring you some, baby. I was like, 'Take that,' " he said, miming karate chops that were so comical we both had to laugh.

"Orlando, what are you doing here?"

"I came to see you." His eyes had locked into mine. He had nice eyes, large and deep-set. His lips were almost the same color as the rest of his face. I was having a hard time taking my eyes off his lips.

"This is my place of business."

"Look, Keri. Can we have lunch or something? I want to talk to you. I miss you."

"We don't have anything to talk about. Let's not keep going in circles. "

"You know I liven things up for you, baby. I already made you smile."

Making me smile had never been Orlando's problem. When we met eight years ago, our relationship was a laugh a minute. Orlando had been starring in a popular sitcom for nearly four years. He was a sought-after actor in his late thirties. Movie offers were coming in. He was nominated for an Emmy. At the ceremony, we sat right next to the entire cast of *Cheers*. His world was glitzy and glamorous, but I knew where I fit in. From the time we met at a late-night restaurant, both of us waiting for a table, I realized what he saw in me, what he wanted from me. I was a woman who didn't glitter for the world, just for him, a woman who could make it through the hard times.

He wanted to marry me. If he'd asked me once, he'd asked me too many damn times. I'd always turned him down. Not because I didn't love him but because I believed that Trina should be out of the house before I took a husband. And there was the matter of Orlando's career and his finances.

Orlando didn't win the Emmy, and the following year his show ended. He kept expecting to land another starring role, but he began to do guest spots. The movie offers dried up. He did a few commercials and a lot of theater. He still worked, but the projects had dwindled and his earnings were nowhere near what they had been. He wasn't broke, but his budget was tight.

"You have a degree," I reminded him one night, after six months had passed without one single job. We'd been together for three years, and I was alarmed by Orlando's denial, his lack of productivity. He dreamed Willy Loman dreams. His next big role was always around the corner.

"I know I have a degree," he said, his eyes going a little cold.

"You could get a job. You could teach acting. That would allow you some time for auditions."

He took that the wrong way. Turned it into my not believing in him. It became a theme, my not believing in him. That was the night I realized it wasn't the money, it was Orlando's desperation, so quiet and so deep, that I couldn't abide. No, I'd told him that night, I just don't believe in *us*.

"I'm not going to lunch with you, Orlando."

"Are you okay? Everything all right with Trina?"

"Trina's fine, and so am I. How are the boys? I saw PJ riding in a car on Crenshaw a couple of weeks ago." Just saying PJ's name made me smile.

"Yeah, he was probably on his way to get his tattoo."

"What kind of tattoo?"

"The wrong kind. Lucy called me and said he had the words FUCK YOU tattooed on his lower back."

"Oh, my God. So I take it Lucy's on the warpath."

"You got that right," Orlando said.

Orlando's ex-wife was not an overly patient woman, nor did she sub-scribe to modern child-rearing practices. When her sons were younger she didn't spare the rod. A tiny woman, she nevertheless packed quite a wallop. I'd been a victim of her wrath one night when she had followed Orlando and me to a bar. In the ensuing argument she stuck to her theme, which was that if Orlando could afford to buy me a drink, he could pay his child support on time. Before I had time to express sisterly solidarity, I was the recipient of a great deal of the drink that she tossed in Orlando's face. She later apologized, but I'd always questioned her sincerity.

"On the other hand, Jabari is rolling. Every college in the nation wants a piece of him." Orlando's older son was gifted both academically and athletically.

I could see PJ with his scrawny teenage body, all decorated with tats, swaggering down high school halls, his pores exuding do-or-die bravado. He would stumble through life, learning everything the hard way. His older brother, stable, dependable Jabari, was risk-aversive. PJ was my favorite.

Orlando sighed. "Well, I guess I'll go eat my lunch all by myself. Lis-ten, I start rehearsals for a play. Will you come see me? Think about it," he said, when I didn't respond.

We stared at each other. He wasn't really handsome; his features weren't chiseled enough for that category. Just shy of six feet, broad in the shoulders with a bit of a belly, he exuded power without doing much of anything. Orlando was the kind of man who opened his front door when the bell rang without asking for a name or looking through a peephole.

"That man!" I said after he left. Frances just laughed. "You just don't know," I said, and she laughed harder. "Is that stain out yet?"

She shook her head. "I've tried everything. Whatever it is don't want to come out. In fact, I think it's worse."

Back in the office I examined the jacket. The spot was spreading.

Instead of a dime, it had now grown to the size of a quarter. I picked up the jacket, folding it across my arm. "I'll take it down the street." Most repairs we tried to fix in-house. But the cleaner's at the end of our block specialized in hard cases. An ancient Jamaican man was the commander of an arsenal of solutions and potions that made most dirt disappear. "The Old Man will get it out," I said.

At one-thirty, I tossed the jacket onto the backseat of my car, drove down to a little restaurant near the hospital, and had lunch. I left my car on the side street and trudged over to Beth Israel's Weitz Center. Usually I waited for Trina outside, but by three-ten, when she still hadn't come down, I decided to go in. Occasionally she dallied to talk with some of her group mates or to one of the counselors. Today wouldn't be the first time I'd had to get her.

Jasmine scented the air as I climbed the stairs. Inside, I walked past the security guard, beyond the station where a Japanese woman with a kind face handled insurance and payments, down the hall to where the partial program was located. There was no one at the front desk, and when I glanced quickly around the large area into the various rooms, there were people milling around but no Trina. A dark-haired woman emerged from one of the offices in the back, and I recognized her as the program coordinator.

"Mrs. Whitmore, is it?" she asked. Her British accent made her words sound somewhat formal.

"Elaine, please call me Keri. I came to pick up my daughter. "

"I was going to call you tonight, Keri," Elaine said.

"You were?"

"Do you have a minute?"

"Sure, but I'd like to let Trina know that I'm here."

"Trina's not here, Keri. That's what I want to talk with you about."

Gonegonegonegonegone.

"What do you mean, she's not here? Where is she?" My words shook out, one tremble at a time.

"No one knows. She and another client didn't come back from the last break, which was at one-thirty. The two of them usually go out on the patio and smoke. They've become friends."

Elaine was speaking, but her words seemed one long incomprehensible jumble. My mind was a vast empty cavern with only one echoing sound: *Gonegonegonegonegone*. I felt Elaine's hand on my arm, guiding me toward an area with sofas and chairs.

"Why don't you sit down," she said.

"No. No, thank you."

"These things happen," Elaine said, "and there may be a plausible explanation. Don't jump to conclusions."

"All right," I said.

Gonegonegonegonegone.

"Trina is doing exceptionally well here. She's quite forthcoming. She contributes a great deal to group discussions. She's one of the leaders."

"Maybe, maybe, maybe—"

"Calm down," Elaine said.

Yes, calm down. And then I bolted, out the door, down the hall, past the guard, down the stairs, into the dazzling sunlight and jasmine-drenched air, dreading the moment my feet hit the pavement because I didn't know where to turn.

There was a time when I had known how Trina would react to every situation, but that time had passed. The era when I had known the friends she hung out with and the places she might be was a far-off country. Trina's friends had moved on. She went only where I took her. She was in a rebuilding phase of her life. The first step was taking responsibility for her healing. The next was forming relationships, becoming more independent, regaining her autonomy. She had been inching closer to that place called normal. Now normal had been sold deep south.

My tears were rising as I stepped onto the sidewalk. Above me a jacaranda tree loomed, its purple blossoms my personal sky. Already, a heavy haziness was settling in my mind. *Please don't let the madness start all over again.* Then I saw her. Trina was sitting across the street on the ledge of the short concrete wall that bordered the portion of the parking lot that faced Weitz Center. Next to her was a woman who appeared to be in her early thirties, dark and heavy with a loud shriek of a laugh. They were both carrying Macy's bags. "Trina," I called.

She looked up and smiled; then she and the woman walked across the street to me.

"Mommy, this is Melody Pratt. Melody, this is my mother, Keri Whitmore. Mommy, I told Melody that you'd give her a ride home."

Did I smell liquor? Were their eyes glassy? Were their words slurred from an afternoon of self-medicating?

"I'd really appreciate it," Melody said. She turned to Trina.

They knew that I knew. I could tell by their friendly, phony smiles. Where had they been besides shopping? What had they been doing?

"It's nice to meet you, Melody."

Trina slipped her arm through mine. I breathed deeply to detect weed or alcohol, then stared into her eyes. Were her pupils dilated? "Don't be mad," she said. "Melody and I skipped the last hour of group."

I modulated my internal screaming, made my voice sound normal. "Really?"

"They were just talking about the same old stuff they always talk about, so we went to the store. I told you that I needed a top. Look."

She opened the bag and pulled out a pale yellow blouse.

"Nice," I said.

She beamed, then retrieved a smaller bag from inside the larger one and handed it to me.

A lipstick. Just my shade of red.

"Thanks, honey. You know," I said, looking at Trina, "I have to get back to the shop. A couple of clients are bringing in clothes. Where do you live, Melody?"

"In Compton."

"Compton! You come all the way from Compton to Beverly Hills?"

"The program out my way was full."

I looked at my watch. It was three-twenty. The trip to Compton and back to the store would take at least an hour and a half, maybe more if I ran into traffic. My first client was due at four-thirty and the next at six o'clock.

My daughter's smile was bright and expectant, manipulative. Regardless of what it had taken away, mental illness had conveyed to her a kind of protracted childhood, a long pause filled with delusions of grandeur, no responsibility, very few apologies, and endless adventure. And to me it should have bequeathed an elastic sense of gratitude for life's most minuscule concessions: My daughter was standing right in front of me; I didn't have to go looking for her. Instead, I felt anxious. *When is she going to get back to normal?*

. . .

"BE GRATEFUL," MA MISSY TOLD ME ONE MORNING, WHEN my mother's semiconscious body was lying across the living room floor. She was breathing, but we couldn't rouse her. It was important for her to wake up, wash up, get dressed, and accompany me to school, as she had promised that she would. She was supposed to meet my teachers, sit in the back of the room, and smile when she saw my papers with stars hanging up on the bulletin board, smile again when she heard all the good things the teachers had to say about me. But she wasn't moving, only moaning as I shook her. Ma Missy called her name, softly at first and then loudly. I began to cry. Ma Missy stopped calling my mother and put her arms around me.

"Be grateful, baby. One of these days she'll be all right, and you won't even remember the bad times. Plenty things worse than a drunk mama. Be strong, girl."

But I had never learned to be grateful for having less than I really wanted.

"WE'RE GOING TO HAVE TO HURRY," I SAID, PICKING UP MY cell phone.

Once we reached the car, Trina and Melody sat in the back together, their loud conversation a kind of voluble stage for me to pitch my thoughts against. From time to time they would lower their voices and whisper, reminding me of two conspiratorial teenagers, plotting against the adult.

Compton always surprised me. The neighborhood seemed less the subject of the bicoastal gang warfare of rap lyrics than a blue-collar version of the American dream. Away from its hardscrabble commercial strip, with its row of fast-food restaurants—that high-fat staple of urban America—Korean mom-and-pops, overpriced gas stations, and more beauty salons than beauty, the LA version of "da 'hood" looked like a PG-rated movie. I let Melody out in the middle of a block of neat bungalows, in front of a gray house with a postage-stamp lawn bordered by roses and the ubiquitous impatiens that claimed every garden in LA as home.

"I sure do appreciate the ride," Melody said, as Trina exchanged her seat for the one beside me. "Drive safe." She smiled, then waved green dragon-lady fingernails in my direction.

"Trina," I said, when we were halfway down the street, "you've had perfect attendance at the partial program. You should be very proud of that. Now"—I hesitated, searching for the right words; Trina's therapist had told me that she needed my approval—"you must stick to the program schedule and stay until the end of every session."

"All right," she said, her voice soft and petulant.

I looked at Trina. Such a pretty face.

"We had lunch with Daddy," she said. "Aurelia came too. When he called at the shop the other day, we arranged it."

"Oh."

"He didn't know I was ditching group. I thought we'd get back in time, but we were having fun. It was kind of a delayed birthday celebration."

"Was Melody with you the entire time?"

Our eyes met; our lips twitched: We were still in tune. Trina and I snickered. Clyde was from the Booker T school of black upward mobility. According to him, if people remained on the bottom it was because they wanted to be there. He'd adopted this philosophy after he learned there was money in conservative politics. Now he had a syndicated radio show from which he broadcast his right-wing sentiments during drive time, Monday through Friday. The talk show, his books and speaking engagements, not to mention his very public anti-affirmative-action campaign, had made Clyde popular and rich. Or unpopular and rich, depending on your party affiliation. Clyde had switched parties, switched streams, and was off course, as far as I was concerned. He was a man with a hole in his soul.

Trina giggled. "Dad pulled me aside and he was like, 'So, do you and Melody hang out together? I mean, she's a lot older than you, isn't she?'"

"What did you tell him?"

"I was like, 'Dad, we don't hang out, per se. We just go to Crazy School together.' You should have seen his face, Mom. Anyway, they were both nice to her. They didn't act stuck up or anything, even when she started speaking Ebonics."

"It's a miracle," I said. Trina made a face. "Mom, you shouldn't stay mad just because you and Daddy broke up before he got rich."

Before Daddy got rich. The transformation occurred after two failed businesses and reasonable success with a third. Just a chance encounter made all the difference. He'd run into a fellow alum. Coffee and conversation followed. Then came lots of cocktail parties with people who frightened me. An invitation to work on a political campaign followed. Keep an open mind; there are rewards, the fellow told him when he balked. Don't do it, I advised. But Clyde's mind had already opened. Something else had closed. Soon I was another thing he'd outgrown.

"I'm not mad," I said, and Trina rolled her eyes.

We were waiting at the corner light. Beyond Trina, on a sidewalk strip of lawn, stood a lemon tree, filled with blossoms. I rolled down the window and took a deep breath. I'd once read that lemon was the strongest of all flavors, not curry or chocolate or coffee. Plain old lemon, which grew anywhere there was warm dirt, could overpower all other tastes. The red light faded to green. Just before driving off, I spotted a heart and two sets of initials carved into the tree trunk. Below them was a hole, the size that a bullet might make.

Trina was quiet during the ride to the shop and stayed in my office, flipping through a magazine, until we closed. The phone was ringing as I drove into my garage, and by the time I got inside there was a message on my answering machine: *This is Mattie. Please come to the meeting tonight. Gloria and I want to see you. Milton, too.*

The dinner with Marie, Brooke, and Nichelle was on my kitchen calendar. Old friends. New friends. Old life. New life. I called Marie, who had already come by the store, bought the shoes, and reconfirmed our dinner date, hoping she wouldn't be at home. But she answered the phone, listening politely as I explained quickly that I wouldn't be able to go to dinner. Something had come up.

"We really wanted to see you," she said.

If my mind had been clearer, maybe I would have addressed the hurt trickling through Marie's statement. As it was, I was mostly concerned with getting off the phone. "Oh, we'll get together, girl."

"No, we won't."

"This is just a very busy time for me."

"We're all busy."

Eyes shut, I visualized Marie, Brooke, and Nichelle, eating in some restaurant, laughing about nothing at all. They'd be talking about casual things, even when they brought up their children. I still couldn't say Trina's name without holding my breath. We had been very close once, bonded women. Soon, Trina would recover, catch up, resume her life. When she got back to normal, all the way back, when the bad days faded like ink in the sun and God handed me my freedom papers, then I'd go to dinner with Marie, Brooke, and Nichelle. Then I'd be casual again.

3

Milton, my friend Gloria's husband, was introduc-
ing the speaker, the famous UCLA professor of psychiatry Dr. Henry
Gold, as I tiptoed down the aisle of All Souls Presbyterian Church,
where the support group was held the last Wednesday of every month. A
small dapper man with a calm air, Milton spoke in a monotone as he
listed the speaker's outstanding accomplishments in his field. From
time to time, he glanced at Gloria, who was seated near the front, and
she would smile and nod. Dr. Gold had already begun speaking when I
slipped into the fifth pew and settled into my seat. I had left the house
late, running back inside several times to get my glasses, a liter of water,
keys. My procrastination was deliberate. The meetings had fallen off my
list of things to do. Already, my mind had begun drifting.

Usually, the support group met in the basement, but that smaller
space couldn't contain the crowd gathered to hear the "internationally
renowned" Dr. Gold. He appeared to be in his forties, a big man whose
voice vibrated with such a hearty cadence that his pronunciation of the
polysyllabic brand and generic names of the latest psychotropic drugs
bounced off his tongue like lyrics to a heartfelt rap. The newsletter had
billed him as "an orthomolecular psychiatrist, an innovator in the field

of brain diseases who has done extensive research on the impact of nutrition on bipolar patients."

"How is mental illness linked to nutrition?" he asked from behind the pulpit.

I opened my schedule book to the blank pages in the back, my pen poised loosely between my fingers. In the darkest days, when the only thing worse than not knowing Trina's whereabouts was being a witness to her manic acts of self-destruction, when seventy-two-hour holds became twofers—therapeutic benefit for Trina and my only possible escape—I would have sat rigidly in my support group chair, straining to hear while thinking, hoping, praying that the knowledge of whatever expert who stood before me might be the salvation I was seeking. Some of the people around me were Clenchers, leaning forward in their chairs, forgetting to take a breath as their muscles locked. Others were cowering on the edge of their seats, as if furtively seeking to ward off the next unexpected pounding of waves they couldn't see from an ocean they couldn't control.

Listening to the ebullient doctor from UCLA rattle off a vitamin regimen for the mood-disordered, I felt myself being pulled back into bleak waters. Strange how the same thing that once kept me afloat now had the power to make me feel as though I were sinking all over again. I stood up, glad that I was at the end of the pew, and walked quickly down the aisle with my head bowed. I knew my face revealed I was desperate to leave, and I didn't want to advertise that to the rest of the group. Making my way to the stairs, I went down to the basement, a large empty room, and took a seat in the back. I'd wait here for the forty-five minutes that the meeting would last and then hang out with Gloria, Milton, and Mattie. I closed my eyes.

The rich, fragrant aroma of percolating coffee and the faint, sweet odor of the cookies and fruit that would be served after the meeting filled the area. The basement was directly below the sanctuary. Dr. Gold's muffled lecture wafted downstairs, but at least I didn't have to watch the hopeful, straining to hear the restorative miracle in each word.

My head was falling forward in a nod when suddenly I bounded straight up. Above me was the unmistakable tone of discord. The words *crap* and *jerks* and *so-called experts* were hurled through the floorboards like spears. A few minutes later, heavy, deliberate footsteps were descending.

"Keri?"

The white woman in front of me wasn't so much standing as she was looming, a wounded lioness pressing against her cage. My name was a snarl in her mouth. There was an unlit cigarette between her two fingers, and she flipped it back and forth furiously. She was tall and a bit overweight, with frizzy hair that was growing out of the blond dye job that someone had administered too many appointments ago. Her hazel eyes were partially hidden by drooping eyelids above and dark circles below. Whatever age she was, she looked older.

"Bethany," I said. "How have you been?"

She nodded, a clipped, jerky gesture that underscored the tension that was tightening the muscles in her face, the cords in her neck. In the world of the Serenity Prayer, tranquillity was definitely not her goal. Bethany was the rabble-rouser of the group. At every meeting she railed against insurance companies and psychiatrists, medications and rules. She waved her cigarette and ignored my question.

"That Dr. Gold is full of shit. This fucking group is full of shit."

She didn't lower her voice. Bethany wasn't looking for a response, just an opening. My head tilted slightly. From that angle, her rage was palpable, bristling on her face like a skunk's raised tail.

Wham! The heel of her hand hit the back of my folding chair. "This is such a sick joke. He's talking about nutritional supplements, the latest this, the latest that, the marvelous advances. How the hell do we get them to take anything? Tell me that. Dammit, we're all here because the people we love won't take their meds. That's why their lives are a mess, and that's why our lives are a mess. If the expert isn't going to address that one salient issue, he might as well stay away from the party."

The chair's last vibration subsided just as Bethany's rant ended. I half expected some angry church administrator to burst into the room and demand that we settle down, which would have been futile. What was inside Bethany couldn't be called to order. I knew from previous meetings that her daughter was a wild marauding schizoaffective—a mixture of psychosis and mood disorder, not necessarily at the same time—zooming full throttle toward the abyss. The emotions registering in Bethany's tired eyes and pressed lips vacillated between outrage and hysteria. I knew how bad it could get, and it was clear that Bethany was living in that deep gully. There wasn't a rope long enough to pull her out. I reached up and squeezed her hand.

"It is what it is," she said grimly. "How's your daughter?"

I didn't want to tell her, didn't want to make her feel worse than she already did. "She's doing okay," I said.

"You're so lucky. Angelica is still . . . way, way, way out there."

Her face was exhausted. She seemed completely drained, as though someone had siphoned from her everything that made her human.

"I'm sorry. She'll come around. She's still young."

She looked as though she needed to be touched. I stood up and hugged her. I'd been a masseuse once, in another life, right after my college years. My grandmother had had arthritis; it comforted her for me to rub her back and shoulder blades, and it soothed me too. So I took a class, and then another, and after a while friends and friends of friends were calling me, setting up appointments, paying me. My first job in LA—after Clyde, Trina, and I moved there from Atlanta—was working as a masseuse in a hot Beverly Hills day spa. Clyde thought it was a pink-collar job, that working with my bare hands demeaned him as he moved up. He reminded me that I had a college degree and nagged me to quit. A public relations firm hired me; later I opened the store. But soothing bodies will always be my gift.

I kneaded the area on Bethany's back between her shoulder blades. The knots I felt had absorbed a lot of tension that would take weeks to rub out. When I was just getting started as a masseuse, I'd touched a woman where her emotional pain was stored and she began crying hysterically right on the table. With Bethany I stopped rubbing after a few minutes; it would have taken very little for her to become unhinged.

"You have to take care of yourself," I said, which was support-group speak, better than English for easy detachment. I tried to step back from Bethany, not wanting to think about her pain, let alone see it. Her sorrow was a skin I had partially molted. But Bethany wouldn't release me. We stood there hanging on to each other, while above us we heard the commotion of people getting out of their chairs. In a moment they would troop down to the basement en masse.

"Angelica's becoming a monster," Bethany whispered against my neck. "She goes into bars and starts physical fights with anybody: men, women. She's attacked me." Her sunken eyes filled with tears. "It's not as though what she has is a death sentence. Why won't she take her meds?" She pulled back from me and stared into my eyes. "Why? She's not so far gone that she can't see what a mess her life is. Do they forget what normal feels like?" She took a breath, flipping her cigarette up and down. "And then they give us this asshole, telling us about vitamins."

She wiped her eyes, squared her shoulders, and dropped my hand.

"Look at this," she said, turning so I could see the back of her head. I tried not to gasp. There was a large bald spot near the top.

"It'll grow back. You need to stop worrying. Listen, the kids are on their own timetable. Angelica's not dead. She's not in jail. Be grateful for that. She's still here, so she has a chance to begin again."

"Like your daughter?"

I nodded. "Six months ago, if anyone had told me that my child would be where she is now, I don't think I would have believed them. My hope was gone at that point. This is a kid who'd beaten me up, was smoking dope on a daily basis, was hanging out with the dregs of the earth."

"Promiscuous?" Her voice dropped when she pronounced the word.

We both looked at each other and breathed deeply. It didn't matter that hypersexuality was a standard part of the illness, this tragic impulse we couldn't take in stride. Bethany saw what was in my eyes: Don't go there.

"What am I supposed to do, leave this up to fate? I'm supposed to say the goddamn Serenity Prayer while my child destroys her life because her fucked-up brain keeps telling her she's okay?"

"It's hard, but what else can you do?"

"Not everybody sits around waiting," she whispered, then glanced around her. "There are other alternatives." Bethany must have seen the question in my eyes, but she didn't answer it. "You haven't been to many meetings lately. I think you feel the same way I do about this crap. You just don't know it yet."

"No," I said quickly. "You're wrong. The group helped me. I couldn't have gotten through this alone."

She gave a short laugh; then her face went grim. "There's all kinds of ways not to be alone," she said. "Better. There is such a place. It's not just a rumor some shrink got started. I will do whatever I have to do to get there," she said.

"You can't make it happen."

"Yes, I can."

Her intensity sent a tremor through me, like when I heard Aretha sing "Respect" for the first time. I watched her as she walked away. She moved like a warrior woman, with long, purposeful steps, as though she were on her way to someplace very specific. *Yes, I can.* Wherever those words led her, it wouldn't be an easy journey.

People were already filling up the basement. I looked around. The meeting was on the west side of town, land of high real estate, fair-skinned people, and the coldest ice. Part of me resented having to trek all the way from Crenshaw to get help for my child's issues. But the truth was, mental illness had a low priority on my side of the city, along with the color caste and the spread of HIV. Some things we just didn't talk about, even if it was killing us. So I had to come to the white people, who, although just as traumatized, were a lot less stigmatized by what-ever went wrong in their communities. All this is to say: It was easy to spot Gloria, Milton, and Mattie in the crowd.

Milton gave me a quick kiss on my cheek. "You're looking good, girl," he said.

"Welcome back, stranger," Gloria said.

"You look great," Mattie said.

I twirled around. "Armani. Retails at twenty-four hundred. On sale for three twenty-five. Take it home tonight."

"What will *you* wear?" Gloria asked.

"Your money," we all said together.

Mattie and Gloria cracked up.

"Let's go get something to eat," Mattie said.

"Listen, you girls go on," Milton said. "We're having a quick com-mittee meeting about the state conference. Mattie, can you—"

"I'll take Gloria home," Mattie said.

"Thanks." He hesitated for a moment, then kissed his wife's mouth. "You behave yourself," he said. Gloria gave him a loving shove.

I left my car where I'd parked it and got into Mattie's ten-year-old Caddy. She drove a few blocks and then pulled up in front of the restau-rant bar and grill that was our favorite hangout after meetings. The aroma of garlic and roast chicken assailed us as soon as we entered. The waitress led us to a table in the center of the room. We each ordered a glass of wine. Before we drank a sip, Mattie took our hands in hers.

"Dear Lord, we are praising your name, and we are in awe of your power. We ask that you bless the women seated at this table. Give us strength for our journey. Bless our children, keep them safe, Lord. Let no harm come to them, and let them do no harm to anyone. We ask that you lead them to their healing. Restore their souls and their lives. Finally, Master, give us the joy that passes all understanding. Don't let our children's problems rob us of our joy. We're grateful for all your many blessings. Amen."

"Amen," Gloria and I said.

Discovering one another had been like falling in love. The desire to help our kids and survive their trials was the heat that forged our passion; our mutual pain was the greatest attraction I'd ever known. The joke we told at that first support group meeting was that we were the only black people in America willing to admit having mental illness in our families.

"Hell, being black is hard enough," I'd said. "Please don't add crazy."

In those first months, not a day went by when we weren't on the phone in constant three-way calls. Sometimes Milton joined in; other times only the women spoke. At times we did more crying than talking, but sometimes we laughed. The pull of that tripartite romance had waned for me; it had been replaced by my daughter's healing. But I had come tonight because of Mattie's request.

When the waitress appeared for the third time, Mattie and I asked for hot chicken sandwiches. Gloria said she wasn't hungry and requested another glass of wine.

"So, Trina's doing okay?" Mattie asked.

I nodded. "She's taking the meds, working the program. She's supposed to start school this fall."

"God is good," Gloria said, in a way that let me know she wished that God had been as good to her.

"How's her dad," Gloria asked, "Mr. Anti–Affirmative Action?" She shook her head and laughed a little.

When people made derisive comments about Clyde, I always

wanted to say, But he's not really like that. I had to bite my tongue time and time again, because I kept forgetting that Clyde no longer reflected me.

"Still in denial," I said.

"How's Wellington?" I asked Gloria. Her twenty-three-year-old son had schizophrenia.

"Homeless," she said tersely, gulping the last of her wine. She motioned to the waitress to bring her another. "He came by my house two weeks ago." She shook her head. "Filthy. Looking terrible. Smelling bad. I think he's on crack."

The mentally ill sang duets more often than solos. They harmonized with self-medication that temporarily helped them hit their notes, only to lead to even more brain discord later on.

Gloria took the wine from the waitress before she could put it down. As she gulped it, red drops spilled onto the table. She didn't notice. "He wanted to come in and eat, take a shower."

"Did you let him?" I asked.

"The girls did. They're still the adoring little sisters. Milton wasn't home, so it wasn't very smart. Anything could have happened. But he was so dirty. I gave him a scrub brush and some Pine-Sol. He was one funky brother."

We started chuckling.

"That bad?" I said, still laughing.

"Shiiiit. Dove ran out the door; Lifebuoy jumped out the window. Dial was going for the liquor cabinet."

We hooted.

"And he had the nerve to get an attitude with me," Gloria said, shaking her head. "Anyway, he took a shower, had a shampoo. I washed his clothes, fed him, and sent him on his way. Haven't heard from him since. My sister said that she saw him downtown last week, and he looked as though he'd been beaten up."

"Oh, God," I said.

"Maybe you should get conservatorship," Mattie said. "You could have him put in a locked facility."

"That's a hard choice to make," I said. Locking up your own kid— the thought made me shudder.

"Yeah." She finished her glass of wine. "You know, Wellington didn't like to bathe when he was a kid. I'd send him up to get a bath and brush his teeth, and he'd just put on his pajamas and get in the bed. He was always so surprised when he got busted. 'Aw, Mom, how'd you know?' I'd say, 'Knucklehead, the soap is dry. The tub is dry. The washcloth is dry. The toothbrush is dry. Duh!' He didn't voluntarily clean up until he hit puberty and discovered the ladies. Then we couldn't get him out of the bathroom. Some girl must have given him some in eleventh grade, because after that Milton and I used to call him Mr. Obsession for Men."

"He's so handsome," I said.

We'd all shared pictures of our children.

"Yes, under the grime he's a good-looking guy. Under his dreadlocks, he's got a sharp but malfunctioning brain. I'm trying to get him into another living place, but to qualify he has to be sober for thirty days. And then, you know, when he was living at the last one, the people didn't run a very tight ship. I know for a fact that some of the residents smuggled in alcohol, including my son. So . . ." Her voice trailed off. "How's Nona?" she asked Mattie.

"Nona's holding on. I visited her at the prison two weeks ago, and she looked good."

"Were you able to get her into the mental health section?" I asked.

She shook her head. "There's a waiting list."

"How much longer will she be in there?"

"Three months."

Gloria and I made noises in our throats. Nonverbal empathy.

"I think if she weren't in jail she'd be dead," Mattie said. She chuckled. "It's cheaper than A Caring Place. I'm still paying that off. Six thousand dollars for a four-week stay. That's room and board, group sessions, private counseling, family counseling. The insurance is only paying half, and it took about twenty phone calls and I don't know how many letters to get them to pay anything. I'm in yet another support group: Mothers of Mentally Ill Inmates."

"You mean, Mothers of Mentally Ill Inmates with Bills," Gloria said. "After a while, support groups will replace families. It won't be about who you're married to. All the official forms will ask for date of birth, social security number, and support group affiliation."

We laughed hysterically. We always either laughed or cried like crazy whenever we got together.

"Seriously, though, we need to start a group in the 'hood," Gloria said. " The Come Out of the Closet Support Group."

We all chuckled.

The waitress appeared with our sandwiches. Gloria asked for another glass of wine.

"It's always going to be like this," she said, taking a sip.

"Oh, honey—" I began.

She waved her hand. "No. No, I've made my peace with it. I'm not looking for Wellington to get any better. Milton's the optimist in our house. I'm the realist." She glanced sternly at us. "So don't think you have to give me some kind of pep talk, because I'm fine." She looked at Mattie. "Did you tell Keri about Ray?"

Ray was Mattie's estranged and soon-to-be former husband. "What?" I asked.

"He moved in with Carolyn. He bought her an engagement ring. And she's pregnant."

I might have been a little out of the loop, but no part of the announcement was a surprise. It was clear to me early on that Mattie's husband was in the process of moonwalking out of her life and away from their daughter's mental illness. I'd met Ray and Mattie together the first time I attended a support group meeting. He was fine, an aging pretty boy, tall and chiseled with a wide smile: an amiable guy. But I knew the minute I shook his hand that he didn't have the fortitude for whatever lay ahead. We were all at the beginning of a journey none of us had chosen to take, and I sensed that he would get off the train the first chance he got.

"The funny thing is—well, maybe not so funny—that the mental illness comes from his gene pool," Mattie said.

"It's never us. That's the rule," Gloria said, and we laughed.

"Seriously, his mother hasn't left her house in about five years."

"What's that, agoraphobia? That's not mental illness," I said.

Mattie raised her eyebrows.

"Technically, it's a phobia," I said, "not a brain disease."

"He's also got a sister who is classically bipolar, seasonal affective disorder and everything. Every fall she flatlines; come spring, she's danc-ing on the ceiling. So anyway—"

"You don't seem all that upset," I said.

"In a way it's anticlimactic," Mattie said. "It was hard being alone at first, but now I'm okay. And it's been—what, six months? I was afraid Nona would have a bad reaction because she wasn't doing well at the time, but the breakup didn't make her any worse. I mean, she's in jail. What could be worse than that? Except, I truly believe that God placed her in jail for a reason. To keep her alive, for one. To gain perspective, maybe. I don't know.

"Anyway . . . a lovely man has come into my life. I kept running into him at the auction house. A couple of times he outbid me. The last time it happened, we got to talking, and he invited me out for coffee. And—there you have it."

"Good for you," I said. "What's he look like?"

"He's white, shorter than I am by many inches, not all that cute; however, when we get together I can't stop laughing. And he brings the thunder and the lightning to the sheets."

"Whoa," Gloria and I said.

"Oh, and he's got money. Boyfriend owns many apartment buildings."

"Whoa," we said again.

"Does he know about Nona?"

Mattie shook her head. "No need. By the time she comes home, the affair will be over. This isn't serious. This is fun."

"Well, you deserve some," I said. "Everybody needs some heat under the sheet." We laughed. "I talked to Bethany tonight."

Mattie rolled her eyes. "That woman needs meds."

"You think so?" I asked.

"She's a little . . . I don't know. I'm not saying she's mentally ill, but she's definitely out there. Going off on the speaker. That wasn't called for."

"After she cussed out Dr. Gold, she came downstairs and hinted to me that she knew some alternative ways that would help her daughter."

"You're going to look up and see her on *America's Most Wanted*," Mattie said.

"Yeah, maybe so," I said.

I was ready to leave after Gloria finished her fourth glass of wine, but she ordered another. Three pairs of eyes met: Mattie's, the waitress's, and mine. I started to say something, but Mattie put her hand on my arm and shook her head.

"I'm driving," she said.

"Don't worry about me," Gloria said. "I'm fine."

She didn't have a problem standing up or even walking to the door, but once she got outside, she began to crumple, then fold. Mattie had walked ahead to bring her car around and had just turned the corner when Gloria started going down. I grabbed her arm, but her legs began buckling and she would have landed on the sidewalk if a man and a woman hadn't been walking past us toward the restaurant. Gloria fell against the man, who was wearing a fedora, low on his forehead; he grabbed her by her elbows and pulled her up. Then he looked at me.

"Keri."

"Orlando."

The woman, who was standing behind him, seemed to perk up when she realized that we knew each other. She was young and unsmiling. She folded her arms as Orlando tried to keep Gloria from falling.

"Are you all right?" he asked, peering into Gloria's half-closed eyes.

"It's not a medical emergency," I said, trying to keep her steady. "She's just had a little too much to drink."

"I'm all right," Gloria mumbled.

"Where are you parked? I'll walk you to your car," he said, then turned to his date. "I'll be right back. Just going to help out these ladies."

"Thanks, but our other friend is getting the car. She should be here any minute."

Orlando was now supporting Gloria by letting her lean against him. If he moved, she would topple over.

"I think I'd better stay put until she gets here."

Behind him, the unsmiling young woman coughed a little.

"You look good, Orlando," I said, loud enough for Pretty Young Thing to hear. "How's PJ?"

"Do I know you?" Gloria asked, tilting her head and thrusting her face close to Orlando's chin.

The grin appeared slowly, just a tiny twitching of his lips at first before it finally took up his entire face.

"Gloria, this is Orlando Hightower. He's an actor. You probably saw him on television. He was in *And Baby Makes Eight*, and he's done a lot of movies."

"I *loved* that show," Gloria said. "I was mad when they took it off."

I calculated we had ten seconds before Orlando's fedora split.

"Here's our friend," I said as Mattie pulled up in front of us.

Orlando put his arm around Gloria's waist and guided her toward the car. Watching them, I recalled how hot Orlando's hands could get. How that heat got trapped inside me. He situated Gloria in the back of the car, buckled her seat belt, and closed her door.

Orlando looked good standing under the streetlamp. "How's PJ?" I asked again.

" 'Lando," Pretty Young Thing said.

"I'll be right with you," he called. "PJ is PJ," he said to me, then extended his hand.

"Wasn't that the guy who came with you to support meeting a couple of times?" Mattie asked when I slid into the seat beside her. "Weren't you two going together?"

"We broke up about six months ago."

"He seems like a nice brother."

"He's a lot of work," I said. "Maybe that's why he needs a young girl. God bless her, she's got more energy than I do."

"I'm having a party." This from the back of the car. I'd missed the resurrection.

"When?" I asked, turning around.

"Friday at eight o'clock. This is your only invitation. Potluck."

"I'll make some chicken," Mattie said, "and I'll bring my friend."

"I'll bring some monkey bread," I said.

TRINA WAS IN THE FAMILY ROOM WHEN I GOT HOME, AND the telephone was ringing. My daughter seemed oblivious to ringing phones or anything other than the TV show she was watching.

"Keri."

I recognized the voice immediately. "Hi, PJ. We saw you in the car the other day. How are you doing, sweetie pie?"

"I'm cool. How's Trina?"

His voice had deepened since the last time I'd spoken with him. That was only six months ago. Fourteen. It seemed impossible that he was only six the first time we'd met. Four more years and he'd be going off to college.

"Oh, honey, you sound like a grown man." Tears gathered. I had no idea where they'd come from. "Trina's right here. Do you want to talk to her?"

"No. I mean, yeah, but I want to talk to you first."

Covering the phone with my hand, I took several deep breaths. "What's on your mind, honey?"

"Um . . . I just want to say that—um, maybe you could call my dad sometime. I mean, you know, just to talk."

"Oh, sweetie."

"Just to talk."

"Well, I talked with him tonight, if that makes you feel better. We ran into each other at a restaurant."

"Oh, yeah." He seemed to brighten a bit. "He's in a play."

"He told me." The tears were returning. I couldn't outrun them. "Do you want to speak with Trina?"

"Yeah."

I handed Trina the phone, and in a moment she was laughing.

There was an empty pizza box on the coffee table and dirty dishes next to it. I ignored the mess, concentrated on my breathing, and sat down on the sofa beside her. The Russian psychologist told me that mentally ill people relapse and go off their meds because they aren't ready for the responsibilities that come with being sane. He advised me not to expect too much too soon. That was tricky. Looking at Trina, I saw the daughter I'd always had and felt the same expectations. But she wasn't ready to meet them yet.

Trina hung up the phone after a few minutes. As I moved closer, she sidled away from me and then rose. Moments later, I heard her going up the stairs. Good, I thought, checking my watch. She'll be in bed by eleven. I slid over to where she'd been. The cushion was still warm. Orlando's face came to my mind, his laughter filled my head. Or maybe it was PJ's laughter. I was still hearing the sound of it when I opened the side door to the yard, unlatched the gate, and dragged the two garbage cans down the driveway to my sidewalk. I wondered how long he and Pretty Young Thing had been dating and what PJ thought of her.

I was almost at the door when my nostrils began to tingle. Faint, so faint. Barely perceptible. Easily misidentified. It could have been perfume, or incense. Or marijuana. Beyond my yard, I heard a squeal of brakes, the laughter of young people. But the odor didn't disappear with them; it followed me back to my house and hovered just below Trina's window before drifting away.

I stood absolutely still, didn't move until I was breathing again. Once inside, I counted the pills in the bottles on my breakfast room table, the mood stabilizers and the antipsychotics, and counted them again. The television was playing in Trina's room. I knocked on her door and opened it before she responded. Watch your mouth, I told myself. Don't accuse her of anything.

She was sitting on the floor, cramming potato chips into her mouth from a bag beside her. Strewn across the rug were a few open magazines, but she wasn't really reading them or watching television. "I thought you'd be asleep," I said, putting my hand on the back of her neck. She was hot. Beneath the skin, her blood was racing. It wasn't fever, what I felt. Something else.

"I'll go to bed soon."

I sat down on the floor beside her, trying to get close enough to smell her breath, her hair, her clothes. "Give me a hug," I said, reaching for her.

She shifted her body away without looking me in the eye.

"I'm thinking about something," she said, her voice a harsh whine. I heard her muttering, the words unintelligible but not the disrespect. She stood up, went into her adjoining bathroom, and slammed the door shut.

That night I waited for her to creep into my bed, but she never came. The first time I checked her room was around midnight. Trina was in the bathroom, singing loudly. An hour later, when I peeked in her room, she was dancing, flailing her body from side to side, kicking her legs high, spinning around and around and around. I used to love to watch Trina dance, but now the sight of her frenzied movements frightened me.

Calm down. Anybody can have a sleepless night, I thought, creeping back to my room. It doesn't mean anything. I didn't actually smell marijuana on her, just in the air around her, near her. The voice in my head grew louder, defensive. *She's been taking her medication, going to the program. Don't jump to conclusions. Have a little faith. Even people with normal brains can have an off day.*

The memories came back to me so suddenly, so viciously, that I realized they'd been lurking in my mind all along. I closed my eyes and saw Trina, her face garish with makeup, her tight see-through clothes a public invitation, rushing through the house on a manic tear. If she got out of control again, how long would it take to get her back on track? If she stopped taking her meds, what would make her become compliant again? How many times would I have to call the police? How long would I have to wait until she met the criteria for a seventy-two-hour hold?

God, I can't go through this again.

I dozed for about an hour. When I woke up, I went straight to Trina's room. She wasn't there. I ran through the house, calling her name, but she didn't answer. When I looked in the garage, my car was still there, which meant she'd either walked somewhere or called someone to pick her up. Outside, the street was dark, empty. There was just the sliver of a moon and barely any stars. Glancing at the clock, I saw that it wasn't quite three. She could be anywhere, doing anything. Perspiration began dripping down my back. I got dressed and taped a note to the front door: *I'll be right back.* Then I got in my car and drove through the streets in the early dawn: around the corners, up and down the hills. I didn't see anyone. Few cars drove by.

There was more action on Crenshaw: The sanitation workers were going about their work, all-night greasy spoons flashed their welcoming light, and people, mostly young men, milled about, striking quick clandestine deals in the shadows. But I didn't see my child.

I headed south, grateful that there was so little traffic; I could drive slowly, stopping at every bit of movement I saw along the way. The vendors' area was deserted. No T-shirts hung on the chain-link fence. No tapes or CDs were available from the rear of vans. Then I saw Crazy Man, his head thrown back, his mouth open wide. When I rolled down the windows, I could hear his bellow of a laugh. Standing next to him was Trina.

She was sullen on the way home. Her closed mouth was half pout, half snarl-about-to-happen. I had spoiled her great adventure. I knew better than to offer a commentary.

Trina ran upstairs to her room as soon as she got inside the house. The door slammed, cracking the shell of silence that had enveloped the place. I crept up the stairs with aching limbs, feeling as though I'd run for miles. Trina's room was silent. I sat on the top stair, the one closest to her bedroom door. I sat there and I waited, like some ancient, scarred slave who'd run away too many times not to know the bloodhounds already had her scent.

4

I FELT SOME TREPIDATION AS I KNOCKED ON TRINA'S BED-
room door later that morning, but she emerged dressed and ready to
go to the partial program. She seemed surprisingly calm. Her eyes,
though, were unfocused. Behind her, the room was in complete disar-
ray, ripped apart by unseen gales, invisible hurricanes. The natural
disaster appeared to be purposeful, as though Trina had set out to see
how much disorder she could create. She didn't do much talking and
refused to eat the scrambled eggs and toast that I prepared for her. While
I ate, she went outside in the backyard and smoked a cigarette. Only a
few weeks earlier, she'd been talking about giving up the habit. That
would be a conversation for another day. I was frightened. On top of
everything else, one sleepless night had the power to upset an emotional
system that would always be fragile. Trina's sanity was maintained by her
regimen of proper diet, enough rest, psychotherapy, and pills. And so
was mine.

Please be okay, baby.

Trina was silent as we drove past the hucksters on Crenshaw Boulevard. In the bright morning light, Crazy Man was like a silhouette posed
against a white sheet. The block was awhirl with the motion of haphaz-

ard commerce. Only he stood still, his eyes cast down, his jaw slack, his expression vacant and sad, giving no hint that he comprehended the scene in front of him. People walked around him, deliberately not getting too close. Had he ever been diagnosed? Had he ever taken his medication? I wondered if his mother lived in perpetual mourning for him, a woman who couldn't detach or give up, whose birth pains were still coming.

When I parked in front of the Weitz Center, Trina got out without saying good-bye. She ran up the steps leading to her program two at a time, and the big glass doors closed behind her. Ten minutes later, my eyes were still riveted to that spot. After twenty minutes, I drove off.

"You're looking sharp, boss," Frances said when she saw me. She held a portable steamer in her hand and walked slowly from rack to rack, zapping wrinkles. From time to time she ran her fingers through the dark hair that trailed down her back.

"Thank you, darling." I was wearing a light blue pantsuit, business-like with the jacket, casual without. I was prepared for anything. *I will not think about last night.* If Ex-boyfriend dropped in and wanted to take me to lunch, well. . . . I looked like a Pretty Young Thing my damn self.

"Did the Old Man say he could get the stain out of the jacket?" Frances asked.

"It's still in my car. I'll take it in today." I looked around. "Where's Adriana?"

"I don't know. She had a date last night."

"Same guy?"

Frances nodded.

"Did she tell him?"

Frances shook her head. "I don't think so."

Once inside my office, I made myself a cup of peppermint tea and called Trina's psychiatrist. Dr. Bellows had been monitoring her medication ever since she'd become compliant, interpreting her monthly blood tests, making sure that the psychotropic drugs she ingested didn't wreak havoc on her liver. He titrated the dosage up or down as her moods escalated or subsided. It was just a little after nine and naturally he wasn't in his office, so I left him a lengthy message describing Trina's behavior, asking him to call me as soon as possible.

Trina's therapist, whose job it was to unravel the complicated skein of emotions Trina's brain was constantly knitting, wasn't in either, and I left her the same message. I repeated it again for Elaine, the program director at the Weitz Center, adding an urgent postscript.

"Please keep an eye on Trina today. She was up all night, and I'm afraid that . . . that . . . I'm afraid. . . ."

I closed my eyes. Saw Trina, her mouth gaping and twisted, screaming curses. Saw Trina with her weapon of choice, the telephone, calling, calling, calling, way into the night. Felt Trina's fist crashing into my skull. Heard her screeching laugh.

"Just—call me."

Customers began drifting in at ten. A client I'd been expecting came in with a Vera Wang gown while I helped a woman choose between two dresses. Frances was busy. Adriana still hadn't shown up or called. I excused myself from the customer, ushered the client into my office, and returned to the floor, banishing the annoyance that was sitting between my shoulder blades.

Half an hour later, Adriana rushed through the door. I gave her a look, and she got pink in the face. "Oh, Keri, I'm so sorry," she said. "Traffic."

"Mulholland Drive has been waiting for fifteen minutes in my office."

"Oh."

What in her voice, in her face, made me look past her, out the picture window, to see him walking away? Just a man on a street, going somewhere or nowhere. What made me think that he'd been with her? What was in his walk, his carriage, his profile that made me think—no, made me know—that he was dangerous? I watched him until I couldn't see him, and then I began to watch her.

Most employees who'd pissed off the boss would steer clear. Not Adriana. For the rest of the morning she was bringing me tea and scones, trying to make me laugh and being so solicitous that eventually she wore me down.

"You can quit sucking up now," I said when she offered to buy me lunch whenever I was ready. I was sitting in my office, pricing half a dozen new items. Adriana hated to upset me, mostly because she felt she owed me so much, which she really didn't.

. . .

SHE'D WALKED INTO THE STORE THREE YEARS EARLIER, applying for the job of sales assistant in a soft baby voice. I'd had to ask her to repeat herself. She was only twenty-three at the time, a pretty girl who wouldn't look me in the eye. The résumé she presented showed a gap of several years between the last job she'd held and the present. When I questioned her about it, she told me that she'd been at home in Minnesota helping her aging parents. Her excuse made me wonder. I didn't hire her.

Adriana returned several days later, with two more rejections under her belt. She waited until I finished ringing up a customer and then tapped me on my back. We went into my office; I closed the door. She must have thought I'd be the most understanding.

"I want to tell you the truth," she said.

I figured she'd admit to a string of firings and that, after prodding, she'd confess to inefficiency.

Surprise, surprise!

"I've been working as a call girl," she said in her soft voice.

"How did that happen?" I asked.

It was the same old sad story: Stepdaddy liked to play touchy-feely and Mama liked to play blind. By seventeen she'd left home with dirty handprints on her body and mind. She told me her tale with no tears, no gulping for air. But her face wasn't hard either, which impressed me.

Nobody ever sets out to become a prostitute. It's the place they end up, like Denny's at midnight. Given my own Former Fast Girl credentials, I had no desire to judge someone for getting paid for what had once been my favorite hobby. Yeah, that was twelfth-grade me, with my bare feet sticking out the back window of somebody's daddy's fogged-up gyrating Ford. That was college me, downing way too much Jack and waking up smooshed against some frat boy I barely knew. And that was old-enough-to-know-better me, sneaking into the motel with Sally Sue's husband. Or was it Ruby Begonia's old man? Me again, looking in the mirror, seeing nothing but ugly. For quite a while, that was me. Clyde had helped me to heal. Things shifted inside me after Trina was born, kind of like my own personal tectonic plates. I had fresh joy to push away the memories of bad times. Trying to make life better for Trina, I outgrew my own pain. Until the baby died.

Clyde, Jr., was our second and came four years after Trina was born.

He was fat and round and sweet, a pleasant, cooing baby. One night his cooing stopped. Crib death is a quick death. The slow death came later.

"Look," Adriana had told me, "I've made a lot of bad choices in my life, but I'm trying to get straight now."

"Are you on drugs?" I asked.

"No."

"No?" I waited.

"I've been clean and sober for about a year."

"Are you in a program?"

"Narcotics Anonymous."

"So you want to work here with me?"

She nodded.

"And then what? After you outgrow an entry-level position that doesn't pay all that much, what then? Suppose some guy comes in here. How do I know you won't proposition him?"

"I'm supposed to take things one day at a time," she said.

"I'm not. You're young. You seem intelligent. Think about school. I'll let you know about the job."

"I will work so hard for you," she said.

Hiring Adriana proved to be a good move for both of us. She really was ready for a change. I kept mentioning school, and after the first year she enrolled in college at night. She brought me her grades: all A's and B's, and when I praised her she seemed to float. And, except for the occasional tardiness, she was a hard worker, always trying to please me. Maybe too much. But now I wondered if a man with an evil profile was lurking in her life.

In some ways Adriana was like a second daughter, one who had chosen me for a mother. Maybe it was because, after all her other potential employers had turned her down, she had come back to me with the truth. I worried about her. She always seemed so lonely. Adriana never mentioned hanging out with the girls. She seemed not to have a life apart from the store. From time to time she spoke of going out with a man, but it never went any further than two dates. It was on the second date that she always revealed her past.

"Why do you have to tell them anything?" Frances asked when Adriana informed us of her policy. "It's not like you're going to marry them."

"Suppose we're out somewhere and some john comes up to me?"

"Just say, 'You must have me confused with somebody else,'" Frances said.

Adriana shook her head. "I don't want to live a lie."

"That ain't a lie; that's your business," Frances said.

Frances and I kept rooting for the Third Date Man, but so far he hadn't materialized.

Adriana wasn't the only redeemed soul working with me. Right before I hired her, Frances had lived in a shelter for battered women. She'd landed there after she fled from her first husband's fists and finally his weapon. Her social worker was one of my customers. She'd told me about Frances's situation and convinced me to hire her. I never thought about why the three of us came together, but people come into each other's lives for a reason. If it's not clear in the beginning, all you have to do is keep on living.

I WAS STILL PRICING GARMENTS, MY HEAD BENT OVER A beaded silk purse, when I felt a hand on my shoulder. When I looked up, Frances was smiling at me. "Somebody's here to see you," she said.

"Orlando?"

I smiled to myself, feeling smug.

She shook her head. "It's your ex."

As in husband, not boyfriend. My heart pumped a little bit harder. I put my jacket back on and pressed my lips together quickly to maximize their color.

When Clyde saw me, his eyes widened just enough to let me know he thought I was looking good. Which made me smile.

"Sorry I didn't call. I was in your area and, uh—I just—"

"Is something wrong?" He rarely came by, and never without calling.

"No, I just—have you had lunch?"

The restaurant was in a strip mall off Wilshire in the heart of Koreatown. The owners, former guest workers in Japan, had learned the art of making sushi from the masters and brought their skills to the west. The place was located down the street from spa row, where new immigrants had opened luxury massage parlors that catered to an arriviste clientele as well as anyone looking for the cheapest body scrub in town. Koreatown had risen like the phoenix from the fires of 1992. That year rioters enraged by the verdicts that had exonerated the LA police, whose video-taped beating of Rodney King had been seen around the world, unleashed their fury on a group they viewed as exploiting them in their own neighborhoods. Although their gripe was with those Koreans who'd established mom-and-pop stores in black and Latino communities, charged high prices for goods, and never hired any of the people who lived in the area, rioters and looters traveled to Koreatown to exact their revenge. Businesses were destroyed, and so were dreams. But now the area seemed to be surging with an abundance of shops and malls, offering everything from clothes to electronics to karaoke-infused happy hours and barbecue à la Seoul. The Koreans had survived the fires of 1992, and in the process they'd internalized an American mantra: A setback is just a setup for a comeback.

It was a lesson few of the looters had learned.

As we sat down, Clyde appraised the restaurant and the waiters bustling back and forth. "Now see," he said, leaning across the table toward me, "I'll bet you anything that everybody here is a family member. That's why Koreans are so successful. If black people would just—"

"Clyde." I wasn't in the mood for one of his "Up, up, ye mighty race, you can accomplish what ye will" speeches, but he ignored me.

"—stop complaining and learn from these immigrants, they'd be better off."

"They?"

Clyde sighed. "The secret of Korean success is hard work and unity." He sat back in his chair and gave me a self-satisfied smile. "Do you still like eel?" he asked.

"Love it."

"Okay, we'll get the elephant roll," he said, marking off a tiny square. "How about yellowtail?"

I nodded, glad his diatribe had ended, watching his fingers as he held the pencil; he clenched it. When he looked at me, he seemed awkward, as though he'd spoken out of turn and regretted it. The waitress appeared; he ordered, didn't say a word, and began eating as soon as the food came. I didn't feel uncomfortable with the silence. Even when we were married, Clyde wasn't much of a talker. He was too busy hanging out in his own head to let me in.

"Do you want to know how Trina's doing?" I asked.

"Yes, of course." He looked sheepish, as though I'd caught him in a lie.

If I tell him the truth, we'll just argue, I thought. "She's fine; she's just fine." He nodded absentmindedly; he hadn't been listening. "What's on your mind? Why did you invite me to lunch?" When he looked at me, his face was troubled. "What?" I asked. "What's wrong?"

He stared at me a long time. "Aurelia wants to leave me."

"I'm so sorry. What happened?"

"A lot of stuff happened. She wanted a baby, I didn't. That was major. But I told her I didn't want kids when we got together. She hates all the functions and appearances that I have to make because of the job. She says I don't give her enough of me."

"You can't be in a relationship with someone if you're chasing dollars and fame twenty-four/seven."

"She knew what my life was like when we got together."

"Aurelia is your fourth wife. Doesn't that tell you something?"

He grew quiet. I knew he was going through the roll call of ex-wives in his mind.

"Yes, it tells me something."

"Have you tried marriage counseling?" Clyde had refused to get help for our marriage, but I hoped he was more open now.

"I'm not into that," he said. "I was hoping maybe you could talk to her."

"Me?" I said, feeling angry all of a sudden.

"Aurelia likes you. She respects you. She'd listen to you."

"And what am I supposed to be saying?"

"That I'm a good person. That she should stay."

"Clyde—"

"She and Trina have always gotten along so well. It might be difficult for them to have a relationship if Aurelia and I aren't together. You know how that goes. I don't want Trina to have another loss."

So many conflicting emotions bombarded me. I felt sadness and a rush of excitement, but mostly I felt angry that once again Clyde was asking me to pick up the pieces. "Will you at least consider therapy?"

His face darkened. "I told you. I'm not into that."

"Your kid sure had to get into it."

"That's because you forced her to go."

"And if I hadn't, do you know where she'd be?"

"She'd be fine. Probably better off without some shrink putting weird ideas in her mind."

"You're a piece of work, you know that? Trina needs counseling, and she needs medication. And you—"

"All right. All right. We can talk about that later. Will you just do me this one favor? Please."

To end the argument so soon was a letdown. Venom was still coursing through my veins. Once Clyde tapped my rage, it was hard to stop the flow, but I swallowed my retort and ate my sushi. Neither digested well.

Home is the place where, if you have to go there, they have to take you in. Was I still home to Clyde? Was that why he'd come to me?

We were young together, Clyde and I. We were poor together. In our time we made love that set the roof on fire. The memory of it warmed me still. But I didn't want to remember. I was Clyde's first wife. There had been three others. Our time had passed. That's what I had to keep reminding myself.

When I returned, the store was full, phones were ringing, and Adriana had one question after another for me. Frances informed me that both Dr. Bellows and Trina's therapist had left messages. And, of course, when I called them back, only their answering services were available. I stayed in my office, returning calls and hoping to hear from anyone on Trina's health team. Frances popped in from time to time, pretending that she was looking for something, trying to act busy when her real intention was to check on me.

Elaine from Beth Israel's Weitz Center was the first person actually to speak to me. Trina was where she was supposed to be and hadn't gone AWOL during her cigarette break. Elaine listened quietly as I described Trina's behavior the previous night, her irritability and insomnia. I didn't say I suspected that Trina had been smoking weed, however, because Elaine might have kicked her out of the program.

"Look, Keri," Elaine said, when I had finished talking. "Your daughter has a brain disease. Every day isn't going to be the same for her."

"How has she been acting today?"

"She's been absolutely fine. Maybe a little bit hyper, but you're going to have to relax, dear. Her healing is *her* job, not yours."

I didn't feel quite as dismissed by Dr. Bellows, when we finally spoke later that afternoon. I told him about my suspicion that Trina had been smoking pot.

"Could it send her into an episode?" I asked.

Dr. Bellows sighed. "Yes." He was quiet for a moment; then he proposed increasing her antipsychotic from five milligrams a day to ten for the next few days. "Get her to her psychologist as soon as possible, so she can talk about whatever it is that's bothering her."

It was a good plan, and I hung up feeling relieved. My relief gave way to frustration when I learned that her therapist would be on vacation for the next two weeks. Trina was really attached to her. It would be very unlikely that she'd open up to anyone else, including me.

Frances poked her head inside my office.

"You okay?" she asked.

She didn't wait for me to answer before sitting down on the chair next to my desk. "When my nephew was on drugs, every night was crazy. I can't even remember the number of times me and my sister would get in the car and go riding around looking for his dumb butt. Delores started beating on him in the middle of the street one night, just as he was coming out of some get-high place. She tore him up. But you know what? He was right out there the next night doing the same damn thing. All Delores did was make herself crazy, along with a few of her family members. And for what? When the drugs kicked his ass to the point where he couldn't stand himself, that's when he got clean."

She looked at me and smiled.

"Trina's gonna do what she's gonna do. And you can't stop her." She leaned over the desk and put her hand on mine. "She's going to be all right. You need to stop worrying about her and live your own life."

Why did people always tell me that everything was going to be all right with Trina, as if their saying it could make it come true, as if the sheer force of their good wishes would eliminate even the possibility that my child's illness wouldn't cut loose and boogie her right into an irreversible tragedy?

"You're right," I said. "Now get to work. You're not getting paid for therapy."

Sometimes even the best intentions got on my damn nerves.

. . .

A LITTLE AFTER FOUR O'CLOCK, ADRIANA WALKED INTO my office. A customer had asked to speak with me. I didn't recognize the thin, weak-looking person she pointed out, but the woman smiled when she saw me walking toward her. Her smile was familiar.

"Keri," she said, extending her hand, "I'm Rona. It's been a few years."

"Oh, Rona," I said, trying to place her while she hugged me. There wasn't much to hold on to. Her emaciated body felt as light as a clump of rags in my arms. It occurred to me that she'd been one of my massage clients. A flash of memory revealed her body as once strong and powerful. Something had taken her way down.

"I've been sick," she said when I let her go. "I'm on chemo."

"I'm sorry to hear that."

"Your store is lovely," Rona said. "When I get my weight back, I'll buy something. But I came by today to ask if you still do massages. I've been feeling so bad, and I remembered your golden touch."

"Oh, Rona, I haven't done a massage in so long. I'm so busy with the shop—"

She began nodding, as though agreeing with my decision. "I understand, I understand," she said.

Adriana was suddenly there, her hand on my arm. "You have a telephone call," she said.

"Excuse me," I said to Rona, who watched me walk back to my office.

Elaine spoke in clear, short sentences, the way she'd been trained to do. Trina had started escalating not long after we'd spoken. She'd cursed a counselor and hit another patient. She had run through the first floor screaming that they were all a pack of devils. Elaine had called security. Two guards had escorted her to the upstairs ward, where she had been placed on a seventy-two-hour hold.

I remembered when Trina had wandered off at the flower mart, the homeless man she had been speaking to, the quick furtive way she had slid her hand into her pocket. What had she hidden there? Was it the joint that undid her? Or maybe Melody was the source. Weed from da 'hood. That fit. It didn't much matter now.

"With mental illness, you have to allow for setbacks. The way is rarely smooth," Elaine said.

"I know."

"Once Trina is stabilized, she can resume the program. This isn't the first time something like this has happened," Elaine said. "Be glad she was here."

Yes. Be glad.

"It's probably for the best. Maybe this stint in the hospital will teach Trina once and for all that she has to be vigilant about taking care of herself."

I thanked her and clicked off the phone. Adriana was still standing there, closer than before.

"Uh—" I began, then stopped to concentrate on my breathing: in . . . out . . . in . . . out. "Trina's had a relapse. She's in the hospital."

"Go see her. Frances and I will take care of everything here," Adriana said.

All the months of healing seemed to fade away, like the end of a really good movie. I rushed past Adriana, past Rona, who was still standing right where I'd left her, out the front door onto the parking lot. Only when my key was in the ignition did logic began to kickbox with my emotions. The hospital had her insurance information. Afternoon visiting hours had ended long ago, and the next visiting time wasn't until seven. Going before then would be useless. Even if they let me in, my presence wouldn't change a thing. My presence wouldn't cure Trina. My head pounded against the back of the seat. Once. Twice. It wasn't hard enough to evoke the sweet release of weeping. Whatever tears I had left remained lodged inside of me. I thought about calling Clyde, letting him know what had happened. I actually dialed his number on my cell phone but then changed my mind.

That other bad time, fourteen years ago, came back to me. "Clyde, the baby, the baby—" I had to start over and over. He kept shouting, "What? What? What?" Louder each time, more afraid each time. Each shout made me take longer until I had gagged up the words. "The baby died."

Clyde wouldn't look at me after I said it; he shook his head as if he hadn't heard me correctly. He began shaking right in front of me, his body quivering with spasms he couldn't control. He wouldn't go with me into the bedroom where the baby was lying. When the ambulance came, too late, I had to talk with the men, listen as they told me what to do next. Clyde went into his office and closed the door. I came in later, to check on him, to let him check on me. I was holding Trina. Clyde wouldn't look at us. I remember he wasn't crying or talking; he was working.

I got out of the car, slammed the door hard, and went back inside.

As soon as I entered, Adriana was next to me. "I'm going home," I said. "The visiting hours aren't until later. Don't you have a test tomorrow?"

"Yes."

I stared at her.

"I studied," she said. My eyes were still on her.

"Who was that man?"

She shrank back, turned her head.

"There are people in this world who live just to see you fall. They make their money on weak people. Go to a meeting tonight."

"All right."

Rona hadn't moved from the middle of the floor. She was standing still, watching the swirl of activity around her. My words came out in a rush. "I can do you right now. At my house. You'll have to follow me in your car."

My massage room was on the first floor, right off the family room. I had to wipe the dust off the table and lay down a clean sheet. I checked my oils and put on a soothing CD as Rona sat on a chair in the room. She might have been in her middle or late forties, but her demeanor was that of a much older woman. Her head was covered with a woolen skullcap that she kept on even after she disrobed. Usually, I left the room while the client undressed and returned after she was on the table under the sheet, but Rona needed assistance.

Comforting a body is like cooking a good meal. The ingredients have to be lined up, the utensils prepared, the fire hot enough. Mostly, the chef has to be in the right frame of mind. I needed to concentrate on something outside of Trina and me.

I washed my hands and let warm eucalyptus oil flow into my palms. "Let me hear you breathing, honey," I said. The sound was wispy, filled with frail tremors. "That's right. Deeper, now. A little deeper."

I could feel the fear in her as soon as I put my palms on her feet. Her entire medical history was in the palms of my two hands. Even though I hadn't used my skills in a while, they hadn't disappeared. Her headaches, the childhood asthma, the ringing in her ears, her latest bout with cancer, and the one before that were right at my fingertips.

"Relax," I whispered. "Just let go. Close your eyes and picture the sea."

My thumbs sank into the knots above Rona's shoulder blades and rubbed the swollen muscles, back and forth, until they were putty, malleable, pressed out, serene. I employed the lightest touch. My breath matched the movement of my thumbs, the in-and-out motion of her rib cage, the ticking of the clock, the New Age music on the tape. I felt myself surrendering to the rhythm of the breath and realized that Rona's pain served me.

"Just rest for a while," I said. She nodded. When I turned to leave, to give her privacy, she caught my hand with hers and placed it on her head.

"There. Please."

The cap came off with a quick, smooth movement. Her head was round, muscled, with just the thinnest veneer of pre-Afro fuzz. It was a head that yearned for heat and comfort. I rubbed her with my knuckles, creating tiny concentric circles of warmth all over her scalp. Rona lay perfectly motionless.

"Thank you," she said when I finished.

I left her alone for about fifteen minutes, so she could recover. When I returned she was sitting up, still naked, her stomach shrunken, her skin sagging below the fresh scar on her belly. Her purse was beside her. She had a piece of paper in her hand. She passed the paper to me, and I realized it was a check.

"No. It's on the house," I said, handing it back.

She shook her head. "I want to come back," she said. "Keep it, please."

I looked at the check again. "Your last name is Tubman? Are you related to—?"

"Harriet?" She shook her head. "No. You asked me that the first time we met."

"Your family isn't from Canada, is it? Didn't I read that she settled there after the Civil War?"

"I don't know. I always thought she died in Buffalo."

"Maybe," I said. "I'm forgetting my history."

"Didn't you go to Spelman?"

"Yes."

Once we rediscovered that we were Spelman College sisters, Rona and I chatted as though we'd been dorm mates, reminiscing about the president, the choir, and the white dresses we wore at the induction service.

"I want to go to the homecoming in October. Are you going?" Rona asked.

I shook my head.

"You should come. Anyway, I want another appointment," Rona said. "In a month. Is that okay?"

"A month is good. Call me for the exact time and date."

"I couldn't have done what she did," Rona said, putting away her wallet. "I'm talking about Harriet Tubman."

"Me neither. Most people can't even free themselves, let alone somebody else."

5

AT EXACTLY SEVEN O'CLOCK, I MARCHED RESOLUTELY UP the steps of the Weitz Center, walked through the double doors, and there I was, back in that old familiar world: fifth floor, domain of foreign-born psychiatrists and psychologists, nurses, orderlies, and the homegrown mentally ill. The same bald-headed Ghanaian who'd been guardian of the sign-in sheet the last time Trina was on hold was sitting behind the little table. He gave me a nod of recognition, opened my purse, and rifled through it. Finding no contraband—no alcohol, drugs, sharp instruments, or enough rope for either a hanging or a self-flagellation—he passed it back to me. I walked over to the locked double doors, pressed the buzzer on the wall, and waited until another accented voice, this one Nigerian, told me to come in.

"Hello, Elijah," I said to the nurse who greeted me.

The small dark man smiled at me from behind the nurse's station and gave me a sympathetic look. I'd met him during Trina's first hospitalization, and he'd comforted me back then.

"I saw your daughter when she came in this afternoon. So sorry she's back here. I thought she was doing the program downstairs, that everything was fine."

"Everything *was* fine," I said. The words came out as wailing. The tears surprised me. I hadn't been aware that any of this was so close to the surface.

"You mustn't cry," Elijah said briskly, as though he were appealing to my sense of logic. "Maybe she'll get better."

"I don't understand. She seemed to be doing the program, staying sober."

"It's hard to stay sober, especially when you have a mental illness."

"Yes. Yes. It's just that you live with somebody and think she's doing one thing, committed to one thing, and it turns out that she's not."

"Welcome to the world, babygirl," Elijah said. His Yoruba-soaked English was without a trace of humor. He handed me a tissue. "She's outside, in the smoking area."

The hallway that led to the outdoor smoking area was a long one. To walk down it was to return to a house I'd once lived in. Same old marks on the walls, the carpets. Same old bewilderment befuddling my brain.

There! My first celebrity sighting! The aging actress whose heyday had been in the forties and fifties, when Dorothy and Lena couldn't get much silver-screen love, was walking toward me, holding the hand of a younger, catatonic version of herself. The daughter, her face puffy, her body bloated, moved slowly, with uneven steps. The mother's eyes met mine and locked in silent commiseration. When she passed, I recalled that she'd won an Oscar, but I couldn't name the movie.

Fat zombies, anesthetized by meds that slowed down their metabolism, roamed the halls. A young boy, barely five feet six inches, lumbered toward me, weighing at least three hundred pounds. Another woman, scarcely out of her teens, her huge belly sagging toward her thighs, guzzled a soda from the machine. It had always angered me that none of the psych wards or residential treatment centers was proactive in keeping weight off their mentally ill patients. Their meals were a carb fest, their exercise programs a joke.

Smoke assaulted me as soon as I opened the door at the end of the hall. The room of inhalation and exhalation, where all had the free pass of a nicotine high, was filled, as usual. At least ten people were crowded around the big table that was in the center of the small atrium. Scanning quickly, I didn't see Trina. A second look revealed my baby in a corner chair, her face somewhat obscured by grayish plumes of smoke. She turned away from me. Seated next to her, very close, was a young man who was puffing away.

"Trina."

Her name resonated in the air between us, like a dare that takes some consideration. Her quick finger tapping was freighted with lethargic mania, subdued by meds but not banished. Her eyes still held out the promise that she might try to scale the building and then leap. She wasn't cured, just contained, and couldn't yet be trusted. She blew smoke defiantly in my direction.

"Trina."

Her eyes tried to fool me. But behind the wide-open stare were two shuttered windows. Around me there was shuffling at the table, the soft rustle of hospital gowns, the swishing back and forth of the requisite hospital slipper socks. Curious glances were coming my way from Trina's community of sufferers. I lowered my voice and forged ahead. One-way conversation had its merits.

"Elaine called and told me what happened. Don't feel bad, honey. It's just a little setback, that's all. You'll get right back on track."

Rah, rah, rah!

Trina stubbed out the cigarette she was holding and lit another one. I reached out to take it away from her, but her glare, pure unadulterated essence of pissed off, stopped me. Maternal instinct held no power here.

"Sorry," I murmured. "I don't want you to become a chain-smoker, just because you don't have anything else to do."

Around the table, heads tilted my way. Smoke settled into my cropped curls.

"Trina, would you come into the multipurpose room with me?"

She didn't move. I felt the young man's eyes. He was handsome and grungy; his knee pressed against my daughter's leg. I sighed and settled into the groove in the wall I was leaning against, breathed in addiction and mayhem on pause, watched the people watching me. They were all there. The ancient schizophrenic, Medusa of the Homeless, her rheumy eyes alert to the faint whispers that still resided inside her. The unipols, wrist slitters, trigger pullers, and overdosers who were on the verge of embracing life again. There in the corner, the young one, Little Miss Schizoaffective, manic enough to be bipolar, psycho enough to be schizophrenic—but not quite. At the table, their eyes still wet with craving, twelve-stepping for all they were worth, the addicts: heroin, cocaine, crack, meth, painkillers (an oxymoron, for damn sure). Crazy was not a useful word in this place. Seventy-two-hour holds demanded specifics.

Trina got up suddenly. Stomped out of Smokers' Paradise and down the hall to her little corner of the world, a twin-bedded cubicle with a cubbyhole bathroom. I trailed her right up to her door, which she slammed vigorously in my face.

I hadn't expected to become the enemy again. Weren't those days over? Silent treatment and screaming fits, her palm striking my cheek— wasn't all that finished? Elaine had said a setback. But blowing smoke in my face, not speaking, her silence quivering with hostility—this was starting over.

Tap, tap, tap. Not too loudly. Didn't want anyone to notice. *Tap, tap, tap.* A bit harder. Sore knuckles seemed a fitting beginning. A nurse walked by.

"We don't allow visitors in the rooms," she said. She stood stiff and stern. No getting past her.

"Right," I said, stumbling down the hall.

Something bad was going to happen. The signs were all there: massa was on his deathbed; mistress was crying. Auctioneers and lawyers were assembled on the veranda. I could feel the overseer's eyes assessing the value of my flesh, her flesh. This wasn't my first plantation. Deep South, that's where I was headed.

What I needed was a swamp and a star.

Visiting hours weren't over yet. People were still coming in as I trudged down the hall toward the exit. All the visitors looked worn out and sad, old slaves who'd been worked to death. Nobody ever looked pretty or vivacious on the psych ward. Didn't matter how damn good-looking you were on the outside, once you set foot on the ward, all the ugly and tired that had been lying dormant inside you jumped up in your face and took up residence.

Never look in a psych-ward mirror.

I stood by the metal double doors, waiting until someone buzzed me out. There was a sign that read ALERT! THIS DOOR MUST BE LOCKED AT ALL TIMES. When Trina was on hold at Daniel Freeman Hospital, there was a sign next to the exit that read HIGH ELOPEMENT RISK. When

I read it, my first thought was: Who'd want to get married in a place like this?

"Keri!"

As I stepped off the elevator, the flash of a familiar smile greeted me. "Bethany!" I said, once she released me.

"My daughter just signed herself in yesterday," she said.

Her face seemed internally lit. Everything about her seemed lifted, as though some invisible hand had realigned her spine, propping up her body and her spirit. Bethany looked ten years younger than the last time I'd seen her.

"That's great," I said, sounding to myself as automatic as a stamp machine. There was no place in me to absorb good news, at least not someone else's.

Bethany didn't seem to notice; she was spilling over with the excitement and happiness elicited by her recent reversal of fortune. She wasn't really listening to me. She wanted to plow ahead with the retelling of her miracle. That's what we do, I thought. If we mothers of the unstable survive our children's madness, we examine it, dissect it, and put it back together, embellishing and polishing whatever good we can extract, presenting that semiprecious stone to an audience we hope will not judge us. How brave and pitiful we are.

"I thought the mania would never break. It just had such a hold on her. And then the drugs too. To tell you the truth, I think it was the drugs that brought her here. I've never seen such despair in all my life. She didn't get out of the bed for three days straight. I know she was thinking about suicide. I kept talking and talking and talking. You know," she said, giving me a cursory glance, "saying all the things they taught us in support group that I never thought would work. Only finally it did, and she told me she wanted to come in."

"So she's not on a hold?"

"Voluntary."

Meaning she could walk out of the Weitz Center whenever she got good and ready. I turned away from Bethany. Didn't want her to see the doubt shining in my eyes.

"That's just wonderful," I said, fiddling with the strap of my purse.

"You just don't know. Well, of course you do." It came to her then, a reality bite in the midst of her spiel. "What are you doing here?"

"My daughter had a little episode."

"Oh, no! She was doing so well. This is probably just a blip on the radar. She'll get right back on track."

"Yeah." She didn't want to hear the details, didn't want my sadness to bring her down. I understood.

"Listen, I've got to get upstairs."

Bethany got on the elevator, and I went out the front door.

The traffic on La Cienega Boulevard was mercifully swift, and whatever music was playing on the radio blended in with my thoughts. I didn't sing along. My nose was still clogged with the sterile hospital odor. I rolled down my window and let the breeze clear my mind.

My house seemed wintry once I was inside. Even after the heat had been on for more than an hour I was still trembling, sitting on the sofa wrapped up in a blanket I couldn't even feel. There were things that needed doing. I was hungry, for starters. The phone rang several times; I couldn't make myself answer it. The sofa had claimed me. I watched television with the remote in my hands, click, click, clicking away.

AFTER ABOUT AN HOUR, THE PHONE BEGAN RINGING AGAIN.

"Hello." My voice sounded strange even to my ears, the voice of some escapee, lost in the swamp, trying to rise from the depths of scum and quicksand to reclaim her humanity.

"Keri?"

I had to crawl through mud to connect to that voice, wipe away the sludge in my eyes, clear my throat.

"It's Orlando. How are you doing?"

His name was a whiff of fragrance, a snatch of a dance tune.

"I'm . . ." A throat full of tears. It would be dangerous to speak. "I'm okay," I said finally.

"I was wondering if we could get together, maybe talk a little bit."

I thought of Pretty Young Thing, the way she had stamped her feet and pursed her lips. "Oh, you still talk to grown women," I said.

He laughed. "You're not going to hold that against me, are you?"

"Let's put it this way: It's been duly recorded."

Orlando laughed again. "Yeah, that was a mistake. I was just lonely. Guess you don't get lonely."

The fast girl in me, eager once and wet, was draped in black. Flirting is a foreign tongue to a mourner.

"Orlando," I said, and then paused to wait out the crack in my voice that was threatening to undo me.

"You don't sound good, baby. Is something wrong?" He didn't give me a chance to answer, or even to think. "I'm coming over there."

Instinct took over. "Yes. Please."

Or maybe it was just plain old desire, pushing everything else out of the way.

6

ORLANDO FILLED UP MY DOORWAY, AND HIS EYES SEEMED
to read my mind. We reached out at the same time and touched each
other like two blind people. His hands pressed against my back; my fingers gripped his shoulders. The image of Pretty Young Thing popped
into my mind, but I didn't have the energy to hold a grudge. After a few
minutes, he pulled away and held me out in front of him. "Trina's sick
again."

"Yeah."

He led me to my family room sofa, and we both sat down. "Is she in
the hospital?"

I nodded.

"When did she go?"

"Today."

I explained what had happened, without elaborating. I didn't
have to.

"You know what you need?"

I let him talk me into the idea, sell it to me in a slow, patient way,
even though I had already acquiesced in my mind, and both of us knew
it. He waited while I put on a warm-up suit, and then we drove to a park

on the edge of Beverly Hills. There was just enough light from the streetlamp that we didn't break our necks as we made our way onto a circular running path.

The track was half a mile long. Orlando was beside me when we started out but quickly distanced himself. Initially, I was walking as he ran. He doubled back and gave me a shove.

"Run, girl!"

So I did. It hurt at first, not so much in my legs as the breathing and knowing that there was so much ground to cover, such a hard row to hoe. Then I settled in, concentrating less on what lay ahead and more on the step I was taking.

Orlando had a smooth, easy gait, and he was fast. He ran like a man who got joy from the wind in his face. In certain spots, where there were only dim shadows, he was almost invisible, his dark skin blending into the night. I lost sight of him. "Orlando," I called.

"I'm right here," he said, touching my shoulder. "You all right? When's the last time you ran?"

"It's been a while. I get on the treadmill, though, every morning."

"Yeah, but that ain't like running in the open. This is better for you, baby, especially when you have something on your mind. It helps you to focus."

He reached out, squeezed my arm, and took off.

I went around six times; Orlando completed ten rounds. Both of us were sweaty and panting when we finished. And hungry.

"There's some turkey chili at home," I said.

"Your chili?"

"Uh-huh."

He grinned. "Maybe we'll pick up some fries to go with it."

We debated about which fries we should get and ended up at an all-night deli in the Marina. We polished them off in the car.

At my house Orlando ate two bowls of chili, pushed back the chair from my breakfast room table, and said, "Now I need to go running again."

"Everything I cook is low-fat," I said. "You're my diet buster, buying French fries."

"Aw, baby, you look good." He reached across the table and took my hand, rubbed each one of my fingers. "How are you feeling?"

"A lot better. Thanks for taking me out."

He looked at the clock on my kitchen wall. It was after eleven. "What are you doing tomorrow?" I asked. Questions about Orlando's day had to be posed carefully. Any references to work or auditions had to be introduced by him.

"I'm looping early."

Orlando's voice-over work was his bread and butter. His was the voice of several cartoon characters. He announced for radio ads and even filled in background crowd voices. In past years the work, along with a few television guest spots, had given him a decent income, but he hadn't booked a show in a while, and the last time we'd spoken, even the voice-over jobs seemed to have dried up.

"Oh, that's great."

He stiffened. "I still *do* work, you know. Looping isn't a cause for celebration."

"Orlando—"

"The has-been actor still gets jobs."

Los Angeles: City of Fragile Egos.

"Orlando—"

"I'm not as big-time as your ex-husband, but I still work."

"You're not a has-been, and I'm not coming to your pity party. I've got one of my own to attend. And as far as Clyde is concerned—"

He leaned across the table and grabbed my hand. "All right. I'm sorry. Party canceled. Both of them. Okay?"

He kept rubbing my hand, making circles on my palm. After a while, we both got up and sat down on the couch.

The telephone rang.

"You have a collect call from—"

I immediately visualized Trina, wearing a green gown, pacing the hallway of the hospital, the pay phone receiver in her hand.

"—it's your mother."

The voice was thin, hoarse, but I knew it instantly. Gone was the vocal dexterity necessary for midnight howling and predawn screaming. On the other end of the line was an older, wiser woman, entering her second decade of sobriety. She went to meetings now and memorized slogans and prayers, ambled through life twelve steps at a time. My mother wanted to make amends. She was in dire need of my touch, my benevolence. And, if I could spare it, a little extra cash.

"Will you accept the charges?"

And just that quickly, whatever kindness had been deposited in my spiritual account evaporated.

"No."

If Ma Missy had been alive, she would have shaken her head, admonished me for my meanness, reminded me that the woman on the other end of the line was still my mother. "She's trying, Keri," Ma Missy would have said. As if trying in the present erased the years of not trying that had comprised my childhood. If Ma Missy had been sitting in my kitchen when my mother's call came, we would have argued. Although she'd protected me from my mother when I was a child and had even evicted her from her home, Ma Missy would always be her champion for the simple reason that my mother was her daughter. She could forgive her everything; that's the nature of motherhood. I, on the other hand, was a wronged child. And without Ma Missy to guilt-trip me into submission, my baser instincts took over.

Not that I hadn't spoken to my mother in the past. The call that came right after Thanksgiving, eleven or twelve years ago, when she was fresh out of the first rehab that had ever really taken hold and I was young enough to believe in a new beginning—I took that one. Talked for hours. Listened to her apologies, her tears. Cried some of my own. I flew back to Atlanta during a sweltering August. We went to lunch, to church, got our hair done, and shopped at the outlet mall. She borrowed a friend's car and drove me to the airport and cried again when I left.

She visited LA when torrential rains obliterated the sky. We went to a dripping Grauman's Chinese Theatre and, given a sunshiny reprieve, toured Disneyland. The two of us did every mall in the city and some in the suburbs, went to the movies, and sat up late at night watching television and talking. She told me she was sorry for all the pain she'd caused me, said she was proud of the woman and mother I'd become. She cried; oh, how she cried! Before she went home, I made up my mind to forgive her.

And then she fell in love. At sixty-three, when she should have been prepared to devote her entire life to apologizing to me for the pitiful mother she'd been, she met a man. "In recovery, just like me." They had so much in common, right down to their tiny fixed incomes. Once again, I was replaced.

Abandonment redux.

"Your mother?" Orlando asked, when I sat back on the sofa.

"Yes. And I don't want to talk about it."

In the past Orlando had stood squarely on the side of rapprochement. But then, his mama had been good to him.

"My baby's getting it from all sides. Come here, girl."

His hand was warm on the back of my neck. I let him kiss me, and then I kissed him back. We kissed some more, and we touched some more. My body was twitching, all that heat inside me struggling and pushing, yearning for someplace to go. I pulled away from him.

"Are you sleeping with that girl?"

"What girl?"

"The little jailbait mama you were hanging with at the restaurant."

"I only went out with her twice."

"You didn't answer my question."

"No."

I looked at him.

"I didn't sleep with her." He started laughing.

"She turned you down, didn't she?" My turn to laugh.

"Yeah, she turned me down after she saw me talking to you. Told me it was obvious that we were involved. I had it made until I ran into you. Who have *you* been sleeping with?"

"Oh, let me try to remember their names."

I stood up first. And then he followed me. My sheets were cool, fresh. His body was familiar, strong. His heat warmed me. We knew the best position for both of us. My crying didn't throw him. He didn't let it throw me. I could feel him bearing down, pushing past all tears, taking me with him, claiming me all over again.

"So, it's you and me, right?" he said, just before we fell asleep.

I thought about Pretty Young Thing draping herself all over Orlando. I thought about all the faceless Pretty Young Things in the world. He knows me, I thought. He knows everything about me and about Trina. I thought about PJ: closed my eyes and saw his grin, saw his face, so sad sometimes he worried me. Did Orlando ever see that sad face?

"All this back-and-forth, break up and make up. . . . We need to think about hooking it up."

The picture that formed in my mind was the same one as always. I saw Clyde, his bags packed, walking out. Then Clyde's face changed and it was Orlando heading for the door, leaving me alone, bereft. A family that included a man who stayed put was a dream that had exploded in my face a long time ago. I wouldn't risk that pain again. "Jumping the broom" to the land of matrimony wasn't in my future.

"I'll think about it." It was what I always said.

7

WE MADE LOVE AGAIN AT DAWN, THEN DOZED UNTIL WE were awakened by a buzzing sound from Orlando's PalmPilot. I felt his kisses after he left, one on my forehead and one on my cheek. Maybe it was their wetness that kept me awake. Maybe something else.

The morning came with clear skies, birds chirping, and a fist called Depression that crashed into my skull. Already, there were grooves in my brain where it fit. I pulled the covers up and waited, trying to remember the feel of Orlando's legs across my thighs, but that memory had faded. No use running, nowhere to hide. More than the blows, the familiarity made me go limp, give up. The way the thing called my name. So seductive. Good morning, heartache; wasn't that the way the song went?

Mean D was ruthless but not creative. The methodology was fairly predictable. Out of nowhere the inevitable masochistic questions insinuated themselves in my brain. If I had done this . . . If I hadn't done that . . . Nothing is as resilient as a mother's guilt. It's that trick birthday candle that keeps flickering back on no matter how hard you blow. Only a few hours into a seventy-two-hour hold and already the guilt— ancient, primordial maybe, but so maternal—had begun stabbing me in all my vital organs. Months of reading books about mental illness, months of support group, of psychotherapy, of assiduously learning that Trina's problem was not of my making (all together now: "I didn't cause it, and I can't cure it!") was flung right out of my consciousness against a bleak sky. The jazz of my present existence scatted only one refrain: *WhatdidIdowrongwhatdidIdowrongwhatdidIdowrong?*

The possibilities made up a list as endless as a cheap wine hangover. Was I absolutely sure that I'd smoked my last and final cigarette at least six months before conceiving Trina, the way I liked to recall, or was nicotine still floating through my system at the moment of conception? Forget about nicotine. What about the occasional joint I'd been so fond of? Could I pinpoint my last high? Why had I been unable to give up coffee when I was pregnant? Had that caffeine rush given me a jittery fetus who later became . . . ? The questions gave birth to more questions, and my masochism escalated in brutality. Why had I been in such a damn hurry to get back to work after Trina was born? Why hadn't I stayed home with my daughter until she was five, six, ten, eighteen? How well had I known her babysitters? Which one of them had smacked her, locked her in a closet, touched her private parts?

The *if only*s followed the questions. If only I'd breast-fed longer. If only I hadn't sent her to that first school with the mean teacher. If only I'd tried to work harder on my marriage. If only I hadn't been so busy.

High-stepping through my mind next came the parade of other people's Perfect Kids. The infants, offspring of my friends and family: always cooing, always adorable. The toddlers with their new teeth and new words, running to embrace life. The preteens. The teenagers. Ah, worst of all, the finished products of twenty-one. My first cousin's Princeton graduate: perfect. My neighbor's budding actress: perfect. My hairstylist's son, working on his master's at USC: perfect. All the perfect products of good mothers, which I, obviously, was not. *What did I do wrong?* It was the chorus to an unlucky song I couldn't stop singing.

My mother never sang that song, I thought. She was remorseless, a woman who did her dirt and kept on stepping. When I told her once that giving birth to me didn't make her my mother, she had shrugged her shoulders. Why couldn't I be more like her?

Somehow, when I faced these moments, I always wanted to talk with Clyde. He alone could bear witness. He alone could exonerate me.

The ringing telephone was a stay of execution.

"Hey, girl. You were on my mind."

Mattie's early-morning greeting, cheerful as it was, didn't abate my blues.

I told her about Trina.

"Look, she's had months of being on meds and going to therapy. She wants to go to school, to get her life back. Trina's not going to jeopardize what's she's built for herself. Don't you think she likes feeling normal?"

"I don't know. The night before she went in, I think she was smoking weed."

"How do you know?"

"I smelled it outside her window."

There was silence on the other end of the line. Even the most optimistic Child of God on the planet had to acknowledge the lure of weed to the manic.

"She only gave it up once," Mattie said. "Took me three attempts to quit smoking."

"I'll hold that thought."

"Nona is doing okay," Mattie said.

More guilt assailed me as soon as she mentioned her daughter's name. Nothing like your child's bipolar relapse to make you a self-centered depressive. I hadn't given Nona a thought.

"That's great," I said, maybe a little too enthusiastically.

"She's getting out early. In two weeks, maybe."

"Is she going to stay with you?"

"Where else?"

"She has a father."

"With a new wife. Ray doesn't want her there. I don't want her to go where she's not welcome. God never gives you more than you can bear."

"Why do people always say that? There have been times when I'm far past what I can bear, and you've been there too."

"We're still standing, and we're stronger."

"How's your friend?" I asked, sidestepping a philosophical discussion.

"Sizzling. You'll meet him tonight at Gloria's party."

"Tonight?"

"Yes, honey, tonight. You said you'd bring monkey bread."

"God, I'm glad you reminded me. I have to find out when Trina leaves the hospital."

Mattie started laughing. "When Nona gets out, I should ask the warden if her cell is available."

"I'll take the top bunk."

I LEFT AN INVITATION TO GLORIA'S PARTY ON ORLANDO'S answering service, hoping he wasn't busy, and then slid back under the covers. Finally, I called Frances at the shop and told her to expect me in the afternoon. "I guess Adriana told you Trina's in the hospital again."

"She'll be all right," Frances said, which is what she always said. "I'm more worried about you." She paused. "Some guy was with Adriana this morning when she came in."

When Frances described him, I could feel my heartbeat quicken.

I STAYED IN BED UNTIL NOON. THEN I GOT DRESSED AND drove to the hospital.

When I stepped off the elevator on the fifth floor, a man was bent over the sign-in sheet at the desk outside the locked doors of the psychiatric ward. When he stood up, I could see his face.

"Clyde."

"Trina called me last night and told me she was here. What happened, Keri?"

"She was at her program, and she started becoming manic."

"Why didn't you call me?"

"I—"

"I'm her father. I have a right to know. There was no reason to have her put in a psychiatric hospital."

My voice began to rise. "She hit somebody. And for the record, I didn't *have* her put in the hospital. The group leader did. But I agree with her."

"So what if she hit someone? Maybe the person deserved it. Maybe he did something to her. I'm getting her out of here."

"Clyde, Trina was smoking marijuana. That may have been what triggered this episode."

"She doesn't belong here."

"It's only for three days. They'll get her back on her medication. That's what's essential. You don't understand."

"I'm signing her out," Clyde said, staring at me.

"You can't do that, Clyde. Nobody can. She's on a three-day involuntary hold. The law says she has to stay here."

"Damn!" His frustration was etched into the lines across his forehead.

I put my hand on his arm, mostly to calm myself. "Let's just go see her."

He pulled away from me. "You go first."

Trina was sitting in the television room, drinking a soda. The same young man who'd been with her in the smoking area had his hand around her shoulder; when he saw me, he pulled her closer. Trina was talking to him in a normal voice, her back to me. His expression made her turn around.

She glared at me so furiously I stepped back. I was carrying several fashion magazines, which I'd brought for her. Instinctively, I clutched them against my chest. Trina flounced off the sofa and walked away, leaving me alone with the young man.

"Why won't she talk to me?"

It was an involuntary question, about as useful as praying to the moon. For a moment, he looked bewildered; then he smiled, and I could see two things: Trina's new friend was handsome, and he was my enemy.

"We both get out tomorrow."

I passed Clyde on my way to the social worker's office. He was pacing and looking at his watch. In theory, we should have gone to plan Trina's aftercare together, but it was clear we weren't playing on the same team.

Rosario Perez's office was located on the second floor of the Weitz Center. One of the psychiatric facility's many social workers, she didn't remember me, but I remembered her, and not just because of her blazing red hair. I'd sat in her office during Trina's first hospitalization, and she'd made me believe that everything would be all right. Looking at her now, I felt bitterness. At nine o'clock in the morning, Ms. Perez's desk was piled high. She gave me a blank stare.

"Mrs. Whitmore," she said, her tapered fingers drumming against the folder that was spread open before her.

"I've spoken to you before," I said. "When my daughter was here last summer."

She nodded, scanning the folder.

"Your daughter is bipolar. She was taking part in the partial program downstairs." Here, she made a little sound of sympathy and looked my way. "Do you have a plan for her care when she leaves tomorrow?"

"I don't want her to leave after just three days. I'd like the hold extended," I said quickly.

"You're familiar with the process."

I nodded.

"Tomorrow there will be a hearing to determine if your daughter should stay or go. She'll have representation from the court. Frankly, I don't think they'll keep her."

"She's not taking her medication."

Mrs. Perez closed the folder. "How do you know that?"

"I can tell. Maybe she's taking some, but I think she's cheeking most of it."

Mrs. Perez sighed. "This isn't a perfect system. Your daughter is"—she flipped through her papers—"eighteen. We can't force her to take medication."

"She attacked someone," I said.

Mrs. Perez nodded, glancing at Trina's chart. "But she hasn't done that since she's been here. If your daughter hasn't swallowed the medicine, she's at least put the pills in her mouth. She's gone to some group sessions. The best thing for you to do is to get her reinstated in the partial program. Mostly likely, she can get back in as soon as she leaves here. Why don't you speak with Elaine?"

I sighed. "When can I pick her up?"

"Assuming that her hold isn't extended, tomorrow, anytime after five." She shook my hand, her face impassive.

THERE WASN'T MUCH HAPPENING AT THE STORE. A FEW CUStomers were milling around. Adriana sat behind the register looking bored. There were things that needed to be done, letters I should have written, papers that needed signing, but I ended up standing next to her.

"What's going on?" I asked.

"Nothing. It's slow."

"With you."

She looked surprised, then lowered her eyes. "Nothing."

"I care about you, Adriana. Keep going to the meetings. Talk to your sponsor. I don't want to see you get caught up again. "

"I won't," she said, but there was no conviction in her voice.

THE SWEET DOUGHY SCENT OF BAKING BREAD WAS WAFTing on the breeze that blew over Ninety-first Street in Inglewood. The aroma hit me before I opened my car door. The street wasn't beautiful, just a row of one-story wooden cottages and neat linoleum-square lawns. A solid blue-collar community, nothing remarkable about it, except that the air the denizens breathed was enriched and made luxurious, like the ermine collars of royalty, by the labor of Monkey Bread Man.

My after-work timing was good. On weekends and holidays there was usually a long line wending its way from the small porch to the house that smelled like smiles and heaven. On this Friday evening, there were only three people ahead of me. It was a pleasant wait.

"Hello, darling! What can I do for you?"

Monkey Bread Man stood in the middle of his living room, surrounded by scores of bundt-cake-shaped loaves wrapped in heavy aluminum foil. I'd never even heard of the rich, sweetish yeast bread before I moved to California. Now I couldn't imagine any celebration without it.

Everywhere I looked there was bread: stacked up against the walls, shoved inside the fireplace, piled against the windows and on top of the sofas and chairs. There was scarcely any room to walk except for a narrow pathway from the door to the center, where the ebullient master baker stood, clad in a white apron, its center pocket bulging with bills. Monkey Bread Man ran a cash business.

"Two large," I said.

He gave a nod to a small boy, his grandson, whom I hadn't noticed standing near a chair. The youngster picked out two cakes, put them in bags, and handed them to me.

"That'll be—" the boy began, then looked up at his grandfather.

"Twelve and twelve," the Monkey Bread Man said, tapping his finger against his head.

"Uh, twenty-four dollars," the boy said. He looked to be about seven or eight.

I handed him a twenty and a five, and he passed the money to his grandfather.

"Teaching him the business?" I asked.

He nodded. "Trying to keep him busy," he said. "You don't keep them occupied, the streets will be raising your children. Then you gotta fight the streets if you want them back."

He nodded as he put the money into his apron pocket and handed me a dollar in change.

"That's why I keep this one right where I can see him. 'Cause I done fought the streets once."

The bread was still warm when I set it on my kitchen counter. The aroma followed me to my bedroom, curled around me as I stripped. It was no less intense when I'd finished showering and began to dress.

The party was in the standing-around-talking stage by the time I got there. Mattie and her heat-in-the-sheet man had already arrived. He said his name fast: Roger or Richard. He was a backslapping kind of man, loud voice, megawatt smile. Short on looks, long on charisma. They were in the living room drinking margaritas. Mattie looked happy. So did Roger or Richard.

Gloria was cooking, a glass of wine in one hand, a big spoon in the other. Mattie followed me into the kitchen.

"Smells good," I said, "and I'm hungry. How are you?"

Gloria shrugged, took a sip of wine, and kept on stirring. "I'm doing fine and getting ready to do better. What's up with you?"

The thought of laying down my burdens was appealing. Rehashing them would have been a more appropriate term. Gloria listened attentively; then she put down her spoon, walked over to the counter where there were at least half a dozen bottles of champagne and wine, poured a glass of Chandon, and handed it to me.

"You got twenty-four hours left, girlfriend. You might as well make the most of them."

"I'll keep Trina in prayer," Mattie said, "but Gloria is right. Tonight you need to party. Feel free to borrow Roger for a spin around the floor. He's quite the stepper."

"You said he wasn't cute. I think he's nice-looking," I said, knowing I was lying.

"In a Johnny Cash kind of way," Mattie said, shaking her head. "Don't worry, he has many fine attributes to recommend him."

As if on cue, Roger appeared with Milton, and we all toasted, talking and laughing until Gloria had finished cooking; then we helped her put the food, plates, and silverware on the table. When I went back into the kitchen, Orlando was standing there.

"I figured I'd find the true sisters in here," he said, then held out his hand, pulled me to him, and kissed my cheek.

I reintroduced Orlando to Mattie and Gloria, then introduced him to Roger and Milton. The men immediately separated from the women and began discussing the merits of the Lakers.

"The guy you're with looks familiar," Gloria whispered.

"He should," Mattie whispered, and I began laughing.

"What?" she asked.

"He was the man who helped you into the car two nights ago, when we went out to dinner after the meeting and you had too much wine."

"Oh, God. I hope he doesn't recognize me," Gloria said. She looked at me. "Damn. You work fast."

"I knew him way before that. Don't you remember? He came to a couple of meetings. We've been on and off for years."

"Wasn't he on that show?" Gloria asked.

I nodded. "He's done a lot of television, movies too." Why was I feeling proud?

Mattie winked at Gloria. "So now you're on?"

"Yeah, we're on again."

Gloria suddenly clapped her hands. "You guys get out of this kitchen and get the party started. Gentlemen," Gloria called, and the men looked up, "the ladies want to dance."

We dutifully moved into the family room, where a young twenty-something DJ with baggy pants and braids in his hair had set up his equipment. Up-tempo beats blared from his speakers. Orlando took my hand and led me to the floor.

Orlando's steps had been honed on Big Shoulders rhythms. My Buttermilk Bottom style was more easygoing. But we melded on the dance floor. Freestyle, that's how we grooved best. No rules, no regs, no patterns.

The floor was crowded when we decided to take a break. On our way back to the kitchen, Orlando saw a woman he knew. I was used to his many spontaneous reunions with people who'd worked or gone to school with him or shared a moment of his life. When the next record came on, he asked if I minded if he had a dance with his old friend, and I didn't mind at all. Even when he was dancing with someone else, Orlando seemed to be standing next to me.

Milton grabbed my hand when he saw me alone, and we began twirling across the room away from Orlando and his home girl. That's how it happened that I was the one to see Milton's eyes grow large as he looked beyond me, beyond the crowd of Electric Sliders, the conversationalists, holding up the wall with their chitchat, to the munchers, tearing through Gloria's offerings of barbecue chicken, greens, and potato salad to the sofa. Seated there, his hands folded in his lap as though he'd just concluded a prayer, was Milton's son. Wellington wasn't dancing or eating or chatting, just looking straight ahead at nothing in particular. There were people on either side of him, but he remained apart from them, his eyes empty and disconnected.

"Wellington is here," Milton said quietly. "Let me go speak with him."

I trailed Milton as he walked over to where his son was sitting.

"How are you, son?" he asked, his voice quiet and calm.

Wellington didn't answer.

"Would you like something to eat?"

Wellington hunched his shoulders and leaned back. The people close by listened for a moment and then began to drift away.

Gloria rushed over. "Wellington, are you—"

"He's okay, honey," Milton said. "Leave him alone for now."

"He just came in. The door must have been open."

"We'll deal with it later." He patted his son's knee. "You okay, buddy?"

Wellington didn't look at either one of his parents.

Gloria sighed. "I don't know," she said. "I don't know."

"It's all right," Milton said. He pulled Gloria to him and gave her a hug. "Don't worry. I have his meds upstairs."

People started coming up to Gloria and Milton, telling them good-bye. I felt hands on my back, and when I turned Orlando was smiling at me.

"What's going on?" He looked at me and then at our hosts.

"Everything is fine," Gloria said.

"You sure?"

She nodded. "Go dance."

The music was slow. The crowd on the floor had thinned out, so we had more room. I could dance and watch Gloria as she sat on the sofa with Wellington, who wouldn't look at her.

"Is that her son?"

I nodded.

"Off his meds?"

"Yeah."

The record had ended. The rest of the couples had drifted from the floor. We walked over to the sofa. Wellington was sitting quietly, Gloria on one side and Milton on the other.

"What are you going to do?" I asked.

Gloria looked up and smiled. "Everything is under control." She patted her son's knee. "We'll be all right."

"Well, I can stay," I said.

"No," Gloria said. "You've got Trina to deal with tomorrow. Finish your date, honey. Have some fun tonight." She grabbed my hand and pulled me close to her. "Milton and I may go for conservatorship."

I nodded as I let the word make a home inside my mind and renewed the options: Let the kid run wild; lock the kid up. Conservatorship. Maybe that was my North Star, if I needed one.

Orlando and I stayed the entire evening. We danced by ourselves in the middle of the floor. We drank more wine and ate more food. After the rest of the people had gone, we helped clean up and then played bid whist with Mattie and Gloria while Roger watched and told jokes and Milton sat with Wellington. After one game of cards, Orlando stood in the middle of the floor and performed Hamlet's soliloquy. Then he sang "Killing Me Softly" in a lustrous tenor. Our little group applauded and whistled, all except for Wellington, who stared straight ahead, his mind tuned in to other voices.

When I got to my car outside Gloria's house, Orlando said, "Do I follow you or do you want to follow me?"

One of the smart things Orlando had done when he was making money was to forgo the requisite star's mansion in favor of a triplex. He lived in one unit and rented out the other two, which provided him with a modest income. His unit was the most spacious of the three, and he'd decorated it in a spare masculine style: white walls, dark furniture, giant-screen TV. Everything was neat, and when he opened his refrigerator there was cooked food in covered pots.

He took out a bottle of wine and poured a little into two glasses.

"This week I have an audition for a sitcom pilot," he said. Before I could say anything, he added, "Don't ask. Very dumb plot. But I'm auditioning for the producers."

Saying lines for the producers was a step above auditioning for the lowly casting agent. Orlando was telling me that he was still somebody in the business.

"Congratulations."

"So I am, once again, a man with prospects. Ebb and flow, baby."

He grinned at me, and I prayed for him on the spot. Asked God to give him the gig, just to keep that grin on his face. That grin would be good for PJ.

"Well, here we go again," I said, as we sat on his sofa sipping the wine. "Fasten your seat belts, it's going to be a bumpy ride." He knew who I was talking about.

"Oh, that," Orlando said. "Love you, love your kid. Let me amend that: Love you; won't punch your kid out. Ain't that the way it goes?"

I took his hand and kissed each knuckle and then his palm. "That's the way it goes."

8

ORLANDO WAS STILL ASLEEP BESIDE ME WHEN I CALLED
the hospital the next day. I recognized the voice of the Nigerian woman
who answered the phone at the nurse's station at the Weitz Center. She
was austere, by the book. A million ways to say hello in Yoruba, and
she couldn't think of one. Maybe the residual affects of colonialism or
the British school system had messed with her mind. Sister wasn't giving
up no love.

"Hello, Ms. Shonibare, is Elijah there?" I asked.

"Elijah is busy with patients."

"May I leave a—"

"Try again in forty minutes. He takes a break then." She hung up.

After ten minutes, I dialed again. This time the voice was lighter,
speaking English words with the rhythm of Tagalog. I pictured the small
Filipino man, Marco.

"Hello, Marco, this is Keri Whitmore. We've met before. My daughter, Trina, is on the ward."

"Oh, yes. How are you?"

"I'm fine. I'm calling about Trina. How is she today? Has the psychiatrist been in to see her? I don't think she's taking her meds. When I
saw her last night, she was very wired."

My hands opened and closed as I spoke. He paused, and I pictured him reading the chart.

"Mrs. Whitmore, did you know that your daughter hasn't listed you?"

"What do you mean, she didn't list me? I'm her mother."

"She's eighteen. She's an adult. If she doesn't list you, I can't give you any information."

"I know that you check for drugs. Was anything in her system?"

"Mrs. Whitmore," he began.

I knew what that pause meant.

Only days before, we had celebrated her birthday. Now those digits meant that my child was out of my control.

"But I'm her mother. She lives with me. She's my dependent. I'll be paying her bill, whatever the insurance doesn't cover. I have a right to know what's going on. She may be coming home tonight. I have to know what I'm dealing with."

"I'm sorry."

I sat up in the bed, still holding the receiver in my hand. Orlando's eyes opened, then closed, then opened again.

"What's going on?" He sat up.

"They won't tell me anything because she's eighteen."

He tried to pull me to him, but I was too edgy to be comforted. I got up and began to dress.

"Don't you want me to fix you something?" he asked.

"Thanks. I'm okay."

"What are your hours today?"

"Saturdays are eleven to seven."

"There's a rehearsal for the play this afternoon," he told me, as he walked me out. "I'll be at the theater from about one to five. If you need me, I'll have my cell on vibrate."

At home, I paged Trina's psychiatrist at the hospital. Five minutes later he called me back, sounding harried. He had seen Trina. She appeared to be responding to the meds. He'd upped the antipsychotic to fifteen milligrams. Dr. Bellows didn't have time to talk, to discuss my fear that Trina wasn't really taking her meds. He insisted that she was responding, suggested that I was overreacting. He wouldn't tell me what was in her lab report.

"Keri, I know this is difficult. Try to stay calm," he said.

Who was I before my child became mentally ill? Did people speak to me in platitudes then? Did they hand me pity as though it were a cup of coffee I needed?

"Is there any possibility that the hold can be extended?" I asked. "Would you recommend that?"

"Yes, I will. But you know this is a legal matter. She will be represented."

In my old life, my complaints were mundane: the cost of shoes I coveted, a fickle lover. My girlfriends—Marie, Brooke, Nichele—and I had spa dates together. We went to the movies. We had lunch or dinner or drinks. What did I cry about then?

By late afternoon I was in my office, examining two cocktail dresses that a new client had brought in. Frances came in and gave me a long look. "Trina's a smart girl," she said. "She'll get it together."

"I don't know what the next few days are going to be like," I said. "You may have to be in charge." I lowered my voice. "How does Adriana seem to you?"

"She's being tempted. Can't say if she's given in or is about to give in. I just don't know."

I nodded. "I've been talking to her."

"Me too." She sighed. "What did the Old Man say about the jacket?"

"I'll take it now."

I wasn't ready for the sunshine. As I walked the half block to the shop, the heat and the brightness felt oppressive. It was the kind of happy-looking sunshine that makes Angelenos feel smug enough to ask dumb questions about Americans who live in intemperate climates. "Why would anybody ever want to live there?" they ask as they rush off to the beach in February in their topless jeeps, never grasping the concept that some people actually thrive on weather that matches their mood. Everything inside me hurt. I needed needle-tipped winds and gray skies in the worst way.

Behind the counter, the Old Man was eating a sandwich. When I held up the jacket, he put down his food, pulled out a moist paper towel from a package, and wiped off his hands carefully.

"Very beautiful," he said.

He was a short dark-brown man with a sad, creased face.

"It has a stain," I said, pointing to the spot. The Old Man took the jacket from me and studied it for a few seconds. He carried it to a picture window and stared at it some more. "Is this blood?" he asked.

"I don't know."

"Might be some kind of ink." He shook his head. "I don't know if I can get this out. It seems to be set."

"You can't get it out?" The Old Man had never been stumped before.

"Didn't say that. Said I don't know. Whatever is in there, don't want to turn the fabric loose. That means I have to kind of pry it from each thread, but gently so I don't do further damage. I got the chemicals. It's a matter of how to apply them. Got to be real careful. You want to leave it here, I'll do my best. But I can't give you no guarantee."

I left the jacket, went back to the shop, and jumped each time the telephone rang. Ms. Perez called late in the afternoon. She was brief and to the point. The hold was not going to be extended. Trina could be picked up any time after five o'clock.

"By any chance, do you know if marijuana or anything else was found in her system?"

"Mrs. Whitmore, you could be looking at illness, plain and simple. Your daughter may have been taking the prescribed medicine, not using drugs, and she still might be having problems. She has a brain disease. There could be lots of reasons to explain why she escalated. I know this is hard, but try to—"

"If you know this is hard, why don't you help make it easier? She's just a social security number to you, but I'm her mother."

My voice was louder than the decibels allowed in the store. "What?"

Adriana was standing in the doorway when I slammed down the phone.

She put her finger to her lips, then whispered, "Somebody to see you. She said she's a friend. Marie?"

"How loud was I? Did she hear me?"

"She just came in a minute ago. I can tell her you're busy."

Marie appeared in the doorway. "Keri?" Her voice was tentative, as though she didn't know what to expect. Clearly, she'd heard me. "I was in your area. Just wanted to say hi. Did I come at a bad time? Is everything okay?"

In your world, I thought. Moneymaking husband. Kid pledging a sorority. There is the shimmering land of Normal and then there is this place I live, built on the toxic waste of chaos. No use acting as if they are sister cities. They're too far apart for visits.

Why on earth did she keep reaching out?

"Everything's fine. I'm sorry about the other night. I wish I'd known that you were coming. I'm late for an appointment."

I didn't suggest we do dinner at some future date. My tone was distant and cool on purpose. My eyes ignored the hurt in Marie's. What was her pain compared to mine? *Let's end this now.*

I GAVE MYSELF THIRTY MINUTES TO REACH THE HOSPITAL. Driving over, I tried to do what Frances seemed to think I was capable of doing: I took deep breaths and let them out slowly. I told myself, This too shall pass. But I didn't believe it.

By five-fifteen, I was standing in front of the nurses' station, waiting for Trina to be released. It was dinnertime, and the ward was quiet. Nobody was wandering the halls. Nobody was screaming. So I didn't have any difficulty hearing the nurse.

"Your daughter left about an hour ago," she said.

Her words flogged me, tore my skin, drew blood.

"You just let her go by herself?" I was astonished.

"She's an adult," the nurse said.

I glared at her. "My daughter has a mental illness."

"Mrs. Whitmore, there's nothing I can do."

She walked away. A tremendous flash of heat surged through me, and my head seemed to explode. There was a bench behind me. I sat down on it and tried to keep from thinking, from crying, from screaming.

"Mrs. Whitmore." Elijah smiled at me. "Your daughter left with a woman. Dark and heavy, much older than your daughter."

"What was her name?"

"I don't know. But"—he bent closer to me and whispered—"she's stayed here before. I remember her face."

. . .

It took more than an hour to get to Compton. Once in the neighborhood I was confused, trying to remember where Melody lived. So many little cottage-lined streets, one graffiti-covered wall after another—I was Alice in Wonderhood, falling down the rabbit hole. Everything seemed to meld together after a while. Then I turned onto a street that did seem familiar and zeroed in on the peeling gray house in the middle of the block.

A woman answered the door after the third ring. Behind her was the low chaotic rumble of bickering children.

"Can I help you?" she asked.

She didn't smile. Deep lines ran from the base of her nose to the edges of her lips. Her body was heavy-breasted and bulky. As she spoke to me, she twisted her neck to keep an eye on the children, and when she turned to face me she winced, then began rubbing her neck. The circles beneath her eyes seemed to have been drawn with charcoal.

"I'm looking for Melody Pratt. Does she live here?"

"Melody ain't got back yet." The woman tilted her head, and her eyes slowly traveled the length of my body, sizing me up in a way that let me know that whoever came asking for Melody was suspect.

"She and my daughter attend the same program together."

She nodded, and then our heads were bobbing to the same rhythm, and we were making soft noises that got stuck in our throats.

"I'm Melody's mother, Celestine. You wanna come in?"

The house was cramped and smelled of years and years of fried everything. The sofa in the living room seemed to have caved in under the weight of the piles of clothes it held, a wobbly tower of children's shirts and dresses and pants. The kids themselves, a boy of about seven and twin girls who looked to be five, emerged from a room in the back and stared at me.

"Y'all go back in there and watch your video," the woman said. "And be quiet. Yeah, they Melody's kids." She motioned for me to take a seat in a chair in the corner that was also filled with laundry. "Just put that stuff on the floor."

Celestine nodded as I explained what had happened. While I talked, she got me a cup of tea, barked orders at her grandchildren, led me into her small kitchen, pulled out a stool for me to sit on, and began chopping onions, frying potatoes and hamburgers.

"You kids come on in here and eat," she called, and the three children appeared. Celestine gathered chairs from another room and assembled them around the dilapidated table. She nodded toward the boy. "Say the blessing." She turned to me. "Have some."

"Oh, no, thank you. I'm not hungry," I said. We went back to the living room.

"Melody's been doing pretty good the last few months, going to the program every day, taking her medication. Every time, you think it's going to be the last time, and then—" she shook her head. "My brother was just like Melody, except he never did get straight with his medication. Just flat out wouldn't take it. And he had his time with drugs, just like Melody."

"How is he now?"

"Dead. Shot hisself."

There was no noise coming from the kitchen. Celestine walked over and looked inside. "When I don't hear them I get nervous." She smiled a little and rolled her eyes, and for a moment she was just another doting grandma. "Your daughter got any kids?"

"No."

She didn't comment, leaving me to wonder whether my answer implied that I was fortunate or unfortunate.

"Don't stress yourself out," Celestine said as I was leaving. "Melody get here when she get here. Same with your girl. Social worker told me you gotta pace yourself, otherwise you end up getting broke down. Right before Melody got into that program, my pressure shot up so high the doctor was talking about putting *me* in the hospital. I gotta take care of *me*. Yeah."

Celestine sounded as though she'd been to group.

BACK HOME, I SAT IN THE GARAGE IN THE DARK FOR A few minutes before I heard my doorbell ring. Hurriedly I unbuckled my seat belt, unlocked the door, turned off the alarm, and raced around to my front door. Peering through the peephole, I spied a halo of Afro blocking out everything else from view.

"PJ! What on earth?"

"Can I come in?"

"Yes, sweetie. Of course." We hugged. "Are you hungry?"

He sat at the breakfast room table and plowed into a huge bowl of ice cream and a whopper slice of cake. PJ's appetite was legendary. His MO was to eat slowly, letting his food settle before he shoveled in more.

"How did you get here?"

"Walked."

"Your mom know where you are?"

He shook his head.

"PJ!"

"She's not even home. She's on a date with her new boyfriend."

"Well, she ought to know you're here. Did you tell Jabari?"

"He's at a study group." PJ looked up from his ice cream. "Can we play Scrabble?"

I searched his face. "We can play for thirty minutes, and then I'm taking you home."

The boys had learned to play Scrabble at my house. Jabari, uncharacteristically, was a mediocre player, but PJ excelled. In less than twenty minutes he was ahead by thirty points. He was intense and fast, skilled at using one or two letters to create multiple word sets. Where other people saw only an opportunity to turn in all their letters, he saw a way to score.

"You think you're going to beat the professor, boy? Never happen." My twenty-four-point word narrowed the gap.

He searched the board, looked at his letters, then stared at me. "Keri, I think—I mean, I know—"

His tone alarmed me. There was so much sadness in his face. "What, sweetie?"

"I'm gay."

It took a moment for me to process the words. PJ stood up. "I gotta go."

"Wait a minute. Wait a minute." I grabbed his hand. "Sit down." He looked terrified. When he was seated, I asked, "How do you know?"

"I just do."

"But how? You're only fourteen. You may be mixed up about your sexuality. You barely *have* a sexuality."

He shook his head. "I"ve known for a long time. I don't like girls that way. I like boys."

I stared at PJ a long time. What does he want from me? I wondered.

While I was searching his face, he began sobbing. I put my arms around him and held him as tightly as I could. "It's all right. Have you told your mom and dad?"

"No," he said, between sniffles.

"They need to know."

"No. They'll hate me."

I pulled away from him. "They won't hate you, PJ. They're your *parents*. Nothing you do can make them hate you, not even a tattoo that says FUCK YOU. We all just want you to be safe."

He gave me a tiny smile for my efforts. "I'm celibate."

"Tell your parents," I said.

DRIVING BACK FROM PJ'S HOME, I TRIED TO REVIEW HIS behavior from the time I'd known him. Hadn't there been any signs? Had I been clueless? Why hadn't Orlando or Lucy seen anything? Poor kid, I thought. Carrying that weight all by himself. And why was he so afraid of Orlando knowing? Lucy, I could understand. But Orlando was Mr. Bohemian Actor. We'd never discussed homosexuality, but he had gay friends in the business. He couldn't possibly be anything but accepting. I sighed, trying to segue from one child's problem to another's. The phone rang at eleven o'clock. I was sitting in the bed with the lights out and the covers clutched tightly. The phone was right in my lap.

"Trina?" I said, gulping air, trying to breathe.

"She left."

I couldn't make out the woman's voice, couldn't connect it to a face, a body, anything except me. She breathed the way I breathed; she sounded the way I sounded: sucked out and empty. I only knew she wasn't talking about Trina.

"Who is this?"

She didn't answer. I had to piece together who she was from the weight of her voice, the rawness in her tone.

"Bethany?"

"That same night I saw you at the hospital, that same night after she checked in, by the time I got upstairs she'd gone. Signed herself out. Hospital couldn't keep her because it was voluntary."

"Right."

"They didn't even call me because she's an adult, and she signed herself in—"

"Listen," I said, cutting her off, "I can't go there with you tonight. Today kicked my ass. My kid left the Weitz Center on her own and is out there somewhere, doing God knows what. So that makes two of them. Do you understand?"

I could tell by her voice that she looked old again. "Do *you* understand?" she said. "That makes two of *us*."

9

THE PHONE RANG ON MONDAY MORNING BEFORE EIGHT o'clock. I heard the children in the background before I heard Celestine.

"Your baby get home yet?" she asked, but before I could reply she excused herself. "Y'all be quiet!" The drone of childish voices diminished for a few moments before the decibels rose once again. "Lord have mercy, Jesus." She paused. "You still there?"

"She didn't come home. Did Melody?"

"Yeah, she come in right after you left, but your daughter wasn't with her. She told me she dropped her off on the corner near some guy's house. Somebody she met at the hospital."

"Oh, God," I said. Long lean Boy Man popped into my mind

"I got the phone number." She read it off. "Melody didn't want to tell me, but I stayed on her until she did. She said that the guy was either bringing your child home last night or to the program today."

"Thank you."

"Hey, next week it might be me."

But it's my turn now. Plan A: Go to the Weitz Center. Park. Wait. See if Trina shows up. Go on to work if she does. Come back at three o'clock. Park. Wait. See if she will get into my car. Plan B: Pull the covers up, way up. Breathe through sheets and blankets for the next twenty-four hours, coming out occasionally to imbibe from the ancient bottle of Jack Daniel's left by an old suitor.

Plan B was very appealing.

There was a lot of traffic near the hospital. Not one parking space to be found on the street in front of the Weitz Center, so I parked around the corner and walked back. I passed two young doctors, leisurely strolling toward the hospital. The words *script* and *green light* floated in the air as I passed them. The movies beckon to everyone in LA. I waited outside the building for fifteen minutes before I saw Melody trudging toward the steps.

Her eyes avoided mine. Her answers were monosyllabic. She seemed taken aback when I climbed the stairs with her. Maybe she was afraid I was going to tell on her, get her kicked out of the program.

"I just want to see if Trina's upstairs." She nodded uneasily.

Group had already started. The door to the room near the entrance was open. Inside, twelve people had formed a circle. They were talking about anger, things to do to control it.

I asked to speak to the director. Elaine came out of a meeting to see me, walked toward me with her hand extended, ushered me into her office with a solicitous smile. Elaine nodded sympathetically, listened attentively. These things happen. Yes, yes. She became vague when I asked about Trina's returning to the program. She mentioned the prerequisite of thirty days of sobriety, the possibility of urinalysis, the fact that two other people had entered since Trina had gone to the hospital, bringing them to capacity. And then it was my turn to nod, to say, "Yes, yes," to rise, because Elaine had to return to her meeting.

Nobody answered the phone at Boy Man's house. Six attempts as my car idled in traffic. The phone rang and rang as the light changed from green to red and then green again.

What was he, a bipolar on a manic tear? A schizophrenic with just enough meds in him to silence his inner voices? A crackhead, a speed freak, an alkie? How would his mental state undermine my child's thought processes?

Were they using condoms?

I glanced at the clock: a little after ten. Clyde would be on the air, spouting his brand of neoconservative invective. I didn't usually listen, but now my fingers pressed the dial to his station. His voice filled the car. He should be *here*, I thought. I gripped the steering wheel and tried not to feel the anger that was suddenly flooding my body. We should be going through this together.

It was what I had thought the first time. As I picked out the tiny casket, made the arrangements, cried, Clyde avoided me. He worked. When it was over and our baby boy was in the ground, Clyde worked even harder.

I called his private line during the news break. "Is Trina with you?" I asked as soon as he said hello.

"No. Isn't she still at the hospital?"

"They let her leave yesterday. Nobody had to sign her out, because she's eighteen. I went to pick her up, and she was already gone. I think she's with some guy who was in there with her."

"I can't talk now. I've got to go back on the air."

"She's missing." Damn him for not understanding.

"Keri, don't get dramatic. You're the one who put her in the hospital in the first place. I told you she didn't need to be there."

"You don't understand what's—"

"I've got to go now."

Moments later, he was addressing his audience, warning them about the dangers of liberalism.

Orlando would have said, Don't worry, baby. He would have rubbed my back and poured me tea or wine, watched me from the corner of his eye. He might have sung to me.

Adriana met me at the door of the shop.

"What?"

"Trina called."

"How long ago?"

"Ten minutes."

"What did she say?"

"She just wanted to speak to you."

"Did she say where she was?"

"You don't know?"

I shook my head. Then everything in me started shaking.

"Keri, you okay?"

"Yeah." Her eyes roamed anxiously over my face. "I'm okay. What?"

"I guess this is what my mom went through. For years she didn't know where I was."

"When's the last time you saw her?"

She shook her head. "Long time."

"You ever talk with her?"

"A couple of years ago. On Christmas Day. There wasn't much to say. She's still with him."

"How's the guy?" I asked, trying to change the subject.

"What guy? Oh, the guy from school. That's over. Won't be seeing him again."

I didn't have to ask the reason.

We both turned when the door opened and Juicy, Coco, and Spirit came trooping in. Adriana's former colleagues always came on Monday. Not every Monday, because sometimes they worked on their days off, especially when big conventions were in town, but at least once a month they'd come in to shop. Frances came out of the office. She frowned when she saw them, then looked at me.

I watched them as they browsed. All were welcome in my store, but some were not trusted. Spirit went for the shoes. Coco looked at purses. Juicy examined the gowns. They giggled and danced in the mirror, then sidled up to Adriana and whispered and giggled some more. Adriana's facial expression was a somber contrast to theirs, but after a while she began smiling and laughing with them. I'd read somewhere that it was difficult for a hooker to leave the business. That fast, hard life was as addictive as crack. One crab had escaped the barrel. From across the room, I could see their claws. Adriana saw me watching them.

"Adriana, I need you to make a quick run."

They didn't stay long after she left, and they didn't buy anything.

She came back soon after they were gone, bringing me the tea and cookies I'd requested. Every time I looked up she was there in my doorway, hovering.

"What's up?" I asked the third time she showed up.

"You don't have to worry about me. Nothing Coco, Juicy, or Spirit can say to me would make me want to go back to that life."

"They're recruiting, and they're going to keep on. I don't want them ever to catch you at a weak moment."

She just looked at me, smiled a little, and shook her head, as though there was no such thing as a weak moment. I knew better, of course. I knew the power of that split second when you vacillate between right and wrong, go or stay, yes or no, and end up colliding with tragedy.

ORLANDO STOPPED BY AT NOON. WAS I READY FOR LUNCH?

"Trina's missing," I said, and hurriedly explained. If I went to lunch, Trina might show up at the shop, and if I wasn't there, she might leave.

"Come on. Take a break. Take your cell phone. Trina knows the number."

I allowed myself to be soothed by his words, to think of myself temporarily as something more than just a mother.

From the corner of my eye, I spotted Frances watching me, no doubt reading my lips. Her hands made a shooing motion.

"I'm not really hungry," I said.

His palm on the small of my back moved me forward. "Then we'll just walk."

We window-shopped. The block the store was on was lined with clothing boutiques, a jewelry store, a couple of restaurants, and a bakery. Orlando led me into each one. The bakery at the end of the block sold hot and cold drinks and sandwiches, as well as baked goods. Orlando bought tea, coffee for himself, and a huge chocolate chip cookie. We walked two blocks to where there was a small courtyard with a fountain and some benches, sat down, sipped our drinks, and shared the cookie.

"Junk and caffeine," he said. "Does a body good."

"How was your rehearsal?"

"The usual first-run-through chaos, including an asshole director and a diva female lead who is oh, so grand."

"Who is she?"

When he said the name, I'd never heard of her.

"Exactly. She's from New York."

I wondered whether he was getting paid, but I didn't dare pose the question.

"Yes, they're paying me," he said.

"I didn't—"

"I can read your thoughts." He looked at me. I didn't say anything. "Do you want to know how much they're paying me?"

"No. No."

We both laughed. I had been married to a man who loved money, and I could sell in my sleep. For me, work had to pay the bills.

"One hundred seventy-five dollars a week. I'm going to spend it all on a big drink."

"As long as you're cool with it, I'm cool with it." That, of course, was a lie. I wasn't cool with anyone who settled for less than what he wanted.

"I love performing, Keri. It's in my blood."

All over Los Angeles, people were muttering the same thing as they slung hash, waited tables, and yearned for their big break. All that hoping and praying just to get to do what they had done when they were kids in their sixth-grade play. But Orlando had had his big break already. Meanwhile, there was more money in teaching. Or real estate. Or selling cars. Why couldn't he learn to love another profession? I had. Well, maybe I didn't love selling, but I was fine with it. The man had a degree. One hundred and seventy-five dollars a week wasn't a job, it was a hobby. But I didn't say that, and I tried real hard not to think it.

"Tell me about the play."

"It's a musical called *Up at the Club*, and it's about how this guy wins and loses and wins Ms. Right. I play a bartender at this club in the 'hood who gets the young people back together. I'm the voice of wisdom and reason. It could be entertaining if they'd tighten up the script a little bit and the director would let the actors act."

"When do you audition for the sitcom producers?"

"Next week."

He started describing the TV series; it really was pretty dumb. And I knew Orlando knew it.

Our cups were empty. I picked them up and tossed them into a nearby receptacle. "Walk me back," I said, and when we got back to the shop, "I'll call you if I need you."

THAT EVENING I SAT IN MY KITCHEN, HOLDING THE PHONE, listening to the police officer say it was too soon to list Trina as a missing person. Even when I told him that she'd been released from a mental hospital two days ago, he said it made no difference. "Call back after seventy-two hours, ma'am." Twenty-four hours more. He didn't tell me how to spend them.

I kept moving. Paced to the refrigerator and back to the sofa. From the sofa to the refrigerator to the phone. Food was in my hands, my mouth, at all times. Popcorn, raisins, ice cream. Eating was my Prozac. In between swallows, I called the number that Melody's mother had given me.

Mattie, Gloria, and I did a conference call. Mattie prayed fervently, something about God's awesome power. The message was always the same: Don't give up hope; things will get better. And then there was the black Baptist postscript: He never puts more on you than you can bear.

I plunked myself down on the sofa in my family room and stared at the television set, letting the portable phone rest on my lap. So this is how the kid turned out, I thought. My sweet, sweet baby. Ballerina princess at eleven, cheerleader at fourteen, nutcase at eighteen. So this is how my life turned out. I dialed Boy Man's number again. No answer.

I called Clyde, hoping he'd heard from Trina but also needing to hear his voice. He loved the child I loved. I didn't share that with anyone else. Aurelia answered the phone. As soon as I heard her, I remembered my promise and was sorry I'd called.

"Oh, Keri," she said, "Clyde isn't here." There was a slight hesitation and then she said, "How's it going?"

It was her halting tone, along with the hesitation, that made me realize that Clyde had probably asked Aurelia to call me and she didn't want to talk with me about her marriage.

So we were in agreement.

"Not that great, actually. I just wanted to know if Clyde had heard from Trina."

"Heard from Trina? What's wrong?"

"Clyde didn't tell you that she left the hospital and didn't come home?"

"I didn't even know she was in the hospital. When did all this happen?"

She got the abbreviated version of the story. And I could hear her anger in the inflection of her voice. Aurelia liked Trina. Whenever Trina had been sick in the past, she'd always come to visit. She didn't bother making excuses for Clyde.

"I don't understand that man," she said with a sigh.

"That makes two of us."

After I hung up, I wanted to go to sleep instantly, not to have to think another thought. But there was nothing in the medicine cabinet to take the edge off my mind. The top drawer of my bathroom cabinet was filled with rollers, bobby pins, do-rags, and hair gel. Nothing in the second drawer but perfumes I could no longer stand. The third drawer was a catchall, a bin full of junk. The third drawer technically classified me as a pack rat, but not a very discerning one. No sleeping pills, no tranquilizers. Had I only imagined that they were there? Benadryl! It had expired three years earlier, but I took two anyway, and then another, since the potency had been compromised.

The first faint veil of grogginess felt sweet. Bright buds of sleepiness played with my mind, but the flowers never bloomed. The three expired capsules left me groggy as opposed to unconscious. I was tempted to take more, one or two more, maybe three or four more, tempted to explore how deep grogginess can get before it surrenders to sleep.

After the officer, the same officer who'd been answering all night, said, "Lady, you need to calm down," after he firmly and convincingly told me there was nothing that he could do or that any other officer could do until the proper time had elapsed, after I'd hung up and hadn't dialed the police or the boy for fifteen minutes and the last little time capsule kicked in, I had a moment of clarity. I went to the computer and checked my e-mail.

Bigtime@aol.com. The address wasn't familiar, but the tone of the message was:

I hate you. If you try to find me, I'll kill myself.

I had never imagined Trina in a place with a computer. Her deranged wildness sharing space with technology seemed incongruent. I stared at the message for a moment, then pressed KEEP.

She's eighteen. I can't make her do anything. My head started shaking of its own accord, as though agreeing with the words in my mind.

There was another e-mail, from Rona. She'd forwarded information about her Spelman reunion and added a personal note:

I've been feeling a lot better since you massaged me. I'll call
for another appointment soon. You have gifted hands. I thank

you, and great-great-great-grandmother Harriet thanks you!
Rona.

What would Harriet do with this? No time to plan. Nowhere to run.
But the same imperative, the same need to cross the border. To save herself. To save another.

10

I FELL ASLEEP AROUND 3 A.M., AND THAT'S WHEN THE phone started ringing. Music blared from the receiver into my ear. Glass broke in the background, crashing against loud, angry voices. There was yelling and shrieking, lots of shrieking. Of course, she didn't say anything. Just screamed and hung up.

And called again. And again. For two hours. Trina's psychotic tease: I'm alive, but maybe I'm in pain.

"Trina, come home!" My voice echoed against a blast of music, more yelling, and then a dial tone.

After the eighth time, I took the phone off the hook.

A week on meds, and she would apologize. A good night's rest would make a world of difference. But she wasn't ready to come down. I had to stay alive while she was up there, whirling in the sky, a sparrow on speed.

A child's death isn't always necessary for a mother to grieve.

Ma Missy mourned her baby girl for years. My mother. Emma. Such a beautiful alcoholic. She reserved weekends for her binges, sitting by the window after work on Fridays, sipping scotch and milk or scotch and soda. Sometimes she drank gin, Tanqueray, or wine. Ma Missy would watch her ominously, waiting for fireworks or tears, which were always preceded by voluptuous laughter. There was a tipping point. One extra swallow could turn a good time into something too ugly for a kid to see. Ma Missy knew the timing. Maybe it was something in my mother's eyes that alerted her, the curl of her bottom lip. One minute Emma was chuckling and the next a snarl would break from her pretty mouth, and my grandmother would snatch me away, direct me upstairs, where I would creep to the landing and listen to Ma Missy, pleading with her daughter to stop drinking, to get herself together, to change her life.

I can't remember how long Ma Missy begged, but I do remember that there came a point where she simply stopped, accompanied me upstairs on Friday and Saturday nights, closed her bedroom door, and watched television with me. With my brain clouded, I wondered why she had given up and how many years had passed before she did. Maybe there was some sort of epiphany. Maybe it was just precise arithmetic: subtraction. Years to go from years lived. Or maybe her craving for peace of mind overcame her maternal instinct.

After one Saturday night not too much different from the others, she lifted my chin in her hands and spoke directly. *I won't give her my life, and I won't give her yours.*

"Keri will stay with me," Ma Missy told Emma.

"She's my child," my mother said, her voice trump-card sure and petulant.

"If you want to fight me," Ma Missy said, "one of us will not be alive when it's over."

My mother packed her bags the next day.

I remember the shock in Emma's eyes and the pain and rage in my heart, because, drunk or sober, I wanted her around. If she was around, I could tell myself that she loved me more than the bottle. It took a long time for me to understand Ma Missy, let alone forgive her. Maybe I was forgiving her now.

THE NEXT TWENTY-FOUR HOURS WERE ENDLESS. THEY segued into semicomatose afternoons and evenings. Orlando provided respite. I didn't hear from Clyde, except on the radio.

I was the last one to leave the shop on Tuesday night. Maybe I lagged behind because I didn't want to go home, to call the police and remind them that seventy-two hours had passed and they could officially begin looking for my lost kid. Suppose they didn't find her? Most of the cars in the parking lot were gone. The night was clear and scented with jasmine. It was dark and quiet until a white Ford suddenly turned in from the street, picking up speed as it drove straight toward me. Somebody was leaning on the horn. There was no time to be afraid, to cry out, to move. The car stopped inches from my feet. The horn faded away and horrible laughter split the air.

Trina jumped out of the car. Boy Man remained in the passenger's seat. Reefer scented the air as the door opened.

Trina swaggered toward me. "Been looking for me?"

She had on the same T-shirt and jeans she'd been wearing when I'd last seen her, only now the T was torn, a deliberate tear to create cleavage. Trina's breasts swelled above her shirt.

I spoke very carefully. "Trina, I want you to come home."

"If I come home, you'll call the cops and get me locked up."

"No. Just come home and start taking your medication again."

"I've been taking it."

"Trina—"

"Trina what?"

Her voice rose, and she stepped closer to me. It was too dark to see the pupils of her eyes, but I didn't have to.

"Come home with me."

"Fuck you!" Her rage splattered the air. "Are you my mother? Tell me the truth. Are you my mother?"

"Trina, what are you talking about? Of course, I'm your mother."

"No, you're not." She turned to the boy in the car. "She's not even my real mother!" she screamed. She turned back to me. "Bitch, you stole me from my real mother, and now you want to lock me up!"

"Trina, calm down."

She was so far beyond any possibility of tranquillity. Trina raised her hands. The blows were rapid, like a sparring boxer's: *bap, bap, bap*. Too quick for pain. No sound except retreating footsteps, a slammed car door, a fast getaway. She left behind air that dripped with perfume.

"Trina!"

I stood in the parking lot, rubbed my shoulder, picked up my purse, turned around toward a rustling sound. My body buckled toward the woman standing in the doorway, clutching a briefcase, watching me. What was on her face that wasn't discernible in the shadows, horror? Disgust? Did she feel anything as she stood in the dark, judging my life? Rage and shame fought for space in my mind. The woman was still standing in the doorway, looking straight ahead as I drove away.

When we spoke by conference call that evening, Gloria and Mattie assured me that Trina would come home. We talked strategy. Milton got on the phone and said I should alert the Systemwide Mental Assessment Response Team, SMART, the county department of mental health's mobile response unit, even before Trina returned, so that if she showed up within the next few hours I could use the attack as a criterion for another seventy-two-hour hold. I asked about Wellington and Nona. I don't remember what they said. After we hung up, I realized that the roles had switched. They were fanning flies in the big house; I was sweating in the field. At least for now, they were the lucky ones.

The lucky ones are never a comfort.

I looked up Bethany's name on the support group's roster. When she answered the telephone, her voice sounded as though the mouth it was coming out of was bruised. A swollen slash, not a mouth. Each word a unique wound, painful to hear. Did I sound like that?

We didn't talk long, not more than a few minutes. Really, we were just checking in with each other, the way the poorest Africans in Zimbabwe do. They ask in their language, *How are you?* and the answer is always, *I am suffering peacefully.*

Bethany's renegade spirit surged forward right before she said goodbye. "I will not live like this," she said.

TRINA ARRIVED AT MY DOOR LATE THAT NIGHT. THE WILDNESS in her eyes was a tide that hadn't ebbed.

"I'm sorry. I'm sorry, Mommee. Let me come home. I just want to come home." She threw herself against me. Her head against my chest felt warm, familiar. My fingers were in her hair before I even closed the door. She pulled away, stepped back, and the light from the ceiling highlighted the fresh bruises on her face. Trina must have liked my look of horror. She began smiling.

"Mommee, that boy I was with started hitting me for no reason."

This was probably a lie, at least the no-reason part. In the kitchen, Trina couldn't sit still long enough for me to press ice against her eye, against her forehead. She squirmed after about ten seconds and then got up.

"You have to go to the hospital."

She clung to me, her hands around my waist. "No, Mommee. Let me stay here. I'll get back on the meds, I promise."

She was manic and high. None of her words meant anything.

"I'll go back to the program tomorrow," she said.

"You have to take your medication right now," I said.

"Okay."

While I was getting the medicine, I called SMART. In twelve minutes they had arrived, with two officers from the sheriff's department. The counselors, a man and a woman, asked me a few questions as we stood in the entryway. Had Trina tried to hurt herself? Had she tried to hurt anyone else? I told them about the attack in the parking lot. The officers appraised me silently.

No blood. Damn.

"Well, ma'am, there's no evidence that she hurt you. Did anyone see her hitting you?"

The woman's face flitted across my mind. "No. But she's been fighting with someone else. When she gets manic, she'll pick fights."

"Did you see her fighting?" the woman asked.

"Her face is bruised. I saw her a few hours ago, and she didn't look like that."

"Is there the possibility that someone beat her up?"

"She probably started the fight."

"But you didn't see her fighting?"

"Look, my daughter just got out of the psych ward three days ago. They should have kept her. She's supposed to take medication, and she hasn't been taking it. She needs to—"

"Ma'am," the man said, "where is your daughter now?"

Their expressions revealed nothing. I was afraid of what they were thinking.

When Trina saw the police officers and the pair from SMART, she glared at me. Mom had betrayed her again. One of the counselors asked how she was feeling, and she didn't respond. She knew they needed a reason to send her back to the hospital, and the quieter she was the less likely they'd find one. But silence can't live where mania resides.

"There's nothing wrong with me," Trina said finally, her words hot and loud. "She just calls you guys for attention."

"What happened to your face? Were you fighting today, Trina?"

"My mother pushed me, and I fell."

"Trina, " I said, "that's not true."

"Yes, it is. Ever since I was a little girl, she's been hitting me. She hates me. That's why she's always trying to send me away."

"Do you want to hurt yourself, Trina?" the man asked.

"No. My mother hurts me. She hurts me all the time. Why don't you lock her up?"

"Trina—" I began, and then stopped.

The woman from SMART closed the notebook she'd been using. "Ma'am," she said, "may we have a word with you?"

As we walked to the front door, she placed a card in my hand. "I can see that she's ill," the woman said. "If she decompensates further, please give us a call. Take care of yourself. I'm sorry we can't help you now, but our hands are tied."

"Fucking bitch!" Trina screamed as soon as the door closed.

It was useless to protest the tone, the language, the disrespect. I didn't have the energy. Too busy drowning in what-ifs: What if she hits me? What if she takes the car in the middle of the night? What if her mania kills us both?

"You have to take your medication if you want to stay here," I said during the first lull.

"Fuck you!" Her eyes dared me to respond. The strong desire to draw blood was in her eyes. "You're not my mother. You killed my mother, and you killed my dad."

"Right. You need to get out of my house. Go back where you stayed last night."

Her eyes moved fast, from corner to corner, settled on mine, then looked away again.

"I don't have to go anywhere."

"Yes, you do." My head started throbbing, which was how I knew that I was shouting. "This is my house, and you're eighteen. Get out."

She walked away from me, climbed the back stairs to her room, and slammed the door.

An hour later I offered her a glass of water and three tablets. "Take this or you have to go," I said when I opened the bedroom door.

She measured my will with her eyes and then took the pills from my hand. But Trina wasn't hollering uncle. I watched her put the medicine in her mouth and take a swallow of water. The antipsychotic was a knockout punch and I'd given Trina a double dose, but by 3 a.m. she was still awake. Noise from the television and her CD player drifted throughout the house. The light on the telephone didn't go off. Trina stayed awake all that night, talking, laughing, singing, dancing, smoking cigarettes and weed. I was awake too: locking up the wine and champagne, hiding the sharp knives, writing my things-to-do list:

1. Turn off long-distance service.
2. Turn off DIRECTV service.
3. Make sure batteries in fire detectors are working.

I was busy. Listening. Anticipating. *This will go on and on and on.*

I I

THE CALLS BEGAN TO COME THE NEXT DAY AND CONTINUED
unabated for nearly a week. Aunt Celia. Cousin Bobby. My gynecologist. A former neighbor. They could have formed their own little support group: Alliance of the Harassed. Brett, Marie's daughter and Trina's old friend, was among them. Hearing her plaintive "Mama Keri," I raked my scalp with my fingernails until I drew blood. Brett and Trina had played together as girls, and the sound of my name in her mouth rendered me a trespasser in a world where I no longer belonged. I could lay claim to her cheerleader past, but the spirit of the fresh clean start in the world of adulthood that she evoked was something I could only covet. Her tentative tone, hesitant hello, and useless chitchat, her stammering tongue as she tried to ease into the reason for the call, made my shame as palpable as the trickle of blood dripping down my head, the stinging in its wake.

What she wanted—no, what she expected—was what they all expected: Mama magic. They might as well have said, "Make her stop." They wanted protection from Trina's ranting and raving and 4 a.m. calls. Listening to people describe—some with glee—the extent of my child's madness gave me the sensation of being trapped in a tiny airless room.

In a spate of twenty-four hours she'd cussed them out and threatened them. Make her stop! She had called dozens of times in one day. Make her stop! I was her mother, and they believed in the inherent and absolute power of a mother's role. Brett gasped a little when I said, "There's nothing I can do. She's been very upset recently. I advise you to hang up on her and take your phone off the hook after midnight."

Delivering my calm, rational statement, I felt as though I were speaking of someone in the abstract, not my child.

"Oh, Mama Keri, I'm going to pray for her," Brett said.

It was what the old Trina would have said, the one who went to church, sang in the choir, and was kind and unfailingly polite to seniors and children.

Trina's old boyfriend from high school called. With him, there had been no screaming, just pure seduction that had continued unabated. Telephone stalking. He'd heard that she was—well, kinda whacked-out. He'd seen her earlier in the day, acting real strange.

How strange was she?

Walking-down-the-street-telling-people-her-mother-was-a-demon strange. Wearing-enough-makeup-for-three-circuses strange.

He assured me that *he* could turn everything around. Trina was still a good person. Maybe if he hadn't broken up with her the way he had, her mind would be okay. When I assured him that Trina's recent troubles had nothing to do with his breaking up with her, he sounded dejected. In subsequent calls, his concern gave way to annoyance and then disgust as Trina stepped up her campaign. She wouldn't leave him alone. Couldn't I control her?

No.

After the fourth conversation, I asked him not to call again.

Practical measure against mania number one: No long distance! I switched to calling cards, which I kept in a secret place so Trina couldn't dial people all over the country. She made the most of what was available locally. My friends, of course, were the most fun. I was her only topic: "Did you know my mother used to beat me? Did you know she hates me? All she cares about is her shop. She's not really my mother. She slept with all my boyfriends."

I was afraid to leave Trina alone when I went to work but more afraid to take her with me. She plucked those fears like a reincarnation of Jimi Hendrix, wearing out his guitar strings with his agile fingers. "I'm taking my meds" became a daily refrain that she'd sing even when the scent of a noonday joint still hung in the air. When I came home at night and stepped over the dirty clothes she'd thrown on the stairs, when I wiped off the butter smeared on the kitchen table and counter, discovered that the chicken I'd set out for dinner had been doused with ammonia, when Trina yelled and menaced, slammed doors, blasted music, couldn't sleep, cursed me, threatened my life, threatened suicide, wave after wave of fierce trembling would work its way up and down my body.

God, you must have me confused with somebody else. You couldn't possibly mean this for me.

"YOU CAN'T TAKE CARE OF TRINA ALL BY YOURSELF," FRANCES told me one afternoon. Trina had been home for a week. "She's wearing you out. I can see it in your eyes." The store was empty. Adriana was at lunch, and we were standing by the register.

"I've told you I can't find any place to put her. The hospital won't take her. Her old program won't take her. What am I supposed to do?"

"She has a father. Send her over there, at least for a while. Let him figure out something."

At the thought of Trina living with Clyde, even temporarily, I instantly registered a veto. Who would supervise her medication, make sure she ate, didn't have caffeine, didn't sneak off at night? Only a mother's vigilance could keep Trina's demons at bay. Even though Trina's behavior was beyond my control, the thought of her being with Clyde gave me a strange, empty feeling, as though I'd been thrown away. I wanted to take care of Trina. When she got better, I wanted it to be on my watch.

"Clyde can't handle Trina," I said, with what I hoped was an air of authority. Frances just rolled her eyes.

We were both momentarily distracted by the sound of laughter. Adriana's smile was so big she could barely fit through the door, and the man walking next to her seemed just as happy.

I looked at Frances.

"She met him at her meeting."

I didn't voice my sentiments, but Frances read them anyway. "Don't get so excited."

Adriana introduced me to her lunch date. The four of us chatted briefly. He was from Oklahoma, had served in the Gulf War, was renting an apartment in Mar Vista, and worked as a computer programmer. I thought my questions were subtle, but when he left Frances said, "Did you forget to ask him his blood type?"

"He's just a friend," Adriana said.

All that grinning? Just a friend?

"Seriously, I've known Jason ever since I started the program. He already has a girlfriend," Adriana said.

"You want everything to be perfect, don't you?" Frances said to me later.

A few hours later, just as we were closing up, we heard a tap at the window. Adriana had already left. When Frances unlocked the door, Orlando and his sons walked in.

The last time Orlando, his boys, and I had been together, we had all gone to see a movie and had dinner at my house. Jabari, PJ, and Trina had played games in the family room while Orlando and I argued quietly in the kitchen. We hadn't raised our voices or changed the expressions on our faces. But as he and his boys were leaving, PJ gave both of us a penetrating stare. "Why aren't you kissing good-bye?" he asked.

Orlando had rushed the boys out, but I could see sorrow in PJ's eyes as he waved to me.

Now I kissed PJ's cheek first and then Jabari's.

"You look nice, Keri," Jabari said.

"You're taller," I said to Jabari. Then I turned to PJ. "What's all this?" I asked, brushing my finger across his faint mustache. He tried not to smile, to hold onto his impassive too-cool-to-care expression, but below the new growth a shadow of a grin emerged.

"Yeah, he thinks he's a man now," Orlando said, and he was grinning too. "I got two men, but nobody's paying rent."

Orlando stepped in front of everyone and launched into a monologue about manhood from a play or a movie no one had seen. The boys shifted their feet and rolled their eyes and tried to endure the two minutes their dad was onstage. When he was finished, Orlando, who had stepped away from the rest of us, turned to his sons. "Remember that?"

"Yeah, Dad," Jabari said. PJ only grunted.

"That's a very famous scene," Orlando said. Then he shrugged. "Anyway."

"You guys want some apple juice? I have some in the back," I said.

"No, thank you," Jabari said.

"How's Trina?" PJ asked.

"Good-bye, everybody," Frances said. She gave a little wave before she closed the door behind her.

I glanced at Orlando's face, wondering how much he'd told the boys. They had always liked Trina.

"She's not feeling well right now," I said.

"We just popped in to say hello," Orlando said. "We're on our way to the mall. Real men need new athletic shoes." He put his arm through mine and guided me a few steps away. "How *is* Trina doing?"

I shook my head.

"Bad?"

"*Really* bad."

He gave me a quick hug. I was grateful he didn't say that everything would be all right. "The boys wanted to see you," he whispered. "I told them we were back together." He studied my face. "So what's the plan?"

"Get her back in the hospital long enough to make a difference."

He squeezed my hand.

"So the sitcom audition went well?"

He recounted every detail, then repeated the lines that he remembered. Told me how much the producers had loved him, how he had nailed it.

I'd heard it all before, so I knew how to listen and not listen, how to make noises in my throat that passed for interest. In the years since we'd been together and not been together, I'd learned what Orlando hadn't learned: not to get invested in an audition. There was no use in two of us getting bent out of shape because of a rejection we failed to see coming. Los Angeles was filled with hopefuls—and with the passed over. Sometimes I wondered how the city managed not to topple, not from earthquakes and mud slides but from the weight of all those hurt feelings, all the would-be stars who hadn't gotten the part.

"Dad," Jabari said.

"Okay, let's go," Orlando said. "I'll call you tonight."

I nodded. "See you soon, guys," I said to the boys. As they submitted to another hug apiece, I caught PJ's eye and silently questioned him. He shook his head.

"Tell Trina I said hello," PJ said.

I was walking them to the door when the ringing of the cell phone clipped to my waist startled me.

"Keri, it's Dora. There's some folks at your house, people I don't think you'd approve of."

"What?" Orlando asked.

"I have to go. That was my neighbor. There's some strange people at the house."

"I'll follow you."

There weren't any cars parked outside when I drove into my driveway. That was a good sign. Even better, when I went inside, the house was in one piece. Trina was in her bed, under the covers. She answered me in short incoherent sentences.

"I don't know," I said to Orlando, who was standing in my living room. The boys were in the car. "Everything seems okay."

The doorbell rang. When I opened it, my next-door neighbor was standing there. She told me she'd seen several strangers coming out of my house, "homeless-looking" people. Mrs. Winslow was in her early seventies but still quite chic, a jazzy oldhead mama who worked out and did yoga and had told me time and time again to call her Dora. She and her husband, Calvin, liked to get dressed up and go out. They gave card parties and barbecues. On weekends, their grandchildren came over. I think I must have swayed a little, because suddenly her arms were around me and she was patting my back, murmuring, "All right. All right now." She sounded her real age then, not the one she liked to project.

Her fingers were soothing, a balm for my spirit. I wanted to breathe in the warmth of those pliant fingers, her take-charge thumbs. They hypnotized me a little, dulled my senses, muffled sounds.

"What?" Her voice was just above a whisper, for my ears only.

"I said, 'You younger women had all those options. Walked out on your husbands because you wanted to be so much.' I heard about your store. Might have worked out better if you'd stayed home and raised your kids."

She spoke evenly, never stopped rubbing my back, and gave me an odd, surprised look when I pulled away. Mrs. Winslow stood in my entryway for a while before she finally closed the door behind her.

"What was that all about?" Orlando asked.

"You need to go," I said. "I'll be all right. I'll call you later."

"You go upstairs and talk to her. I'll leave if everything is okay."

"Nobody's been here," Trina said, her eyes jumping up and down, her hands flailing out and slapping against her thighs. She stormed out of her bedroom and into her bathroom. I heard her stomping around, talking loudly. I knew she was lying.

"It's all right," I said to Orlando minutes later. "You can go."

FRANCES ASSURED ME THAT SHE AND ADRIANA COULD MANage things, so I stayed at home for a few days, babysitting Trina. Guard duty would be more accurate. Watching, waiting, trying to come up with a strategy. I called around to price private-duty nurses and security guards. Too expensive. All the residential treatment programs required a face-to-face interview to determine "if the prospective client will be a good fit."

Thank you for your time.

During the weeks when Trina was still living under my roof, I called SMART at least half a dozen times. Each time they arrived in a timely manner and were unfailingly polite. Somehow, Trina was able to pull herself together in front of them. "Ma'am," they'd say, "your daughter doesn't meet the criteria."

No slit wrists for her; no bullet wounds for me.

OF COURSE, THERE WERE QUIET SPELLS, DAYS WHEN TRINA'S madness was too much even for her and she'd take a double dose of antipsychotic and sleep for twenty-four hours straight. She didn't leave her room to eat; she didn't bathe. I didn't coax her to do either. Even days when her body odor filled her room, I kept silent. The lure of peace was too seductive.

"I'm taking my meds again," she announced one night, after two or three days of relative quiet. I'd just turned off the television in the family room and was about to go to sleep. Trina called to me from her room, which was at the top of the back stairs. Her door was partially opened, and she was lying across her bed. "Did you hear what I said, Mommy?"

"Yes, honey."

"Come here, Mommy."

I went into her room. Trina had picked up all the clothes that she'd dumped on the floor. The top of her bureau was neatly arranged: comb and brush here, perfume there. The air smelled fresh, soapy. Trina had bathed and combed her hair. She was wearing jeans and an ironed shirt. When I sat down on the edge of her bed, she threw her arms around me and kissed my cheek. "You're a good mommee," she said, resting her head against my chest.

I went to bed, warning myself not to feel better. That would be like Sally Hemings sending out wedding invitations.

The next morning, when Trina woke up and came to me with a glass of water and swallowed her pill in front of me, I tried to kickbox the hope that surged through me. Get back! But what's a foot against hope?

Trina swallowed medicine, and my day became full of smiles and sunshine. "Maybe it's over," I told Mattie. A few days, of course, wouldn't banish mania. It would take weeks for the meds even to begin to be effective. Still, Trina's intent was important.

Mattie's own daughter was peaceful, compliant, and living at home. Gloria's son was back at his board and care, once again attempting to be sober and medicated. My friends' children were finally getting it. Why not Trina?

What followed were days when my shoulders steadily crept downward and my breaths became steady and even. I worked a full day here and there, instead of my recent split shifts. The headache that had taken residence above my left eyebrow began to recede. At night I slept.

One afternoon, I went to Orlando's apartment. There was barely any conversation between us. We made love quickly and efficiently. For so long I'd forbidden myself to want Orlando, the smell of him, the weight of him, his voice when it was low and throaty, the taste of me on his tongue. But that day he was my drug of choice, my self-medication.

"You ain't fooling nobody," Frances whispered when I returned to the shop. "Look at you, just smiling all over your little self. Must have been good."

"Mind your business," I said.

Throughout the good times and the bad times, Clyde never called me, although I knew he spoke with Trina, if not regularly, at least often enough for him to be able to gauge her mood fluctuations. I'd heard her talking with him, jumping from one topic to the next, her mouth going a million miles an hour. Listening, I thought to myself: Do you get it now?

I CAME HOME ONE EVENING, AND BOY MAN WAS STANDing in my kitchen. Up close he looked like insufficient funds, a bounced check on weed. "Why are you here?" I asked.

Before he could answer, Trina came clickety-clacking down the stairs. High high heels, red red lips, bright cheeks, a dress the size of a Ritz cracker, eau de weed clinging to her. Here we go: takeoff. *Whoosh*.

"Trina," I began, placing myself between her and Boy Man.

She waved her hand, which was a warning that said, I can become a fist.

"I don't want you to go out, Trina. You're not well."

"Bitch, *you're* not well."

"She's not well," I said to Boy Man, who stared back with interest. "If you leave here, you can't come back," I said to Trina, my voice shrill.

The door slammed and then again, against the inside wall as I yanked it open way too hard.

The car was in the driveway, the motor running.

"Trina! You come back here!"

I could hear her laughing; they were both laughing. I raced around them, got to the car before they did and stood in front of it, my arms stretched out wide. Jesus on the cross, right?

Trina had the nails.

Glancing back, I saw jazzy Mrs. Winslow watching from her window. Across the street, another neighbor's shade was raised. Two car doors slammed. I didn't move. Boy Man backed up, went around me.

"Girl, your momma crazy," he said, as he took off.

Getting there.

My body was shaking as I walked back to my house. Something beneath the quivers broke through the band that held my mind in place when I saw Mrs. Winslow still peeking.

"What the hell are you looking at? She's not some freak!"

She slammed her door. I slammed my door.

Trina returned the next day, disheveled, glassy-eyed, stoned, and manic. I was sipping coffee in the kitchen when she came in. The hot liquid sat on my tongue, unswallowed, as I watched her.

"I'm taking my meds," she screamed, pulling out a bottle of the mood stabilizers from her purse. She poured herself a glass of water, then shook two pills into her hand and gulped them down. "See?"

I left for the store knowing she would sleep but not sure for how long. I canceled with Orlando. By the time I returned home, Trina was walking out the door again. Another night, another rendezvous.

The next day at work I called a list of board and care facilities and visited a few during my lunch hour. They were all horrible, straight out of *One Flew over the Cuckoo's Nest,* inhabited by unkempt women with missing front teeth, men who sat still as warthogs, looking for prey.

She can't live here, not my baby!

I called Mattie that night. "Come to the meeting next week," she said. "You're under a lot of pressure."

No. I was underwater.

Melody's mother, with her grandchildren yelling in the background, listened to me.

"Do you think that maybe Melody could talk to her, try to get her back on track?"

"Well," Celestine began, then excused herself as something crashed behind her. She was gone for a while. When she got back on the phone, she sounded like someone who'd just pulled a double factory shift. "The thing of it is, Melody's doing good. Yeah. And I don't want her around nobody who ain't. You talking about Melody influence your daughter, suppose your child influence mine? And me with these grand-babies, too."

"You have a point. Didn't mean to—"

"All that wildness. I'm not going down that road no more. Melody know that too. If you don't take your meds, better find you another home. Yeah. Maybe that's what you need to tell your girl."

Right.

"You living the good life up there in the hills. You probably got the money and the insurance to go along with every little crazy thing your child do. Me, I ain't got it like that. I can't be bailing nobody out time after time after time. Uh-unh. No. I told Melody: You don't stay on your program, you on your own, and all Mama want to know is do you want to be cremated or buried. I'm serious. When somebody black get to acting a fool out in these here streets, the cops gonna shoot 'em and go on about they business. Just like they killed that man over on Crenshaw."

"What man?"

"Some man on Crenshaw yesterday, near where those guys be selling stuff. He was trying to fight people, acting all crazy. Somebody called the cops, and they shot him. Yeah. They say the man used to walk up and down Crenshaw Boulevard all day long."

I could taste fear in my mouth as I drove toward home. Maybe I began to grieve in my car, shedding tears for Crazy Man, crying hard, as if I knew him. Or maybe I was crying because I didn't want to know him.

Several scattered bouquets marked the spot where Crazy Man had been killed. There was dried blood on ground so close to where I lived, it might as well have been right at my front door.

"He was going off," Mr. Bean Pie said. "Started screaming and hollering, talking about the CIA was after him, that we was all working for the CIA."

"Then he started tearing down the street, pulling off his clothes," CD Man said.

"By the time the cops came, he was near butt naked." This last contribution from one of the Incense People, who added, "But they ain't have no right to shoot the man, even if he was crazy. I got me a cousin act just like him."

Don't we all.

It could have been Trina, I thought. Those words bombarded me for the rest of the day. My child could have been the one being buried. She could have walked out of my house, bent on mayhem and destruction. There wasn't anything I could do to protect her. But Clyde could. He was bigger, stronger. He was a man. He could push Trina out of the way, bar the door with his body if she threatened to leave. Maybe Frances was right.

I called him in the morning. He came to get her that evening. Stood stiffly in my entryway. Clyde had never been inside. For six years, Trina had run out to him. His head moved jerkily as he looked from wall to wall, from room to room.

"It's beautiful," he said. "You always were a great decorator."

"Thank you." The compliment gave me a feeling of satisfaction, which I didn't expect and didn't want to understand. "Clyde, she needs supervision. Someone has to give her the medication. She has to go to bed early. She needs to eat well and no caffeine. She really should be in a facility."

"Let me handle this, Keri."

Trina was packed and ready. Excited. She raced down the steps. Her anticipation made me feel lonely, but I talked myself out of it. Had a great big smile on my face and waved hard as they drove off. Waved and wiped tears. Wiped tears and powdered my face, put on lipstick, sighed in the mirror.

I called her every day for five days. After the second day, Trina refused to speak with me. On the second day I spoke with Clyde, who said everything was fine. Yes, she was taking the medication. No, he wasn't giving it to her; Trina was taking it on her own.

"Is she sleeping at night?" I asked.

"Of course she is," he said.

THE CIRCLE OF CHAIRS IN THE BASEMENT OF THE ALL Souls Presbyterian Church was wide, and every seat was filled. There was no speaker scheduled. People were free to share what was on their minds, and when I walked in late, a man was standing in the center of the circle. "And now, we're going back and forth with Social Security. My son worked for at least eight years before he got ill. He paid into the system, but they're giving us the runaround. As many of you know, he won't get medical benefits until he's been on disability for two years. Right now, the residential treatment center is charging an arm and a leg."

There were groans of recognition.

"We're being eaten alive. But except for the money, things are better."

The man sat down. A woman raised her hand. Straight black hair, Asian eyes. "I'm Soon. My son is thirty-five and has schizophrenia. Right now he's not taking his medication and is completely out of control. He was put out of his sober living home because the manager discovered some crystal meth in his drawer. So then he was on the streets for about two weeks until I could find another place for him, which I did. The new place?" She shook her head. "I tell you, it's so interesting to me, this whole concept of sober living. Sometimes I think they ought to call it *whatever* living, because so few of the managers really care about sobriety. Anyway, keep the prayers coming. Thank you for listening."

When Mattie whispered for me to share, I pointed to my wristwatch. Mouthing, "I'll call you," I fled up the aisle and out the door.

The telephone began ringing as soon as I got in the house. I thought it would be Orlando. He'd been staying over the last few nights. But the call was collect.

"Mommy," Trina said, her voice amped up with excitement, with manic pleasure. "I'm in jail, and I need for you to come get me right now."

"What happened, Trina? What jail? Where's your father?"

"I didn't do anything, anything, anything. Get me out of here. Right now!"

"Where's your father? Why are you in jail? What did you do?"

"They said I stole something from Saks. You get me out of here!" she bellowed.

Shoplifting. I could barely breathe. "Does your father know where you are?"

"No. He went out, and Aurelia wasn't there. He left me with the housekeeper."

I tried to ignore my rage and concentrate on my leverage. "I will not bail you out unless you agree to go to the hospital."

"I don't need to go to any damn hospital."

"Then stay in jail," I said. Dial tone.

Will you accept the charges? Part two.

"You are going to the hospital, Trina. If you leave, I'll revoke the bail, and you'll be arrested again. And you'll stay in jail. Do you understand me?"

"Yes, Mommee."

The jail was on Martin Luther King Boulevard. The bail bondsman didn't arrive for more than an hour, even though his office was right down the street. As soon as he came in, shaking the building with his slow, heavy steps, he disappeared downstairs to take care of the bail and didn't come back up for another hour. Sitting in the waiting area, I tried to make my mind go blank, to pretend that waiting for my kid at the police station was as normal as tap water. He returned with bad news: He did not accept personal checks, and he didn't take credit cards.

"My bank is closed. I can't get more than three hundred dollars out of the ATM machine. I don't want her sitting in jail overnight."

"Sometimes that's the best thing for them." When he looked at me, there wasn't a trace of kindness in his face. "Is there somebody you can call? Is the father in the picture?"

"Yes. No. Jesus." Just hearing the word *father*, I could feel anger exploding in every part of me.

Orlando wasn't at home; his cell phone went right to message center. I didn't leave a message. Neither Mattie nor Gloria answered. Frances had just bought a house, and I knew she didn't have any money to spare. Adriana. The name lingered in my mind. I didn't want to put her in jeopardy.

Bethany answered on the third ring.

"I'll be right there," she said, after I explained what had happened.

She handed me an envelope as soon as she walked in the door. "What's she in for?"

"Shoplifting."

"Poor baby." She was quiet for a moment. "We found Angelica," she said.

"Where was she?"

"On the street."

"Where is she now?"

"At my house. I've got friends staying with me on rotating shifts. So what's your plan?" Bethany asked.

I sighed. "I'm going to take her to the hospital. She said she'd go."

"I'll go with you."

The bail bondsman disappeared downstairs again, and when he came back up, he told me that Trina would be released after she signed the paperwork. "Nice doing business with you," he said, pressing one of his cards in my hand.

Another hour passed before Trina emerged. From across the room, all I could see were her lips, bright orange and shiny. The closer she got, the more colors I saw. Blue eyelids. Rust-colored cheeks. Black eyebrows. Trina was giggling at some private joke.

"We're going to the hospital," I said, taking her arm. "This is my friend Bethany. She loaned me your bail money." Bethany took her other arm.

She didn't resist. Trina got into the front passenger seat of the car and buckled up her seat belt. In between the giggling, she sang. Bethany sat right behind her. I watched the traffic and Trina, but I couldn't do both at once. At the second red light I heard a sound. *Click, click.* The seat belt. *Bam!* The door. Trina running, getting smaller and smaller.

The back door opened, and Bethany sprinted after her. As I watched, my car stood in traffic, not moving, cars around me blaring their horns. Finally, I parked and waited for Bethany to come back, hoping that she wouldn't be alone. Loud rhythm and blues blared from the radio. Vintage Al Green just added to the confusion.

"Make me wanna do right. Make me wanna do wrong."

I visualized Bethany tackling Trina to the ground. Had a crowd gathered to watch the fight? A heat flash rose up and began exploding as little pinpricks of moisture erupted all over my body. I got out of the car, just to feel the air on my face, and peered up and down the block. Bethany trudged resolutely toward me. My child had been swallowed up by the Los Angeles night.

We rode around for half an hour. Nearly eleven and Crenshaw was slow but not deserted. Steel shutters had come down on the furniture and wig stores hours ago, but the fast-food joints and video stores, the liquor store that took up an entire corner, were still open.

It was easy to hide out in LA, so much space, so much indifference. People were used to the bizarre here, the pre-rehab antics of stars in trouble. A pretty girl with too much makeup, too much cleavage, talking fast, not making sense, would attract attention but not the kind that would result in someone coming to her aid. In Atlanta, people were always watching, at least in Southwest, where close-set houses squeezed lives together and somebody's grandma was always sitting on the porch. There the word would have spread like the dope man's phone number.

The neighbors had certainly talked about my mother. I remembered a sweaty summer night filled with stars and lightning bugs. The porches that lined our block were filled, the people driven from their hot homes to the cooler night air. Heavyset matriarchs and sedentary patriarchs sat on wicker chairs enjoying their iced tea, the faint breeze.

Then from our house two bodies spilled from inside onto the porch and the street. My mother—hair done, tight dress and high heels, red lips and powdered face—ready for action, for a night of drinking. Ma Missy—do-rag, housedress, house shoes, grim face—hell-bent on stopping her. What a diversion they were as their arguing suddenly escalated. Ma Missy raised her open palm and *whack!* Right across my mother's face. Suddenly the entire block had a focus, and every breath was heavy with judgment.

"You ready to act like you got some sense?"

By that time, Ma Missy had my mother on the ground. But the ultimate answer was no. My mother jumped up, pushed Ma Missy, and ran down the street.

"I'm a grown woman, Mama. Do whatever the hell I want to do," she called, then cut butter all the way to the waiting car.

In the morning as I walked to school the children, ones I thought were my friends, fell silent as I approached. My best friend, a girl who lived two houses from ours, put her hand in mine; I found the gesture annoying and tried to pull away, but she was determined to stick by me and wouldn't let go. At the end of the school day, though, I took the long way home by myself.

I THOUGHT OF MY MOTHER AS BETHANY AND I DROVE, MY mother clean and sober, her resilient demons finally vanquished. Her words on the telephone replayed in my mind. "It's your mother." That phrase was so seductive, so powerful. "It's your mother."

I let Bethany off in front of her car. Bethany smiled. "What are you going to do?" she asked.

"I'm going to wait until Trina meets the criteria for a hold, and then I'm going to try to get a conservatorship."

"Listen to me. Mental illness is in my father's family big-time. My dad has schizophrenia. His father committed suicide. His sister had bipolar; out of her four children, two are ill. I'm telling you: Fuck a hold. Fuck conservatorship, which could take months, years to get. Do you want your child to be well, to be safe?"

That word again. "Bethany—"

She wouldn't let me speak. At the base of my skull a punishing headache was being born. Maybe that's why everything Bethany said seemed to have an echo, why her words overwhelmed me. I tried not to listen, but Bethany was so loud and I felt so weak. I couldn't summon the energy to ignore her. The night in front of me was a long horror. My house would be dark and quiet, my bed like a prison. Trina wouldn't be back until she came back. I knew I'd never revoke the bail and have her arrested again. I didn't have Orlando. I didn't have Clyde. If Bethany stopped talking, I'd be alone with my aching head, my weak body that couldn't fight off undue influence.

"I want you to meet some people," she said.

12

BETHANY GOT LOST ON HER WAY TO MY HOUSE THE NEXT day. She called me from her cell phone three times, and each time she was farther away than the last. The first call was from Crenshaw.

"There's all these guys standing on the sidewalk, and they have, like, T-shirts hanging from a wire fence. Where the hell am I?"

"You went too far south," I said.

"What is this pie they're selling? Bean pie? I'm getting one."

"Turn around and make a left onto Stocker."

She called back to tell me she'd just passed the biggest liquor store she'd ever seen in her life. Maybe she stopped in, because she went right by my house. Her next call was from Slauson.

"I'm in the parking lot of Seven-Eleven," she said.

"Stay there. I'll come get you."

When I pulled up beside her, she had all the windows in her car rolled down and she was sitting in the front seat smoking.

"I bet you think I'm an idiot," she yelled. That cracked her up. I could see her laughing in my rearview mirror as she followed me home.

"What is this neighborhood?" she asked, as soon as we got to my house. "It's fabulous. Look at that view. Amazing."

"View Park."

"I never even heard of it," Bethany said. It was the first time I'd seen her enthusiastic about anything other than creating a ruckus. She stood in my driveway, gazing at the downtown skyline. nodding her head up and down, her expression one of amazement, as if something fantastic had jumped out of the woods and startled her. "So did you find your child?"

"Not yet."

"Let's go," she said.

Bethany's car was a junkyard on four wheels. There were newspapers and magazines, empty hamburger cartons, crumpled bags that had held French fries or potato chips, candy bar wrappers, crushed soda cans, several purses, two pairs of athletic shoes, a dirty jacket, and tufts of fur, lots of fur. The stale cigarette smoke went right to my head, and I started sneezing immediately. She didn't apologize, just told me to dump everything in my seat onto the floor, which pretty much left me with no place to put my feet. Bethany was oblivious to my discomfort in more ways than one. She's a weirdo, I thought to myself. And I was a fool for being with her.

She drove west to Santa Monica, parked her car, and then we walked several blocks to the beach, sitting down on a bench that faced the water. All around us people jogged and skated, bicycled and walked. Stretched out like an endless ribbon was the calm, predictable Pacific.

"I thought we were going to a meeting."

"We are," she said. "See that guy over there by the wall? Walk over to him."

"What—" I stopped. Not twenty yards away, a man with a baseball hat pulled low over his eyes was standing by the wall. I hadn't expected some clandestine secret-password FBI kind of scene. Bethany saw the doubt in my eyes. She looked around and gave me a shove.

"Go," she said.

The man started talking as soon as I walked over. He sounded like John Wayne in an old Western. I looked down at his feet, expecting to see boots and spurs, but he had on sneakers. If he knew how to rope a steer, it didn't show in his face.

"My name is Richard. My son is twenty-two. He has bipolar with borderline features." He spoke quickly, faster than the Duke would have. "I tried to get help through the usual channels. Nothing worked out. The kid would act out, terrorize the family, tear up the place. I'd call the police, and my child never fit the criteria. When they did place my kid on hold, it was never long enough. I found friends, people willing to take a risk."

"What?" I couldn't concentrate.

He didn't look up. "Don't ask any questions. Just let me talk. The friends told me about a place where I could take my kid. At this place, there are psychiatrists and mental health workers who don't abide by the rules. They have a different take on mental illness. They believe in intervention. They don't believe in the hitting-rock-bottom theory. They helped me save my kid's life. My kid is taking his medication, going to school, doing well."

"I—"

"The people who helped me can help you too. That's all you need to know for now. It's been nice talking to you."

He walked away.

Bethany had the bean pie on the bench when I sat down beside her.

"I should have gotten a knife or a fork or something."

"Who the hell was that?" I asked.

"I can't tell you any more than he told you. But the people he told you about help people like us."

"What do you mean, people like us?"

"People with mentally ill family members who are fed up with waiting for the system to act."

"Who is that guy? What people are you talking about? What is this all about, Bethany?"

"If you're interested, you can come to a meeting."

"Interested in what? I thought that *was* the meeting. What the hell are you talking about?"

"Listen to me, Keri. There are people in the world who don't believe in the way this country deals with mentally ill people. And they can help us."

"How? How do they help us? Can they get my kid on a hold? Can they help me get conservatorship? My kid is missing. Can they find her?"

Bethany shook her head. "That's not how they do things. They're way outside that box."

"If you can't tell me any more than that—" I rose.

"You got a radical problem, you need a radical solution. The Weathermen. Symbionese Liberation Army. The Panthers. Civil rights movement. They didn't wait for the system to give them what they needed."

"Well," I said, "here's the thing: When radical white people get tired of being radical they get to be state senators, or they write books, or if push comes to shove they can move to Oregon and hang out for thirty years before the FBI finds them. Radical black people get killed."

Bethany stared at me as though fire were shooting out of my mouth. Maybe she was pondering what I'd said, or maybe she was just trying to figure out how she could eat the pie without a knife and fork.

Minutes later, we were both scooping up bean pie with our fingers.

"Nobody's going to get killed. But there are some risks involved, as with anything that's worthwhile," Bethany said. "I never thought about things being more risky for black people, but I guess that's valid."

Between us, we finished off nearly half a pie. Afterward, we were quiet, just sitting and looking at the ocean.

"I figure whatever this group is doing is illegal. Right? You're snatching people who are over eighteen and forcing treatment on them. Does that about sum it up? Come on, I'm not stupid. What do you do, shove the kids in the trunk and take off in the night to parts unknown?" When she didn't respond, I continued, "I can't get caught up in anything like that. Period."

Bethany nodded. "That's what I said at first."

"Are you involved?"

"Are you in or out?" Bethany said, imitating the lines from a movie trailer.

"So you've already done whatever it is that this group does and now you're recruiting?"

"I'm not recruiting, I'm trying to help you." Bethany sighed. "Angelica is in a very scary state. She finally crashed. She was pure mania for so long, and then she just crashed. She's in the midst of a terrible depression. It's a good day if she brushes her teeth. Very scary."

She stopped talking and put some pie in her mouth but didn't chew it.

"It's awful watching her go through this. I have to get her some real help, and I can't do it alone. Are you in or are you out?"

She looked at me, and I stared back at her. She was willing to trust a bunch of radical strangers with her child's life. What would it feel like to be that daring? I envied Bethany her ability to invent an option, even if it was a crazy one. Me, I followed the rules, even when they made no sense. I cleared my throat. "I'm going for conservatorship."

13

BY THE TIME CLYDE RETURNED MY PHONE CALL, TRINA HAD been AWOL for nearly twenty-four hours. For some reason, when I spoke with him, I wasn't furious. His absence was work-related, of course, some celebrity golf tournament he'd agreed to host. When I told him that Trina had been arrested and was now missing, he was speechless. When he could finally speak, he seemed dazed.

"I'm so sorry," he said. "I just didn't realize."

"If she calls you, please—"

"I will," he said. "And if she—"

"I will."

During that day, as customers searched through our racks, I called the Office of the Public Guardian six times before I finally reached Herbert Swanson. I had found his business card inside a zippered compartment of a purse I hadn't carried for months. Conservatorship would give me the legal right to place my child in a locked facility, to force her into a place where she would receive her medication regularly. The Office of the Public Guardian was charged with helping people get conservatorship. Listening to him, a picture formed in my mind of a man with a telephone growing out of his head, a silver motor tied to his back, zooming from meeting to meeting. Sitting at my desk at the store, I filled him in on Trina's background, the progression of her illness, and the recent events that had led to my call.

Eight months earlier, when the Office of the Public Guardian's representative had come to the support group meeting, Trina had just left the hospital and was beginning the partial program at Weitz Center. The night that Herbert Swanson gave his presentation was the first evening I'd left Trina alone in the house since she'd come home. I was a little distracted, listening to him outline the legal remedy for the mentally ill who were out of control. I remembered leaving early that evening and rushing back home to find my daughter calmly watching television in my bed. I snuggled in beside her, grateful that I would never need the card I'd taken, because my bad times, Trina's bad times, were behind me. Now every molecule in my body was paying attention to Mr. Swanson.

"Where is your daughter now?" he asked when I'd finished.

"I don't know. We were on our way to the hospital last night and she jumped out of my car. I haven't heard from her since."

He made a noise that meant Wow! or Good Lord! or something like that. "And you want to go for LPS conservatorship?"

"Yes."

"It's a pretty difficult proposition without your daughter being on a hold."

"What do I have to do?"

"First of all, she must be evaluated by a psychiatrist who is on staff at a designated hospital. I can send you a form to give to the doctor. Once it's filled out, you mail it to my office with a request for an LPS conservatorship. The court will then give you a hearing date. Your daughter will have to be personally served with the papers, because she has to be present in court."

So simple, so straightforward. So impossible.

"Mrs. Whitmore, if I were you, I'd try to get her placed on a hold. Once your daughter is in the hospital, everything will be a lot easier. The psychiatrist there can do the paperwork."

"What do you think I've been trying to do for the last month and a half? Every time I call SMART or the police, they refuse to take her. Somehow she manages to pull herself together when they arrive, so she doesn't fit the criteria."

"You're going to have to lower your voice, Mrs. Whitmore."

"Sorry."

"Mrs. Whitmore, if your child is as sick as you say she is, there will come a day when she won't be able to control herself. Really, it's easier to get an LPS if your daughter is in the hospital on a hold."

"But how—"

"If your daughter has a psychiatrist who is on staff at one of our hospitals, talk with him about supporting you in getting a conservatorship. Establish a relationship with the SMART people. Be persistent. When you finally make the call, tell them where you wish to have your daughter taken. When she gets to the hospital, call us. You'll get a court hearing. And then it's up to the judge. I wish I could speak with you further about this, but I'm late for a meeting. I want to warn you, Mrs. Whitmore. There's no such thing as miracles. Mental illnesses can transform people. You may not be able to get back the daughter you have. You may, as the saying goes, have to learn to love a stranger. Good luck."

RONA WAS WAITING FOR ME WHEN I PULLED INTO MY DRIVE-way that evening. She was seated inside her car, reading a magazine. The night before, she had called to remind me of the appointment she'd made a month earlier. She'd lost more weight, enough for the skin around her mouth to fall slack, enough to remind me that other people had problems even more urgent than my own.

"Trina," I called as soon as I stepped inside. No answer.

Rona had trouble getting onto the table. Her left arm was swollen, and her legs seemed to be stiff. When she was settled, I ran my hand over her shoulders; she flinched, which told me that she expected pain. My touch became lighter and lighter. After a while, her skin seemed to loosen beneath my hands, and her breathing regulated into an almost silent purring. Midway through the session, she fell asleep, waking up moments after I'd finished.

"Girl, I feel so much better. Chemo is a bitch." She laughed, struggling to sit up. "Did you send in your reservation?"

"My reservation?"

"For the reunion in October. I'm going," she said in her soft, wispy voice. "I'm definitely going."

"My life is a little up in the air right now," I said.

Rona looked at me for a few seconds, then started laughing. Miniature rusty wheels began rolling in her throat. The sound clanked and cranked its way to the surface. Tiny, joyful spasms erupted from her. Such unexpected happiness from a shaking bag of bones.

"I can relate to that," she said, and laughed some more.

THE NEXT DAY, I REPLAYED IN MY MIND MR. SWANSON'S marching orders for LPS conservatorship and tried to reach Trina's psychiatrist. Dr. Bellows wasn't at his office, and we played phone tag nearly all day before I finally faxed him a quick note describing Trina's situation and asking for his cooperation on my decision to get conservatorship. Around four o'clock, I drove to his office, where he was in practice with two other psychiatrists and two psychologists. At the sign-in window, a young Latina handed me a clipboard and asked me to add my name to what was a very long list. Every non-Latino physician in Los Angeles had a Latina working in his office. The object was for her to bring in her family and friends, thus expanding the practice to a population that might not have been reachable otherwise. In Dr. Bellows's office, there wasn't one seat available in the reception area.

From time to time, other doctors appeared behind the window, but I didn't see Dr. Bellows until two hours had passed. That's when I glimpsed him through the partially opened door that led from the waiting room to the treatment areas.

"Hey, just a moment, ma'am," the receptionist called, when she saw me going toward the doctor.

Dr. Bellows looked startled when he saw me. With so many faces in his life, so many names and sad stories, mine didn't register immediately.

"Keri Whitmore, Trina's mom."

He nodded.

I spoke quickly, filling him in on what had been going on with Trina. Thirty seconds, max. "I've been calling. Did you receive my fax. Will you support me on conservatorship?"

He hesitated. Looked in another direction. The receptionist appeared behind him.

I spoke even faster. "Because if you aren't willing, I need to know."

"Miss—"

When I looked at her, the receptionist stepped back.

"You need to calm down," Dr. Bellows said. To me.

"I'm calm," I said, facing the doctor. I turned to the receptionist. "I'm calm."

"Miss—"

"*Whitmore!*" I heard myself in the absolute silence that followed. "I'm sorry. Didn't mean to scream. So sorry."

The assistant eyed Dr. Bellows. Everything around me seemed to slow down. Dr. Bellows whispered that he remembered Trina. He promised to fill out the papers whenever I got them to him and to testify on my behalf in court. He apologized for taking so long. He asked me if I'd heard of my support group, and I told him I was a member and attended the meetings from time to time.

"We all need a little help sometimes," he said. "Take care of yourself."

The doctor glanced at the receptionist, who took my arm in a firm grip and led me back into the waiting room, where people sat up straight and alert, averting their eyes when I passed.

MY HOUSE WAS QUIET WHEN I GOT HOME, BUT THERE was evidence of chaos wherever I looked. Pieces of a broken cup lay shattered on the kitchen floor. The refrigerator door was flung open. Waste floated in the guest bathroom toilet while water ran in the sink. Somebody was speaking loudly, rapidly behind a closed door. The phone line in Trina's room was lit up.

I flushed the toilet, turned off the water, closed the refrigerator door, and began picking up the broken pieces but then stopped. My fingers felt cramped and sore. My back hurt.

I called Clyde. "She's back," I said.

"How is she?"

"The same."

"I'm sorry," he said. "Sorry about the way I am. It's only that if I stop moving—"

"I know," I said.

In my bathroom, soaking in the tub, door locked, I reviewed my to-do list: The countdown for conservatorship was on. I had a psychiatrist who would sign the papers whenever Trina was brought in. All I needed was another seventy-two-hour hold.

Standing outside Trina's door, I could hear her talking on the telephone to someone. Her words were racing. Stay inside tonight, I thought. Call people, talk fast, scream sometimes. Be safe.

A long time ago, one of the speakers at the support group told us we shouldn't let our relative's illness become our lives. But Trina *was* my life, and I didn't want to learn to love a stranger.

14

THE GRADUATION CARDS HAD BEGUN ARRIVING IN LATE May. High school. College. The children of my friends were growing up, moving on. Their proud parents trumpeted the news.

I crumpled the announcement cards in my hands. Piercing paper points stabbed my palms. Sharp edges cut my fingers. Another reason to cry. Everybody's damn kid was graduating. I mailed check after check. At the bottom of my cards I wrote "Congratulations," followed by gay exclamation points.

God, please, don't let me be like this. Please take this envy from me.

Meanwhile, Trina was relatively quiet. Behind her bedroom door she mumbled and shuffled back and forth. She played her CDs and the television, but the sounds emanating from her quarters were subdued. My shoulders shouldn't have come down, but they did. I shouldn't have mistaken a period of calm for healing. But I couldn't help thinking: *Maybe today is the day I'll get her back.*

My birthday wasn't as bad as I thought it would be. I received roses from Clyde and a bottle of perfume from Orlando, a bracelet from Adriana and cards from Frances, Mattie, and Gloria. Trina stayed in bed all day long, so at least the house was peaceful. At eight o'clock that night, I was putting away my dinner dishes when the doorbell rang. Moments later, PJ was standing in front of me, holding a bouquet of flowers.

"Happy birthday," he said after I let him in. He handed me the flowers.

"Thank you, PJ. How did you get here?"

"I walked."

"Does anyone know where you are?"

He shook his head.

"You hungry?"

He sat down on one of the high chairs at the kitchen counter. I warmed up leftovers: chicken, rice, greens. PJ dug in as though he hadn't eaten in a week. Watching him, I remembered all the times I'd cooked for him and his brother, all the times they'd gone to sleep in my guest room. Orlando's sons and my daughter had laughed together over bowls of ice cream, over Monopoly boards, and while watching videos. Orlando and I used to marvel at how well they got along. Even when we weren't together, the kids always managed to maintain their relationship. Just before Trina had gotten ill, she'd gone to the movies with the boys.

"Is Trina crazy?"

I was bent over the dishwasher, and that's the position I froze in. "Who told you that?"

PJ looked bewildered. He hadn't expected questions. "I heard."

"Oh, really? From whom?" I straightened up slowly and walked over to PJ.

He stared back at me, unsure of what to say.

"Was it your dad?"

He shook his head. "Jabari said he heard somebody say that."

I didn't know I'd been holding my breath until I heard myself exhaling. "Trina's going through something, PJ," I said, hesitating, trying to pick the best words. "Her mind is kind of overloaded, and she's not thinking clearly."

"Is she going to get better?"

I hesitated again, this time to wait out the tears that were stinging my eyelids. "I think so."

PJ stared at me hard, perhaps sensing my unsureness, my helplessness.

"So, PJ, what's this I hear about a tattoo?"

"Aw," he said. His face registered a mixture of bravado and embarrassment.

"So let's see it."

He lifted his shirt and turned around. Written with a flourish across the small of his back were the words FUCK YOU, just as Orlando had described.

"PJ, you want to tell me why you put that on your back?"

His reasons weren't coherent. Something about everybody did it. He mentioned several rappers. He sounded angry when he was talking. And then he sounded sad.

"My dad was mad about it at first. But then, it was like, whatever. He's got an audition, so whatever. He's got to rehearse, so whatever. Anyway," he said, after a moment of silence passed between us, "I might have it taken off when I get older and start working a regular job and stuff."

"I can't wait for that day."

PJ looked at me, and a grin spread across his face. I hugged him, and he hugged me back.

"Have you had that conversation yet?" I asked.

He shook his head, then looked at me. "You don't know how hard it is just to say it to myself. You're the only person I've told. My brother doesn't even know. People are going to start treating me differently. Everybody's not like you. Can we not talk about this?"

I nodded.

"Is Trina home?" he asked.

I sighed and let him go. "She's sleeping right now." Before he could ask me any more questions, I said, "Let me take you home."

"I HAVE SEEN THE TATTOO," I TOLD ORLANDO LATER THAT night, when we spoke on the telephone.

"PJ's tattoo?"

"The very same. He came over tonight. He walked."

"Really. He misses you."

"Yeah. I miss him and Jabari too. So I fed your hungry boy and then I asked to see his tattoo. He said he might have it taken off when he's older. So I took that as a sign that he regrets the whole episode. If I were you, I'd casually approach him about removing it in a couple of months. Maybe just the two of you could go do something together that would get him in a talking mood."

"All right. Thanks. Oh, the rehearsals are going really well. They've invited a lot of television and movie people for opening night, which will work out great since it's so close to pilot season. Maybe I can go right from the play into a series. That's the point of doing these hundred-and-seventy-five-dollar-a-week gigs. Exposure, baby. I got you sitting right up front on opening night."

"Have you heard back about your sitcom audition?" I knew as soon as I said the words, as soon as I heard him inhale, that he hadn't made the cut.

"I couldn't be as dumb as they wanted," Orlando said. Then he switched topics, going on and on about the play. Several times I tried to break in, to tell him about PJ and how he wanted to know about Trina, but he was wound up, ready for his close-up, so I just let him talk. Maybe that's how it had always been with Orlando and me. There were times when I just let him talk, but I wasn't really listening and he didn't really care.

I felt lonely after I hung up the phone, a feeling I couldn't shake off in the days that followed. In the past I'd prayed for as much silence and avoidance as Trina now began doling out. She didn't scream; she didn't curse. Only now I needed for her to get out of control, to break my windows, yell and scream and threaten me: to meet the criteria. But she was quiet, talking on the telephone, leaving water running, not flushing toilets, but doing nothing that would have gotten her put on a seventy-two-hour hold. So I waited. Maybe she was waiting too.

It occurred to me that I hadn't smelled weed in days. Whoever had been supplying her had cut her off, or maybe she was worn out from climbing up the drug staircase, hopping from cigarettes to liquor to weed and who knew what else. Each step had promised tranquillity, a restoration of balance. Each step had lied. The staircase was circular. The drugs calmed her initially, then set her off.

In her current state, Trina was relatively tranquil because she wasn't stressed out. Her room, equipped with a television, CD player, and telephone, her current drug of choice, was devoid of triggers. Her mealymouth mama, passively accepting her highs, her lows, making no demands, walking on eggshells with skill and interminable patience, wasn't upping the ante.

If she was ever to be my pearl again, I had to be her grain of sand.

There was risk involved, of course. She could become manic and still not meet the criteria. I could create a monster I'd be forced to endure.

Since she'd been off her medication, Trina never cleaned up the kitchen. From the garage door one evening after work I observed the usual chaos: dirty dishes swimming in oil-slick water, food smeared on the counter, cabinet doors wide open. I took a deep breath. My fury was effortless, a vein just waiting to be tapped. I screamed my displeasure from the bottom of the back stairs all the way to the top, where I pushed open the door to Trina's room and yelled some more.

She was in the bed watching cartoons, giggling like a toddler. Her first glance was filled with curiosity, as though Mom was just another form of entertainment. She actually chuckled. I stormed across the floor to her bed and yanked the covers off. She jumped up.

"Leave me alone, you bitch!"

"This is my house, and I won't let you turn it into a garbage can. Go downstairs and clean up that kitchen right now."

"Fuck you!"

"Don't you dare talk to me like that."

I moved in closer, pressing my chest against hers. She pushed back with her hands. I let them stay on me for seconds, and then I fled downstairs. I called SMART.

Today is the day I get her back.

The team, when it arrived, was made up of people I hadn't met before, a white psychiatric social worker and a Latino assistant. Minutes later two police officers drove up.

"What's going on?" the psychiatric worker asked me, when she came inside. Her name was Hilda Griffin, and she looked permanently weary.

"My daughter has bipolar disorder, and she's not taking her meds. She assaulted me."

"What's your name? What's your daughter's name?"

She wrote them down in a book she was carrying.

"How old is Trina?"

"She's eighteen. She assaulted me."

"What exactly did she do?"

"She pushed me."

"When?"

"Right before I called you guys."

Ms. Griffin tilted her head, eyed me. "Were you fighting?"

"I asked her to clean up the kitchen."

"Where is she now?"

"Upstairs in her room."

Ms. Griffin waited until the two police officers were in the house before she went to look for Trina. My entourage trailed behind me.

Trina was back under the covers, her entire body hidden from view.

Ms. Griffin directed her questions to the lump in the bed. Her voice took on a soothing quality that had been lacking when she interrogated me. Maybe she thought I didn't need soothing.

"Trina, I'd like to see your face, dear. Can you come out from under the covers?"

I held my breath, looking from one authority figure to the other.

"Trina, dear, let's talk. I'd like to help you."

Glancing at her partner, she shrugged her shoulders.

What kind of shrug was that? Was that an "our work here is done" shrug?

"You fellows can leave," Ms. Griffin said to the police.

Shit.

I walked them back down the stairs and out the door and returned to Trina's room.

The social worker and her partner were standing outside the door, which was closed. "I can see there is a problem," she said.

"She hit me," I said. "A danger to others. That's the criterion."

Ms. Griffin placed her card in my palm. "I thought you said she pushed you."

"I—"

"I can't justify taking her in. Not today. Keep in touch."

They went away quickly. And then it was Trina and me: Trina, an irritated wasp; me, the hand that had swatted her.

"Piece of shit."

She came out from under the covers feeling emboldened, empowered. The authorities hadn't taken her away. She was invincible.

Trina screamed until she was hoarse, until I slammed my bedroom door in her face. Any other time, the fight would have exhausted and demoralized me. But not now. Means to an end. Keep screaming, I thought. Only a matter of time and then everything will go my way. Just like potty training.

WITHIN A WEEK I HAD BECOME TELEPHONE FRIENDS WITH Hilda Griffin. I called her every other day to check in, to update, to prove to her that I wouldn't go away. She came on duty after three, and when she was in the field I contacted her by cell phone. After the second call, I felt I had an ally. By the third call, she recognized my voice. She told me about her children, the son who started wetting the bed after her divorce. When she didn't hear from me after three days, because I was busy, she called me.

Trina's rage blew out in twenty-four hours, just another thing she couldn't hold on to. Her general mood was low-grade edginess, a fever that rose and fell. At night I could hear her calling people on the telephone, roaming the hallway, at times singing. She never slept. During the day, she sat at the breakfast room table and wrote.

"It's a novel," she snarled when I asked her about it. Around her feet were wads of paper, literary rejects.

She wouldn't allow me to read her work-in-progress, but I fished several of the balled-up sheets out of the trash can and stole a look. Trina had always been a good writer, but my new reality cautioned me to expect gibberish. To my surprise, the thoughts she'd set down on paper were clear. Actually, her writing made more sense than she did. Everything's not gone, I thought. It's not as though her mind burned up in a fire.

She can begin again. She'll be a famous author!

The next few days settled into a pattern that, if not predictable, was somewhat comforting to me. When I left in the morning, Trina would be writing at the table, her head bent down over her tablet, oblivious to everything around her. When I returned home, she'd still be there. Almost immediately, she'd retreat to her room, where she would play music, watch television, and talk on the telephone until morning.

At least once a day, Clyde called from Seattle—where his show was being temporarily broadcast live from some conservative round table conference—wanting to know Trina's every move. He was like the old me, anxious to interpret every sign as progress. On the third day, he said that Trina's relative silence was an indication that she was calming down. I informed him that depression was the flip side of mania.

"You're so negative!" he shouted.

"This isn't going to go away, Clyde."

"Maybe you don't want it to go away. Maybe you don't want her to be well, so you won't be alone."

"I'm not alone, you asshole. You're the one who's about to be alone."

So much for our truce.

I called Ms. Griffin twice that week to report that my daughter seemed unable to stop writing, that she looked disheveled and didn't bathe. I exaggerated as much as seemed plausible and tried not to think about how betrayed Trina would have felt if she'd heard me. Ma Missy had always told me not to put my business in the street. But that was an old rule, from my old life, about as useful to me as a training bra. The worse off I made Trina seem, the sooner she'd get help. So I didn't tell Ms. Griffin that the house seemed peaceful with Trina's overzealous productivity.

I rummaged around in the cabinet. Felt the hidden bottles with careful fingertips. There. Right there. My hand grasped the slender neck of the bottle. Chivas. Jesus. I remembered Ma Missy handing it to me. Not a gift, a warning. *Don't ever open it; don't be like her.*

I placed the scotch carefully on the kitchen counter and then, just when I was about to walk up the stairs, changed my mind and put it on the desk in my office. My child was smart enough to recognize bait when she saw it, even if she couldn't refuse it. When it was all over, I didn't want her to feel stupid on top of everything else.

It took three days for Trina to find the bottle. But once she did, it didn't take long for her to empty it. It was hard to imagine her drinking scotch, one of my mother's drinks. It was so old school, so East Coast and wintery.

The days of scotch passed quietly. By the third day, when it was all gone and she'd begun to crave the flavor and depend upon the way the alcohol temporarily stilled her mind, she was roaring, a typhoon unleashed upon dry land. Upstairs in her room, she frantically dialed number after number, slamming down the phone again and again. I waited.

On the fourth morning, I woke up feeling chilled. When I checked Trina's room, she wasn't there. She wasn't downstairs either. But the front door was wide open.

I heard her before I saw her. Beyond the driveway, she was walking up the street, her feet bare, a towel wrapped around her.

My instinct was to rush toward her, gently guide her back into the house. Instead, I went inside, picked up the phone, and called SMART. When Hilda Griffin appeared with the police, I heard them ask Trina the date. She stared at them and began reciting the months of the year.

"How old are you, sweetheart?" Hilda Griffin asked.

"I'm sixteen," Trina said.

Thirty minutes later, a subdued Trina was in the back of their car, and I was following them in mine. She was gravely disabled, the social worker declared. She had met the criteria. The seventy-two-hour hold was about to begin, and I knew it would be extended to two weeks. I called Herbert Swanson at the office of the public guardian, and he promised that he would send someone to interview Trina immediately. Breathe easy, I told myself. A court date will be set. Relax. Dr. Bellows will testify.

I called Clyde. "I'm going for conservatorship, and don't you dare try to stop me."

He sighed. When he spoke, he sounded weary. "We have to talk about this," he said.

I knew him well enough not to push it any further, to leave Clyde with a psychological victory or at least with no clear-cut win for me. When I hung up, my mind felt peaceful.

And now the nightmare will end.

Only it didn't quite go like that. Dr. Bellows was at a week-long seminar in Toronto. Trina was a model patient. She took her meds, actually swallowed them—the Haldol, the mood stabilizer, the antipsychotic—and calmed down almost immediately. She made three bracelets for me in arts and crafts and attended groups each day. My newly medicated daughter had great insights that she shared in a well-modulated voice. Her treating psychiatrist was a resident from Bombay, who wore bright green sneakers with his lab coat. He was impressed with Trina's articulation, her beauty, her obvious intellect. He wouldn't give me Dr. Bellows's number in Toronto. No one would.

One morning, the resident said to me, "Mrs. Whitmore, I don't know that I can justify keeping her here any longer than two weeks."

I had tracked him down while he was making his rounds, waited for him outside the doors of the locked facility. When the nurse buzzed him out, I was there.

"She needs help. Please. I'm trying to become her conservator. Dr. Bellows said that he'd support me."

"The locked facilities are awful. I'm sure you don't want your daughter going to one of those places. You probably couldn't live with yourself if you sent her there."

"You don't know what I'm living with now. You have to keep her here. You have to help me."

"We'll see, but the way it's going, she will probably be out in two days. I have to go now, Mrs. Whitmore." He started walking away from me.

One hour, one joint, and she'd be right back where she was before.

"This isn't working," I told Bethany that night. "I can feel it slipping out of my hands. They're going to let her out of the hospital."

"You haven't been listening to me at all," she said.

"I'm listening now."

15

Steal away, steal away, steal away home. I ain't got long to stay here. Gabriel Prosser. Denmark Vesey. Nat Turner. Harriet Tubman. Did they all begin with secret meetings and whispered plans? Did they change their minds more than once? To steal away home was more than a notion.

Halfway to the restaurant, I turned my car around and headed home. What was I doing, speeding down Wilshire to meet a woman I knew to be operating more on rage than common sense? But then I thought about those bright green sneakers, walking away from me in such a big hurry, and turned around again. Whatever Bethany had to offer, at least it wouldn't involve being at the mercy of people who just didn't give a damn.

This time the meeting was in the back booth of a coffee shop on Wilshire, down the street from the behemoth that housed Children's Services. Four o'clock was an odd time to go to a restaurant, but I hadn't eaten since my breakfast muffin, so I was hungry. Bethany was there with a tall pale man named Brad. She introduced me as Keri. When he said hello, his voice was low, a strong voice. His handshake was dry and warm, his grip filled with steady pressure. He had sandy hair and darker eyebrows, elegantly arched. He looked clean and honest, a bit boyish. His chin jutted forward a little.

We ordered food—appetizers, entrees, coffee, and desserts—as if we were coworkers having a friendly dinner, perhaps celebrating someone's promotion. We chatted about the headlines and the weather, about movie stars and the Lakers. Brad didn't clink a glass with a spoon or clear his throat, but I felt the moment that defined our purpose. He put his two hands on the table. They were large hands, with clean, square fingernails and no rings.

His voice was just above a whisper. "We are a group of psychologists and psychiatrists who believe that the mental health system in this country is a sad joke," Brad said. "All the members of our group have worked in hospitals and in a variety of mental health institutions; we've experienced firsthand the wasted opportunities for people to recover." He leaned in. "Recovery is possible for people when the right conditions are present. We assist the relatives, mostly the parents, of people who need an intervention but are too sick to accept help. We forgo the nine-one-one, the SMART people, the conservatorship. We transport the ill person to a safe place: *our* safe place. Once the patient is there, the relative leaves and we take over."

"What do you—"

Brad held up his hand, his face suddenly stern.

"What we do is illegal. We could all go to jail. Kidnapping is involved at times. It is not for the faint of heart, and there are no guarantees."

The longer he talked, the more alive he became. I tried to read his face. Committed man on a mission? Kook ready to spontaneously combust? Reincarnation of John Brown? How would Clyde have reacted to him? Would he consider him a tool of the Left or the Right?

Why should I trust him?

"But we have helped people begin the healing process. We have turned some lives around. I think you have met one of the people we helped. Continue?"

He and Bethany looked at me.

"Yes," I said.

"We have a facility in a remote area. A small staff runs the place. We're completely self-sufficient. We work with no more than sixteen patients at a time. Our patient-to-staff ratio is four to one. That's a lot of care. We are expensive: twelve thousand dollars a month. The average stay is six months to a year."

I think I must have gasped, because Brad stopped speaking, and he and Bethany looked at me. Maybe he was just a salesman, a hope huckster without a Bible. At $12,000, hope was high. Was this a con? I looked at Bethany.

"Anyone who comes to the facility must be prepared to make a commitment," Brad said.

"I'm not rich."

"Most people aren't."

Brad signaled the waitress, then handed her a credit card. When the woman disappeared, he turned to me. "We have two openings now. Can't guarantee how long those slots will be available."

"Where is this place?"

Brad shook his head. "If you decide that we're the right group for you and your loved one, you'll find out that kind of information on a need-to-know basis."

"You do use medications?"

Brad nodded. "Of course. Medication compliance is what we instill in our patients. For most, it's the key to leading a productive life. But we try to prescribe the lowest dosage possible, in order to minimize weight gain and other side effects. We incorporate an array of nontraditional methods as well, including acupuncture, homeopathy, exercise, meditation, and proper nutrition."

"My daughter drinks. She smokes marijuana, and maybe—"

"Most people with brain diseases self-medicate. It's to be expected. We have very strong substance abuse counselors."

The waitress returned and handed Brad his card and receipt. He stood up.

"You have a lot of questions," he said once the waitress had left. "I don't want to answer them just yet. It might be better if you meet some more parents and speak with them. Would you like that?"

"When?" I was multiplying twelve thousand dollars times six months in my head, calculating the equity in my home, the balance in my savings account, the value of my stock portfolio, and the little apartment building I owned in Atlanta. How fast could I liquidate?

Brad extended his hand. "Time is short. Stay here for a while. Some other people will come to speak with you. Good meeting you."

"How did you find out about this place?" I asked Bethany as Brad walked away.

"A friend," she said.

"Have you seen any of the people they've helped?"

"They've helped me already. Some of their people are the ones who watch Angelica for me."

"I don't have that kind of money."

"Talk to some of the other parents."

"But if I don't have the money—"

"Just talk to—" Bethany stopped as a colorfully dressed woman slid into the booth beside her.

"My name is Carleen. Brad said you might want to speak with me."

Bethany didn't appear surprised, but I was taken aback at seeing someone so soon. I didn't know whether I wanted to speak with Carleen. A part of me felt angry and violated that Brad had all the control and things were happening so fast. All I knew about him was his first name. Maybe he was who he said he was, and maybe he was some crackpot who was trying to suck me in.

But I smiled at Carleen as she sat down. She was tiny, with a little thin nose and almost no lips. Her hands seemed to flutter as she spoke, mostly about her twin boys. They had been difficult children, even when they were very young. At eight years old, they started taking Ritalin. For a while they were better, almost controllable, but then they hit puberty and discovered weed, liquor, and Ecstasy. They were diagnosed with bipolar disorder at age seventeen. By that time their family life had become complete chaos. By twenty-one, they'd both been in and out of both hospitals and jails. At that time, she couldn't imagine their lives improving. She said the program had saved her sons.

"Did you try to get conservatorship?" I asked.

"Sure. I have conservatorship now. They were in a locked facility for a year. They seemed better. I let them come out. Took them to another facility. No locks. They weren't able to maintain their sobriety. They'd leave the premises and get high. After a while, they stopped taking the meds. Everything started all over again. A friend told me about Brad's program. I made the arrangements, and it's been five—no, six—years, and they are still medication-compliant and drug-free."

For a minute I couldn't speak. It was bewildering to think that conservatorship didn't bring complete deliverance.

"What about failure rate? The group can't possibly help everybody."

"I don't know about that," Carleen said. "I only know about my case. I had no contact with any other parents or kids. The program is strictly anonymous."

"What about when you visited?" I asked.

"I never visited the site. I'd meet my sons and the counselors somewhere that was neutral."

"So I guess you think it was worth the twelve thousand a month?" I asked.

"I paid about thirty-five hundred," she said.

Bethany's expression didn't change.

"They told me it cost twelve thousand dollars a month."

"They told me that too in the beginning. It's a test, to see your level of commitment. There's a sliding scale. If you can pay, fine; they accept the money. But they have donors who finance them. Nobody is ever turned away because of money. I know that this is a lot to absorb. Would you like to talk with someone else?"

"Yes."

Twenty minutes after Carleen waved good-bye, a Latino man—Francisco—appeared at our table and sat across from Bethany and me. Thirty minutes after he left, an older white couple showed up, Fleur and Larry. Their stories were similar to mine. Sick loved ones, a system that had failed them, nowhere to turn. And then suddenly a light. I was suspicious of the light.

Maybe I'm being brainwashed, I thought, when people kept coming. In my mind, all kinds of scenarios played out. Maybe the group was a cult. Suppose I took Trina there and they took out her organs and sold them. My mind was putting up a valiant effort, fighting with all it could muster the inevitable conclusion that came from feeling my back against the wall.

"What other choices do they give us?" Carleen had asked me before she left.

Harriet probably said that.

"THE BEST TIME TO DO IT WOULD BE TOMORROW NIGHT," Bethany said when we were alone. "When you pick her up from the hospital, Angelica and I would meet you with Brad. We'd just keep going."

"What do you mean, we'd travel together?"

"There are two openings, yours and mine. How long do you think they'll be there? We have to make a move now. "

"I can't do that."

"Yes, you can. Just toss some clothes in a bag. A pair of jeans and some tops. The same for your daughter. They'll give her pajamas and toiletries."

"I have a business to run."

"Leave someone in charge. You won't be gone that long. Better sooner than later, Keri. At least now she has some meds in her system. A week from now that may not be the case."

"I have to go," I said, and stood up.

"If you leave her to the system, she will be lost."

"Let me think."

It was impossible to process everything I'd heard. Nothing was linking up in my mind. Clyde would have ripped Brad's presentation to shreds. But I couldn't even contact Clyde if I wanted to. He wasn't answering his cell phone. I called Orlando on my way to the hospital. He was in rehearsal and couldn't really talk, except to go on and on about what a good role he had. Hanging up, I felt frustrated. Ma Missy should have been with me. She could have read Brad, told me if he was for real or not. But Ma Missy wasn't here, and I had no one to help me make the most important decision of my life.

TRINA WAS TAKING A SMOKE BREAK WHEN I GOT TO THE hospital. "I'm ready to go home," she announced when I sat down with her in the television room. "There's nothing wrong with me, and I don't need to be here."

"Trina, you have a mental illness—"

She waved her hand, as if shooing away a pesky fly. "No, I don't. I just shouldn't have smoked weed, that's all. I think the guy who gave it to me laced it with something. Come early tomorrow; then we can go to IHOP. I'm fiending for pancakes."

"Things are going to be different when you come home, Trina. You will have to take your meds, start seeing your therapist regularly, and there can't be any cursing, violence, drugs, or drinking."

Even I recognized that my words held no authority. I wasn't telling her, I was pleading with her. Mother as supplicant.

"I know," she said blandly.

"I'm going to type up a contract, and you're going to sign it," I said. "And if you break the contract, you're going to have to find another place to live."

"Okay." She stood up. "So come get me early, so we can have some pancakes." Trina licked her lips and rubbed her tummy. "Yum-yum."

If she'd been eight years old, I would have laughed.

"So they are sending her home tomorrow," Elijah said as I was leaving. He shook his head. "She's not ready yet. So many times, when they send them away, they're not ready. Then they just come back. On and on and on. In my country, we are not so developed. We don't have special places, special medication for the ones with the mental illnesses."

"What do you do with them?"

Elijah shrugged. "We just let them be. Sometimes, the less hope, the better."

The testimonies of strangers formed a merry-go-round in my head. Richard. Carleen. Francisco. Fleur. Larry. They'd all ridden out the horrors of *before* and grabbed the brass ring of *after*. But what guarantees did I have that one day I'd count myself among them? Maybe I'd end up with the others whose first names had been withheld, the ones for whom the program had been just another failure.

Option number two was simpler: Start again. Go back to support group. Call the SMART people. Wait. Call them again. Hope that she meets the criteria, that she is swallowing the bottle of pills or punching me as they come through the door. Hope that she gets put on a seventy-two-hour hold. Hope that the hospital has a psych bed available and that the meds don't work so fast that she's totally lucid after three days, too lucid to stay longer. Pray that the hospital decides to extend her hold and that the patient's rights advocate is lazy. Pray that Dr. Bellows will do all the paperwork, come to court, and testify on my behalf. Pray the judge will see things my way. Wait. Hope. Pray. Trust the system.

At home, I began cleaning. My drugs of choice: Windex, Pine-Sol, Murphy's Oil Soap. The vacuum zigzagged all over the family room. I folded towels and put them away. I threw out old food in the refrigerator. My inner obsessive-compulsive was in charge, anxious to cross off everything in the cleanup to-do list. The goal was to keep moving until the ache had transferred from soul to muscles. The point was to change the focus.

Orlando rang the bell close to eleven. He was on a high, still in character, still spouting lines. We made love right on the family room couch. It felt different, the way he stroked me, the way he sucked my nipple and rubbed my ass. Then I realized that he was fucking me the way the man in the play would have done it.

I liked it.

Orlando fell asleep on the couch. Toward midnight, and still with energy to spare, I approached the pile of unopened mail and magazines, letter opener in hand. Five days' worth of mail. But what was this?

> *Dear Keri,*
>
> *Happy birthday! Sorry this is late. I know you think I wasn't the greatest mother, but I have always loved you. I am trying to make amends for the past. I just wish that you could find it in your heart to . . .*

I crushed the paper in my hand. My fist closed over it and smashed down some more.

Later, when I'd try to remember exactly what propelled me over the edge, I could never say with any degree of certainty what final wind blew me there. All I knew was, my child would never be able to say I didn't try hard enough. A click went off in my mind, and I was racing across the plantation in the dark.

16

THERE WAS NO TIME TO MULL THINGS OVER THE NEXT morning. Five minutes after I told Bethany my decision, we were on a three-way phone call with Brad. Thirty minutes later, I was seated on the same oceanfront bench where I'd heard the first testimonial. Bethany sat on one side of me and Brad on the other. I handed him a check for twenty-five hundred dollars, what he'd determined I needed to pay each month.

"Tell me what will happen," I said to him.

"Tonight I'll meet you in the parking lot of the hospital. You need to arrive there by cab. Tell your daughter that your car is in the shop and a friend will be taking you home. Bethany and Angelica will already be with me. I'll drive everyone to one of our houses. Your daughter will meet with a psychiatrist while she's there. You'll stay at the first house for a few days and then move on to another and then another until you reach the destination. When you're almost there, someone will take your daughter the rest of the way alone, and you'll return home."

"Like the underground railroad," I said.

Brad smiled. "Actually, that's the model."

"What do you know about the underground railroad? " I asked.

Brad hesitated. "I'm not much of a history buff. It was a means of freeing slaves, getting them north to Canada. Harriet Tubman was the most famous conductor on the railroad. I know that much," he said. "It seemed an appropriate model for what we do. Mental illness is a kind of slavery. Our movement is about freeing people too. We won't always have to hide and run and do our work in the dark. The day is coming when people with brain diseases won't be written off or warehoused, when everyone will know that recovery is possible."

He seemed to be speaking only to me.

"Where is the place? How far away?"

"Can't tell you that. It's for everyone's protection."

"How will I be able to contact her?"

"Someone will call you twice a week. You can talk with your daughter then."

Before I responded, Bethany chimed in. "Think of how many times you haven't known where Trina was. There have been weeks when Angelica was missing. At least, this time around, you'll know she's getting help."

That made sense.

"You came to us for a reason," Brad said, wrapping his fingers around my wrist. His touch surprised me; it was so unyielding. "If we go away, that reason will still be here. You have a mentally ill daughter with a history of noncompliance with her medication regimen and all the concomitant chaos this usually entails. There is no end in sight. You can start again with the SMART people and seventy-two-hour holds, or you can try us. We will not wait for her to hit bottom. We'll reeducate her so she accepts her diagnosis, takes her meds, and gets therapy. There's no guarantee that what we do will work for your daughter, but we're used to success."

He let go of my wrist, but, looking into his eyes, I felt he was still holding me.

"If she could just get back to being who she really is. Everything is waiting for her. She can start where she left off. She can still have the life I dreamed of for her."

"Or maybe she'll have a new dream." He spoke in a gentle voice.

"So many things could go wrong."

"Look," Brad said. "Everyone who will be with you is trained in worst-case scenarios. I personally transported three people with their parents at one time."

"Have you ever lost anyone?" I asked.

"No one has ever died under our care, if that's what you mean."

"What's the worst thing that ever happened?"

"On the road?"

I nodded.

"A patient with schizophrenia got a knife and assaulted his father and the person from the program. They both had to have stitches."

"What happened to the patient?"

"Our person managed to subdue him and take the weapon. He called for backup, who came, gave the patient a sedative, and took parent and driver to the emergency room."

"How did you get into this?" I asked Brad.

"The hard way."

I knew what that meant. "How long would I be gone?"

"Three to four weeks."

"When would I have to leave?"

Brad looked at his watch. "What time are you going to pick up your daughter at the hospital?"

"Around seven o'clock, assuming she'll still be there. The last time she just left without me."

"Then we'd go to Plan B," Brad said.

"Will it just be you, Bethany, and me?"

"Don't know yet. This afternoon I'll call someone at the hospital for an assessment of your daughter." Seeing my surprise, he added, "We have people everywhere.

"I'll meet you in the parking lot at ten after seven. Be packed and ready to go. Make sure your daughter's been to the bathroom. Bring as much medication as you have. You can get more on the road. Need to ask you a few things." He looked at me sternly. "Will you be able to be away for four weeks?"

I nodded.

"Do you or your daughter have any physical problems that I should know about?"

"No."

"Have you ever been arrested for or convicted of a felony?"

"No."

"Do you have a plausible excuse for being away that you can tell anyone you feel needs to know?"

"Yes."

"Have you told anyone about this?"

"No."

"Don't."

IT WAS NEARLY ELEVEN O'CLOCK BY THE TIME I REACHED the store. In the trunk of my car were three suitcases, one filled with enough of my mix-and-match clothes to last for several weeks. Two others contained a summer and fall wardrobe for Trina. Adriana was at the register, and Frances was in the back, altering a woman's dress that had come in yesterday. In my office I busied myself with payroll and writing checks, but still I heard the familiar voices.

Juicy and Coco and Spirit were standing near the purse display, chatting with Adriana. Juicy seemed to be telling a story, one she acted out in pantomime. When she finished, the other women roared with laughter. I'd never heard Adriana laugh so exuberantly. Customers in the store turned to stare at them. I did too. Spirit's arm was on one of Adriana's shoulder's and Coco's was around the other. Juicy pressed against her. They formed a tight circle. Family.

They could reclaim her, I thought. They wouldn't have to promise her anything but their arms around her shoulders. I'd been thinking that Adriana had been saved, that I had saved her. That was my delusion.

"Adriana," I said, after Frances had helped the other customers, "I need you."

Keeping an eye on the girls, I called Frances over and led her and Adriana to the office.

"I've made arrangements for Trina to stay in a mental health facility for a while. I'm going to take some time off."

"You going back east?" Frances asked.

"I don't know. Maybe."

"You want us to go visit her at the hospital?" Adriana asked.

"No. She's not in any shape to see anyone. I'll tell you when." Peering out the door, I saw Coco waiting near the register. "Frances, go help

Coco." As soon as Frances left I turned to Adriana. "Cut them off," I said.

"What?"

I nodded toward her friends. "They want to bring you back down to their level. They don't want to see you living clean. That's why they keep coming here."

"I'm through with all that."

"Stop seeing them," I said.

She stared at me for a very long time. "I can't do that," she said. "They're still my friends. I'm not like them, but I can't just dump them."

I wanted to tell her that she couldn't trust them. I wanted to grab her by her shoulders and shake and shake until she got it. But I had a hard row to hoe ahead of me, and I needed all my strength. "They're not your friends. They don't love you. They can't even love themselves," I said.

But she didn't believe me.

TRINA WAS WAITING FOR ME AT THE HOSPITAL, PACING BACK and forth in front of the nurses' station. Her face was scrubbed clean; her smile was subdued. She called me Mommy and kissed my cheek. I wanted Clyde with me. Here's our kid, I'd say, the wonderful one, not the other one. She was utterly compliant and controllable, not a person in need of an intervention. But I knew things could change in two seconds.

Puff. Puff.

"Go to the bathroom," I said.

"Why?"

"We're not going straight home. My car's in the shop, and a friend is picking us up."

She walked back to her room and as soon as she disappeared my phone rang. It was Orlando—himself, not in character.

"Where you been, baby? I've been trying to catch up with you all day."

"Orlando, I really can't talk right now. I'm running. I put Trina in a mental health facility, and I'm taking off. I need to get away. I'll call you when I get there."

"Where you going? Are you coming to the opening?"

"I don't know. I don't think so."

I could see his face, the dejection in his eyes. I was his favorite audience. Trina was walking toward me. Orlando's next question was forming in his mind.

"Orlando, I have to go. Talk to PJ, okay? He really needs you. I'll call."

Elijah was sitting behind the sign-in desk. "Young lady," he said, smiling at both of us, "you take care of yourself. Do what you need to do. I don't want to see you back here again."

Trina giggled.

"Don't worry," I said. "You won't."

17

THE EVENING AIR WAS CHILLY. HOSPITAL STAFF AND VISI-
tors milled about. Across the street the emergency room was packed.
Brad was standing in front of the door that led from the hospital to the
parking lot. When he saw us he said, "There you are," grabbed Trina's
hand, and shook it. "Brad," he said, "your mom's friend."

"Brad who?" she asked, and I thought, *We're not ready for her.*

"Sebastian." The name slipped off his tongue so easily, I almost
thought it was real.

Trina gave me a look, and I knew she was trying to figure out who
Brad was and how he fit into my life.

"This way," Brad said, leading us across the parking lot, down a dark
row of cars until we were in front of his blue Explorer.

He held open the door. In the backseat, I could see Bethany and
Angelica, who sat apart from her mother. Trina looked at Brad and then
at me. She didn't move. She looked from me to Brad and then back to
me again.

"Why didn't you drive? I don't want to be with a stranger."

There was outrage in her voice, the two-year-old who would scream
until she turned blue. Had she taken her evening pills?

"I don't want to go with him," she said.

Above us, the sky was cloudy and dull; the sun had disappeared. Behind us a siren cut through the air.

"Trina," I said, "you're being rude. Brad is doing me a favor. My car is—"

"There's nothing wrong with your car. Why didn't you ask Adriana or Frances? You could have called Orlando."

She began backing away. I wanted to reach for her, but I couldn't feel my arms. Nothing on my body seemed to work. I had a fleeting vision of Brad dragging her to the car as Trina screamed her head off.

Brad pulled out a pack of Marlboros and offered one to her. "When you get in, I'll explain everything," he said.

"I can smoke in the car?" Trina asked, taking a cigarette. She was looking at me.

Brad nodded. I nodded.

Trina climbed into the seat behind Brad, the middle row. When she saw Bethany and Angelica her body jerked, and I could tell she remembered the older woman.

"They're friends of mine," Brad said.

I sat beside Trina, and Brad got behind the wheel. Click! Click! The power locks sounded. I glanced behind me. The locks were childproof. Only the driver could open them. Moments later, cigarette smoke wafted throughout the car.

"Who are these people? Where are we going?" Trina asked, exhaling the words with the smoke. She stiffened as we turned onto the freeway.

"Trina, your mom has been really worried about you," Brad said. His voice sounded reassuring. "She doesn't think you're getting the kind of help that you need at the hospital. I suggested that she take you someplace where you can get proper treatment."

"Are you going to kill me?" Her tone was high-pitched and frantic.

"Trina!" I said. She'd made outlandish, paranoid statements before, so I wasn't completely surprised.

"We're not going to kill you. Your mother and I want to help you."

"Where are you taking me?"

"To a place where you can get help," Brad said.

"I don't want to go. You can't make me go. I'm over eighteen." Her head twisted from left to right, from Brad to me. "Take me home. You have to take me home."

"Trina," Brad said.

"No. I don't want you talking to me. I don't know you. Mommy, make him take us home."

"I love you very much. You have to trust that I'm doing what's best for you. I want you to have a good life. You haven't been having a good life recently. You're sick, honey."

I looked at Brad. Does he know what he's doing? Can he handle her? Trina reached for the door.

"Take your hand off the handle. I control the locks. You may not know me, but you need to trust that your mother has your best interests at heart," Brad said.

His voice was Papa Bear strong. In the dim car, Goldilocks scowled and raised up from her seat.

"It would be a mistake for you to try to run."

Trina slid back into her seat behind the driver.

"Other side," Brad said. Trina slid over.

What was in his voice that made her do that?

In the rearview mirror, Brad smiled. I felt Bethany's hand squeezing my shoulder. I turned my head to acknowledge her. Angelica stared at me. The light from the parking lot revealed a thin, hollow-eyed young woman who might have been pretty at one time. Her lips were moving rapidly, but I couldn't hear what she was saying.

"There are some rules," he said. "I want us all to be safe. Number one, you cannot leave this car for any reason. Number two, you must take your medicine. Number three, you must do everything I tell you to do."

What kind of training did he receive? What courses did he take? Did he make A's? Why didn't I ask more questions? What made me trust him?

"You're the devil, and you're trying to kill me," Trina said. She turned to me. "And you want him to do it."

She glared at me. The meds hadn't fully kicked in yet. Trina was still manic, and I was still her enemy.

At the first red light, I saw Brad reach into his glove compartment and pull something out. With quick, deft movements, he turned around to face Trina, then leaned over.

"Ow!"

Bethany began patting me. Beside her, Angelica sat as though frozen.

Passing streetlights revealed a flash of something shiny. I could see the needle in Brad's hand. His jab into Trina's bare upper arm had been deliberate and quick. Trina started crying after she got over the shock, which was before I got over it.

"Trina, that was Haldol I gave you. You've probably gotten it before at the hospital. It will calm you down and make you sleep," Brad said.

She looked at me. "It was poison. Why are you letting this man kill me?"

"Trina, I want you to get well," I said.

Twenty minutes passed before I heard the soft snuffling sound that Trina makes when she's asleep. By that time I was calmer, more in control.

"Why did you give her that shot without even asking me?" I asked, my voice low. "How did you know that the hospital hadn't already given her something?"

"I'm a psychologist, Keri. I can tell when a patient is manic. If she'd been sedated, your daughter wouldn't have been acting like that."

"They give the kids shots at the hospital, and they don't tell us a thing," Bethany whispered.

I wasn't used to this new Bethany, who rubbed my shoulders and whispered. I liked the less subdued version, the woman with a butcher's knife of a mouth.

"Listen, let's get one thing straight: I don't want you giving anything to my child unless you clear it with me first." I looked from Brad to Bethany.

"From time to time, I'll have to make decisions quickly. You are going to have to trust me," Brad said.

"How many times have you done this?" I asked.

"Enough times," he said.

"What does that mean?"

"It means I know what I'm doing. I'm not a novice. I'm not interning. Been through this process dozens of times. And whether you want to or not, you're going to have to trust me. Period. If you can't do that, Keri, I can drive you home or wherever you want to go, right now."

I couldn't go home, and he knew it.

"Going to need your wallet, your money, and your cell phone, Keri."

"What are you talking about? I'm not giving you — "

"It's for our protection, Keri," Bethany said.

"So I'm walking around with no money and no ID. How does that protect me?"

"We've had cases where patients have stolen their parents' wallets and identification in an attempt to leave the program. They call people on the cell phones. I keep the wallets and phones in a safe place, and at the end of the trip I return them."

"I have a business. I have to be in contact with people. I always answer my cell phone. If they don't hear from me, they might report me missing."

"Keep your phone for now. We'll work something out. But I'd like your wallet."

I fished around in my purse and handed Brad my wallet. He glanced at me and kept driving. He'd called my bluff, and I'd caved. His profile as we drove was resolute, his chin strong and determined: the hero under pressure.

I was the runaway, hidden in the back of the wagon under the hay. That was me, holding my breath, saying my prayers, trying to make it to a safe haven.

18

TRINA DIDN'T STIR FOR NEARLY THREE HOURS. BETHANY and Angelica were slumped against the backseat. Around midnight Brad took an exit off the 5 and drove down a two-lane road for about forty minutes. I must have dozed myself, because I wasn't sure where we were when he pulled into a dark driveway that led to a one-story ranch house, surrounded by a garden full of very tall sunflowers. Brad knocked at the door while everyone else remained in the car. The window was down, and I heard someone ask who it was.

"A friend with friends," Brad said.

When he said that, Bethany woke up and looked around.

"I guess we're here," she said. She looked at me. "Wow."

"Yeah."

"This has got to work."

It was the first time she'd voiced anything other than absolute faith in the program.

A woman opened the door. From the light in the house I could see that she was wearing a Black Dog T-shirt and khaki pants. Her hair was thin and chopped off and had been combed flat against her head. The lipstick was worn off her lips, but she had big, pretty teeth and a smile that reminded me of good news. I heard Brad call her Jean. He hugged her tight against his chest and then let her go real fast. A man came out and stood beside her. Brad beckoned for Bethany and me, and the men helped Trina and Angelica out of the car and brought in our suitcases.

Food was waiting for us, set up nicely in a bright yellow kitchen with yellow and white curtains at the window. There was salmon, broccoli, a baked potato. All seven of us sat down. Trina was just barely awake. Her eyes fluttered as she looked at the food.

Angelica's eyes brightened when she saw the spread. Bethany had told me that Angelica had used methamphetamines. She had the lean, sunken look of a drug addict. Her appetite proved that she was able to exchange one addiction for another. She piled her plate, ate every bit, and then loaded on more food. Angelica ate like a lower-rung mammal, without regard for good table manners. Bethany watched her, then looked around to see our reaction. Her embarrassment seemed incongruent with her go-ballistic personality. But there it was for all to see: maternal shame. Not even badass mommas were immune.

Jean served us, and her husband, Eddie, poured small glasses of orange juice. They had a tiny poodle that barked a little bit and stayed close to Jean. Nobody said much at dinner. Trina didn't touch her food. She slumped in her chair and closed her eyes.

"Honey, aren't you hungry?" I whispered.

"It's poison." She glared at me, then turned her head.

"Would you rather have something else?" Jean asked Trina. "We have a frozen pizza. I could make you a big salad. Or a bowl of cereal: Cheerios."

"There's ice cream," Eddie said.

They were like enthusiastic foster parents, anxious to have the new kid fit in. Trina ignored them. Jean and Eddie smiled at each other and then at me.

"Well, you get hungry, you just let me know," Jean said. She sounded southern.

"I'm hungry," Angelica said. "I want ice cream."

As Jean was handing Angelica a bowl of vanilla ice cream, there was a knock at the front door, and in a moment a tall man with a headful of curly gray hair and deep-set eyes strode into the kitchen. He was carrying an old-fashioned doctor's bag, which he set right on the table.

"Good evening, everyone. I'm Wilbur," he said to Bethany and me. "I'd like to speak with you both for a moment."

We followed him into the dining room and sat down at an antique oak table.

Wilbur appeared to be in his late fifties or early sixties. He shook hands with a powerful grip. "I need to draw some blood from your daughters to check their medication levels. What have they been taking?"

Bethany spoke first, listing Angelica's medications. I was amazed. There were two different mood stabilizers, an antidepressant, an antipsychotic, and something for sleep—at least five different pills twice a day. A real cocktail. If the number of pills was an indication of the severity of the illness, Angelica was a pretty sick young woman. At least Trina only takes four pills a day, I thought, feeling momentarily superior, then stopped myself. I didn't need to play my-kid's-not-as-crazy-as-yours.

I told Wilbur that Trina had been compliant for months until she started smoking marijuana again. He listened attentively as I described the recent changes in her mood and behavior, the uncontrollable mania that had brought us to the program. "She was just on a hold. I picked her up from the hospital at seven, so she's probably got some medication in her. Brad gave her a shot of Haldol."

"How does she seem to you?"

"Paranoid. She called Brad and me devils. When she gets like this she'll say I'm not her mother."

Wilbur nodded. "Will she physically attack me?"

"She's hit me a couple of times. I don't know if she'd try that with you. But she won't be a model patient, that I can guarantee."

He looked at Bethany.

"Angelica is dual-diagnosis. She's going to be craving meth. The meds may mitigate that somewhat, but it will still be there. She's a flight risk. Don't turn your back on her."

"What about Trina, any drugs?"

"Marijuana. And if she has the opportunity, she'll drink. I don't think she's addicted to either one, though. Maybe I'm in denial. Oh, and she'll run too if she gets the chance."

"More something she does when she's manic," Wilbur said.

"Exactly."

"Okay. I need to draw some blood. Brad will help me. I think it's better if you're not in the room. All right?"

"All right," I said. Bethany nodded.

I shouldn't have acquiesced so quickly, I thought when Wilbur walked away. Shouldn't we have demanded to see his license, his board certification? Something.

"Are you okay with all of this?" I whispered to Bethany.

"Brad told us that there would be a psychiatrist," she said as my body tightened and I held my breath. "By now Trina could have jumped out of your car, disappeared to God knows where. Right at this moment, you could be on the phone calling all over, trying to find her. And as far as I'm concerned, Angelica would have been dead if it weren't for the program. They're safe. We know where they are, and they're safe."

Safe. Yes. This was all about keeping the girls safe.

"It's going to work out."

Yes.

"Breathe, Keri."

That's what I did.

Brad and Wilbur took the girls into one of the rooms in the back. Trina was angry and wide-awake. She cursed the men loudly, while I sat at the kitchen table with my head in my hands but still breathing. Jean came in and sat down beside me. She had a cup of coffee for both of us. "She's a beauty, your girl," Jean said finally.

My thank-you was barely out of my mouth when I began to cry. It had been so long since anyone had said anything nice about my child.

"You're doing the right thing," she said, then added, "It was my son. Eddie and I put him in the program about ten years ago. Ryan was out of control, really, really crazy."

"He's—"

"Schizoaffective disorder. It's a good place. Maybe not for everyone, but for my boy it was a good place."

"How long did he stay?"

"A year."

"And you and Eddie didn't know where he was?"

She shook her head. "Nobody can know that, sweetheart. Sometimes Ryan still gets confused in his thinking, but that's to be expected.

He was in the service when the illness started manifesting: air force. He got an honorable discharge. After he came out, he wound up working for Sears. He lost that job. Ryan was living with us for a while, but his behavior was very unpredictable. And then he started getting violent and really bizarre. We tried to get him help, but he was homeless for about eighteen months. Eddie almost died, literally; he got very sick from the stress. When we found out about the program, things started to turn around. Ryan got better. Eddie got better. Are you married, honey?"

"I'm divorced."

"Where is he? Why are you going through this alone?"

I started to say, I have Bethany. "That's a good question," I said.

"Does he know what's going on?"

"He doesn't completely accept that she has mental illness. He doesn't know about any of this."

"You shouldn't have to do this alone, sweetheart." She sighed. "The parents go through one part of hell and the kids go through another. Tell you the truth, I think we have it worse than they do. At least when they're spinning out of control, they're in their own little world, imagining that they're okay. But we have to stand there and watch them and love them and know we're helpless."

Trina had stopped screaming. I could hear footsteps coming toward the kitchen. Wilbur and Brad were on either side of Trina. Her mouth was grim and furious.

"I'm afraid that Trina isn't very happy with me right now, Keri. I'll get the results tomorrow," Wilbur said. "I'll come back in the morning. Meanwhile, I'd like to give Trina a little something to help her sleep."

"She had Haldol not too long ago."

"We just want to get her through the entire night," Wilbur said.

How much Haldol were they giving her? I wondered. But I found myself nodding. *Sure. Drug her. Keep her quiet. Give us all a rest.*

Were they giving Angelica as much Haldol? If Trina had been a little blond girl, would they have presumed compliance and passivity, been less on guard, treated her more kindly? If I'd been a white woman with a husband, would it have made a difference in what they expected? I studied Brad and Wilbur for a moment, trying to see them through Ma Missy's sharp eyes. Would he have garnered her highest praise?

"Now *that's* a decent white man," she told me once, referring to Mr. Bonds, who owned the children's shoe store in our neighborhood. Decent because he didn't assume she was an idiot. Decent because he didn't try to sell her something she didn't want. Decent because he didn't overprice his goods. And, most of all, decent because he hired my mother as a saleslady. She kept that job for the eighteen months that she remained sober during my eighth and ninth years.

"She's a natural-born saleswoman," Mr. Bonds told Ma Missy. I was with her when he said it.

My mother told me to bring my friends to the store, and I obliged her with a daily parade of eight- and nine-year-olds. I pointed out the pretty lady smiling at the customers and said, "That's my mommy. She wants you to come back with your mothers." And they did.

Mr. Bonds paid her a commission, which increased my mother's enthusiasm. Away from the store, my mother scoured the neighborhood, zeroing in on children wearing worn-out shoes. She took me to the zoo once, another sobriety miracle. While we were gazing at the elephants, she spotted a little boy whose shoes were beyond redemption. As I watched, she went right to his mother and handed her the business card she always carried, all the while touting Mr. Bond's inventory. A few days later she reported that the mother had bought two pairs of shoes from her.

I began taking a detour home from school after Emma fell hard off the wagon. Mr. Bonds had to let her go. She railed against him. "That white . . . ," she'd begin, as if his color was responsible for his perfidy.

"White ain't got nothing to do with nothing," Ma Missy muttered.

How would she have judged Brad and Wilbur?

"Just let two strange white men give me anything," Trina said now, as if she'd read my mind, as if she were my mother's grandchild. She aimed her snarling words at me, like poison-tipped arrows. "You don't care. You don't give a fuck, you devil bitch. You killed my mother, and now you're trying to kill me. Where is my real mother?" Her voice rose in a high shriek.

"Young lady," Wilbur said, "let's not have that kind of language."

Beside her, Angelica seemed subdued, as though her tranquilizer had already taken effect. Jean led us to a room in the back of the house. We followed, with Trina screaming incoherently at the top of her lungs and Angelica lumbering like a zombie. The room could have been a two-car garage that had been enlarged and converted into a barracks. Trina's screams reverberated and were amplified, even though her voice had begun to grow hoarse. The room was spare, with a row of six single beds and six dressers. There was a wooden chair next to each bed and an end table with a lamp on the other side. At both sides of the room were two doors, which I assumed led to bathrooms. The only signs of decoration were the walls, painted a vivid blue, and the cheerful flowered curtains hanging at the windows. Looking out one of the windows into the dark, I could just make out what appeared to be a building. At the foot of each bed was a pale blue blanket and folded blue towels. Jean pointed out the bathrooms and told Angelica and Trina, who had finally become quiet, to use them first. Jean walked to the middle of the room. Brad and Eddie stood at the door.

"Are we sleeping in the same room as that man?" Trina asked when she came out. Her words were slurred from the medication. She looked straight at Brad, who was sitting on one of the beds.

"It's the best thing, honey," Jean said, looking at me.

I was a bit disconcerted myself and didn't know what to say. No one had ever discussed sleeping arrangements.

"Cool," Bethany said. "I need a cigarette."

She went outside for a few minutes, and when she returned Brad was assigning beds. His was after Angelica and Trina's. Mine was on his other side, and Bethany's was last. When Eddie asked Brad if he needed backup, Brad told him no.

"We'll have to lock you in," Eddie said. He closed the door. I heard a click.

"I have a key," Brad said.

My shoulders came down a little.

Brad was the last one to use the bathroom. Bethany and I lay in our beds listening to the shower, the towel rubbing across his skin. He brushed his teeth. In the stillness we heard the tiny clickclickclick the waxed string made as he flossed. He gargled for a long time. An antiseptic, soapy odor floated toward us. We heard him flush the toilet, then spray the bathroom.

Bethany started giggling first. "Fearless fucking leader, we salute you," she said.

"Would you trust your kid with this man?" I asked, and we giggled some more.

It was the beginning; there was still laughter inside us. Later, when we were fugitives, standing at the edge of waters that would not part, we would struggle to remember that sound.

19

IT WAS GETTING LIGHT WHEN I AWAKENED. THE SMALL travel clock I'd placed on the nightstand revealed that it was a little after five-thirty in the morning. The room was filled with snores and snuffles and smelled of commingled breaths, perspiration, and soap. I was the only one awake, which annoyed me. Some part of me expected to see a uniformed Brad pacing the room with a flashlight. Exaggerated fantasy notwithstanding, he should have been keeping watch. If there were an emergency, would he remain unconscious? There would be no going back to sleep for me.

As quietly as possible, I spread my towel on the floor next to my bed, lay down on it, and began an abbreviated, makeshift workout: sit-ups, waist twists, push-ups, some leg lifts. After fifteen more minutes of quiet, intense exercise, I began to stretch myself. By that time, through cracks in the shades, rays of sunlight had begun streaming into the room. I tilted my head away, toward Brad's bed. His eyes were open and watching my every move.

"Oh," I said.

We were staring at each other when I heard the rustling of sheets.

I turned. Brad turned. Angelica came toward us, her lips moving rapidly. She stopped at the foot of my bed and angled her head, as though she were listening to a response.

"Good morning, Angelica," Brad said. "Would you go back to your bed, please."

"Not you," she said. She pointed to me, moved closer, and crouched down to the floor where I was still lying down. Brad got up quickly. "Don't believe what they told you. They're all slave catchers," she whispered. "You'd better run."

"Angelica." Bethany's voice was groggy. She struggled to sit up in bed. "What are you saying?"

But by that time Brad had his arm around her shoulders. "The truth. I'm the only one telling the truth," she said as Brad began to lead her back to bed.

Her face had been less than an inch from mine, close enough for me to smell her tobacco breath. Looking up as she loomed above me, I could see a network of tiny scars on her legs and arms. Nicks. Flicks of the razor. So many small brown marks formed a pattern against her pale skin. At least my kid doesn't cut herself, I thought. There it was again. brain disorder competition. I glanced over at Trina. She was still sleeping soundly.

Outside the door was the hustle and bustle of breakfast preparations. A rich coffee aroma floated through the cracks, with the tap of a fork hitting a glass bowl; a *plop-plop-plop* suggesting scrambled eggs. In a frying pan, bacon sizzled. Silverware and plates clattered against the table. Everything seemed normal except for us. The light coming in around the sides of the shades was not enough sun to warm me or even brighten my day.

"You have to understand," Bethany said later—when we were in the bedroom alone, while Jean, Eddie, and Brad were giving the girls their medication in the kitchen—"Angelica has a borderline personality disorder, thrown in with her schizoaffective illness. She tries to pull people apart. Splitting, that's the term. She's going to try to keep everyone at each other's throats. That's her MO."

"Why didn't you tell me that before?" I asked.

Bethany looked surprised. "What difference would it have made? They're both sick girls."

"She could accuse anybody of anything. She could say I did something to her."

"So could your kid." Bethany met my gaze. "When they're psychotic, they'll say anything. The medication should make it better. And she's going to need intensive psychotherapy for a long, long time. That's the same thing your daughter needs."

I heard what Bethany was saying and what she wasn't saying: Don't try to pull any your-girl-is-crazier-than-my-girl crap. She was right. What good would it do? But I couldn't stop asking questions.

"Is she still cutting herself?" I asked.

"Doesn't everybody?" She stared right back at me. Not blinking.

"You should have told me everything," I said, feeling angry and a little betrayed. "I asked you how she was doing."

"Have you told me every horrible little peccadillo that's been an outgrowth of Trina's bipolar? I mean, come on."

"This is major, Bethany. Borderline is a completely separate illness. I mean, what else haven't you told me? Does she set fires?"

The door opened, and Jean stood there, her hair wet from a shower, no makeup. I could smell her cooking. "Come on and eat, you two." I knew she'd heard us. She tried to play it off with a smile that looked for real.

The scrambled eggs were whites only, and the bacon was turkey. Jean served steamed broccoli as well as grapefruit sections, fresh-squeezed orange juice, and water. Bethany and I sat as far apart as possible and avoided looking at each other. But I noticed we both picked at our food.

There was coffee for everyone and herb tea for Trina and Angelica, which they both refused to drink.

"I want coffee," Tina said.

"I do too," Angelica said.

"I'm afraid that's not going to be possible," Brad said. "While you are with us, you won't be getting caffeine in any form."

Angelica opened her mouth, then closed it.

"We all pitch in," Eddie said cheerfully after we'd finished the meal. "Trina, would you clear the table? Angelica, would you load the dishwasher?"

"You need to walk," I heard Jean telling the girls. The table had been cleared, the dishwasher filled. "The medication slows down your metabolism. If you're not careful, you'll gain a lot of weight. I know someone who put on thirty pounds in a month. He was miserable. We're not going to let that happen to you. You're way too beautiful. Today you're going to walk. Trina, you, Brad, and I will go first. When we come back, Angelica, we'll go out with you."

"I don't want to walk," Angelica said.

"We'll go to the end of the road and back. And then I'll give you a cigarette."

As Jean was offering nicotine as an inducement for overall health and well-being to her charges, I sat down on the porch, watching the walkers and trying not to feel sad.

I figured we were halfway to San Francisco, somewhere off the beaten track. The daylight revealed a house that sat on a hill, surrounded by oaks and eucalyptus trees. Behind it and on either side were acres and acres of huge sunflowers. The driveway Trina, Jean, and Brad were trudging down led to a small two-lane road that snaked its way back to the main highway. The closest house was not in walking distance.

The door opened behind me and Bethany came outside. We glanced at each other for a brief moment, and then she walked off in the yard. A few moments later I smelled the smoke from her cigarette.

It was official: We weren't speaking.

I might have used my time on the porch to reflect on our argument, but as far as I was concerned she had withheld important information. My ringing cell phone was jarring in the midst of such rural splendor and self-righteousness.

"I called you at home," Mattie said. "You're up and out rather early. The store isn't even open yet."

"Had some running around to do," I said.

"Where are you?"

"Listen, can I call you back?"

"Sure. I was just checking on you to see how you were doing and what's going on with Trina."

"I'm hanging."

"And I wanted to tell you that there is a special support group meeting next week at a theater in Westwood. We'll be viewing a documentary about a brother and sister, fraternal twins, who have schizophrenia. They started taking this new medication, and they're supposed to be leading normal lives. Are you going to be able to come?"

"I don't know. I've got a lot of—"

"Now, don't stop coming to group, girl. Just remember how we all were before. Group helps a lot. Don't you listen to that Bethany. Let God be God. You just get out of his way."

"Mattie, I have to go."

When I checked for messages, I saw Orlando had called after eleven the night before. "Hey, baby, where are you?" I could hear people talking in the background. The rehearsal, no doubt.

BY ELEVEN, WILBUR STILL HADN'T SHOWN UP. TRINA seemed to like the fact that I was with her. She was quiet, almost silent, which was a big improvement on her ranting and screaming. We had been seated at a card table, set up in another bedroom. Jean had placed a box filled with beads in the center and instructed Trina to make bracelets. The creative outlet seemed to soothe her. From time to time, Trina had looked up from stringing her beads and given me not a smile but a glance that was not hostile. She managed to brush against me whenever she went to the bathroom, and twice her foot had rubbed against mine under the table. These were small things, but they weren't accidents.

Around eleven-thirty, Jean found Brad, Trina, and me now sitting on the front porch. "Today, I want to get you started on your work," she said. "The program exists because of payments and donations and because of our business. We manufacture something called Health Bars." She passed me a wrapped bar. I recognized the brand. I'd seen them before in grocery and health food stores; in fact, I'd bought them. "The ingredients are sunflower seeds, almonds, dates, prunes, and honey in an oat-bran base. We sell them to a number of local markets throughout the state. We ask anyone who stays with us to help make the bars. At this location we shell sunflower seeds. Other locations have different tasks. The ingredients are combined and baked at the main location and shipped out from there. For the rest of your stay, you'll be working for a few hours a day. All right, follow me."

She took us to the barnlike building behind the house that I'd glimpsed the night before. Once inside I could see that it was a large rectangular room with a gigantic industrial-sized refrigerator and two tremendous stoves. In the center of the room was a long table with plenty of flat surface for whatever work we'd be doing. There was a buzz of Spanish as we entered; several Latinas were sitting at the table, shelling sunflower seeds. There were no cars in the back. I assumed they'd been dropped off and would be picked up later.

It hadn't occurred to me that I had been drafted as a worker as well as Trina until Jean pointed out my place at the table. Music played in the background: Frankie, Ella, Tony, Sarah. I could close my eyes and pretend I was at a club. From time to time, one of the Latinas, a small thin woman with a braid that hung past her hips, would get up, collect the shells, and throw them in a large trash can at the back of the room. Then she'd return, take the seeds, and distribute them to the other Latinas, who chopped them into small pieces.

"I've eaten these bars before," Trina said. "You gave me one on the morning I was taking my SATs. You said it would give me energy."

"I remember."

We smiled at each other. It was nice, that moment when we both smiled. A nice, normal moment, the kind I'd learned not to trust.

Trina stared at me.

"What?" I asked.

"Could these sunflower seeds be poison?"

"I don't think so, Trina."

My response seemed to satisfy her, at least for a while.

I called the store just before lunchtime. Frances answered, her voice brisk and businesslike. We talked a little bit. She didn't ask me any questions about Trina.

"Did the Old Man finish with the jacket?"

I'd forgotten all about the jacket. "Give him a call. You can ask Adriana to pick it up when she gets a break." Something about the slowness of her response alerted me. "Is everything okay with her?"

"She's—I don't know. She seems lost without you, Keri. Nothing to worry about. She's just a little spacy and sad."

"Let me talk with her."

"Hey," I said, when Adriana answered. "How are you doing?"

We chatted for a while about nothing in particular. She asked me how Trina was. Better, I said, which wasn't a lie. Although she said she was fine, Adriana's tone said otherwise. But there was nothing I could do about that.

At one-thirty, everyone assembled for another meal. The kitchen table was laden with platters of chicken, corn on the cob, a mixture of broccoli, carrots, and cauliflower, and a huge salad. Eddie sat at the head of the table and put a cloth napkin around his neck like a bib. Jean served our plates. We were like some bizarre, misfit farm family who'd run out of conversation, except for Jean, who chattered nonstop. She was definitely southern. Every word had a drawl. She talked about the weather and oranges, while the patriarch, Eddie, chowed down and finished her sentences. I kept waiting for them to call each other Ma and Pa. After lunch and cleanup, the girls went on separate walks.

I was sitting on the porch when Brad sat down next to me.

"Wilbur couldn't get the lab work done. He'll be back tomorrow."

"I thought this was going to be a pit stop. You know, go to the bathroom, get some food, and keep moving," I said.

Brad actually laughed. "It doesn't work like that."

"You forget that I don't know how it works, Brad."

He put his hand on my shoulder. "There is a destination, and we will get there. But there's a journey that comes first. You're on the journey now. Relax."

I didn't want the journey. I clamored for the terminal, the place where somebody would fix my child and return her to me exactly as she had been before, so that my life—our lives—could go forward.

"Where are you from?" I asked, trying to forge a conversation to make myself feel less uncomfortable.

He gave a short laugh. "Small farming town. Kind of place that makes you want to aim a gun at the sky and pull the trigger, just so you know you're alive."

"That bad?"

"Even the baseball games were quiet. As a kid I always wanted to stand up in the middle of an inning and scream, 'Get me outta here!' "

"Iowa? Nebraska? South Dakota? North Dakota?"

"Can't get into that." He paused. "Are you and Bethany having some issues?"

His question surprised me. I hadn't realized that the silent treatment Bethany and I were doling out to each other had been noticeable. "We had a little discussion this morning," I said. Brad stared at me without responding. "I was upset because she didn't tell me about all of her daughter's problems."

"I see," Brad said.

"I didn't know about this whole splitting thing."

"And if you'd been told?"

"Maybe I wouldn't have come. I don't want Trina around somebody who's that sick. Don't get me wrong: Trina has an illness, but she's not that bad."

"Okay."

"Trina will be going back to school in September, to Brown. She's a National Merit Scholar."

"Keri, we're going to do everything we can to ensure that both Trina and Angelica can have good futures. Trust us to do our work. And we'll trust you to do yours. But you know, there can be no healing without acceptance."

I TOOK A WALK, A MINDLESS TREK TO THE ROAD AND BACK. Five times in all, fast enough to work up a light sweat and hear my own breathing. Leaning against one of the oaks, I pulled out my cell phone. There were messages. Orlando had called again. And PJ.

I dialed PJ's cell phone. Fourteen years old and his own cell—but thank God, because the alternative would have included the possibility that I'd have to say hello to his mother. And ever since the drink-in-my-face incident, Lucy had been on my list of people to avoid at all costs. PJ's phone rang, rang, and rang some more; then I had to listen to about eight minutes of gangsta rap before I could leave a message.

After dinner we watched movies. Jean and Trina played more Scrabble, and Angelica worked on a puzzle. It was clear to me that some kind of bonding was taking place between Jean and my child. I wondered if this "station" was the first stop for everyone, so that all the runaways could benefit from Jean's inner Earth Mother.

Yawning and stretching, Trina seemed calm enough as she got ready for bed. It didn't appear that she would need Haldol tonight. Bethany, the girls, and I had changed into our pajamas in the bathrooms while Eddie, Brad, and Jean posted themselves like sentinels in the bedroom.

"Why does he have to sleep in here with us?" Trina asked.

"It's best," Brad said.

"It's not best," Trina said. "You snore and you talk in your sleep."

"Sorry about that."

He rooted around in his bag for a moment and then opened a small plastic container and offered it first to Trina and then to me. Small, round pearly globs of wax.

"Earplugs," he said. "Roll them in your hand until they get soft, then stick them in your ears."

I took two and began rolling. Trina stared at Brad defiantly.

"I'm not going to run away," she said.

"I'm sleeping in here tonight, Trina," Brad said. There was an air of finality and authority in his tone that I admired. If Trina had been hectoring me, the argument would have gone on and on. He extended the container toward her again; Trina rolled her eyes and refused the plugs. Then she began pacing, as if she'd shrugged off all traces of sleepiness.

"These people are crazy," she whispered, leaning over my bed. From the corner of my eye, I saw Angelica sit up in her bed and lean forward.

Brad looked at Trina, his head tilted a bit, as though he was measuring something from a distance.

"Really," I said.

She began shrieking. "They're trying to kill me!"

Brad got up from the bed, moving very carefully.

Her eyes were large, bold, daring me to contradict her.

"Trina . . ."

"Last night they came into the room. They tried to make me drink something."

"Really."

"Yes!" she screamed, over and over.

Brad took a few steps toward Trina.

"Get the fuck away from me, you devil!" Her body tilted toward the door. She began to shriek. Outside the room, Eddie and Jean came running. The key turned, and then they were inside.

"Trina," Jean said, taking my daughter's hand. "Trina," she said, in soothing, dulcet tones.

I sat and watched. Brad and Eddie held her. Jean talked. A few minutes later, Brad gave her another shot of Haldol. How much was that? Too much? Not enough? I hadn't risen from my bed.

.   .   .

I SAT IN THE FAMILY ROOM AFTER TRINA CONKED OUT. JEAN came in offering peppermint tea, two steaming cups on a tray with painted roses on it. She sat next to me, her thigh pressed against mine, even though there was plenty of room.

"She was such a smart little girl," I said to her. Trina's report cards, the pinnacle of my motherhood. "Trina made straight A's all the way through school."

Jean stared at me for a moment. Then she laughed and bumped against my thigh with hers. "Those days are gone, sweetheart," she said, still chuckling; she stopped when she realized I wasn't laughing. "What I mean is, move forward," she went on, her tone gentle. "Appreciate what she's got going for her right now, right in this moment. She's a tremendous survivor, dear. They all are. She has battled hard to be here. Respect that. Straight A's? That was then."

"I'm not talking about some inner-city public school wizard who didn't crack a thousand on her SATs. Trina scored fifteen thirty-five out of a possible sixteen hundred."

There, I thought. There.

Jean opened her mouth and then closed it. She reached for my hand and squeezed it. I pulled away. There was condescension in her touch. She knew I'd felt it.

"My son was an average student, average ballplayer, average kid. But he had a killer sense of humor. He could turn everything into a big laugh-in. At the dinner table, he'd keep Eddie and me in stitches. We just knew he'd grow up to be a comedian. He started playing the comedy clubs in college, and he was doing great. Then he was diagnosed with schizophrenia. We had some bad days, real bad. But now my son works, he has his own place, he has friends. He has a different life; I've accepted that. For your daughter, more is possible. Bipolar isn't the same as schizophrenia. But I had to accept my child's diagnosis, with its limitations."

That's you, I thought. My child will recover; her life will move forward.

"My son is independent. He lives in a duplex next door to his sister. He takes his meds on his own. He has a part-time job. And he has a girl-friend. So."

So I'd slit my wrists if that was Trina's future. Maybe she saw that in my eyes. She smiled at me. "Trina's life has value just as it is, Keri, the same value it had when she was making straight A's and got into Brown."

"Don't tell me what to want for my child," I said. "And don't tell me what to want for me."

Jean just nodded and smiled her "it's all good" smile. "I didn't mean to upset you, sweetheart."

For some reason, after she left, I thought of Crazy Man, lumbering down Crenshaw Boulevard, out of his mind and unperturbed, maybe even happy at times. Did his chaotic life have value?

I knocked on the barracks door to get back in. Bethany opened it, which surprised me. I'd expected Brad.

We stared at each other until I looked down and then away.

"She'll be okay," Bethany said. She waited, waited until I looked straight at her. It took a little while.

"Yeah," I said.

20

Dr. Wilbur arrived the next morning. Trina was doing yoga with Jean and Eddie in a multipurpose room at the back of the house. Angelica, Bethany, Brad, and I were shelling sunflower seeds in the Health Bar factory. The doctor asked to speak with Bethany first. Neither the music nor the aromatherapy had soothed Angelica; she seemed agitated. She had been mumbling to herself while Bethany sat next to her. After her mother left, she stared first at me and then at Brad.

"Where did my mother go?" she asked, looking at me.

"She went to see the doctor; she'll be right back," I said.

"She'd better be careful. That doctor is a rapist. He tried to rape me when I got the medicine. He wanted to feel me up."

"Angelica, you finished shelling your pile?" Brad asked.

The anger that flared in her eyes was sudden. "I want money for this." She waited and then stood up. I heard a zipping sound. In what seemed like less than ten seconds, Angelica was completely naked.

"Angelica, you need to put your clothes back on," Brad said.

"This is all they really want," she said, looking at the Latinas, who averted their eyes and whispered softly in Spanish. She dug her nails into her arms and began scraping them against her skin, making angry red streaks. She didn't draw blood, but that was only because her nails weren't long and sharp enough. Brad rushed over and grabbed her wrists and held them behind her back, which is what Bethany saw when she walked in.

"Angelica," she said, from the doorway.

Angelica's body was sunken, carved. Illness on display. ¡Dios mio! one of the Latinas said, her words underscored by nervous laughter. Bethany made an attempt. "Angelica . . . Angelica. . . ."

"It's okay," I said to her, and turned to Angelica. "I'll help you get dressed, and then you can have a cigarette."

Angelica stood perfectly still for a few moments and then bent down, picked up her clothes from the floor, and handed them to me, one at a time. "Who works for free?" she asked me.

I was pondering her question when I saw Wilbur at the door, beckoning me. The psychiatrist led me back to the barracks, where he sat down on the plain wooden chair closest to the door. There was another hard-backed chair right next to his, and I sat in it.

"The blood tests reveal that your daughter has only trace amounts of medication in her system."

"What does that mean?" I asked.

"It means it will take six to eight weeks for the meds to be at a really therapeutic level. You say she was in the hospital recently. For how long and what did they give her?"

"The same drugs you're giving her, lithium and olanzapine. She was only there for seventy-two hours, and I suspect she was doing some cheeking."

Wilbur nodded and jotted something on the small notepad he was carrying. "I'm going to switch her to an antipsychotic that dissolves instantly on the tongue."

"I didn't know there was such a thing," I said.

"It's been around for a while. Unfortunately, the mood stabilizer isn't available in that form. We're going to have to make sure she gets it in her. Jean's pretty good at that."

"How long before she stops being so paranoid and impulsive?"

"Remember, it's not every day that she gets taken someplace against her will. Most of us would be upset."

He had a point. Maybe I had become so used to dealing with Trina's abnormalities that I'd overlooked the fact that her brain could still react normally to life's ups and downs. If my mother had snatched me off the street and driven me to parts unknown, I'd be screaming, too.

"Some of Trina's problems can be worked out with medicine, and some will take therapy, Keri. She's fortunate. Bipolar disorder isn't curable, but it's highly treatable. Is there anyone else in your family with a mental illness?"

I shook my head.

"No? On her father's side?"

"Oh, well, they're all a bunch of nuts. But," I said, seeing Wilbur lean forward with interest, "I'm talking about garden-variety crazy, as in 'Will you loan me five hundred dollars that I know you know I have no intention of paying back?' That kind of crazy."

Wilbur laughed. "I'm familiar with the type."

He stared at me in the way counselors do when they're trying to elicit more conversation. But I had caught myself before I told him that my mother didn't hesitate to beg me for money. The last person on earth I wanted to talk about was Emma.

Not talking about her didn't mean I wouldn't think about her. Later—after Wilbur had described in detail the stages of Trina's healing; after he'd answered my questions, the ones he could answer; after he'd assured me that I should have faith in both the program and Trina's ability to heal—when I was alone, that's when my mother inserted herself in my mind.

Good ol' Emma, pressing so hard against my thoughts that I could see her slim frame, resent her for still looking good, hear her wisp of an almost-old-lady voice pleading with me to answer her calls, give her another chance. My list of rebukes was as much a part of me as my skin.

But you left me home alone when I was three. You didn't come to my open house at school when I was five, six, seven, eight, nine. You threw up all over my prom gown. You were drunk at my graduation. You didn't show up at my wedding. You didn't come when the baby died.

As I sat on the hard-backed chair, my arms began to ache. That's where the hurting always started.

I put on the sneakers and jogging suit I'd brought, and when I went outside the cool morning air on my face startled me in a good way. Music was playing. I could hear Jean encouraging someone, with her soft, gentle "That's right, sweetheart. That's just perfect." There was no one in the front part of the house, no one to watch me go out the front door.

I ran through the rows of sunflowers. Ran fast, without stopping. I sweated a lot, and after a while my muscles began to strain and hurt. That kind of pain was welcome, it really was. That kind of pain didn't make me remember things I didn't want to remember; it didn't cause me to mourn a man, a marriage, and a child.

When I got back to the house, Bethany was standing on the front porch. "They were looking for you," she said.

"Who?"

"Brad, Jean, and Eddie. They don't want us to go wandering off. Somebody might see us."

"Out here? We're in Boonieville."

Bethany shrugged. She lit a cigarette. "Listen, that's what they told me."

"Where are the girls?"

"Angelica is making jewelry. Trina's working. They're all right. Nobody's screaming. Nobody's naked. Nobody's hacking away with the razor blade."

"Bethany, I'm sorry about what I said."

There was silence for about five seconds.

"Don't you just fucking hate it when they get naked in front of company?" Bethany said. We laughed. "What did the doctor say to you?"

"That Trina doesn't have the proper level of medication in her system. He asked me about my family background, if anyone else had mental illness."

"My whole family has it, both sides. My dad had six siblings and only two don't have some kind of brain disease. They covered it up with drinking. My sister's son was strung out on crack when he died. He was manic and high, and he either fell or jumped from a rooftop parking lot."

"Oh, my God."

"Yeah. So that was—what, six months ago? When that happened, I started making plans to get Angelica in the program. A nurse on one of the psychiatric wards had told me about it a long time ago, but I never followed up."

"Your aunts and uncles who were alcoholics, did they ever get a diagnosis?"

"Some of them. You know, someone would be hospitalized—once, twice—and then the attending psychiatrist would say, 'It appears that so-and-so has bipolar disorder, or depression.' He'd prescribe medication, and they'd take it for a little while and then stop, and the craziness would start all over again. They'd rather admit to being drunks than to having mental illness."

The craziness in Ma Missy's house, without long pauses or any reprieve, came to mind. I considered for a moment the possibility that Emma's drinking masked deeper pain, but I didn't probe very deeply. I wasn't prepared to empathize with a woman I despised.

For much of the day, Jean and I stayed clear of each other. Being around Jean made me feel as though I needed to explain myself, a feeling I hated. Maybe she sensed my resistance. She wasn't as garrulous as she'd been the day before.

Dinner that evening was sumptuous. In a low bowl, Jean had arranged cut flowers surrounded by tiny green oranges as a centerpiece. There was a curried spinach and potato casserole, fried trout with some sort of lemony sauce, corn on the cob, and homemade corn bread. For dessert, Jean served pears poached in apple juice, cinnamon, and honey.

Trina didn't say a word at the table. She ate mechanically, two helpings of everything that was offered. I sensed that she was wired and fractious and that whatever was on her mind would bear monitoring. Jean followed her when she got up from the table. While I was loading the dishwasher, I could hear the one-sided conversation. Her tone was pleasant, as though she expected a response from her listener. A few minutes later the front door opened, and when I looked out the picture window in the living room, Trina and Jean were walking toward the road. When they returned ten minutes later, Trina went back to the room with Brad, and Jean came into the kitchen.

From where I sat, I could see that Jean's face was serene as she began putting away the leftovers and wiping off the stove. Maybe she never really expected much out of life, I thought. Maybe that's why she can be content with her sunflowers and her boy who will never be the same.

"How did you get Trina to take a walk?"

Jean looked surprised, then thoughtful. "I don't know. We were talking, and then I just took her hand and said, 'Let's go for a walk,' and she came with me. It helps not to be Mom," she added.

"Right."

"Are you still angry with me?"

"I'm not angry with you," I said, rinsing plates and putting them in the dishwasher.

Prickles of annoyance pulsated just below my skin. She was trying to lead me down a touchy-feely path I didn't want to follow. I could feel my cell phone vibrating in my back hip pocket and took it out.

"Keri?"

"Clyde, where are you?" I could have bitten my tongue. I didn't want him to ask me the same question.

"I'm back in LA. I called the store. They told me you were away. Where are *you*? Where's Trina? How is she doing?"

"She's with me. I'm . . . we're . . . she's getting treatment."

"Where? Why didn't you tell me about this? You're going to want me to pay for it."

"No. I can manage."

For a moment he was silent. Disappointed, no doubt. "I'd like to see her this weekend."

"This is a different kind of place. For the first couple of months they don't allow visitors."

"What the hell are you talking about? How did you find out about this place?"

"One of my support group members sent her daughter here. I've met a lot of people who had family members come. It's a great facility."

"I want to talk to my daughter."

"It's not possible right now. You're just going to have to trust me."

"You always need to be in control," he said. He hung up without saying good-bye.

Jean didn't pretend to be occupied with busywork. She stared straight at me as I pocketed my cell phone, making me feel self-conscious.

"That was my ex-husband. He doesn't know about any of this. He's upset because he can't talk with Trina."

"Ex-husbands can be a challenge to your sense of harmony."

There was no sense of irony in her comment. Maybe that's why we both laughed.

"You've been married before?" Ma and Pa Kettle weren't their only ones? This was a surprise.

Jean gave a short laugh. "Honey, Eddie is my fourth and last husband. We've been together for twenty years; that's twice as long as any of the others."

"So he's not your son's father."

She shook her head. "That would be husband number two, Ralph. He lives in South Africa. Does something with diamonds. Makes a ton of money. He still sends me some. Of course, he doesn't come to see his son—who Eddie raised, by the way. Ralph gets to absolve his guilt, and I'm grateful for the cash, because sometimes Eddie and I run short. People do what they can do, dear."

Jean had inserted her little New Age lecture so subtly I almost didn't notice the message she'd planted. Maybe I was ready to hear it. "I want to stop being angry with Clyde. I try. My rage is like a drug for me. I take a hit, and then I'm out of control."

"I've done a lot of things that I've regretted when I'm angry. If your ex doesn't hear from his daughter, is he likely to go looking for her?"

"No one knows where I am," I said. "Not even me."

"There's a lot at stake," Jean said.

21

WE STAYED WITH JEAN AND EDDIE FOR A WEEK OF WHAT I suppose was a kind of orientation. Whether I was becoming oriented was hard to tell. Institutionalized was more like it. After the first two days of waking up when we pleased, a 7 a.m. bell suddenly rang out on the third day. And it kept on ringing, despite Trina's groans and Angelica's slow rise from the bed. The honeymoon was over. We were now expected to help prepare all meals under the supervision of Jean, the cooking machine, who instructed us in low-fat, low-cal methods. Cleanup was shared as well. And, of course, we shelled sunflowers.

I hadn't expected that cracking open tiny seeds for hours at a time would be rewarding, and initially it wasn't. That first day, my fingertips were cut; my neck ached from bending over the table, and Angelica's constant muttering got to me. But on the second day things seemed to flow well. After a while, the work became soothing; by the third day I was looking forward to sitting at the table.

The girls seemed to be responding well to the program. Angelica muttered and stared and dug at her flesh and Trina continued to accuse Jean of trying to poison her, but not as often and not nearly as vehemently as before. Healing in mental illness comes in stages and degrees. Both daughters were taking their medication. Most significant of all, the stretches of normalcy, or what might be normalcy for either of them, began to lengthen.

"When she gets that blank stare and her foot starts tapping, Miss Angelica is getting ready to go off," I said to Bethany, who nodded her head in agreement.

I didn't make any attempts to calm Angelica; I left that to Jean and Brad. But once or twice, when I saw wildness in her eyes, I patted her hand and rubbed her arm, and that seemed to soothe her. After a while, I began to watch her for signs of trouble. A couple of times while we were working, I got up from the table and massaged her neck and shoulders. The smile she gave me—well, I could tell what God meant for her to be.

After a few days passed, Trina's coherent periods began lasting for at least fifteen or twenty minutes at a stretch. During those times, anyone eavesdropping on her conversation might have thought her colorful as opposed to crazy. She took her medication without protest. She and Jean bonded over long walks, yoga, and Scrabble games.

"I see progress," Bethany said. We were standing out back, looking at the mountains.

"You can feel it. They're getting better."

It was as though we were looking at the entire world through gauze. Our daughters' responses to medication, good food, exercise, and the lack of controlled substances softened everything for us. As they became more normal, we became more relaxed. Smiled more. Laughed more. Trusted that we'd made the right choice, that everything would come out okay.

When I finally called Orlando, we hadn't spoken in days. He answered his cell phone on the second ring.

"Baby, where you been?" he asked.

"I—"

"I've been calling and calling. What's going on?"

The suspicion in his voice flowed right through the cell phone.

"I'm doing some traveling. Visiting. I needed to get away."

"What is it that you don't want to lie to me about?"

"I'm not with anybody."

"I didn't mean it that way, and you know it."

"Well . . ." Damn his intuition. I wanted to tell Orlando what was going on. Of all people, he would keep his mouth shut. But I couldn't.

"I needed to be by myself, just to clear my head. I'm not out here party-ing. And you have your play."

"So why didn't you just tell me you needed to be alone instead of having me wondering and worrying about you? I've been calling you all week long. You can't drop off the face of the earth, girl. There are people who care about you."

"I'm sorry, Orlando. I'm with Trina, looking into the best treatment for her."

"Oh."

"Jabari and PJ doing okay?"

"Girl, these rehearsals have been—"

Irritation sliced my throat as I swallowed. I thought of PJ's trou-bled face, the secret he felt he needed to harbor. "Orlando, please talk with—"

I heard someone calling Orlando's name. "Places, everybody."

"Listen, I have to go. Call me when you get a chance. And say a prayer for me. I love you, baby."

He hung up before I had a chance to respond.

ANGELICA WOKE UP SCREAMING THAT NIGHT. NIGHTMARES are a fixture in the lives of the brain-disordered. Trina and Angelica had been moaning in their sleep the entire week we'd been at Jean's.

Brad rushed to Angelica and immediately put his hand over her mouth.

"You have to stop yelling now. Do you understand me?" he said.

"Hey!" I said. His hand across her mouth looked tight, like some-thing that would leave a mark. I was already out of bed and moving toward them.

"We can't have that here," he said to her, to me. His voice was like the palm of his hand: hard, breathtaking. I didn't take another step.

He removed his hand and what came out of Angelica's mouth was a gagging sound and then a torrent of words.

"They were pulling my legs apart, trying to stick their dicks in me. Their hairy dicks. A lot of them. They smelled so bad," she said, her voice rising to a wail. "They tried to stick everything inside of me: dirt and leaves and glass bottles. They were fucking me with glass bottles. Big old nasty monster men. They didn't care. They didn't care."

The declaration subsided and the muttering began, Angelica's own private conversation. Haldol couldn't be far behind.

Bethany was next to Angelica by the time she began sobbing. I came to life too. "It's all right. It's all right," she said, over and over, while I patted and rubbed and Trina sat up, her eyes half open, her sleep broken, and Brad stood there, his resolute chin thrust out.

Wilbur rushed in and I told him what had happened, including Brad's response. He and Brad took Angelica from the barracks into another room, and Bethany followed them. When they brought her back she was subdued, her muttering mere whispers. Bethany shushed her with "Aw, honey. Aw, sweetie. It's okay. Everything's okay." Jean and Eddie stood guard.

Outside the room, I heard Brad, his voice controlled, his deliberate words pitched against Wilbur's angry criticism.

"She was jeopardizing all of us. You never know who is driving by, even this late at night. We're not completely isolated." I didn't hear Wilbur's response. But after a slight pause, Brad said, "I've made my decision."

IMMEDIATELY AFTER DINNER THE NEXT EVENING, BRAD quietly instructed Bethany and me to get our things together. We would be leaving in an hour. We had been with Jean and Eddie for one week. Progress had been made. Two steps forward, one back. Better than I had expected. So I was hopeful about what lay ahead. I packed in silence next to Bethany, keeping my questions inside my head.

"Are we going home?" Trina asked me as we got into the car. "I'll take my meds when we get back home."

Her words were a siren's song. But I'd been dashed against the rocks once too often. No, I was in for the full ride.

"We're not going home just yet, Trina," I said.

Her face grew dark, her eyes stormy. "Where are we going?"

Brad walked over. "Going to a place where you will get more help. Trina, I want you to relax. Be grateful."

I could have told Brad that my child wasn't grateful, not yet. But his chin jutted forward, an indication that he was in the fearless-leader zone. It was only when we were getting into Brad's SUV that I learned that Jean would be traveling with us. The news pleased me. Even with her Earth Mother tendencies, Jean's presence was welcome because of the continuity she provided for Trina.

We were about to pull off when I heard Eddie yelling. Brad rolled down the window.

"Back tire's flat," he said.

It was a miracle he saw it, as dark as it was. We all piled out and stared at the tire, as though looking at it would repair it.

"Take our car," Eddie said. "You can't go without a spare."

Their car was an old Volvo station wagon. Brad, Trina, and I sat up front. Jean, Bethany, and Angelica sat in the back. Brad played one jazz CD after another. Highway 5 to Sacramento, the signs read. I paid attention for a while, until I fell asleep.

Around two-thirty, I woke with a start. The car had stopped. Angelica was screaming again. Amid the confusion, I heard Trina, her voice whiny and petulant. She needed to go to the bathroom.

We were now traveling along a two-lane highway; I could see a few lights in the distance. There were signs advertising gas and lodging ahead, but Brad drove right past the lighted area and didn't turn off until several miles later, onto a pitch-black road with huge fields of low-growing plants on either side. The air was thick with the scent of citrus. Angelica's conversation with her nighttime assailants continued.

Brad pulled over to the shoulder, stopped, and got out. There were no other cars on the road. He went around to the back and opened the trunk. When he reappeared, he was carrying a roll of toilet paper in his hand. He opened the door for Trina and waited for her to get out. Jean opened her door. Angelica's keening split the air. Brad didn't see Trina's eyes when she realized that the toilet paper and the unlit highway were the only accommodations she would be afforded, but I did. I thought about her request to go home and reached out to grab her arm—my fingers grazed her skin—but before I could connect, Trina had hurled herself from her seat to the ground. She began running and screaming at the same time. It was startling, the sound she made: an eagle suddenly escaped from its cage in the zoo, a shriek of panic and euphoria as the freedom stung her face.

Brad, Jean, and I took off after her, yelling for her to stop. Of course, she just ran harder, zigzagging from one side of the road to the other like a wild bird trying to outrun a hatchet. We were still calling out when we saw headlights coming right toward us.

"Help! Help! Help! They're trying to kill me! They're trying to kill me!" Trina waved her arms and jumped up and down, racing toward the oncoming vehicle.

The car, which was about half a city block away, slowed down. Brad, Jean, and I all inhaled at the same time. Trina ran to the driver's side, banging on the window. Behind her, Angelica wailed.

"They're devils! They're devils! Help me, please. Save me from the devils!"

I could see the driver now. Horror and fear stained the woman's face like makeup. The vehicle stopped for a moment. I gasped. Just that quickly, the car accelerated and sped past Trina, coming straight toward us. Brad shouted something, and the three of us scattered as the car barreled down the road.

Trina was hysterical, screaming and running in the dark. Brad finally overtook her. He held her, his hands gripping the backs of her arms. She sat down on the ground, in the middle of the road, refusing to move, so we lifted her up and carried her back to the car.

"We're trying to help you. Shh, shh, baby," I said.

Brad's mouth was tight and grim as he gave both Trina and Angelica shots of Haldol. Bethany was leaning over her daughter, her arms around her neck. Trina was mercifully still, resigned that her escape had been foiled. She whimpered for a while and then grew quiet. Brad's face was tense, like a bank robber's when the getaway car is missing.

Trina could have been killed, I thought. The car could have run right over her. Jean and Brad couldn't have done a damn thing about it. They possessed ideals, not power. Suppose I had died? What would have happened to Trina?

The next time I looked at my watch it was 5 a.m. and the car had stopped in front of another farmhouse surrounded by a field.

"A friend with friends" I heard Brad say. A front door opened, and once again we were ushered in.

Jean offered to make sandwiches, but no one was hungry. A man who introduced himself as Pete led us through a dimly lit house to a bedroom where four single beds were lined up. Another barracks. He disappeared before I could get a good look at him. At the window, blackout shades were drawn.

Jean and I helped Trina change into her pajamas while Angelica and Bethany were in the bathroom. Trina didn't want to brush her teeth or wash her face, but Jean succeeded in persuading her without raising her voice. Through the wall I could hear Brad filling Pete in on our backgrounds, carefully not mentioning that the wild child sleeping in one of his beds had just jeopardized the entire program. Pete didn't say much. Maybe he was used to being given psychological profiles of strangers before dawn.

I met Brad at the door when he came into the room. "Trina could have been hurt," I said, my voice low, my back to my daughter, who was lying down but not asleep. "That car could have hit her. Or suppose the woman had opened the door and driven off with her? I didn't know it would be like this."

Brad's hand reached for me, pulled me away from Trina. "There is risk involved in what we do," he said. "You knew that."

"I didn't know. I didn't know that this—I want to go back," I said.

"Back to what?" Brad asked.

"I just want to take her home. This isn't working."

"No," Brad said.

"What do you mean, no? I'm taking her back home."

Jean suddenly appeared at my side. "This is mental illness, Keri; the behavior is unpredictable. That's part of it," she said. "That will always be part of it, no matter where you go."

"What do you think will happen if you take her home now?" Brad asked. "She has to get enough meds in her system before she'll be willing to stay on them. She is still manic, still paranoid, still psychotic. If you take her home now, as angry as she's feeling, she might call the police and tell them you kidnapped her."

"She could do that anyway."

"No one who completes the program has ever done that," Jean said. "You take her home now, and you'll have to go back to square one. Trina has a mental illness."

"You keep telling me what I know."

"Do you?" Brad asked. When I didn't answer, he said, "It will never go away. Recovery for Trina will be ongoing for the rest of her life and the rest of yours. It will take years. Those years can be disappointing or painful for you or they can be productive, maybe even joyful. It depends on your attitude."

"There is nothing wrong with my attitude," I said.

"You're like a lot of parents. You think your daughter's bipolar disorder is your personal tragedy, but it's not. It's Trina's. She is the one with the brain disease, not you. You want the bright child back, who attends Brown and gets straight A's. Well, don't we all. You have to accept Trina the way she is. She's not something you ordered from a catalog. She's a gift from God. You need to treat her that way."

"I love my child."

He put his hand on my wrist. "I'm not talking about love. I'm talking about reverence for her life."

Brad squeezed my wrist and then let me go.

When I looked at Brad and Jean, I realized they wanted me to surrender my dreams of Trina's complete recovery. Maybe that was another reason to leave.

"I think we should all get some rest," Jean said.

"Is there anything to drink around here?" I asked, looking at Jean. The question didn't appear to throw her.

Brad stayed behind with the girls. Jean, Bethany, and I went to the kitchen and sat at a large round claw-foot table. Jean went right to the cabinet above the refrigerator. It was high, so she used a small ladder. She pushed aside bottles of apple juice.

"Rum or vodka?" she asked.

We opted for rum and mixed it with some fruit juice we found in the refrigerator. Sipped it for a while before anyone spoke. The fuzziness began permeating my mind, filling it with sad music. What's the use, what's the use, what's the use? was the refrain.

"They all try something, honey. Tomorrow will be better," Jean said.

"It just goes on and on," I said. "One minute she seems perfectly normal and the next—"

"—she's running through the world naked with bloody legs." Bethany looked at me. "Yeah. Be grateful for your own sack of woes. I'd trade places with you in a New York minute."

I let that sink in, but the words didn't make me feel better.

LATER, WHEN THE CELL PHONE RANG, IT WAS FRANCES, HER voice not cheerful. "Keri, I hate to call you when you're taking your break, but I just . . . I don't know what's going on with Adriana. She's, she's—listen, those so-called friends of hers, they won't leave her alone. Every time I look up, they're right there. And I've seen her with that guy more than once. It's like they're stalking her. Like they know her protection is gone and they're moving in for the kill. She's acting so strange. Coming in late to work, acting spacy. Girl, Adriana's in trouble."

"I can't help her," I said, maybe too fast. Maybe too hard. On the other end of the phone, Frances was quiet.

"I know that. The only reason I'm calling you is that I don't want you to be shocked when you get back," she said finally. "It's just—damn, it's hard to see someone falling through the cracks right before your eyes."

When I hung up I said one of Mattie's quick prayers. There should be a patron saint for wayward girls, a celestial guardian for strippers, porn queens, hookers, junkies, and those whose brains spew out dangerous impulses. What's a mother to do against those tragic impulses? What kind of protection can I offer?

I sat down on the side of Trina's bed. My body felt stiff and heavy. She was lying there, still not sleeping. I didn't know what she'd heard. My fingers made a trail down her arm. She flinched but didn't pull away. I took her hand in mine and began massaging her fingertips and then the joints of each finger.

"Why can't we just go home?" she asked me. "These people are devils." She began to cry, silently at first, and gradually the sound became a little louder. "I never thought my life would be like this." She wiped her eyes and became silent again.

"Everything is going to get better, Trina. You'll see. I know you think you hate me now, but I had to do this. You're going to have a good life again. You have to believe that."

Trina stared at me; then she took my hands and placed them on her head. I thought of Rona then, her small fuzzy head. Poor thin tired Rona, battling a wildfire in her body, hoping desperately to make it to her reunion in October. Wouldn't that be a small thing for God to grant? "Could you manage that one tiny thing?" I said aloud. Trina looked at me. I began massaging again. My energy passed from me to her. My peace, my power, eased across my skin to hers. Was she feeling me?

22

DESPITE JEAN'S COAXING, TRINA REFUSED TO GET UP LATER that morning. I didn't really feel like moving either. As I lay on my narrow bed, Bethany and Angelica were dressing under Jean's watchful eye. They were off to the salt mines. I'm sure that somewhere on the premises there was a room for shelling, a space for yoga and games and crafts.

You've seen one underground railroad stop, you've seen them all.

I could hear Bethany and Angelica talking. Mostly, it was Angelica, carrying on at least two conversations, one with one of her invisible friends and the other with Bethany, who was trying to distract her. I stole a look at Angelica. Damn. How did Bethany stand it? The voices, the catatonic stares, the meth habit. Sunken cheeks and burned-out eyes, stringy hair she probably refused to wash. Her teeth were stained, a yellow that made me want her not to smile.

At least Trina was still beautiful. At least she looked normal and clean. She could carry on a decent conversation. If she walked into a store, no one would alert security. It wasn't right to compare them, but I couldn't help myself. I needed to feel superior.

Closing my eyes, I recalled going to the movies, a drink after work; I recalled seduction and quick, easy fucking. Good times seemed so far away.

"Are you okay?" Bethany leaned over me. I could smell her perfume. She was still putting it on, even on this unscented journey of ours.

"I'm just tired. Everything caught up with me all at once."

She gave me a look that told me she understood. Behind her, I could hear Angelica muttering at the unseen.

"You're not going to go home, are you?" Bethany asked.

Now that someone besides Brad was calling my bluff, I had to consider my words and ultimately confess that I'd been premature in my thoughts and certainly in speaking them. If I went back home, Trina would be worse off than before. She had just enough medication in her system to keep her out of the hospital and not enough to maintain her at home unless she continued to take her pills. Given her recent track record, I couldn't count on her to do that. So here I was: stuck.

"No," I told Bethany. "We're staying."

She patted my shoulder.

"Actually," I said, "I was thinking about calling my boyfriend for phone sex."

Bethany gave me a look of pure amazement. "God bless you. I haven't thought about sex in so long."

"Are you married, Bethany? I've never asked."

"My husband died five years ago, but we were living completely separate lives at the time. We hadn't slept together in years. He had someone, but I didn't. Too caught up in Angelica's illness. And then I have another daughter. She's older."

"Mom."

We both looked up at the same time. I gasped; Bethany didn't. A naked Angelica was standing in the doorway of the bathroom. Her legs were dripping blood in four or five places.

I got out of bed. "I thought you got rid of everything sharp. What did she use?"

"I don't know."

I called Brad and Jean; they came running. The cuts weren't deep. Jean applied peroxide and Band-Aids. Brad found a sharp rock in the wastepaper basket.

"Come on, honey," Bethany said to Angelica when she had dressed and the excitement was over. "Let's get some breakfast."

Trina never woke up. I went back to bed.

Trina and I dozed for maybe two hours before Brad and Jean came in to wake us. When we were ready, they escorted us to a very large eat-in kitchen where fruit, juice, coffee, herbal tea, muffins, cheese, and oatmeal were waiting for us. Trina dug right in, but I wasn't hungry.

"It's good, Mom," she said, as though we were sitting in a restaurant. Moments like that threw me off, normal moments that appeared so suddenly.

Normal didn't hang around long. Trina refused to go to yoga. She screamed that she wanted to go back to bed. After a while, I saw Jean walking her toward the barracks.

I sat between Angelica and Bethany at a long table in a room in the back of the house. The new shell game was almonds, cracked the old-fashioned way. Even though the nutcracker they handed me was deluxe, the job was tedious. I mean, it wasn't picking cotton from sunup to sundown; it wasn't fingers split open from the sharp bolls. It was just a pain-in-the-ass job.

"Full bucket means done," Brad told us.

I ended up cracking nuts for almost four hours and working up a pretty good sweat. Brad never mentioned our late-night conversation; in fact, he didn't address me directly at all. Halfway through my tour of duty, he left the room, and the tall man I'd caught a glimpse of the previous night took his place.

"I'm Pete," he said, as he sat down across from me. "You didn't come to breakfast, so I haven't welcomed you." He smiled and extended his hand. The hand I shook had soft skin and a powerful grip.

"Thank you." My words sounded too spare. I should add something. Underground Railroad Etiquette 101. "Thank you for opening up your home to my daughter and me."

"You're more than welcome," he said.

When he smiled, I realized he was handsome. His smile lit up his face, so that his dark eyes, aquiline nose, and wide mouth were highlighted, almost airbrushed. His skin was olive, a color that made me wonder what family tree he claimed.

When I handed Brad my full bucket, Angelica was still staring at the ceiling, the pile of almonds in front of her untouched.

I was surprised to find Wilbur inside the barracks with Trina. We'd driven for at least five hours to get to Pete's house, and I had assumed the girls would see a new psychiatrist.

"Hello, Keri," he said. "Trina, I'm going to step outside and talk with your mother, all right?"

We went outside to the corridor and moved away from the barracks door.

"Brad told me about last night, and I talked with Trina about it. What do you think happened?"

"I'm not sure what you mean. She jumped out of the car and took off. That's what happened."

"Right," he said, nodding. "Has she ever done anything like that before?"

"Run away? Sure. Whenever she gets manic, she takes off. She's a flight risk until she's stable."

"Right. I've decided to increase her mood stabilizer. We're still not going to see the real effects for six to eight more weeks, but the boost should cut down on the impulsive behavior. I'll be staying here until you leave, and I'll be keeping an eye on her."

"Should I try to get her out of bed?" I asked.

"No. Just let her be for a while."

I decided to walk. The terrain wasn't as mountainous as it had been at Jean and Eddie's. There were mountains way off in the distance, but the house and the surrounding property sat on flat land. Behind it were rows and rows of almond trees. The program's philosophy seemed to be: Shell what you grow and put it all in the Health Bar.

A huge magnolia tree, with branches and leaves that looked able to cover half a basketball court, was growing between the house and the almond orchard. A woman sat on a chair in the shade its leaves provided. I could hear her calling, trying to say something I didn't understand. When I got closer, I realized she couldn't articulate the words she wanted to say. It turned out that the chair was a wheelchair. The left side of her body seemed to be lower than the right, as though someone had put rocks in the pockets on that side. I assumed she was recovering from a stroke.

I smiled, and her face twitched slightly. Her eyes responded; they were large, dark, and luminous. And even though her face was slightly lopsided, and it was an older face, there were traces of beauty left in it still. She had turned some heads back in the day. There was a sturdy plastic lawn chair next to the woman, and I moved toward it, my back still facing the house.

"I see you've met my wife. Cecilia, this is our guest, Keri." Pete had come up so quietly I hadn't heard him.

"Nice to meet you," I said, smiling as his wife made a guttural sound.

Pete carried a tray, which he placed on his wife's lap. On it were a bowl of chili, toast, and a salad, as well as a glass of orange juice and a cup of black coffee. He pressed the edges of a napkin into the opening of Cecilia's dress and began feeding her, blowing on the food each time before putting it in her mouth. She seemed able to chew only a small amount at a time, and it took forever for her to swallow. When Pete held the cup of orange juice to her lips, some of the liquid spurted out of her mouth and dribbled down her chin.

"Had a little accident, huh?" Pete asked, wiping the drops from her face, dabbing softly at her skin. Cecilia's lips twitched.

It took a long time for Pete to feed his wife. I watched, because . . . why did I watch? Their tenderness took me by the hand, drew me in. At first I thought the giving was in one direction, but then I witnessed her energy flowing to him, the pleasure he received from watching her eat, from looking at her, remembering her beauty or still seeing it. Behind us the leaves of the almond trees rustled, and the breeze carried the faint sweet odor of their fruit.

"It was nice meeting you," I said, rising to leave. I took her hand in mine. Hers was cold, so I rubbed it to warm it up, an involuntary gesture. Cecilia closed her eyes, and I took her other hand and rubbed it too. Cecilia's hands told me a lot about her pain, her state of mind. I kept rubbing, pressing down on certain spots on her palms. My fingers worked their way up and down her wrists. No one said a word until I let go.

"You seem to know what you're doing," Pete said.

"Yes, I do."

"How was that, honey?" he asked his wife.

Her eyes were closed; she made a contented sound.

"Do you want to go back to the house?" Pete asked. She made another noise and he said, "Well, I'll check on you later."

As we were walking, I got a really good look at Pete. He was tall and straight, with no fat around the middle. His hair was mostly silver; the face it framed was calm, unlined, and handsome. He could have been fifty; he could have been seventy. I could see African, Native American Indian, and European in his features.

"So where did you learn acupressure?" he asked me.

"I went to massage school in another life."

"Did you work for a spa or do it on your own?"

"Both. When I started out, I worked out of my house; later, I was at a day spa. Very posh. I was in public relations for a while. Then I opened a designer resale shop and pretty much stopped doing bodywork until a couple of months ago, when an old customer of mine looked me up. She has cancer and is going through chemo. She talked me into working on her. I don't think your wife is aching, but she's stiff. Has she been ill long?"

"She's been the way you see her now for four years. But she was getting ill long before. My daughter will be thirty-eight on her next birthday. Trudy was diagnosed with schizophrenia when she was seventeen. Cecilia and I did everything we could to help her get treatment. She was a beautiful girl, just about to go to college. She was, of course, noncompliant with her medication regimen. We put her in facilities where she could get care; she walked out. This went on for years. There were times when she went missing, when she was homeless. Horrible things happened to her, things no one could have prevented.

"When she was first diagnosed, my wife and I were living in San Francisco. I'm a physician, a nephrologist. I owned three dialysis centers in the city, and plans were under way to open several in Los Angeles. I was earning more than two million dollars a year. I served on boards, and I was a member of several elitist organizations. We belonged to a country club. Cecilia was a real estate agent, selling multimillion-dollar properties. We were a very successful couple.

"As our daughter's illness progressed, both of us began to get ill more frequently. Colds, lots of colds. Flu. Numerous viral infections. And terrible headaches. I began to realize that if I didn't pace myself, I would die. I let go of the boards, the organizations. I sold the three centers and cut back on my practice. I stopped taking every telephone call my daughter made. But my wife tried to hold on to everything. If the telephone rang at three a.m., my wife took the call, and she wouldn't stop listening until five. She couldn't accept the fact that Trudy wasn't going to fulfill all our dreams. When you love someone who has a mental illness, there comes a point at which you must detach in order to preserve your own life. My wife couldn't do that."

He reached out, as if to hold on to something, and then returned his hand to his side.

"What happened to her?" I asked.

"Massive stroke. That's when we came out here."

"You think it was your daughter's illness that caused her stroke?"

He shook his head. "It was her reaction to it that made her sick. We all have the potential for pathology in our bodies. Cells can react negatively at any given time. Stress can set those cells in motion on a journey to self-destruction. Each one of us is responsible for defending our own bodies from that kind of assault. My wife wouldn't rest. She wouldn't eat well. She wouldn't guard her emotions."

"Will she get better?"

"What you see is an improvement." He smiled.

"How is your daughter?"

"Better. She lives in a group home just outside of Phoenix. I see her once a month. We talk on the phone every Sunday. She has a peaceful life. Sometimes, that's all you can ask for."

"Did the program help her?"

At first I thought he hadn't heard me, he took so long to answer. "Yes, but time helped more."

"Why do you work with them?"

"Why do I work with them since they didn't deliver back to me the daughter of my dreams?" He laughed. At me. "I believe in what they are trying to do. Early on, my wife and I encountered the kind of mindless bureaucracy that can frustrate anyone with a sick child. Don't get me wrong: There are good hospitals, good doctors, wonderful treatment facilities. Once we got the right information, I must say that the system worked very well for us, up to a point: patients' rights. Patients' rights often clash with what's best for a mentally ill person. Once, after we succeeded in getting our daughter on a hold, she refused to see us, told the doctors not to speak to us, and so, of course, they couldn't."

"I've gone through that. I felt like a beggar asking people for information about my child. I begged, and they still wouldn't tell me anything," I said.

"It's hard not to become frustrated. But then I began to recognize that there really wasn't anything they could tell me that was in any way not subject to change within microseconds. They could report that she was fine, had taken her medication, quit smoking, and was winning converts for Jesus, and by the time I'd made it to the hospital to witness the miracle, she'd be racing down the hall naked, screaming curses at everyone she passed. The updates are a waste of time. The system, the illness, the day-to-day management, all of it. It is what it is.

"Growing things provides me with a simple seasonal routine. It's a good routine for someone who is in mourning. You can't always beat what is difficult in your life. Sometimes you have to let it win and shout hallelujah anyhow."

It sounded like giving up to me.

He smiled. His teeth were bright white, a young man's smile. "Will you massage my wife again, while you're here?"

"I'd be happy to," I said.

I'd treat his wife, but I'd never agree with him. I hadn't brought Trina on this journey to accept the cards I'd been dealt. I was here to throw in that hand and pick up the one I was supposed to have.

TRINA WOKE UP IN TIME FOR DINNER. JEAN HAD DONE THE cooking, as she had at her own house. Trina stumbled to the table and ate with her head down. Afterward there were movies and games and beads to string in a large room off the kitchen. Trina sat on the couch and stared at the screen, but I could tell she wasn't taking in anything. Jean tried to talk her into playing Scrabble. She refused, but she did join Angelica at a card table filled with jewelry-making paraphernalia. Angelica had been working on a bracelet pretty steadily for at least an hour. I heard Trina tell her that it was pretty, as she sat down at the table. Angelica thanked her. They passed ornaments back and forth.

The rest of us—Brad, Wilbur, Jean, Bethany, Pete, and I—were in the room with them. Supervising, as it were. We watched movies, read the paper, talked a little, and kept our eyes on the two girls, who seemed to be bonding over colored glass. Jean got up after a while and made some coffee and tea. We supervisors sat around, sipping hot drinks. It was almost like a party, just not a very happening one.

THE DAYS TOOK ON A SERENE RHYTHM. WE AWOKE AROUND eight o'clock and had breakfast. Every morning, Wilbur checked on the girls. Then we all went to shell almonds, although Angelica still refused to do the work. For the rest of us, the hours seemed to have been extended. We shelled until one or two o'clock, and gradually the one bucket became one and a half and then two. Lunch was late, a farmhouse repast of fish or chicken, a salad, and several vegetables. After lunch there was yoga, crafts, art, or reading. At some point early in the evening, I would go into the master bedroom, light some candles, play soft music, and massage Cecilia. Dinner came around seven. Cleanup time followed, and then there were movies and games. At night, Wilbur was prescribing less Haldol for Trina.

For several days, Angelica didn't have any bad dreams. Neither did I.

I made my daily calls right after lunch. The store was the first one. I usually talked with Frances, whose efficient reports always removed any worry from my mind about the business or her ability to handle it. Sometimes Adriana was there, sometimes not. We spoke briefly twice. Adriana seemed anxious. I could tell by her voice that she was uneasy. She made me feel sad whenever I spoke with her.

Once I called PJ. He sounded far away and very young; I could tell he didn't really want to talk. I could hear Lucy calling him. He got off the phone without mentioning if he'd spoken to his mother or his father. But he didn't really have to tell me. I knew he hadn't.

I called Orlando two days after our last conversation. He was at home. He'd just come from an audition.

"It didn't go well," he said, his voice tight.

I should have left him alone. Orlando had his own routine for getting himself out of the bad-audition blues. Instead I was patronizing. I think I said he'd nail the next one.

"Maybe I'll even get my own radio show," he said, his words laced with sarcasm and a bitterness that stunned me. I knew enough not to touch that one. Seconds later, Orlando mumbled a terse good-bye before I could tell him that he didn't need a radio show to impress me. All he needed to do was—what? Stop chasing rainbows? Get serious about life? Give up the one thing he really loved? We'd had those conversations in the past, and I wasn't ready for the repercussions. I had other things on my mind.

Clyde was harder to get hold of. When I did hear his voice on the phone, he had exactly fifteen seconds to give me before he had to go on the air. So I ended up turning on the radio. But listening to his show wasn't a conversation, which was all I really wanted in the first place.

ON OUR SIXTH NIGHT, AS WE WERE ABOUT TO PREPARE FOR bed, Brad whispered to Bethany and me that we should pack up, because we'd be leaving in a little while. I'd just finished massaging Cecilia. As usual, Pete was sitting in the room with us. I watched his face through the light and shadows that the candles made. The thought of leaving them made me feel empty, even though, in a real way, I'd found something I thought was lost. I was like some old pianist who hadn't touched her instrument in years, only to discover that, when she did play, the songs were still there inside her. My hands, my fingers were working again. Rona had given me a sense of what was still within me. Cecilia made me know for sure.

Wilbur had left several hours earlier with a quick wave. I had no idea if I'd see him again. I could hear Jean singing as she cleaned up the kitchen. Brad wouldn't answer me when I asked if she would go all the way with us, but I figured that she would. Then, just as the girls were leaving with Brad and Bethany to tidy the barracks, Jean's cell phone rang. Everyone in the room seemed startled; it was the first ringing cell phone we'd heard other than mine. And then it was comedy time, with Jean running around trying to find it, the rest of us trying to guess where the sound was coming from. And, of course, just as she retrieved the phone, it stopped ringing.

"It's probably Eddie," she said. "He'll call back."

And he did, later that night when we had started to drive north. Trina and I were in the front seat with Brad. Jean, Angelica, and

Bethany were in the back. My child was dozing, her knees bent, her head against my shoulder. If I closed my eyes I could pretend that *peace of mind* was the locomotive I was riding and I could ride that train all the way to a tranquil place. Or at least that was the way it seemed. But that was before I realized the tracks led to a swamp.

I turned around when Jean's cell phone rang and saw her head jerk forward. She said, "Hello, Eddie," and then was silent, as her lips began to quiver and her shoulders tensed. I could hear him through the phone, some of what he said. I heard the word *police* very clearly.

When she hung up, Jean repeated what her husband had told her. The police had come to their house earlier in the evening because a woman had reported what appeared to be the abduction of a young black woman by a white man, three white women, and a black woman in a vehicle with their license plate.

I waded into the swamp as the water covered first my ankles, then my knees, and kept on rising.

2 3

WE RETURNED TO PETE'S HOUSE — WE WERE LESS THAN HALF an hour away — hustled the girls back to the barracks, and left them with Pete. He didn't ask any questions, accepting Brad's "Something has come up" with a nod of his head.

Brad, Bethany, Jean, and I filed into the dining room and sat down at Pete and Cecilia's table. Jean searched all our faces. No one spoke for a moment.

The first thing out of Jean's mouth was surrender. "I think we should drive back to my house. Go to the police. Tell them it was all a mistake," she said. She was looking at Brad, speaking in a low voice.

Brad didn't respond. Jean started to repeat her words, and Brad gave her a look that told her that he was thinking. She stopped talking.

I glaced at Bethany, who was seated next to me. I could tell she wanted a cigarette. "Fuck that," she said. She stood up and began pacing. "I didn't come all this way to go to jail."

Brad ignored her. "The police are going to want to see Trina. She'll implicate everyone." His voice was low, so that we all had to lean forward to hear him.

"If we just tell the police that she was in the midst of an episode, they won't—" Jean said.

"Police don't care about episodes, Jean. They care about the law. Kidnapping sentences are harsh," Brad said.

"Brad—"

"I can't jeopardize the program."

Brad and Jean continued to whisper back and forth, a heated exchange of opinions, while Bethany and I listened. We could lie low at Pete's for a few more days, in hopes that everything would blow over, and then continue on our way. That was Brad thinking aloud. But that would mean explaining everything to Pete, making him an accessory. Technically, Pete already was part of the crime by virtue of being in the program, Jean said. But staying in his house would just get him in deeper, Brad said carefully, as he looked over his shoulder at Bethany and me.

It was one thing to break the law in theory, to feel that the justness of your cause warranted a risk, to view punishment as a remote possibility; it was quite another to sniff the scent of the consequences in the wind that touched my face. That odor filled my nostrils, making it difficult to breathe.

"Look," I said. "I don't know about the rest of you, but this is more than I bargained for. Since my child is the cause of the problem, maybe we should leave."

Brad shook his head, as though that simple gesture were enough to override my decision. "Not the answer, Keri. In her current state, Trina is likely to expose us."

"Who is she going to tell? What could she say? She doesn't know who you are or where she is."

Brad shook his head. "You're not prepared to deal with Trina. She won't be admitted to a hospital. She's not yet committed to taking her medication. You'd be right back where you started."

I could feel myself wavering.

"We need to keep going," Bethany said. "They're small-town cops. How hard are they going to press? I mean, hello, how many real crimes involving dead bodies don't get solved?" When Brad didn't respond, her voice rose. "They're fucking small-town cops, not rocket scientists."

Brad looked away from Bethany and me and kept on brainstorming, as though we'd never spoken. Jean stayed quiet. We could drive to the next stop, park Jean's car, rent another one, and deal with the police when everything was over, he said. Maybe even take Trina back there once she had enough medication in her system to say what was in her best interests. And ours. But there was no guaranteeing that the police would wait patiently for us to volunteer an explanation.

Jean reiterated her original suggestion. She sang her one note in a higher key, this time a shrill soprano. If we went home and faced the music, the police wouldn't believe Trina no matter what she said. Any claims she made would sound preposterous. All they had to do was call some of the hospitals in LA and have them send the records, and it would be clear that Trina had a mental illness, which made everything she said suspect.

The hospitals wouldn't release the records, Brad countered, and if they didn't, what proof did we have that Trina had bipolar disorder?

Anyone could see that Trina had problems, Jean said. Her voice had climbed to a squeaky register, Minnie Riperton notes, only flat. Her hands flailed uncontrollably. Jean's distressed face revealed a woman who was easily browbeaten. At the moment, she was more scared child than Earth Mother, more frantic woman than New Age spiritualist. There was no wisdom in her eyes, just fear. Of the four husbands, my guess was that at least two of them had knocked the shit out of her on a regular basis and she'd gone back for more. Why had I listened to her? Why had I placed my future in her trembling hands?

I could hear the panic in their voices. It grew louder and louder, as did my own doubts. They didn't possess magic—or even answers. Nobody had ever sicced the dogs on them before, and for all their secrecy, their first-names-only and late-night cruising, they were unprepared. And now we were bound together by the same shackles, tracked by the same hounds.

If anything happens to me, Trina will be lost.

"I'm leaving," I said, pushing back my chair. "If you won't take me to rent a car, I'll call a cab."

"With no money?" Brad said.

It was true: Brad had my wallet. It only occurred to me now that one of the reasons Brad had confiscated it was for an occasion such as this.

"We're not going to force you to stay," Jean said, "but we think it's in Trina's best interest and yours if you do. You've come so far. Really, this is no more than another challenge. Honey, if you weren't here, your challenges would be far more perilous. Think about the reason you called us."

"What did Eddie tell the police, Jean?" I asked.

She looked at Brad before she answered.

"He told them that the woman was mistaken: No abduction had taken place, and the people the woman saw—us—were all going on a trip together, on a retreat. He told them Trina was probably just playing around."

"How did the police respond?"

Jean glanced at Brad again. "They said they had thought of that, but the woman was certain the girl was in serious danger."

Jean sounded defensive to me. "What else did they say?" I asked.

"They kept asking questions," Jean said.

"What kind of questions?"

"About the car. Who was driving." She shifted a little; the motion caused small animal noises to escape from her seat. "They wanted to know where *I* was."

"Where *you* were?" I asked.

She opened her mouth and then put her open palm over it.

"Do they know you?"

Something about the way Jean slumped against her chair told me there was more.

"Do they know you, Jean?"

Brad looked at her. Jean's hand came down. Her eyes were nearly closed.

"Oh, Jesus!" she said. We waited. "They've been to the house before."

Of course they had. "Because of your son," I said.

Now her eyes were completely shut, as though she didn't want to see the words she spoke. "No, not because of my son—at least, not recently. Because "

"Jean," Brad said.

It was generic caution, a yellow light flashing: Careful, careful, don't tell too much.

The old rules didn't apply. Jean sped right through. "Three years ago I got arrested for attempted assault. Eddie was seeing someone, a younger woman. I came back from a trip, and she was in my house. I punched her—well, him too, but she pressed charges. So—"

"Holy shit," Bethany said.

"So what happened?" I asked Jean. "You said she pressed charges."

"I plea-bargained. I got probation and community service."

"Are we the community service?" Bethany asked. She hooted, her laughter a sudden burst of noise, like a shot in the night.

"You never told me," Brad said. His tone was flat and empty, somewhere between rage and resignation. His incredulity was palpable. So was mine. How could he not know something so essential?

"They may come after us," I said. It was what we all were thinking. Might as well say it.

"I didn't think that . . ."

Jean's voice trailed off as Brad stood up. We all watched as he left the room.

"Brad is upset. He's invested so much in this. It's his entire life. I mean, he really doesn't have much outside of—" She stopped abruptly and gave us a half smile. "This is bad," Jean said.

She looked so morose, so unlike her "everything's fine" self. I reached out and patted her back. "You and Eddie seem so happy," I said.

Jean looked surprised. "We are, sweetheart. We love each other. I forgave Eddie a long time ago. He hasn't had a bimbo in ages."

"Not every woman can say that, goddammit," Bethany said.

"I was married to an alcoholic who couldn't keep a job and liked to hit me. Next was an alpha male who spent all his time making money and was never around. And then there was Steve, who also had a handy right hook. Eddie and his girlfriends . . . I guess by that time I was tired and ready to make a deal. He was helping me with my son. I was willing to look the other way. But the woman I punched out was just a little too bold. She didn't play by the rules. Funny thing is, after I hit her, Eddie stopped cheating. It was as though he felt my punch, like it went right through that girl and knocked some sense into him."

"Why did you go after the woman when it was Eddie you wanted to hurt? Women always go against each other," Bethany said.

Jean looked surprised. "I didn't want to hurt Eddie. I wanted him to respect my feelings, and I wanted to scare her away. I knew exactly what I was doing. That punch wasn't the result of some heat-of-the-moment passion; it was planned. I was angry that night, but I was in full control. She was a crybaby. She started bawling and Eddie was trying to comfort her and keep me away, so she thought she'd won. But she'd lost. Eddie likes strong women."

"So you forgave him," I said.

"I needed him, and gradually I forgave him. He stopped cheating, and I began to love him again."

A simple formula. Forgiveness always sounds easy, even in the Bible. Especially in the Bible.

"I just didn't realize the repercussions for what we're trying to do," Jean said, her words bringing us back to the matter at hand, which had nothing to do with forgiveness.

The door opened, and Brad returned.

"We're going to stay here," he said. His voice said, I am the leader. It said, I am in control. But something was shifting.

""Tomorrow morning, I want you to take me to rent a car," I said.

"We're staying here," Brad repeated.

"Maybe you are, but *I'm* going home."

"Take your daughter back home, and we can't be responsible for what might happen. You knew the rules when you signed on, Keri. You knew what we're doing is illegal."

"I'm not going to surrender our lives to you, Brad. Listen to me: The police are looking for all of us. That's not some vague hypothetical thing. It doesn't make any sense to stay here. I'm leaving."

"Trina's not in any shape for you to travel alone with her."

"You let me worry about my child."

"The best thing for both our girls is to stay right here," Bethany said, looking at me. "We had a reason for doing this, and that hasn't changed."

"Maybe nothing's changed for you, but it has for me. What good am I to Trina if I'm in jail?"

"Oh, for God's sake," Bethany said. "Nobody's going to jail. Some hick cop gets a little overzealous, and all of a sudden you're talking about jail. That's crazy."

"Black people go to jail in this country for bullshit every day. So don't tell me nobody's going to jail. The way it works in America is, I'd be the only one to go."

They all got quiet for a moment.

"If it's possible for you to go to jail, it's just as possible for Trina to be jailed or killed because she's in the middle of an episode," Brad said. "Not too long ago, the LAPD shot a schizophrenic man right in your neighborhood. Killed him. Do you want that to happen to Trina?"

It took a minute before I realized he was talking about Crazy Man, another minute before I allowed myself to be persuaded by the logic of what Brad was saying. "Never run my train off de track, and I ain't never lost a passenger." That was Harriet Tubman's claim to fame. She was always in charge. My conductor wasn't prepared; his train was in danger of derailment. The North Star couldn't guide him. How could I let him lead me? But what choice did I have?

"Let's just get the fuck out of here," Bethany said. "You're coming, right?"

I sighed, then nodded slowly.

Bethany turned to Brad. "Then we should go now. Let's stick to the plan."

As we walked to the car, Trina was alert and perceptive beside me. She knew that something was up. I could tell by the focus in her eyes, the arch of her pliant back. My child glanced at our faces, saw the tension there, knew things had changed, and sensed an opportunity.

"Will I be out of here in time to go to school?" she asked me. Her tone was conversational and casual.

"I don't know."

"Wherever you were going to take me, you don't have to anymore. I just want to go back home. I'll stay on the meds and go to school. Why are you trusting these strangers? It's not necessary. I'm already better. My good judgment is back."

Trina's clear voice with its reasonable tone was seductive, particularly given the changed circumstances. She wouldn't try to run away again. She'd take her meds and never cheek them. She kept talking, her voice a long-playing CD that soothed and lulled, as the words kept coming without a break in sentences that rolled from one to another without pause. I listened without being persuaded. Mania is a spinning top. Sometimes it looks as though it has run down, but just a little wind can get it going again.

24

THERE WAS NOTHING ON THE HIGHWAY BUT LONG-DISTANCE haulers, rushing by with a *whoosh* of air, oil drips, and prodigious honks. Brad kept to a moderate speed. Not too slow. Not too fast. Not too noticeable.

If I had to put a tag on the mood in the car, it would be regretful. The station wagon was full of unspoken woulda-shoulda-coulda's, sentiments that don't travel well on a mission. Jean was close to tears, but she kept them in; I'll give her that. Brad was stoic and stern, a displaced captain who might have been scheming for a comeback. Only Trina was upbeat, chattering into the night to no one in particular, jumping from thought to thought, each sentence a trapeze she could swing on to the next one. Flying high. One sleepless night, one missed pill, one glass of wine, one joint, one hit of crack or meth or Ecstasy, or one false move could take her back over the edge.

Brad took a dark road. Jean leaned over the seat, retrieved a battered map from the glove compartment, and began navigating. Rather, she attempted to navigate. When we passed the same apple orchard twice in an hour, we were officially lost. Bethany didn't venture an opinion, but Jean, Brad, and I whispered back and forth, hissing and spitting through our teeth until we veered onto a two-lane highway that was a little more traveled.

"I have to go to the bathroom," Trina said. She'd been napping, and now she yawned and stretched.

"I have to go too," Angelica said.

Angelica had been quiet for so long that the sound of her voice startled me. The fact that she could string two coherent sentences together at times and say something absolutely normal struck me as an incongruity of the highest order. After living with her for more than two weeks of baring her breasts, slicing her legs, and talking to invisible people, I had lost sight of her capabilities. Maybe her medication had started working also. I'd been so absorbed with my own child that I hadn't paid attention to Angelica. But now as I looked at her, I could see that her face was fuller, her skin smoother. The hair that had seemed so stringy before was softer looking. The most recent cuts on her legs had already started to form scabs. When she saw me staring at her, Angelica smiled.

"We'll have to find a gas station," I said.

Brad made a little noise in his throat, a slight clenching motion with his hands, his silent no. I understood his apprehension. Anything could happen in a public place. But my bladder was calling, and the thought of three women peeing in the bushes was depressing.

The sun was coming up. An old man in a pickup directed us to a convenience store attached to a gas station. We followed him to a narrow road and beeped our thanks. A mile later, we pulled in and filled up. Brad, Bethany, and Angelica got out first. Ten minutes later, when they returned, a grim-faced Brad motioned that it was Trina's and my turn. We were halfway between our car and the store when the police drove up. There were two cops, a man and a woman. Behind them, separated by a wire barrier, was a huge German shepherd. The woman eyed us as we walked past the car. I smiled; she didn't. The dog began barking when I passed, as though my scent had indicated that I was prey.

I glanced back at the Volvo. Jean's neck was craned toward the police. She was rubbing her pointer finger across her top lip, back and forth, back and forth.

Brad waited outside while Trina and I went into the bathroom. On our way out, he bought some snacks. As we were all walking toward the door together, the cops were coming in, each wearing a holstered gun Brad and I inhaled at the same time. My breath was nose-stinging sharp. I tried not to look at Trina, who was between us.

From the car, the dog was still barking, the sound louder and angrier than before.

"Wonder what's wrong with him," the man said.

"Maybe he's hungry," Trina said. She stood still and smiled at the police.

The police looked at Trina and then at each other.

"Did you feed him?" the woman asked.

"Yeah, I fed him," the man said.

"Did you feed him poison?" Trina asked. "They try to poison me all the time."

The barking was deafening. For a moment that was all I heard.

"Do you want a soda, honey?" I took Trina's hand and led her to the refrigerated section. When I looked back at the cops, they were staring at us.

As Brad drove off, the police were coming out. Nobody said a word for five miles, except for Trina, who kept repeating that the police were trying to poison the dog.

"They're not trying to kill the dog," Angelica said. "They need the dog."

I thought about group, visualized Mattie, Milton, Gloria, and me siting together, listening to a speaker, some expert who had information on the latest medication, the latest study on schizophrenia, depression, or bipolar disorder. For a moment, I longed to be back in that cocoon, telling the others about Trina's bout of paranoia, hearing their voices saying, "Yes, yes, that's just the way it is."

Barking. I heard barking. Jean turned around before Bethany and I did. Right behind us was the police car. We were on a two-lane highway that served as a bypass for an adjacent town. Early-morning traffic consisted of a perfect flow of cars zipping by, the drivers on their way to work, maybe dropping kids off at school. Nowhere in LA did cars move in this unimpeded way.

"How far from here to where we're going?" I asked.

"I'm not sure," Brad said.

I peered into the mirror again. The police car was moving up, cross-

ing the solid yellow line. Why? I heard Jean cursing softly. She was looking out the back window.

"Would you mind not doing that?" Brad said to her.

"How far?" I repeated.

"I don't know," Brad said, his voice a loud snarl.

My heart was beating to the rhythm of fear. When I glanced into
the rearview mirror, the cop who was driving glared back at me with
eyes that didn't blink. His partner was on the phone. Was she talking
about us, checking the license plate of a ten-year-old Volvo, calling for
backup?

Behind me, Bethany drummed her fingers on the back of my head,
rest. When I turned my head, I could smell the nicotine on her fingertips. She gave me a nervous smile.

"Quit it," I said.

I didn't see the turnoff until the very last minute. An exit to the
unknown. A split-second choice: keep going or veer right to another
path.

"Turn, turn, turn!" I said.

Brad kept going straight. "No need to draw attention to ourselves,"
he said.

"Are we lost?" Trina asked.

Angelica began to laugh. Trina joined in. If I hadn't been so distracted, I would have realized it was a bad sign.

"No," Brad said, careering down what looked like the main drag of a
hardscrabble town.

"We're not lost," Angelica said. "We're escaping."

Behind me, Bethany's fingers were silent, her lips tightly bunched
in what looked like a knot.

In group, everyone would wait their turn to rise and recount the tra-
vails of coping with a mentally ill relative. At the end of the evening,
members would leave feeling supported, less isolated. Not hunted. Why
hadn't I made my peace with that? Why had I thought there was the possibility of a quicker fix?

Behind us, the police car made a hard right and disappeared. A hot
flash steamed my entire body. In a moment my forehead was dripping.
They could come back, of course. The cops could be waiting for us at
the next intersection. These roads were their domain, not ours. If they
wanted to find us, they could. We still needed to get rid of the Volvo.

The town faded away after less than a mile, as Jean tried to pinpoint our location on the map. The suburbs were a blink, a couple of housing tracts surrounded by farmland. We found ourselves on a thin ribbon of road, flanked by growing things. We sped along for a good ten or twelve miles, past fields of artichokes and garlic. The odor of the latter seeped through the closed windows, mixed in with the air-conditioning, chilling and assailing our sinuses.

"Pass the spaghetti," Trina said, looking at Angelica, who obliged her with a chuckle.

The next odor—the bracing, pungent scent of unwashed animal flesh and manure—overcame us several miles before we saw the source. "Yuck," Trina said, holding her nose. Cattle. Two hillsides full. The herd was settled, peaceful, content with just sitting and staring and mooing. Acres of dark-brown-and-white hides, legs folded beneath their massive bodies.

I was attacked by a bout of acute envy. Oh, to be able to rest on the side of a mountain, chew my cud, low a bit, and mind my own business. Wouldn't that be the bomb?

We could still smell the cattle for miles after we passed them. The scent was just beginning to grow faint when a red light on the dashboard started flickering on and then glowing steadily as the engine began sputtering and the wheels started to wobble. At the last minute, Brad managed to get the car on the right shoulder before it stopped.

"Are we out of gas?" Trina asked.

Not that simple. The tank was three quarters full. When Brad tried to start the car, it wouldn't even turn over.

All the women looked at him, as though an auto mechanic's skill is an automatic outgrowth of testosterone. I sure as hell didn't know a fan belt from a transmission. When Clyde and I were together, if anything broke I always expected him to fix it. But neither one of us could fix broken things. To his credit, or maybe because of masculine conditioning or pride, Brad went outside, lifted the hood, and poked around inside. He returned to the car within five minutes, *clueless* stamped over his face.

"Can we walk back and see the cows?" Trina asked.

"No," I said.

"It's not that far."

"No!" This time a shout. I turned to Brad. "We can't just sit here."

Brad didn't respond, which infuriated me. I began dialing my auto club on my cell phone.

"Maybe you'd better wait," Bethany said. She put her hand on my hand. I snatched mine away.

"I'm calling the auto club, and I'm not waiting."

"Let's step outside," Brad said.

We walked about twenty feet from the car in silence.

"Why are you acting like such an asshole?" Bethany asked, when we stopped.

I glared at her. "Maybe I'm tired of being with people who don't know what the hell they're doing."

"Wait a minute," Brad said.

"You wait a minute. How could you not know that one of your people had been arrested? You sure as hell asked *me* that. Do I look like someone who has a record?"

"There was nothing about you that—" His face turned red. "Look, we slipped up. I admit it."

"Damn right you slipped up. And my child and I are in jeopardy because of it."

"We're all in jeopardy," Bethany said, "not just you and your precious perfect child."

"What's that supposed to mean?"

"It means I see the way you look at my daughter."

I was quiet for a while. "Look, I just want to get out of here," I said finally.

"If you give me a chance to think, I'll call someone in the program," Brad said. "That's better than risking exposure with outsiders."

"All right." I glanced at Bethany, then turned back to Brad. "I'd like to speak with Bethany alone for a few minutes." Brad walked back to the car. "Listen," I said, "I'm sorry if I hurt your feelings."

"My feelings? Fuck my feelings. Don't you dare write off my kid."

"Bethany—"

"I'm not here because I want her to get a degree from Brown and meet the perfect young man. I want to keep her alive. That may not be enough for you, but it's enough for me."

"Bethany—"

"You should try to see the God in her."

The religious reference took me by surprise. Bethany had never struck me as someone who believed in any power other than her own indomitable will. "All right. I hear you," I said. But really, I didn't.

Trina was begging to take a walk when we got back. She wanted to stretch her legs, smoke a cigarette.

"No," Brad said. "Nobody gets out."

"I'm not going to run away," Trina said, lighting her cigarette. "I just want to walk back and forth a little bit."

"I don't want you going anywhere," he said.

"Just over to that bush," she said, pointing to some low shrubbery about twenty feet away.

"Okay. Just to the bush. I'll walk with you," Brad said.

"No. Just my mommy."

Brad got out and leaned against the door of the car, watching us.

We marched away, Trina puffing as I dodged her smoke.

"Does Daddy know where I am?" she asked.

I didn't answer.

"He'll be mad."

"Trina—"

"When are you going to kill me?"

Good ol' paranoia, banished but not gone.

"I'm not going to kill you, Trina. I love you."

She ignored my sentiment, the logic. "Are you going to let them kill me?"

"No."

"You've been trying to have me killed for so long."

"Trina, why would you say such a thing?"

"Because it's true." She stopped walking, then moved forward, pushing her face closer to mine. Behind her back, Trina flexed her fingers; the knuckles cracked like tiny guns.

It came back to me, the way the group had taught me to respond to Trina when she was manic. An expert from USC had facilitated a session on communication. I summoned his words, played them back in my mind. *Use sentences that begin with I, so that you own your feelings. Agree with her.*

"I can understand why you feel that way."

The words didn't stop her, but she hesitated.

A phone rang; the noise was faraway and tinny. I patted my pockets, then began moving toward the sound in the car. "Come on," I said, taking Trina's hand, pulling her along. "That's my phone."

She wouldn't move.

I saw Brad coming toward us.

"Trina—"

"Are they coming to kill me? Are the killers calling you?"

"I can understand why you feel that way."

"My daddy will save me," she said, falling in step with me.

Right.

By the time we were sitting in the car and I was fumbling through my bag, the telephone had stopped ringing. The numbers flashing belonged to the shop. It seemed so far away: Dolce and Gabani, Armani, DKNY. Another planet. I checked for other messages. Clyde's was a terse two-seconds-to-air time reminder: "Call me." Orlando's was a performance piece: "Hey, baby. I miss you. Hope you're relaxing and clearing your mind. The play is looking good, at least I am. We're in previews this week. I hope you're back for the opening. The kids are all right. Did I tell you that I miss you, baby? Call me."

Me and my men.

I put the telephone back in my purse. Trina was singing a slow hip-hop jam; I heard Angelica joining in. Beside me, Jean tugged at her thinning hair. Above her upper lip were tiny lines I hadn't noticed before. When the tow truck pulled up behind us, we all jumped at the same time. That is, the mothers and the wardens jumped. The daughters were still, even as they harmonized. Their eyes weren't turned toward the road but toward each other.

25

THERE WAS NO FARMHOUSE THIS TIME. NO GIANT SUN-flowers or almond trees. During the trip, I had gotten used to California agriculture and perhaps a little too dependent on the peacefulness of nature. This last stop was on a tree-lined street with houses flanking both sides of the one we entered, a house that smelled of chimney smoke, laundry detergent, and mingled perfumes. This was no isolated retreat but a suburb south of Sacramento. The street thrummed with activity. There were cars in driveways and people coming in and out. Bicyclers, tricyclers, and a trio of skaters vied for space. It didn't seem a good place to be underground.

The house was an old-fashioned ranch, spread over at least half the parcel of land it sat on. It was cheerful; the wood shingles were a freshly painted white. The lawn that surrounded the house was well tended, a bright emerald green. A brilliant burst of roses, azaleas, hydrangeas, and geraniums bordered the walk and the front.

We drove straight into the attached garage. Behind us the automatic door came down with a heavy thud. The pristine exterior belied the helter-skelter look of the interior. From the garage we followed our new leader, Margaret, to a huge wreck of a kitchen. An open loaf of bread and uncovered jars of peanut butter and jelly were on a counter filled with crumbs, balled-up napkins, an empty milk container, and several used glasses. The knife that had slathered the sandwich makings was stuck in the jar of peanut butter. On the stove was a large pot filled with very soft pasta and a sauce that looked like the inside of a vacuum bag plus cheese. *Fettucine I'mafraidof.* The sink was filled with dirty dishes, and an empty cereal box was poking out of a trash can beneath a lid that wouldn't close. We could hear doors slamming, televisions and CD players blaring throughout the house, and what sounded like several arguments going on at once. Young voices called out good-naturedly and irritably for a comb, a blouse, permission, a ride to the mall.

"I have a feeling we're not in Kansas anymore," Bethany said as we got out of the car. She wasn't looking at me.

"Click your heels three times, Mom," Angelica said. She had been walking ahead of Bethany, and she turned her head and laughed. Bethany and I did too. I was as shocked as I was tickled. Who knew that inside Angelica's scrambled brain was a working sense of humor?

"Six," Margaret said when I asked her exactly how many children she had. "Four are teenagers, two in their twenties."

By that time, we'd met her brood. They'd solemnly shaken our hands when Margaret summoned them to the kitchen, where we were assembled. It was Margaret who'd led the tow truck to us and who had collected the bedraggled wayfarers in her van. She was an overweight whirlwind who could house a small child in the crevice between her breasts. She had a head full of graying curls and a mouth that was usually open as she yelled orders to her children. Margaret's volume was always turned way up; when she spoke to me the first time, I winced and stepped back. Her husband was working, she explained. Their reason for involvement was her oldest child, the one whose thoughts matched the speed of light.

"Oh, goodness. I knew for a long time that something wasn't right. A mother knows," she said, clearing the table after lunch, nodding toward Bethany and me as we sat there. The girls were getting their meds from Brad and Jean. Bethany sipped coffee, and I drank tea. Margaret had refused our help, telling us to relax. Watching her, I could tell that she wasn't much of a housekeeper, or at least whatever inclination she had for neatness was no match for the chaos-creating inventiveness of her children. Just the sight of her kitchen counter, piled high with dishes and saucers, cups and silverware, would exhaust most people. Margaret halfheartedly rinsed a few plates and loaded them into the dishwasher, wiped the counters, and poured herself a cup of coffee from an electric percolator near her stove.

"I surrender," she said. "Oh, goodness. What a mess. The cleaning lady comes Monday, thank God." She slumped into the chair next to mine. "How are you two doing?"

"I'm okay," I said.

Bethany didn't say anything. She had her eyes closed, and her chin was resting on her chest.

"Bummer about the car."

"Yeah," I said.

"So, what are your kids' diagnoses?"

"Bipolar disorder," I said.

Bethany didn't answer.

"What fun!" Margaret said. "My son has schizophrenia. You think it's wild in here now? When Conrad was at home, there was nothing but chaos."

"Where is he?"

"In rehab. He's been there for about five months. He just wanted to try marijuana once more for old time's sake. Only, of course, that led to being high for months, getting off his meds, and, in general, being an asshole."

Bethany's head sank lower.

"Didn't he do the program?" I asked.

"About eight years ago. We had seven good years. But even this last year was nowhere near as bad as it was before."

"When is he coming home?"

"I don't know. He's got some work to do."

We nodded at each other, those nods a shortcut language that circumvented conventional get-acquainted chitchat. Not necessary in our world.

It occurred to me that I hadn't spoken to Frances in a few days. After a while I excused myself and stepped into the garage, took out my cell phone, and dialed the store. A woman answered the phone; it took me a moment to recognize Adriana's voice. Every word she spoke was too slow. If her voice had been the sky, it would have been hazy.

"What's wrong with you?" I asked.

There was a long pause. "Nothing."

"You sound so strange."

"There's nothing wrong."

"Is school okay?"

"Yeah."

I didn't trust a word she said, but Frances was at lunch, so there was no way to find out what was really going on. I didn't want to accuse her of anything, but she sounded high. And lost. But Frances wouldn't have left her in charge if she thought something was wrong. So then I didn't trust my own judgment.

"Orlando's son stopped by this morning. He was looking for you."

"PJ?"

"Yeah."

"Did he say what he wanted?"

"Just you." She laughed a little. "We're all lost without you, Keri."

"Adriana, you're not lost." I waited, thinking she was taking her time to respond, but she never said anything. "Tell Frances to call me when she comes back."

I returned to the kitchen. Bethany and Margaret were still sitting there, and I joined them at the table. Bethany wasn't saying much. Behind us in the family room, Britney Spears was crooning on MTV, her voice loud to match the din that surrounded it. Teenagers, a horde of them, were lying on a sofa, chairs, and the floor, shouting and hooting at the screen. As I glanced at the gathering in the room, I saw Trina and Angelica on the sofa with Margaret's children and their friends. Brad and Jean stood quietly on different sides of the room in the back.

"They're okay," Margaret said; I could tell that she was saying those words for herself. "We weren't expecting anybody from the program. When Brad called, everything was so rushed. I forgot to tell my kids not to have anybody over. They're okay."

It looked okay. There were at least twenty young people crowded around the large-screen television, so many that Trina blended in. They were mostly white, a few Latinas, and one black boy. No one seemed to be paying particular attention to her. I heard a noise as two couples danced. Three big empty pizza boxes were on the floor. Crumpled microwave popcorn bags were balled up on the coffee table.

"I know," Margaret said with a sigh, "raised by wolves, the entire pack. Clean up!"

"Mom!" three voices exclaimed. Slowly, legs began to unfold. Boxes, bags, soda cans, and balled-up napkins disappeared. The teens marched into the kitchen with their plates and plastic wear.

"Carl, didn't I tell you to empty this trash?" Margaret called.

The work went very quickly, actually. Trina was intrigued. She cleaned up with the rest. A boy with blond hair took her plate into the kitchen and smiled at her. She smiled back.

"Carl and Chelsea, when that game is over I want you two to clean this kitchen."

Squeals of protest, followed by grunts of acquiescence. Trina's neck swiveled; her eyes glinted. She was fascinated by this domestic show. She'd always hated being an only child, always longed for a big, messy family to lose herself in. Her yearning was an echo from my own soul. Trina's childhood had been populated with imaginary friends. Now her eyes were feasting on the vibrant young people surrounding her as if they were her dreamscape come to life. All those bright faces, smiles, laughter. Some people take this for granted, I thought.

"Do you and your girls swim?" Margaret asked Bethany and me.

"I didn't bring a suit," Bethany said.

"Don't worry about that," Margaret said. She disappeared for a moment and emerged with a cardboard box filled with bathing suits. "Take one," she said. "Call your girls."

Angelica chose a two-piece green and Trina picked out a black one-piece suit. They went to the bathroom one at a time to try them on. Trina came out with a long face.

"Do I look fat?" she asked, standing in the hallway. I could see Brad watching me from the family room.

She looked fine. "No," I said.

"You're just saying that so you can look better than me. You *want* me to be fat."

"Trina, you look very slim. Ask someone else. Would you believe Jean or Bethany?"

"No. You told them to lie."

There it was again, the paranoia, the irritability, telltale signs that all the meds weren't in her system. Maybe her life would always be a seesaw. Maybe I'd look back on this exchange as a high mark. I sighed. "Trina, I packed you some shorts. Do you want to swim in your shorts?"

"No, I don't want to wear any fucking shorts in a swimming pool, so I can look like an asshole and you can look like a beauty queen."

Brad was beside me in five seconds. He strode over to her. "Trina, I'd like you to calm down."

She turned to me. "Why does he get to tell me what to do?"

"Trina—" Brad said.

"You think you're such a fucking hero. You're not saving me, I'm saving you. If you didn't have me, you'd feel like you're nothing."

"Trina!" I said.

She stood there in her little borrowed bathing suit, her shoulders heaving up and down, her face full of Molotov-cocktail rage, her fists clenched for battle. I stepped back.

Jean appeared. "Trina, sweetie pie, are you ready for the water?"

Abracadabra! Peace. Five minutes later, Jean had coaxed her into the pool, and her murderous intent washed away.

"It's going to be like this, up and down, for a very long time. Get into the flow of it," Brad said.

But I was only half listening. I was thinking about what Trina had said, that he needed her. Who was Brad without the program to be commander of?

We went out back, where there was a patio, a pool, and a smaller hot tub, that staple of good California living. The scent of sunscreen hovered over us. Margaret's children and their friends were already in the water. Bethany immediately found a chaise longue to lie on. I jumped into the pool. Floating in the deep end, I closed my eyes and let the water carry me. Across from me, teenagers paddled and splashed and screamed and dived. They talked about their school and their teams, their teachers and their friends. They laughed and teased and dunked one another. Angelica and Trina hung back just outside their circle at first, then moved toward them slowly. I marveled at the ripples they created. I didn't crave ripples. What I wanted was a surface smooth as glass, at least for a moment.

Bethany was still on the chaise longue when I got out of the water. It was hot, and the cool water felt good dripping off my back. Bethany's eyes were closed, her lips were pressed together; she seemed tense.

"Bethany, what's wrong?"

"Migraine," she said.

"You take something for it?"

She nodded. "It's not working."

I took her hand in mine and pressed with my fingers on the area of her palm between her thumb and forefinger. I held it down for about two minutes. "Is the pain diminishing?"

"Yes." She sat up, looking at me with interest.

I kept pressing her palm and began stroking her arm.

"It's going away. Thank you. I can think again. Sometimes they get so bad I want to cut my head off. Where did you learn how to do that?"

"When I attended massage therapy school, they taught us acupressure points."

Bethany looked surprised. "You're a masseuse? Is that what you did before you opened the store?"

"I still do it. How long have you been having migraines?"

"Since Angelica's been sick. She's twenty-six. I've had them for about nine years, on and off. When she gets better, they go away. How's that for a fucking metaphor?" She paused. "If she kills me—I mean, if I get sick from the stress and everything—who'll take care of her?" She paused for a moment to let the anger flow through her. "They can always walk away, can't they?"

"Your husband didn't walk away; he died."

"That was just death imitating life. He never really admitted that there was anything wrong with Angelica. He found a way to ignore what he didn't want to see or feel. Worked twelve hours a day. Played golf all weekend. And of course, he had his diversions. He left me alone with 'the problem,' like it was woman's work. I hated him for that."

"Some guys can handle it, and some guys can't," I said. "My boyfriend's been a rock since the beginning. My husband—my ex-husband—I think he's on the verge of letting go of his denial."

I'd never thought about Clyde as evolving, but now that the words were out of my mouth I realized that his evolution was beginning. For years, I'd not only been waiting for Clyde to change, I'd been expecting it, like a package that someone swore was in the mail.

"If you have a boyfriend who supports you, I'd stick with him," Bethany said.

I smiled, thinking about Orlando.

"I can tell you like him," Bethany said.

"I do, but he's got other issues," I said, with a laugh. "He's an actor who used to star in a popular show about ten years ago, and now he has problems getting hired. He's got an ex-wife from hell—well, actually, she's calmed down a little. His younger son is having problems. And—"

"And with all that, he still supports you? Maybe *you* have the issues."

I let that sink in.

"You're lucky," Bethany said. "If this doesn't work, I'll have to walk away. And then what will happen? She'll become homeless. I'll have to accept that, right? I'll have to accept the fact that I gave birth to the crazy lady and people will laugh at her and exploit her and be afraid of her and not want to be around her. Because if I don't walk away, she'll end up killing me. So the program has to work, because this is my last go-round. After this, I give up."

I sat still, listening to Bethany but not believing that she'd give up on Angelica under any circumstances. She would stagger on, dragging her child and all the fractured pieces of herself behind her. I gave her hand a squeeze. I am lucky, I thought.

"You don't think I could walk away, do you?"

"No," I said.

"But don't we have to, at some point? I mean, are we supposed to take care of them for the rest of their lives? Do we owe them that?"

"Oh, God, Bethany. I don't want to think about it. Let's just get through this."

We both looked up when we heard the shouting. A rousing game of swimming pool dodgeball was under way. Angelica and Trina darted back and forth with the other swimmers. Margaret's boys were not only discreet, they got A+ in security. They flanked Trina and Angelica while they played the game and later when they were swimming and floating. The girls had only to move inches from the pool, and they were instantly trailed. But Angelica and Trina didn't try to go anywhere. They played in the water as long as we let them, and after they got out they collapsed on the plastic chairs, stretching their legs out in front of them, and devoured the potato chips that Margaret set out. I turned my head. When I looked back, Trina was draining a can of Coke.

When I told Brad about Trina's caffeine jolt, he looked disturbed. "Obviously every house isn't as strict as Jean's about nutrition and stimulants. This was an emergency situation. We won't be staying here long, tonight or tomorrow morning at the latest. I'm sure we'll have the car by then."

AS IT TURNED OUT, THE CAR WASN'T READY IN THE MORNing. The Volvo had been towed to a garage in town. It was late that afternoon before Brad received a phone call from the mechanic.

"Transmission," he said, and even I recognized that as bad news when I heard it. Two or three days would be needed to repair it.

"You can stay here, no problem," Margaret said.

"You ever meet anybody so goddamn cheerful in all your life?" Bethany asked me later, when we were sitting alone on the back patio. The girls were with Brad and Jean, doing yoga. "I mean, if six people, two of them mentally ill, came to my house unexpectedly, I'd be giving them the number for Motel Six. I don't know why anybody would sign up for this. Not that I'm not grateful."

"I get the impression that the program recruits from within. So don't be surprised if we're asked to take in people after the girls are better," I said.

After the girls are better. What a beacon those words were. Our world would expand. We would be givers. We could be human again.

Angelica and Trina returned from yoga and shared a cigarette break. They wandered through the yard and chose a spot where they could sit near each other. They appeared to be having a conversation and laughed at times. They were discovering each other, maybe becoming friends. Trina hadn't made a friend in a long time, and she'd lost most of her old ones.

"Wouldn't that be funny," Bethany said when I mentioned it.

There were no barracks this time. That first night, Bethany, Angelica, and Jean were given a room right next to the one I shared with Trina and Brad. Trina didn't protest Brad's presence, although she asked to sleep next to me. Brad put her in the middle of the three single beds. When he went into the bathroom, I could hear Trina mumbling to herself. "Are you talking to me?" I asked.

"I'm saying my prayers."

· · ·

SINCE MARGARET'S HOUSE WASN'T IN THE HEALTH BAR industry, Jean gathered the girls together for what she termed a "group session" right before dinner. Jean, who'd been vacillating between a mental stupor and fits of self-flagellation since Eddie's call, appeared to rally. Never mind that Angelica was more likely to retreat into her shell of self-damage and mayhem than she was to be introspective, group was on the agenda, so group it was. They went into a room in the back of the house, closed the door, and didn't come out for two hours.

After dinner, the doorbell began ringing. "Summer school buddies," Margaret dubbed the friends of her children who sought them out, carrying laptops and books as they trailed through the hall that led to the teenagers' bedrooms.

Trina and Angelica sat on the sofa, watching a movie and talking. I could see them from where I sat in the kitchen. Margaret's daughter came to her, carrying her math book. Margaret shooed her away.

"Do you need help?" I heard Trina ask. The girl showed her the work. "I love geometry. This is how you do it." She explained the steps of the problem to Margaret's daughter and patiently answered her questions. It was an ordinary interaction, lasting no more than ten minutes, but it lifted me through the roof.

Almost as soon as Trina had finished working on the problem, a group of young people trailed into the family room, plopped down on the sofa, chairs, and floor, and began watching television. Trina and Angelica were part of the group. Margaret was passing them snacks and sodas when Jean rushed in, followed by Brad. There were Cokes on the tray. I meant to say something about that. Jean beckoned to me.

"We need to talk," she said.

"I'll watch the girls," Margaret said.

We went into the kitchen, where I could still see Trina.

"The police came back," Jean said.

Brad folded his arms across his chest, lowered his head a bit.

"What do you mean?" I asked.

"Eddie called me. The police just left our house. Somebody saw us with Trina."

"You mean the woman in the car?"

She shook her head. "No. When she was at our house. Somebody saw Trina and me the day we were walking. She started to run away, so I chased her and grabbed her arm. Somebody saw me pulling on her. I don't remember any cars, but I guess one must have passed us that I didn't notice."

"You didn't tell me about that," Brad said.

"It was over in three seconds. She didn't run that far. There was never any danger. It's happened before with other people. I've never told you about those times either."

"Well, you should have. Why did you take her to the road? It was too soon for that. You're the first stop, dammit," Brad said.

"I didn't mean—"

"What the hell are you talking about, you *didn't mean*? You've jeopardized everybody, the entire program. Jesus!"

Jean's mouth twitched. She looked down at her feet.

"What did you learn in training, huh? Keep away from people. It's like a commandment."

Her mouth twisted just a little, and then she was right in his face, snarling like a pit bull. "Don't you dare talk like that to me. I give up my time and take the same risks you do."

So that's how she was. She wore the calm Earth Mother brand well, but there in the dark she morphed into a spitfire right before my eyes.

"I have to go to the bathroom," I heard Trina say. I watched her walk down the hall.

"Look, the car is going to be ready tomorrow," Brad said, his voice lower, his tone softer. He looked at Jean. "We're about six hours from your house, six hours from the site. We'll drop off Trina and Angelica at the site and take the car back to your house. We'll see the police and explain what happened, leaving out a few details."

Jean didn't answer. Brad looked at me. "What do you think?"

"I don't know." The idea that the police were looking for us was one I still couldn't process.

"Tea? Coffee?" Margaret held up a cup. I looked into the family room and didn't see Trina or Angelica.

"Tea," I said.

"What do you want in it?"

"Sugar. I'll get it."

Minutes later, cup of tea in hand, I knocked on the bathroom door. No answer. Knocked again and went in. The bathroom was empty; the window was open.

"Trina! Trina!" As I called, I raced from room to room.

"What's the matter?" Margaret asked, coming out of the kitchen.

"I can't find Trina."

"Maybe she's with one of the kids."

Behind me I heard Bethany, calling Angelica.

We rushed from room to room. No Trina. No Angelica. I heard Margaret loudly asking her children if they'd seen the girls. Which of their friends had left?

Justin.

"Oh, goodness!" said Margaret.

Brad and Jean were waiting for us when we returned to the kitchen. One look at their faces told me both girls were gone. "It's that blond boy," Margaret said to Bethany and me. I remembered him.

I heard Margaret's children talking. I heard the word *stoner*.

Bethany grabbed my hand. The way she squeezed was like screaming.

My cell phone rang. It was Frances. "I've been calling and calling. What's wrong with your phone?" she asked.

As soon as I heard her voice, I started crying. She couldn't make out what I was saying.

"What's wrong?" she kept asking. "Where are you?"

I just cried some more until I could say good-bye and hang up.

Jean stayed behind in case, by some miracle, the girls returned. Bethany and I got in Margaret's SUV. Brad drove. Backing out of the driveway, he caught my eye in the rearview mirror, then looked away.

She'sgoneshe'sgoneshe'sgone. Same sinking feeling as that time at the flower market when she had wandered off while I was bargaining for birds-of-paradise. I looked at Bethany; she stared back at me. By now we should have been used to losing our children. But really, when does that time come?

2 6

THE BLOND BOY LIVED WAY PAST WHERE THE PRETTY
flowers grew. Even in the dark, I could see that the lawn in front of his
house was more dirt than grass, and what grass there was appeared half
dead. There were sheets at the windows, dingy and torn. Paint was peeling all around the sides of the house; the ledges of the windows were the
worst. The wood on the door was splintered; no one answered when we
rang the bell. So the four of us stood there, trying to come up with a
magic word.

Nobody really knew where to go next, but Brad pretended he did.
Around the corner. Around the next corner. To his right, his left. The
park, the 7-Eleven; *zoom, zoom, zoom,* as if speed meant being in
charge. That resolute chin looked as though it were made of chiseled
rock. Bethany and I sat in the back. She held her head. I kept pressing
down on the area above her thumb, but the acupressure wasn't working.
We drove to a mall, which by LA standards wasn't very large. The four of
us fanned out and did a thirty-minute search. Like a storm trooper, I
marched into and out of the hot girls' clothing stores that Trina favored
when she was manic. Saleswomen flinched when they saw me coming,
and shoppers stepped aside. Have you seen a girl, two girls, one is white

and the other is . . . about so tall and so big and very pretty and—No?
Sorry. I raced back to the car, trying to tell myself that Trina would be
waiting for me, because I needed something to keep my legs moving,
my heart pumping. But Trina wasn't there, and neither was Angelica.

Bethany was the last person to return; she was panting, her movements labored. She seemed to favor her left leg.

"You okay?" I asked her.

"Are you kidding?"

"Don't you fall apart on me," I said.

"We're going to find them," Brad said. "I've put out an alert. We
have other people in this area. It's not just us looking for her." His voice
was conversational, but the vein in his neck was throbbing. He was in
charge again.

"Well, then, find them," I said. "Find them before anything bad
happens. Find them so this will turn into an amusing little anecdote I
can tell at select cocktail parties. Okay? You're trained, aren't you?"

"This in no way reflects on the program," Brad said. "These things
happen. We're dealing with—"

"I know what we're dealing with, Brad."

"This place isn't that big, compared to LA," Margaret said. She
started going on and on about her son, how he used to run away when
his meds weren't right. Even the happy endings were irritating at this
point. I saw Bethany wincing.

"Margaret," I said, "your voice is too loud. Bethany has a migraine."

"Oh, goodness. Sorry. There's another place," Margaret went on,
her volume turned down, "where all the kids hang out. A hamburger
joint. Not far away. Well, not all the kids."

No, just the black kids with gangbanger and teenage-pregnancy
aspirations. A mile from the mall, we crossed tracks and landed on the
dark side of town. *Depressed area* didn't begin to describe the urban
blight that surrounded Woodie's Hamburgers, which appeared to be the
only survivor of an economic bomb that had blown up an entire block.
The buildings adjacent to Woodie's were boarded-up tragedies. Woodie's
exterior was none too prepossessing: The front was dirt-colored and
sprayed with graffiti, a crack ran from one end of a large picture window
to the other. The interior consisted of a scarred counter, a few booths,
and a couple of tables and chairs, some of them broken. There was a
greasy fry kitchen in full view of the clientele. Rap music blared, the

lyrics more profane than poetic. The young people who looked up when I walked in—and kept checking me out the entire time I stood there—may have been teenagers, but their souls were much older.

"Jesus," Bethany said, inhaling sharply. She was standing next to Brad, who was making his own quiet assessment.

I was about to return to the car in defeat when I heard the woman behind the counter.

"Margaret, you looking for your son?"

She was scraping well-done burgers from a grill and lowering a steel basket of French fries into scalding grease. The woman was large and moved slowly, and I could tell that none of the patrons would even think about giving her a hard time. Her quick glance sized me up efficiently.

"Charlene," Margaret said. "How are you?"

"I'm doing all right. How about you?"

"I'm good. No, not my son. We're looking for two young women."

"How's he doing?"

"Much better, thank you."

"They was in here."

Bethany clutched my hand.

"A white girl, a white boy, and a light skin-ded girl who favor that lady," she said, pointing to me, "came in here about thirty minutes ago. They left in a hurry."

"Did they happen to say where they were going?" I asked.

Charlene shook her head. "They was looking for something."

"Like what?" I asked.

"What do white boys come down here looking for?"

Our eyes met. "What were they looking for specifically?"

She turned around to check the food, then faced us. "They wanted some weed, mostly. The white girl wanted some meth." She looked at Margaret. "They kids like your son?"

"Our children have mental illnesses too," I said.

"Had me an auntie like that. She was—uh, mentally ill." Charlene had a completely different accent for the words *mentally ill*: proper, refined, an educated woman's language. She was used to saying *crazy*.

"So, are you all like a club or something like that?" Charlene asked.

"No," I said.

I felt Bethany's body brushing against mine. "The white girl, how did she seem?"

"She wasn't talking much."

Margaret thanked Charlene. We headed toward the door.

"Chasing them down don't do no good. Just wear you out," Charlene said.

"I'm her mother," I said.

"Mamas wear out too."

"My son Conrad used to hang out at that place," Margaret said when we were back in the car. "He made all his weed connections there. I met Charlene when I used to go looking for him. When he moved up to meth, the dealers were on the white side of town. Equal opportunity, my dear," Margaret said.

"Every time Angelica seems to have kicked meth, it turns out she was only on vacation. It's a hard, hard drug," Bethany said.

Maybe I should have fallen on my knees right then and there and thanked God it was marijuana Trina was after and not something that would whiplash her and leave her reeling. But marijuana could do that to her. Marijuana and no meds equaled mania plus delusions plus paranoia. Speed and crack would have been worse, but a trip to hell is a trip to hell, no matter what's taking you there.

Brad, Bethany, and I agreed that it didn't make sense to drive back to Justin's house when he, Angelica, and Trina were either parked somewhere in his car smoking weed or else driving around looking for meth. But Margaret said we should go there and wait, in case they returned.

"They wouldn't smoke at his house, would they?" I asked.

"A lot goes on over there," Margaret said.

After Margaret gave us directions for getting to the bus station, the train station, and a couple of other weed-friendly places that the young local like-to-get-high people knew about, we dropped her off at Justin's house, where she'd volunteered to wait while we drove around. Our efforts proved futile. After about forty-five minutes, we returned. Margaret and Justin were standing on the walkway that led to the house.

I could tell that Justin was high. He wasn't cool enough to disguise his spacy expression and the teenybopper buzz that glazed his eyes.

"Where are our daughters?" I asked him.

"They, uh—I was gonna . . ." He looked from Bethany to me, back and forth, like the branch of a thin sapling being blown by the wind. His eyes settled on Bethany's. "Angelica hooked up with this dude at Woodie's. She left with him."

"Where did they go?" Bethany asked.

"I don't know. I don't know. The guy said he'd bring her right back, but we waited and—uh—"

"Did they go to get meth?"

"I don't know."

"Don't lie to me, you little shit," Bethany said. "She doesn't have any money for drugs. Do you know what that means?"

He stood there frozen.

"I could have you arrested for possession," she said.

"Take it easy," Brad said. He faced Justin. "Truth, dude." There was something threatening in Brad's tone. Justin didn't look him in his eyes.

"Yeah, they went to score some meth."

"Where?" Brad asked. He moved closer to Justin. Brad's chest seemed to have expanded.

"This dude they call Rocco has a place."

"Do you know where it is?"

"I can't—"

"You don't have to be involved. Just tell us where it is," Brad said.

"Did my daughter go with her?" I asked.

"She left."

"Where did she go?"

"When we were at Mrs. Schultz's house, she asked me if I had any chronic—uh, any marijuana. So I told her I didn't have any but I knew where we could go get some. And she said not to tell you, that we would be back before you noticed that we were gone. So—"

"Where is she now?"

"After we left Woodie's, we—uh, went to the park and . . ." He lifted his hands up, let them fall, scanned my face, and looked at Margaret. "I mean . . . I was bringing her back to your house. We were on our way." He glanced at me. "But we got to the red light and she jumped out of the car. I tried to find her but the light was still red, and by the time it turned green she was gone."

Gonegonegonegonegonegonegone.

I had my hands on him before I could draw my next breath. "Where did she go?"

"Keri." This from Brad. It took effort for him to loosen my grip on Justin's arm.

I let go of Justin, but not before I completely blew his high.

"Where did she go?"

"After the light changed, I drove around looking for her. I saw her get in a car with two dudes. I tried to chase them down, but they took off."

My knees buckled. I caught hold of Justin's shirt where it covered his belly. I held on, trying not to feel the net that was coming down over me, the rope growing tighter around my wrists. Angelica had warned me about the slave catchers. What she didn't know, what I should have realized, was that I'd never left the plantation.

2 7

I CALLED HOSPITALS FIRST, PSYCH WARDS. MARGARET KNEW the names of three, and then I had Justin go in his house and bring back a Yellow Pages. There were about sixteen hospitals in the area. None of them had Trina.

"I'll have to call the police," I said, leaning against the car.

"What are you going to say?" Brad asked.

"That my mentally ill child is missing. I am not going to mention the program."

I knew, of course, that there would be a waiting period. Twenty-four hours? Forty-eight hours? No. The magic seventy-two. Nothing would happen until time had passed. Time always had to pass.

I called anyway, and after they put me on hold the officer told me it was too soon for them to do anything.

Justin wanted to give us an address and some directions, and go back into his house to see if he could recapture the last vestiges of his high. Brad persuaded him that it might be better to show us the way. He was not a happy guide, nor, as it turned out, a good one. We drove north on the freeway for at least twenty minutes before he realized that we were going the wrong way; then we drove for forty-five minutes in the opposite direction. The exit we took led to an area that was rural and poor. The houses were spread out. There were no real streets. We passed several trailer parks before turning down a long unpaved road that led to a dilapidated small ranch sitting on several acres of land.

"That's it," Justin said. He looked as though he wanted to flee.

There were cars parked in front of the house on what would have been a lawn. An odd odor hung in the air, sharp and pungent. Something was cooking.

Brad parked about fifty yards away; then he got out and strode to the house. Even through the rolled-up windows, I could hear voices and laughter. Everyone got silent when Brad knocked. Two or three guys came to the door. I could hear Brad talking, explaining things in a forceful tone of voice. They closed the door in his face. A few minutes later, it opened.

We heard Angelica before we saw her. Her curses rent the still air surrounding us. When Brad came out of the house, he had his arm around her waist and was trying to hold her against his side. The guys stood at the door watching, not saying anything. Angelica's arms were flailing, and she attempted to kick him as he dragged her to the car. She was wearing jeans and a white shirt with most of the buttons undone. Bethany got out and ran toward them. Brad told her to go back, but she kept running toward them, yelling and screaming incoherently. She rushed past Brad and Angelica and raced up to the three men, who were watching. "What did you do to her?" she screamed over and over, until the men, who never answered, went inside.

When Bethany joined Brad and Angelica, she tried to grab her daughter by the shoulders, but Angelica shook her off. Then she tried to hit her. Brad had to hold Angelica with one hand and keep Bethany away with the other. Margaret and I tore out of the car and pulled her away. She tried to fight us too, but then she got very still and just stood where she was until she stopped weeping.

By the time Brad got Angelica seated in the back between Margaret and me, sweat was dripping off his forehead. Angelica was wild, more agitated than I'd ever seen her. She was muttering furiously to herself and didn't pay attention to any of us, except Bethany. She vented the last of her rage on her mother, who appeared to have slipped into catatonia, her face was so devoid of emotion. Angelica's curses and threats were wasted on her.

Brad went right to his glove compartment, retrieved his hypodermic, and gave her a shot of Haldol. After a while her curses became slurred and softer.

"Do you know where Trina went?" I asked.

I expected some version of speaking in tongues. Angelica hadn't said one coherent thing since she'd gotten into the car, but now she turned and spoke clearly. "She doesn't want you."

Margaret's house was quiet when we returned, but not for long. When Brad tried to get Angelica to take her regular medication, she spit it out and filled the small bedroom with a stream of curses that echoed throughout the house. Bethany trailed into and out of the room, pleading with her daughter to take the pills. Meth-enhanced psychosis was a powerful adversary.

Margaret began cooking, clattering pans and clanging utensils, which didn't completely shut out the din from Angelica's room. Bethany was smoking on the back patio. When I went out there, several butts were on the ground near her feet, and she was lighting another.

"They should be shot, those guys."

"Yeah."

"And they're supposed to be the fucking normal ones."

"Right."

"Like they couldn't tell that she had a problem. Fucking assholes." She took another drag from her cigarette and began muttering under her breath. "I guess I'll have to get her tested."

I didn't answer that one. I had no comfort to give Bethany, so I went back into the kitchen. Jean wandered in, took a look at me, and hovered. Margaret put a cup of tea in front of me. Maybe she thought it would make me feel better. I stood up.

"I need to make some calls," I said. Jean disappeared immediately and returned with Brad.

"I'd like to speak with you, Keri," he said.

"Okay."

"Regardless of what's happened, the confidentiality of the program must be upheld. The situation will be resolved. We'll find Trina. So, I don't want you to—"

"I have to call her father and tell him our child is missing."

"I just want to impress on you—"

"You don't need to impress a goddamn thing on me. You find my child."

"Keri, you—"

"Brad," Margaret said. He looked at her and then at me.

"The program is everything to him," Margaret said, as soon as he and Jean had left and it was just Margaret and me sitting at the table. "His wife left him less than a year ago. That was his second." She sighed and looked at me. "We'll find her. My son used to run away. . . ." Margaret knew I wasn't listening, but she kept talking anyway.

I left in the middle of her monologue. In the bedroom, I tried to collect myself, to practice saying, *Clyde, Trina is missing, and it's my fault.* The phone at Clyde's office rang seven times before his answering machine took the message, which I repeated for his home phone. His cell just rang and rang. My arms began to ache. *I can't lose both of them.*

Orlando answered his phone on the second ring. He said, "Hey, baby, you feeling better?" And he listened when I told him no, no, not better, and explained what had happened, not everything, not the part about the program, just the part where I admitted that Trina was missing.

"Don't panic, baby. You have your cell phone. Maybe she'll call you."

Maybe she'll call me. I thought, She's riding in a car with two strange men. And then I told him everything. While I was talking I could hear him saying *Listen to me, listen to me, listen, listen . . .* But I couldn't listen. I hadn't called to listen to him. I just wanted to hear my thoughts pitched against his voice. I just wanted to know he was there.

"Where are you? How long would it take me to get there?"

"Isn't opening night soon?"

"Tomorrow," he said. "I have an understudy."

"I don't even know where I am, Orlando. Somewhere outside of Sacramento. I don't know the address. I'll call you back as soon as we find Trina."

"No," he said. "Get the address and give it to me. I'll hold on. Go get the address."

I went inside the kitchen carrying the phone in one hand; with the other I looked in a pile that appeared to be mail but turned out to be school papers. In the family room, there was a stack of magazines on the coffee table. I began going through the pile. *Vogue.* Mrs. Margaret Schultz, 13899 Villalobos Road, Corinth, California.

"I'll be there in the morning," Orlando told me.

"All right," I said. "Thank you." I could feel myself breathing again and noticed a pinching sensation in my shoulders as they came down a little.

But I wanted Clyde.

After I hung up I thought about the night Ma Missy put my mother out, how she sat on the sofa in front of the picture window in the living room, smoked Salem cigarettes, one after another, and wailed as though something had been cut from her body. The next morning, she woke me up, took me to school, and went to work. We didn't see my mother for nearly a year. And except for that first night, I never heard her crying again.

I cried a lot. I got bad grades that year. I picked fights with my best friends, and mostly I lost. At night I dreamed of my mother, and during the day I cursed her name in little-girl language. A piece of the woman who had groaned me out into the world was better than an empty space at the table. I pushed people far away, to a place where they could never come back and hurt me. I told myself I would show her; she'd be sorry; I didn't need her at all. One night I slipped out of my grandmother's house and wandered through the streets in the dark. I was trying to find her, but I ended up losing myself. I fell asleep in a stranger's backyard; the police brought me home at three in the morning. One look at Ma Missy's shocked face, and I felt like a failure. No wonder, I told myself. No wonder she left me.

And now I knew that that had been the easy part of my life.

"She missed her eight o'clock," I said aloud to no one. The medication hour had come and gone. Trina wouldn't notice the time. She was high, she had missed her medication, and she was with strange men. Are you praying for me now, Mattie?

I put my phone away and went back into the kitchen, where Jean and Margaret were sitting. Angelica was still cursing and yelling from the room where Brad was watching her. I heard her say something about the FBI having her under surveillance.

"Oh, goodness. How come it's always the FBI and the CIA?" Margaret asked. She was opening what looked like an industrial-size can of ravioli and dumping it into a pot. "How about the SEC or the USDA?"

Jean glanced at her, a slight smile forming. "The NBA, the NFL."

We all began to giggle.

"Don King Productions is following me."

We went on and on, laughing hysterically as we listed more and more ridiculous names. And then we stopped and the kitchen was quiet again, and Angelica was the only one howling.

"I have to do something. I just can't sit here," I said.

"I know it doesn't make you feel any better, but it's all part of the illness," Margaret said. "They drug, they drink, they run and bang their heads against a wall. You just have to step back, not go under with them."

"I am under," I said.

I was ready to renew the search, to sally out again into the strange town on my mission, but Margaret persuaded me to stay put. It was nearly eleven o'clock, she pointed out. All the stores were closed. If she was at someone's house, it would be futile to go looking for her. She might be on her way back here. There was a chance that Trina had seen the address on the front door, noticed the street. If she came back, wouldn't I want to be there?

"Want something to help you sleep?" Brad asked me around 2 a.m.—or, in mental illness time, six hours past meds. Angelica was finally quiet. I was sitting on Margaret's kitchen chair. The only light was from a low-wattage bulb above the stove. Brad held out a pill in one hand, a glass of water in the other. He looked tired under that light. I figured I looked worse.

"No," I said.

"You need some sleep, Keri."

Whatever he gave me cushioned the world in a hurry. So this was how it worked, I thought. It was like taking a big, big shot of double-acting liquor. Everything was soft and grainy, slightly out of focus. I would have cried, but I was too calm. Brad helped me out of the chair, put his arm around my waist, led me to the bedroom, and placed me on the bed. I barely heard the door close.

IN THE MORNING, JEAN BROUGHT ME ORANGE JUICE, COF-fee, and a plate of eggs and sausages. A slight wooziness had settled into my brain. A Haldol hangover, something to be worked off during the day. Jean sat on the bed, watching me. I didn't eat the food. After a while, she took the tray back to the kitchen. It was still too early to call the police. I heard someone at the door, and when I looked up Brad was standing there.

"I went back out after you fell asleep, and this morning too. Want you to know how sorry I am about all this. Truly sorry," he said.

What did he expect me to say, That's okay, don't worry about it?

Brad sighed.

"The thing is"—and here his voice swelled a bit, just enough so his emotions had room to maneuver and settle down—"we have saved so many lives. At least seventy-five since we started. Seventy-five young people who are alive and productive because of the work I do—the work we do."

"I just want my kid back. That's all I want."

"We want her back too. You once asked me how I got involved with this work. My mother had schizophrenia, and she wouldn't accept any treatment. I grew up with a woman who wore way too much makeup, didn't bathe, and had conversations with people who weren't there. Kids at school laughed. The neighbors whispered. For the longest time, I thought I'd done something wrong.

"My mother used to beat my brother and me with anything she could hold in her hands. She'd always say that the Lord told her there was evil in us; she had to beat it out. My brother wound up in the emergency room with a broken arm. My dad lied and said he fell, because he didn't want us to be taken away.

"I can't tell you how many times my father called the police or took her to the hospital, only to be turned away and sent home. The few times she was actually admitted, she wasn't there long enough to do any good. She'd come home and stop taking the medication. Then we'd be right back where we started. We weren't rich. My dad couldn't afford a fancy residential treatment program. It was such a waste of a life—and my father's too. When she died, we were just relieved that the ordeal was over."

He paused. He was trembling. "We have contacts in this city, Keri. Our people are looking for Trina as we speak."

"My mother used to say that Satan sent us to her. I wanted to do good in this world." I thought he was going to cry, and I didn't want to witness that. Maybe he would have, but Margaret appeared, holding my purse. Inside it my cell phone was ringing.

GodGodpleaseGod.

"Keri. I got a call from Trina," Clyde said. "She's at Somerset Hospital in Sacramento, on the psych ward, acute side. She's on a seventy-two-hour hold."

2 8

THE PSYCHIATRIC WARD OF SOMERSET HOSPITAL WASN'T THE freedom I'd dreamed of, but at least I was no longer wading in the water. I could lay down my burden for a little while. A sign-in sheet awaited me with a cold polite African (Ghanaian? Nigerian?) manning the desk. There was the buzzer to press, a nurse to wait for, a sterile hall to walk down, wandering mumbling patients to ignore. There was fear, my steadfast companion, circumstantially amplified this time: *Didtheyhurtherdidtheyhurther?* And in spite of my apprehension, dueling it, the same old hope began leaping up, entirely unbidden, impossible to quell: *Maybethistimemaybethistimemaybethistime.*

Clyde was waiting at the end of the hall. His face was unshaven, his clothes rumpled. He was speaking with a brown-skinned woman in a white coat. She extended her hand when I approached.

"I'm Dr. Natal," she said. "I can tell that you are the mother."

"Is she all right? Did they hurt her?"

Dr. Natal put her hand on my wrist. "No one hurt her."

I heard a high-pitched mournful kind of sound, the kind tired old-school sisters used to make at church, after they'd finished shouting and the nurses were fanning their faces. The way I realized it was my noise was because of the look Clyde gave me, the way he appeared not so much worried as frightened when I began to cry.

"I'd like to see my daughter."

One request, two voices in sync. Clyde was holding my hand.

"She is sleeping right now. Besides, visiting hours don't begin until two," Dr. Natal said to both of us.

Her voice was East Asian and had a lilting quality that turned statements into questions.

I looked at my watch; Clyde looked at his. It was twelve-thirty.

"She called you," I said, looking at Clyde.

Clyde nodded. "Around midnight from the pay phone."

Dr. Natal took us into a small cubicle with a desk, several chairs, and no windows, opened a manila folder, and scanned the contents for a few seconds before closing her file.

"Mr. and Mrs. Whitmore, your daughter was brought in last night. She was paranoid and delusional. Has she had mental problems in the past?"

"My daughter was diagnosed with bipolar disorder about two years ago," I said. "She's had five hospitalizations since then. Six. The last was a few weeks ago at Beth Israel's Weitz Center in Los Angeles. She was medication-compliant for five months, and then a few months ago, she stopped. For the last two weeks she's been taking her meds, but I'm pretty sure she's been smoking marijuana and drinking for the last twenty-four hours."

Dr. Natal smiled. "That will do it every time. Is there the possibility that she took other drugs? Never mind," she said when she saw me faltering. "They have probably already run a toxicology screen."

"How did she happen to get here? Was it voluntarily?"

Dr. Natal opened the folder again. "No. It was involuntary. Two men brought her in. She'd hitched a ride with them and told them she was going to kill herself. Has she been suicidal before?"

"She's threatened. To my knowledge, she's never made any attempts," I said, glancing at Clyde. He was sitting on the chair, straight and stiff as a brick wall.

"One of the nurses told me the men were on their way here anyway, so they brought her in."

Clyde coughed.

"They just happened to be coming to the hospital?" I asked.

Dr. Natal shook her head. "We run a day treatment program here, one for people with mental illnesses and one for addictions. There is a dual-diagnosis section for those who have both. The last meeting starts at ten o'clock at night. It seems that the men who brought in your daughter attend the dual-diagnosis program, so they knew what they were looking at."

"What was she doing in this area?" Clyde asked. "You never told me."

"I—"

"Perhaps you need to talk," Dr. Natal said. "There is a café downstairs where you can have a cup of coffee."

"How did she get here? Were you visiting somebody?"

I looked at him, trying to gauge whether a public place would corral or accelerate his anger. "We need to go outside, Clyde." I looked at Dr. Natal. "I want to talk with you about getting the hold extended. I intend to go for conservatorship."

"What do you mean, get it extended?" Clyde asked.

"You both need to talk," Dr. Natal said. "When you return at two o'clock, ask the nurse to page me."

We went outside to the parking lot and sat in Clyde's car. I told him everything. His cell phone kept ringing, but he didn't answer it. When I was finished, he looked at me for a long time. He seemed in a daze. "I can't believe you did that," he said finally. "You actually broke the law and kidnapped Trina. What do you really know about this group?"

"Before I agreed, I talked to several people whose children had been in the program. They all said it helped."

"Yeah, I guess nobody said that their kid ran away and hitched a ride with strangers while this so-called program was supposed to be on the job."

"Clyde—"

"There were other options, Kori."

"You name them. I have exhausted all of them. She is sick. She stopped taking her medication. All hell broke loose. She was completely out of control. So I tried something radical."

"You could have—"

"I could have what? I did everything I could do. And I was scared and tired. Maybe if you'd helped me more we could have made another decision."

"Don't say I didn't help. She called me, not you."

"Do you want to know why she called you? Because you're the daddy with the checkbook. You ignore the problem, so I'm the one who has to pick up the pieces. You put me in that role a long time ago."

He pushed himself away from me closer to his door. "I don't want to talk about that."

"I had to do everything: call the mortician, pick out the casket, buy the flowers, write the obituary."

"I had to work."

"You *wanted* to work. That was your escape. You never even mourned him."

"I told you, I don't want to talk about that." His voice was raised. His entire body was shaking.

"You left me all alone to cry over my dead son, and you left me alone to deal with Trina. So I'm dealing with Trina. I'm going to get the hold extended, and I'm going to attempt to get conservatorship."

"What is that?"

"It means I can force her to get treatment. I can have her placed in a locked facility."

"Hell, no."

"A locked facility where she will be stabilized on medication."

Clyde shook his head. "One of those warehouses for crazies. I will never allow Trina to go there."

"Then what do you suggest? Do you want her to come live with you and Aurelia?"

His body jerked involuntarily. He looked at me, then slowly lowered his eyes.

"Oh, Jesus."

"She moved out."

We sat in silence for a few minutes.

"Whenever Trina's with me, she seems okay," Clyde said.

"Clyde—"

"Not completely okay, but not bad enough to be locked up."

"Don't think of it that way. Think of it as being kept safe."

"How do you know that? Have you seen any of those places?"

"I wouldn't put her anywhere that doesn't seem safe."

His face said he still needed convincing.

"Look, we can both choose the place, Clyde. "

"I don't know."

Neither one of us was hungry. We sat in the car until it was two o'clock, time to go back inside the hospital. Eighteen years ago, we had both walked down a hospital corridor to take a look at the child we'd created, wishes and dreams in every step we took. Maybe she'd grow up and be an astronaut or Miss America. Everything had been in front of us then. A beautiful, perfect baby: What could go wrong? In this hallway our steps were quieter. We shuffled, weak and weary, our parenthood weighing on us like chains.

But something joyful rushed from us simultaneously, just like the first time, when we saw her. There she is, we thought. Ours.

Trina was sitting alone on a sofa in the visitors' lounge. There were three sofas and two round tables and chairs in the large room. Several patients were watching a big-screen television set that was tuned to a classic movie: John Wayne and Maureen O'Hara. Trina wasn't watching. She was staring at nothing in particular. Her body seemed swallowed up by the gray hospital robe she was wearing. I could tell she hadn't bathed. If I got close enough, I knew, she would smell.

"She looks so little," I said.

She saw us before we walked over. There was a smile for her father, belligerence for me. To never be forgiven wasn't outside the realm of possibilities. I'd made my choice, and now I'd have to live with the consequences. "She doesn't want to see me. You visit," I said. "I'll wait for you outside."

I went to the nurses' station and asked to speak with Dr. Natal. A few minutes later the nurse told me that the doctor would meet Clyde and me in her office after our visit. Clyde emerged about an hour later, looking worn out and sad. "Will she see me?" I asked.

He shook his head. "She thinks you're trying to have her killed. She said some really crazy things. Did a man sleep with both of you?"

"In the room, Clyde, not our beds. It was for security, in case Trina tried to leave or got violent. I'll tell you everything later. We have an appointment with Dr. Natal to talk about the conservatorship."

Clyde flinched when I said the word. "I'm not having her locked up."

"Would you prefer her to get locked up for real? She's already been arrested for shoplifting. Is jail better than a medical facility? That's where she's headed, Clyde, down that slippery slope. She won't get medication or therapy in jail. She'll just get sicker."

"Keri—"

My voice rose. "Or maybe you want her to commit suicide. You heard Dr. Natal. Trina told those men she wanted to kill herself. We've already lost one child. Do you want to lose the other one, so you can leave me alone to grieve all by myself? Walk out on me because you can't take the pain?"

I was screaming by then. Two nurses rushed toward me. Beyond them in the hallway, necks swiveled and all eyes were on us. I didn't care. Something had come loose inside me. I began pounding Clyde's chest with my fists. He tried to grab my hands, but I snatched them away, so he ended up pulling me to his chest and holding me there while I sobbed. When I got quiet, I could feel something jerking inside him, some kind of hard trembling that he couldn't control. After a while he said, "All right. We'll do it your way."

"Mr. Whitmore, are you all right?" Dr. Natal asked, when we sat down in the two chairs facing her desk. Clyde looked shell-shocked and more fragile than I'd ever seen him.

He nodded.

I glanced at Clyde and turned to Dr. Natal. "I've been trying to get a conservatorship of her person, so I can get her stabilized again. If that means putting her in a locked facility, that's what I'll do. I need a psychiatrist to support my claim that she's gravely disabled. Will you help me?" I asked.

"Are you in agreement with this, Mr. Whitmore?" she asked.

He nodded.

"Where do you all live?"

"In Los Angeles," I said.

"You need someone in LA," Dr. Natal said. She leaned back in her chair. "Let's do this. We'll try to get the hold extended. If we're able to do that, I suggest that you transfer your daughter to Beth Israel. I have a dear friend there, a psychiatrist also. I'll give her a call. You've been in touch with someone at the Office of the Public Guardian?"

I nodded.

"Okay, let me see what I can do about getting the hold extended."

"Thank you," I whispered.

"Thank you," Clyde said.

She glanced at her watch. "There's a support group for parents that meets in about twenty minutes. Perhaps you and your husband would like to attend. The nurse can show you where it is."

There weren't many people in the room, maybe a dozen or so. There were several rows of chairs. Clyde and I sat in the back. Rather, I sat and Clyde stood, his brows crowding together over the bridge of his nose, eyes scared, as though maybe he wasn't supposed to be here, and me thinking, Yes, this was exactly where we were supposed to be. I took his hand and pulled him down to his seat. He looked at me, and then he leaned forward as the speaker's voice got louder. Her son, she told the group, had done well in his first year at Stanford, and now—and now—

And then Clyde was shaking again, trembling. I took his hand in mine and squeezed it. He tried to pull away, but I held on until his fingers became limp. When I looked at him, there were tears in his eyes. The woman in front of us turned her head and smiled.

"Welcome," she said, her greeting half grin, half ol'-time religion. Clyde drew back; I leaned forward, toward that blessing. I felt the circle closing. Maybe I was right back where I started. Maybe not. Hallelujah anyhow.

My cell was ringing by the time we reached Clyde's car. I heard Brad's angry, anxious voice when I answered. A man was standing at Margaret's front door looking for me. Orlando somebody. What had I told him about the program?

"He's there to pick me up. Trina and I are leaving, and my ex-husband is with me now. Actually, I was getting ready to call Margaret to get directions. We were on our way over to get my stuff."

His voice was liquid acid. "Neither one of them is supposed to be here. You made the agreement, not your ex-husband or some guy. I can't jeopardize the program by having strangers know our—"

"Look, Brad, Trina and I are leaving."

"You gave this guy Margaret's address, and now you want to bring another—"

"They're not reporting you to the authorities. Damn. They don't have to come into the house. I just want to get our things."

"Why are you leaving? We can wait for Trina's hold to be up. She'll get stabilized in the hospital. You shouldn't go."

"We're leaving."

"What happened was a fluke. That wouldn't—"

"We're going home."

I could see his face in my mind, his eyes cloudy with personal failure. Brad hadn't delivered us safely to the promised land. He'd lost a passenger.

I'd lost something else.

"You did your best. I'm not blaming you. I appreciate all your efforts." I thought about asking what was happening with the police but changed my mind. If I didn't have to know, I didn't want to know. But I did want to speak with Bethany, to tell her good-bye. So when we made arrangements to meet in the parking lot of the mall where we'd searched for Trina, I asked Brad to make sure that she came along.

They were both standing with my bags where we said we'd meet when Clyde and I drove up, but I didn't see Orlando. The van was nowhere around. I told Clyde to stay in the car, which was my final promise to Brad.

"Where's Orlando?" I asked. Brad looked jumpy; he moved his body from side to side and kept pounding his fist into his open palm.

"I gave him directions."

"Why didn't you have him follow you?"

But I knew. Anyone behind him would see his license plate.

Bethany grabbed me in a tight hug. She looked as though she were coming off a long bender. Her cheeks were sunken, and the circles below her eyes were darker than usual. Her clothes were rumpled, as though she'd slept in them. "Thank God!" she whispered in my ear. "How is she?"

"They didn't hurt her," I said, and told her the story, which elicited another "Thank God!"

"Come with us," Bethany said after I'd finished. I glanced at Brad. He looked awkward for a moment, then stepped away.

"No."

"Our girls are hard cases," she said. "Something was bound to happen. It won't be like that this time."

I shook my head.

"We started this together."

"I'm sorry. I'm going back to LA."

"So you're going to try the system again? It didn't work before."

"I know. You still think this is going to work for you?"

"I'm no good with systems. We're going to the site this evening. I'll stay nearby for a while; then I'll come back in a week or so."

"Bethany, we need to go," Brad said.

"How's Angelica doing?"

"She's coming down. I can see depression setting in. Wilbur will meet us tonight; he'll know what to give her."

"Bethany," Brad said. He wouldn't look at me. I was no longer part of his world.

Bethany hugged me again. I ran my fingers over her back, found the knots, and pressed down. Bethany groaned a little. "Come see me when you get back," I said. "I'll get rid of them for you."

"I will."

Clyde wanted to know why we were sitting in the parking lot. When I told him that Orlando was on his way, he looked a little confused. He'd met him years earlier and had even gone to one of his plays, but they hadn't seen each other in a long time.

"Is he still your boyfriend?"

I was taken aback, not by the question but because of the frank interest in Clyde's eyes. He never asked me about my personal life.

I hesitated. I don't know why.

"You guys have been hanging out for a long time. How come you never got married?"

"How come you get married so much?"

Clyde chuckled. "I've been trying to figure that one out myself. I don't think I'll be doing it again."

"I wouldn't bet money on that," I said. "You're the marrying kind."

"Am I?"

"You like having a wife; you just don't want to be a husband."

The words came out before I could stop them. When I looked at Clyde's face, I knew that I'd cut too deep.

"Why does it have to be my fault?"

"How many times have you done this?"

He looked as though he were doing the math for the very first time. "I did the best I—"

"You've never given your best to a marriage. You give your best to making money."

Clyde's face contorted. "I'm sick of hearing this shit. All women want a successful man, but they never want to deal with what it takes to be successful in America. And it's twice as hard for a brother. You don't have any problems accepting the rewards of my working so hard, but when it comes with dealing with the sacrifices involved, all you do is complain. You don't know what you want."

"I can't speak for the rest of your wives, but I never asked you to go slay the dragon for me. You did that on your own, because of *your* needs."

"I did it to take care of my family."

"You left your family, and then you started throwing money at us."

"We were together a long time after—" He stopped, cleared his throat, and grew quiet.

"Say it."

"Say what?"

"Say we were together a long time after the baby died."

He turned his head.

"Don't look away from me."

He turned back, and when he did he looked weary and frightened, which infuriated me more. "What do you want from me?"

"Do you think the only way you can leave somebody is to walk out the door? You were never home. Our world exploded, and you didn't try to help me put it back together. And you didn't try to help Trina, either."

"So I'm the bad guy, huh? Because I don't want to hold on to grief, I'm the bad guy?"

"You didn't share—"

"I didn't share what? I mourned our son, Keri. I still do. I just don't do it the way you do. You mourn forever, and you hold grudges forever. You never want to let anything go."

"What are you talking about?"

"Your mother, for one thing. You were grown up at eighteen, and you're still in pain about your childhood. Damn. How long ago was that? The woman has tried and tried to make it up to you, and you're still so damn angry that—"

"I let her back in my life. She's the one who ran out again."

"No, she didn't. She got married. She didn't make you her number-one priority, and you got pissed off. That's what happened."

"I—"

"Listen, if I failed to grieve with you, I'm sorry. But knowing you, you won't accept that apology, because you like to hold grudges."

I had a hot retort in my mouth, but Clyde put his head against the steering wheel. I couldn't see his eyes. And then there was a tapping on the window, and when I looked I saw Orlando standing outside, looking in at us.

It was awkward with Orlando, who hadn't expected to see Clyde, let alone interrupt us in the middle of an argument. No use trying to act normal when it was so obvious that both of us were upset and one of us was almost out of control. Clyde barely spoke after he rolled down the window. I got out of the car, and Orlando hugged me even though I could tell that he was holding back. He looked exhausted and stressed out. I told him Trina was in the hospital and brought him up to date as quickly as I could.

There were logistics to figure out. Orlando sat in his car while Clyde and I sat in his and decided that we'd both stay to learn if Trina's hold would be extended. If it was, we'd have her transferred back to the Weitz Center. If it wasn't, we'd drive her back to LA and either look for a residential treatment program in a remote spot, or call Brad and say I'd made a mistake leaving, or chain up Trina in my garage.

I got out of Clyde's car and conferred with Orlando in his; he said he'd spend the night and go back to LA in the morning. He called an 800 number for a hotel and found a place that wasn't too far from the hospital. After we checked in, Orlando and I went to get something to eat. Clyde stayed behind to take a nap. We agreed to meet half an hour before visiting hours at the hospital.

I felt more guilty than hungry as I sat across from Orlando. "I'm so sorry I called you. I didn't know Clyde was going to be here. I hate that you're missing opening night. God, Orlando. Are you going to get fired?"

"Nah. I told the director I had a family emergency. They would have postponed it, but tickets had already been sold. Anyway, it's not that big a deal. Don't even think about it. The play kind of sucks." He seemed forlorn.

"Orlando, are you all right?"

"I'm fine."

"I'm sure the play doesn't suck."

"I'm fabulous, but the play sucks. Anyway, I'm here now. It's good to see you, baby."

We didn't talk much. A couple of times when I looked up from my food, Orlando was staring at me.

"I'm okay," I said the last time. When he kept staring, it occurred to me that I might look as bad as Bethany did. It wouldn't be the first time Orlando hadn't seen me at my best.

We took a walk after we finished eating. When we got back to the hotel, there were still a couple of hours before visiting hours started. "I want us to take a nap," Orlando said. So we got in the bed and slept until it was time for me to meet Clyde.

CLYDE WAS WAITING IN THE LOBBY WHEN I CAME DOWN. His rest had done him good. He seemed more relaxed. We stayed away from discussing anything personal while we drove to the hospital. It wasn't until Clyde turned into the entranceway of Somerset that I saw his face begin to take on a grim look, and all the lines of tension that the nap had eased seemed more pronounced.

Clyde went in first to see Trina, and I waited outside near the sign-in sheet. He came back after forty-five minutes and said Trina wanted to see me. She looked bedraggled, her hair uncombed, sleep settled into the corners of her eyes; she was huddled in a corner of one of the sofas in the television room. I wanted to hug her, but her eyes allowed me to come only so far.

"Trina, why don't you give Mommy a hug," Clyde said.

She shrank back.

"That's all right. I love you, baby."

She stared at me with sullen, suspicious eyes. What would it take for that look to recede, disappear?

I didn't stay long.

"She'll get better," I said as Clyde and I were walking down the hall.

Clyde didn't answer.

"The medication has to get in her system. It's a process."

He didn't look at me.

"You never answered my question," Clyde said as we were driving back.

"What question?"

"Why haven't you and Orlando gotten married? Brother drove all night to be with you. Seems like a nice guy."

"He *is* a nice guy."

Clyde smiled. "So you're not going to tell me?"

"I haven't figured it out myself. Why are you so into my Kool-Aid?"

Clyde opened his mouth, then closed it. "Just being nosy."

Orlando was in the shower when I got back to the room. There was a bottle of red wine on the dresser, and a bouquet of flowers, the kind vendors sell on street corners. And French fries, still hot. I popped one into my mouth and then another. He'd found Sacramento's jazz station; the strains of a soft saxophone were coming from the radio. I knocked on the bathroom door, then cracked it. "The flowers are beautiful. And the fries are great. Thank you."

"You're welcome. How's Trina doing?"

"You know. It's day two; she hates me. What can I tell you?"

I heard water running. Orlando came out with a towel wrapped around him. "Your bath is ready," he said, and kissed me.

There were bubbles in the tub and two lighted candles on the sink. I sank into the water, letting the warmth and the fragrance push back some of the worry and tension. I almost fell asleep, but then I heard soft tapping on the door. "Hey, baby, you're kind of quiet in there."

Orlando had already poured the wine by the time I got out. He handed me a glass and held his up. "To better times," he said.

Clink! Clink!

We got into the bed, then sat up with our heads against the back-board.

"How are the boys?" I asked.

Orlando smiled. "Jabari had his football banquet last week. He was MVP."

"All right!" I said. Our palms met in midair.

"So he takes off for training in a couple of weeks."

"That soon?"

"Michigan starts a little earlier than most. You should have heard his acceptance speech. Brought tears to my eyes. Talk about eloquent."

"Wonder where that came from?"

Orlando grinned.

"How's PJ?" I asked.

"Well," Orlando said, "that's a whole other story." He looked at me and put down his glass. "Uh," he said, then stopped, pressed his lips together, and started again. "PJ told me he's gay."

His voice cracked when he said the word. I looked at him, saw his lower lip begin to quiver. He began sobbing. I put my arms around him. I hadn't expected tears. Not from my rock.

"It's going to be all right."

"Oh, God." His head was against my chest, and his voice was muffled. "They're going to call him a faggot." He began sobbing harder. "And there's AIDS. Jesus. Why didn't I know? What the hell was wrong with me, not seeing this?"

"He didn't want you to see it," I said. "What did you tell him?"

He lifted his head and looked at me. "I told him I loved him, that he was my son. What do you think I told him?"

"Did he tell Lucy?"

"We both did."

"How did she take it?"

"You know how emotional Lucy is. But she did say that she loved him." He looked at me. "Did you know?"

I nodded. "I haven't known all that much longer than you. It was easier for him to tell me. I'm not his parent."

"You act like his mother."

I didn't say anything.

"He's the age your son would have been."

I didn't answer.

Orlando put his hands on my shoulders. "Help me get through this."

"You will," I said.

"You don't know how this feels to a man. It's like somebody's tearing my guts out. Who can explain how things turn out?"

"Not me."

"You're a good mother, Keri."

"I was always so proud of Trina. I could point to her and say, 'See, I got something right.' "

"You did a lot of things right. Trina's a wonderful girl when she's not sick. It's not her fault, and it's not yours."

"I know. And you didn't do anything wrong with PJ."

"I know."

His hands stayed on my shoulders for a long time, and then I put mine on his. I looked past him to the dresser with the flowers and more candles twinkling. Then we were pushing each other down, touching kindly, sharing sweetness and heat.

I WOKE UP THE NEXT MORNING TO THE RINGING OF THE telephone. It was Dr. Natal calling to inform me that she had just left Trina's hearing; the hold had been extended for two weeks. She'd already called the Weitz Center and arranged the transfer. I told her Clyde and I would be there shortly to check Trina out.

When I hung up, Orlando was getting dressed and looking at me. "So I take it that you and Clyde are riding back to LA together."

Something in his voice made me pay more attention.

"I guess. Maybe we'll follow the ambulance. I don't know."

"Right. Well, look, I'm going to head out."

"Aren't you going to eat something?"

"Nah."

"Come on. Don't start a seven-hour drive on an empty stomach."

"I'm not hungry now. I'll stop off somewhere later. You need to get going."

I got up, walked to him, and put my arms around his waist. "I'll call you when I get back. Break a leg."

"What?"

"The show. You're going on tonight, aren't you?"

"Oh, yeah, yeah. Thanks, baby."

He gave me a kiss. I thought of it as I was dressing; it was quick and dry, like the kiss a grown man gives his favorite aunt.

Clyde was waiting for me in the lobby.

"Orlando didn't want to eat breakfast?" Clyde asked.

"He wasn't hungry. He's already gone."

Clyde and I argued at breakfast and on the way over to the hospital. He didn't want to have Trina transported by ambulance. He thought we could handle her ourselves. "You were willing to put Trina in a car with strangers, going to God knows where, but you don't think we can handle her?"

"She ran away twice on this trip already. Do you really think—?"

He held up his hand. "You drive. I'll sit in back with her. She won't run away from me."

Somehow, I knew that was true.

Trina looked better when I saw her. She was washed, her hair still damp from a shampoo. She didn't look as though she was ready to attack me, which didn't mean that she was ready to have a friendly conversation. Mostly she talked with Clyde. He was the one who told her that we were leaving, that she was going back to the Weitz Center, and that we were taking her there. She narrowed her eyes and glared at me for moment. I was sending her back to her old plantation with the taste of liberty still in her mouth. But when Clyde told her that it was for the best, she sighed and seemed to settle down. She was quiet as we signed her out and seemed subdued as we walked to the parking lot toward Clyde's car.

"All right," I said, when I was seated behind the wheel. "No stops."

30

IT WAS LIKE OLD TIMES, SORT OF. I'D ALWAYS BEEN THE long-distance driver in the family when Clyde and I were together. Not that we'd taken that many car trips. Clyde liked flying better. He lacked the patience for hours on the road, whereas I always found solace in being able to cruise along with no agenda other than hanging out in my head until we arrived.

Trina slept on and off for most of the seven hours. In the beginning, she sat up and leaned on her father, her face pressed against his shoulder. Later, she lay down on her side, tucked her legs under her hips, and put her head on Clyde's thigh. We'd stopped off at a grocery store before we went to the hospital. As I drove, Clyde passed me a bottle of water, juice, a sandwich, and a piece of fruit. Despite my edict of no stops, we did have to use the restroom once or twice. Clyde and I both took Trina inside a convenience store and waited for her together outside the ladies' room; she didn't give us any trouble. We were on the road around six o'clock when Clyde gave her some medication; she took it without a fuss.

"What is this stuff she's taking?" Clyde asked after Trina had fallen asleep again.

"One controls her moods, the other prevents psychosis."

"How do they work exactly?"

"It's complicated. I don't completely understand it. Basically, she's getting too much of one chemical in her brain and not enough of the other, and the medications help balance her out. They talk about this stuff in support group, but you know me and technical stuff. Plus, I guess I didn't try to focus because I was too busy waiting for the miracle, thinking I'd wake up one day and Trina would be permanently cured. Before this last episode, when Trina had been doing so well for months, I was really convinced that the worst was over."

"Maybe it is," Clyde said. "Is the support group like the one we went to in the hospital?"

"Very similar."

"How did you find out about it?"

"On the Internet. I was surfing, trying to get information about bipolar, trying to find a good psychiatrist, and the group was linked to another Web site I went on."

Clyde was quiet for so long that I thought he'd fallen asleep.

"You've done a lot by yourself, haven't you, Mommyfingers."

The old nickname sounded sweet in his mouth: Trina's name for me when I rubbed her little-girl shoulders. Long-lost laughter filled the car. Mine so loud, I almost didn't hear the echo: "Mommyfingers."

Trina was sitting up, looking at us both, smiling. She had her good memories too.

It was after eight o'clock by the time we got to the Weitz Center. The bed was ready, and after we filled out the paperwork and gave the nurse Trina's clothes, Clyde and I left.

By the time Clyde turned up Crenshaw, the sky was dark. There was a nighttime film crew outside a popular barbershop. Young whites with cameras and equipment filled the sidewalk, and black actors milled about. An evening service was ending at the large apostolic church, and a crowd of people was spilling onto the street. The fast-food joints and mom-and-pop restaurants were all filled.

"Good old Crenshaw," Clyde said.

As he turned onto the street that led to my house, his eyes seemed to

grow hungrier and hungrier, devouring everything he saw. "Are you getting nostalgic for your people?" I asked. He didn't answer. He was still
quiet when he dropped me off, barely saying good-bye.

Inside, the drapes were drawn and the air smelled stale. I opened all
the windows, sat at my kitchen table, and drank a cup of tea. I made
some calls and left a message for Frances, telling her I would be coming
in to the shop in the morning. I called Mattie, as well. I started going
through the mail. When I got tired of that, I lay down on the sofa in
the family room. By the time I woke up, it was after eleven. I called
Orlando.

"We made it," I said. "How was the show?"

"It went well."

"You weren't exhausted?"

"Nah."

"I wanted to thank you again for driving all the way up."

"Hey, you don't even have to go there. I guess you must be tired,
baby."

"I just woke up."

"So I'll let you go. Get some rest. I know you have a lot to do
tomorrow."

When I hung up the phone, I closed the windows. The house felt
chilly.

NEXT MORNING, I ARRIVED AT THE SHOP EARLY, BUT FRANCES
was already there. When I walked in, she was steaming clothes. We
hugged; then she stepped back and looked at me. I knew she was thinking I looked more tired than before I left on my so-called vacation, but
she didn't say anything about my appearance. She asked me about
Trina, and when I said Trina was back in the hospital, she just nodded.

I scanned the store as Frances continued to steam. Almost all the
merchandise had turned over since I'd left, and there were lots of new
things. The place was spotless, the plants looked healthy, and the items
were well placed. When I went into my office, my desk held bank
receipts of the deposits Frances had made while I was away and computer printouts of all the sales. Everything was neat and orderly. "You
did an awesome job," I said to Frances, looking up from my desk.

"I told you not to worry," she said. She was standing in the doorway. "The only downer is the pantsuit. The Old Man couldn't get rid of that stain either." She pointed toward a rack of new clothes that hadn't been tagged yet. The green pantsuit was among them. When I took a closer look, I could see the spot.

"We're going to have to eat this," I said.

"It might sell. Not everybody cares about a little spot. Save it for me. When I lose fifty pounds, I'll wear it," Frances said.

By the time the store had opened I'd already called Dr. Natal's colleague, as well as Dr. Bellows, and left messages for both. I called Herbert Swanson at the Office of the Public Guardian. His assistant assured me that they would send someone to interview Trina and speak with both Dr. Natal and Dr. Bellows. Possibly by the end of the day she'd be placed on temporary conservatorship.

"Then what?" I asked.

"You'll get a court date. After that it's about showing up and hoping for a good judge."

Swing low, sweet chariot, stop and let me ride. I got a home on the other side.

"Where's Adriana?" I asked Frances when I got off the telephone.

She had just finished ringing up a customer and was still standing behind the cash register. "I didn't want to tell you while you were away, but she's been missing whole days, lately."

"Without calling?"

Frances nodded. "She's been looking kind of bad too, like she's not sleeping."

Our eyes met. Frances shook her head.

At the thought of Adriana sinking back into her old ways, her old life, my stomach lurched. "I'll talk with her, get her back into her program, and spend more time watching her."

Frances caught me by my arm. "You already saved her once. You have enough to do to take care of Trina and yourself. You've lost weight. And you didn't need to."

"But she was doing so well," I said.

"She was just playing dress-up," Frances said. "Her new life wasn't real to her. Working a regular job, having a nice boyfriend, making good new friends—all that scared her. She never really committed to it. You wanted it for her. You wanted to give her a cleaned-up perfect life, and she just wasn't ready for it."

"She was already going to meetings when she came to me. She wanted a better life. All I did was show her how to get it."

"I'm not faulting you, Keri. God knows, you helped that girl. I'm saying that if Adriana slips up, she has to take responsibility, not you. And that goes for Trina too."

"I wasn't trying to make her life perfect."

Frances just smiled. She had released my arm. Now she touched the scar on her face with her finger. "You know, everybody gets a wake-up call. This was mine. My ex didn't do this. He blacked my eyes and broke some teeth, but he didn't cut my face. I fell on a piece of glass one time. He was nowhere around. But when I looked in the mirror and saw the blood dripping down, it was like I was seeing my pain for the first time. I didn't leave him right away, but that was the beginning. And I'm telling you, Keri, everybody gets a moment like that. You just have to pray that Adriana and Trina will pay attention when it comes. That's really all you can do."

I mulled over Frances's words as I drove to the Weitz Center. Clyde was waiting for me when I got off the elevator on the psych ward. Although it took Trina a while to come out of her room, when she arrived in the visitors' area she seemed more alert and more communicative than she'd been in days. The room was large and sunny and smelled like the banana one of the patients was eating. Trina chatted about her roommate, an older Russian woman who was subject to crying jags. She was full of ward gossip, claiming that everyone was fighting with everyone else and that most patients were having sex. She delivered this news in the dramatic fashion of a born provocateur aiming for ultimate shock value. Knowing I was familiar with her ploys, Trina looked at her father as she spoke. She was trying to elicit his sense of paternal responsibility, his urge to protect her: *Daddy, get me out of this terrible place.* I'd have to clue him in later. Trina was feeling better; she was dreaming of escape.

After we left Trina, we went downstairs to Rosario Perez's office. The social worker, upon learning of our plans to get conservatorship of Trina, produced a list of institutes for mental diseases, or IMDs. "Some of these are pretty rough places," she said. "The ones I've checked have the best reputations. Good luck."

The first facility was in Culver City on a block filled with flowering jacaranda trees and lawns bordered with rosebushes. The Light House was at the end of the block, after the single-family dwellings had given way to apartment buildings and nursing homes. There were bars at the windows, and from the backyard a cloud of smoke arose from residents on their cigarette break.

The admissions director was brisk and businesslike as she took us on the tour. An antiseptic odor clung to everything we passed. Several men in dull gray pants and shirts were mopping the long shiny corridor. There were chairs alongside the wall and a few patients were seated in them, silently watching the comings and goings of the ward. Black people and Latinos in blue uniforms doled out medication to those waiting in a long line queued up outside a room that was closed off by a divided door. The top half was open, and as nurses dispensed antidepressants, mood stabilizers, and antipsychotics, they hurried people along to their "groups."

Some of the patients standing there could pass for normal. Others shuffled down the halls, mumbling to themselves and leaning away from the people around them. Many of the patients were overweight, some grossly so, and poorly groomed, the clothing and run-down shoes of some giving a hint of the homeless status that had preceded their arrival at the Light House. From time to time someone would shriek, the sound melding with the ordinary workaday din; no one seemed to notice— except Clyde, who stiffened. I saw this visceral reaction for the metaphor that it was: his resolve.

After we thanked the admissions director for her time, after we had left the building and were breathing unsanitized smoggy Los Angeles air, Clyde looked at me and shook his head. "No way."

We toured a second one, a collection of squat one-story cement buildings with a courtyard in the middle, located way the hell out in Pomona, where the afternoon sun was roasting everyone and everything foolish enough to venture outside for more than ten minutes. Clyde took one look at the division of patients—criminal inmates on the west, others on the east—and said, "Let's go."

By the time we got in the car, he was fuming, his words full of spit and rage. "There is no way in hell Trina is going to be locked up with the people I saw in there. I mean, who the hell would mix criminals with people who are mentally ill?"

"They're *all* mentally ill, Clyde, and they're in separate buildings. And who the hell would put mentally ill people in jail in the first place? Let me tell you something: The way Trina was going, only the grace of God prevented her from having a permanent room on the west side. So don't get to feeling too superior, my friend.

"Listen, the Light House isn't the Rolls-Royce of facilities, but it's workable for ninety days, and that's all we're talking about. First of all, it's close. I could go there every day at lunchtime and come back in the evening. You could drop in whenever you have time. Her therapist could visit her. The main thing is for Trina to get back on her medication. Those long lines will help her become compliant."

"How?"

"Because a certain degree of regimentation is necessary for her to get better. Lining up twice a day will impress on her that she has to take her medicine."

"What if somebody jumps on her? What if she's raped? Did you see the women in there? What the hell do they feed them? No. Hell, no. Those people are crazy. Trina just needs a little help and some rest."

"Your daughter has bipolar disorder, just like a lot of those people."

"All right, all right, she has problems too, but I can't let her go there. I just can't."

We went on and on, all the way back to the shop, and we were still at a stalemate when we got there.

"We'll keep her at home," he said, just as I was about to get out.

"Whose home?" I asked.

He looked sheepish. "Well, I was thinking yours. But I could pay somebody to stay there and take care of her."

"Around the clock? Do you know how much money that would take? You'd be bankrupt in a month."

Clyde slumped against his seat. The worst thing anyone could say to him was that he didn't have enough money. "How much does the Light House cost?" he asked.

"The county pays," I said. "The catch is, you have to wait for an opening."

"She sounds stable now."

I groaned. "If she sounds stable, it's because she's in a very structured environment where the meals and the meds and the activities all come at a certain time. If you take that structure away, she'll regress. I'm trying to tell you that the Light House has more pluses than minuses."

"Something might happen to her. She could get hurt. People die in places like that," Clyde said.

"Look at me." When he did, I said, "Trina may die *if she doesn't get help.*"

WHEN ADRIANA HADN'T COME IN BY TWO O'CLOCK, I assumed she wouldn't make it at all. According to Frances, this was her fourth day of not showing up. A crowd of shoppers arriving around noon kept the two of us hopping. After most of the people had left, I turned to Frances. "Maybe I need to hire someone else."

In my office, I dialed Adriana's home number and then her cell. I left the same message on both. "I need you. Please come in tomorrow."

The green pantsuit hanging on the rack seemed to reproach me. No matter what else I was supposed to be doing, it caught my eye. I spent a lot of time staring at the spot, trying to judge how noticeable it was.

WHEN I DROVE UP TO ORLANDO'S THEATER THAT NIGHT, there was a line outside and a throng of happy people milling about on the sidewalk. Some of them were recognizable: television faces from shows that either were in syndication or had gone on to sitcom heaven. As I stepped up to the will-call window, I could hear scattered conversations. The words *agent, casting, callback,* and *for the producers* were used frequently. These were Orlando's colleagues and costars, and some hadn't worked in quite a while. They'd come out both to support him and to do themselves some good just in case a big-time producer really did show up. Many of these actors greeted me; they'd met me often enough through the years.

Orlando's name was prominently displayed on the marquee. One of the continuing perks of having been in a hit sitcom is name recognition. He might not be on Broadway, but in a cast of unknowns he was the clear draw. The theater was a ninety-nine-seater that didn't pay union scale, but at least it was full. That had to make Orlando feel good.

I slipped into my unreserved seat about five minutes before curtain.

The lights were still up. I scanned the audience quickly and heard my name. By the time I figured out where the sound came from, PJ was sliding into the seat next to mine. I had just enough time to give him a quick greeting before the lights dimmed.

Orlando had called it right. The play wasn't good—an implausible story that went on way too long—and he was right about his performance. From the moment he walked onstage until the curtain came down, he took command. He enjoyed himself so much when he was performing. It took so little to make him happy, just a few folks clapping with their eyes on him. I wanted more for him than that.

"So what did you think?" I asked PJ after the last bit of applause had faded. People were beginning to file out, but we sat back down.

"Dad was great, but the play needs work, as they say."

"I agree."

"I saw it last night. They already changed a couple of things," he said.

"Oh, PJ. You came two nights in a row? That's so sweet."

"I kind of like theater," he said.

"Oh, no. Not another one." We both laughed.

PJ seemed settled in a way I'd never known him to be. Since the last time I'd seen him, he seemed to have matured.

"So how are things?" I asked.

He smiled. "I told them."

"And they didn't disown you?" I smiled.

"No. Actually, they were pretty cool about the whole thing. I mean—well, my mom was upset and everything, but my dad was fine. He knows a lot of gay people."

"Just be safe. That's all we care about. Be safe."

By the time Orlando came out, PJ and I were alone in the theater. I offered to treat the three of us to dinner, but Orlando said he was more tired than hungry and still had to take PJ home.

"Do you want to come over?" I whispered in his ear.

"I'm tired, Keri," he said.

"Is something wrong?"

"No."

At home I felt edgy and restless. A glass of wine didn't settle me or block out the thoughts that were bombarding me. Bethany and Angelica. Where were they now? Had I been too hasty in leaving the program? They were probably at the main site by now. Maybe it had been a mistake, not sticking with them.

Or maybe they were all in jail. I'd been so busy with the conservatorship and the store that I hadn't taken time to ponder the possible outcome of Jean's little dilemma. No one had called me. If something had gone wrong, surely Brad would have contacted me. Or maybe not. Being stoic suited him. Not giving out names, taking the bamboo beneath his fingernails without flinching, not being afraid of the dogs yelping at his ankles: that's how he liked to think of himself.

I took my second glass of wine out to the hot tub, feeling very much alone. As the whirlpool jets began bubbling, I started crying for Trina, Orlando, Clyde, Adriana, and me. All the lost people. When the portable phone that was lying on the edge of the tub began to ring, I had just run out of tears.

"Keri? It's your mother. Please, please don't hang up. Please talk to me. Please."

I listened to Emma call my name over and over. I let her beg. Hang up, I told myself. Hang up right now.

"What do you want?" I said.

"I just want to talk with you. How have you been?"

"What do you care how I've been?"

"I do care, Keri."

"No, you don't. You never did. You're just calling me because you're old and lonely. You're probably wondering who's going to take care of you if things get really bad. Well, it won't be me."

Her voice was very soft. "You have a right to be angry with me."

"I have a right to hate you. And I do."

"I'm sorry. Please, let me try to make amends."

"I don't want you in my life." I was shouting.

"All right, all right." She paused. "How's Trina?"

I wanted to tell her that Trina was at Brown University pulling a 4.0 because I'd been a great mother, not some drunk who didn't accept her responsibilities. If only I could have flung those proud words in her face. But I began sputtering and then crying.

"Keri, what's wrong?"

I hung up.

· · ·

BY THE END OF THE FIRST WEEK, TRINA SEEMED MORE SUB-
dued, her psychosis not as evident, except when she asked me if I was
her mother and tilted her head and narrowed her eyes when I said that I
was. I always thought of Emma when she said that, even though I didn't
want to think about her. "Where's my real mother?" she asked me, over
and over again.

A fixed false belief. It came with the territory. In her mind I wasn't
her mother, but at least she wasn't calling me the devil. I was grateful for
any small bit of progress.

Clyde and I visited together at lunchtime each day, and at night I'd
return to visit alone. The afternoons were almost fun, like Family Day at
college. Trina appeared to enjoy us. We played Scrabble and brought
puzzles and ate fruit. Trina talked a lot and laughed when her father
teased her. At night she was more subdued. I usually arrived at eight,
and by the time I got there she'd already had her evening meds, including a tranquilizer. She didn't talk much, but she seemed happy to
see me and listened as I chattered on about the shop. We did girly
things at night. I gave her a pedicure. I curled her hair with electric
curlers, which brought out an appreciative audience. And, of course, I
massaged her.

I started with her fingers toward the end of the first week. She let me
hold her hand without pulling away. My thumb brushed against her
palm, back and forth, back and forth. She didn't resist. Every day I
rubbed her a little more. She grew limp and relaxed under my touch. I
soothed her.

I was doing reflexology one night, pressing against the balls of her
feet. Her eyes were closed. She opened them and looked at me. "What
it is," she said, "is that I start flying. It feels like flying. I'm going up, up,
up, and I can't come back down. So I just go with it. Everything whizzes
by so fast. There's the sky and the trees and the people, and I pass them
so fast. Nobody can make me stop."

I kept rubbing.

"Do you want to stop, Trina?"

"I was supposed to go to Brown, wasn't I?"

I nodded.

"In September."

I nodded.

"But I can't go to school if I'm flying, Mom. All the letters on the page come together and the numbers are jumbled. Nothing makes sense when I'm flying. And I don't know when I'll take off again."

"Take the medicine and you won't fly," I said.

"I can't smoke weed, Mommy."

"No."

"I can't smoke weed and I can't take Ecstasy and I can't drink. All that stuff used to make me feel normal. Now they all make me fly so fast. Too fast. That's what Elton and Thaddeus told me."

"Who are they?"

"They took me to the other hospital. They were nice to me."

"How did you meet them?"

"I hitched a ride with them. They could tell I was flying."

"At the hospital, they told me you were very sad. Did you tell the men that you wanted to die?"

She averted her eyes. "I want to go to Brown. I studied so hard. I passed all the tests, and now I'm not smart anymore."

"Yes, you are."

She shook her head. "I'm so slow, Mom. When I try to think, everything is so slow. I can't remember things I used to know."

"That's just temporary. You've been under a lot of stress."

She sat straight up. "You put me under stress." Her voice began to rise. "You made me go with those people and sleep in the room with a strange man. You stressed me out. I didn't want to go with them. You made me. And now you want to lock me up." The last was a shriek that filled the visiting room. A nurse rushed over.

"You're going to have to keep your voice down or your mother will have to leave," she said.

"I want her to leave. Make her go right now," Trina said.

"Trina, I did what I thought was best."

"You're not my mother, bitch."

It's going to take a while; that's what the nurse told me. That's what I kept telling myself as I drove home. My driveway was dark; the automatic lights hadn't come on. When I hit the remote control for the garage door to open, nothing happened. I looked up and down the block. The streetlights were out and all the houses were black.

"Damn!" I said, with more vehemence than was warranted. I got out of the car, took my keys out, and headed for the front door. When I got to the top of the steps, something moved.

"Keri."

I jumped, and then I looked. "Adriana, where have you been?"

"Keri, I need, uh—" She giggled.

It wasn't so dark I couldn't see that she was thinner, that she was trembling, that something was wrong.

"I cashed a check today, and I was on my way to my car and some dude snatched my bag so now I need some money, and I was wondering—"

"Don't come to me with that bullshit," I said, feeling anger replace my fear. "Just don't. You've been using drugs again. That's why you haven't been to work. I can tell by looking at you."

"No. No, Keri. I'm not on any drugs. The reason I didn't come to work was I've been sick. I had the flu. I meant to call, but I was too sick. And then, as soon as I left the house, I got jacked."

She spoke rapidly, moving from foot to foot.

"Get out of here. And don't come back," I said.

"Why are you gonna do me like that?" she said.

"If you want to get back in rehab, I've got your back. If you want to call your sponsor and start going to meetings, I've got your back. But if you're going to be a whore and a junkie, you're on your own. Don't come here, and don't come back to the store until you're ready to get some help."

"I don't need any fucking help from you, bitch."

It was instinctive. One bitch too many. Past my quota. I grabbed Adriana by her shoulder and slammed her into the door. And then I started yelling.

"You come to me, and I give you a job, get your ass in school, try to show you how to have a decent life. And then you fuck up, get back with your lowlife friends who just want to bring you down, and I'm the bitch?"

She was more shocked than hurt, although I couldn't swear that she wouldn't be black-and-blue in the morning. But the shock kept her still, forced her to listen. Listening, of course, didn't mean a damn thing, not with every cell in her body wanting drugs.

"I'm so sick of you goddam kids. If you want to wreck your life, do it."

I unlocked my door and slammed it in her face. The phone was ringing when I got inside, but by the time I answered it the caller had hung up. Maybe it was Clyde, I thought. He'd told me earlier that he'd be going out of town for two weeks. So much for fatherly commitment. It was better to miss the call, better to realize that I was alone, that I had no backup, that Trina was going to be in and out of sanity for the rest of her life and I'd just have to deal with it. Ma Missy had learned that lesson a long time ago. Why couldn't I? Why did I keep holding out for rescues and miracles and perfect endings? The program had tried to disabuse me of that notion. Jean and Eddie, Pete and Cecilia, Margaret—even Celestine, Melody's mother, frying hamburgers for three grandchildren and holding her breath until her daughter made it home at night—they'd all learned acceptance. Things could be worse. Much worse.

I went into the kitchen, got the bottle of Merlot that was in the cabinet above the refrigerator, and poured myself a glass. I was sipping it and my tears had tapered off when the phone rang for the second time. The area code of the number that was revealed was unfamiliar. But the voice wasn't.

"It's okay. Everything is okay. They went back and worked everything out."

"Bethany!"

"Yeah."

As we talked I could feel myself missing her and maybe missing the dream I'd let go of.

"Tell Brad I said that the hype on Harriet Tubman—the "never run my train off de track, and I ain't never lost a passenger" thing—that had to be PR spin. She must have lost *somebody*."

But maybe not forever.

THE CIRCLE OF CHAIRS IN THE BASEMENT OF THE PRESBY-
terian church was tight and close. Summer was traditionally a slow time
for the support group, a season when attendance was sparse. Those who
came regularly, if they were able, took off on vacations designed to
relieve them of the stress of taking care of mentally ill relatives. Of
course, in many cases, those relatives accompanied the caretakers, in
which case the word *vacation* was a misnomer. It would be more accurate to say that those people went on a trip.

Mattie, Gloria, Milton, and I were not on vacation. It was Mattie
who had reminded me of the regularly scheduled meeting. She'd been
calling me for prayer almost every morning since I'd returned. Now she
held my hand as I sat beside her.

Right back where I started from. It seemed almost surreal for me to
be sitting between Mattie and Gloria, to be surrounded by others with
stories ranging from horrendous to unbearable and, of course, the one
or two people whose loved ones could be filed under *Doing pretty well.*
Not *Flourishing at Brown,* not *Taking the world by storm.* Just *Doing
pretty well.* Regular. Ordinary, as in "The kid no longer breaks windows." As in "She takes a couple of classes at community college and

volunteers at church." The happy endings were when the Social Security disability checks came through before all the money ran out, when Medicare or Medi-Cal finally cranked up, when there was a vacancy at a decent residential treatment facility, when the shrink or the therapist knew what the hell she was talking about. When the kid took the medication on her own, without being prompted, because she knew she needed it. Listening in the tight little circle, I realized there were many people who were holding steady on the seesaw of mental illness. The *pretty well* stories had been attenuated in my mind because I'd been looking for another ending.

I am not alone, I thought, looking around the circle. Not everyone here is sad.

"Your turn," Mattie whispered, and nudged me.

I felt suddenly tongue-tied and foolish. Milton gave me a nod and a smile. "I've been going . . . my daughter and I have been going through a tough time recently. If you recall, she has been diagnosed with bipolar disorder. Up until a few months ago, she was taking her medication regularly and was talking about going to college in the fall. She was— uh, she was accepted at Brown. But then I think someone gave her a joint, which led to her smoking some more joints, and the next thing I knew—"

"You were starting all over again," one woman said.

I nodded. "You got it. She got very hostile. I'll spare you the details. So now she's in the hospital and I'm waiting for a conservatorship trial, which should be coming up in the next few weeks."

"Try not to go on a Thursday. Judge Boch is there on Thursdays, and he's a horrible man," another woman said.

Several others volunteered bits of information about their own trial experiences. Don't be late. Don't expect too much; just because you have a conservatorship doesn't mean everything will get better.

"I feel as though my whole life is crashing. My kid is in the hospital again. My ex-husband, who promised to support me through this, took off for two weeks on some work-related assignment. My trusted and beloved assistant is on drugs after being clean for a long while, so on top of everything else I'm short-staffed at my store. Oh, and my boyfriend is pulling away. Plus I haven't a clue as to which of the institutes for mental diseases I should place my daughter in."

"Not Havenbrook," someone volunteered.

"Is that the place out in Pasadena?" I asked.

"Yes. My son was placed there, and his experience was terrible. Lots of fights. Lots of homeless people. He went there smoking a couple of cigarettes a day; he left smoking a pack and a half."

"My nephew was there. It helped him a lot. He got stable there."

"What about the Light House?" I asked.

Another woman shrugged her shoulders. "I don't know about that one."

"My brother was there for about three years," said a man. "It wasn't a bad place. They took good care of them physically; they got their checkups, went to the dentist regularly. Their best doctor is Dr. Felix. How long would your daughter need to stay there?"

"I'm hoping no more than three months."

"Give her condoms," another woman said. "They can't stop them from having sex in there. And not everybody is healthy, if you know what I mean."

"Maybe you don't need to place her in a locked facility. There are plenty of really good unlocked ones, and they're so much better."

"She'd go AWOL in a hot minute," I said.

"Some of them are pretty far out. There's one in Azusa, up in the mountains."

"Forget it. The waiting list is around the corner."

People called out other facilities where their loved ones had received good care. I took notes. After support group, people crowded around me, squeezing my hand, giving me more information and encouragement. Someone in the group asked me about my insurance coverage, if it was adequate. "It's good insurance," I said.

But not quite good enough, I learned when a hospital administrator called several days later. My insurance paid for only thirty days of mental health or drug and alcohol abuse care per calendar year. When all the hospitalizations were tallied, Trina was closing in on the twenty-five-day mark. "Mrs. Whitmore, we are going to need to release your daughter," a sincere young woman told me.

Release her to where? was my question. They told me that because of the temporary conservatorship, she could be placed in any IMD that would take her. The caveat was that I'd have to pay for it. The county wouldn't pick up the tab until after the judge gave me complete conservatorship. The IMDs, flawed as they were, cost nearly $5,000 per month. My other alternative was to bring her home.

"The hospital has to keep her," Herbert Swanson's assistant told me. "They try to dump patients all the time." There was disgust in his tone.

The hospital social worker didn't agree. She restated their position: Trina would have to leave when her thirty days were used up. "You might want to think about taking her out today. She has only five more days left. If you use all those days and wind up not getting conservatorship, what will you do if she has to be hospitalized again?"

How about I bring her to your house?

I asked Mr. Swanson to call the hospital. Whatever he said worked. Trina was allowed to stay.

Then things began to fall into place. The shift in luck, the appearance of hope on the horizon, took me by surprise. Clyde returned, three days later than he said he would and feeling guilty enough to make a bargain. He agreed that Trina could go to the Light House for ninety days. The next day Trina received a court date.

I'd been visiting Trina twice a day in Clyde's absence. Since her last outburst, she'd been more subdued. She didn't talk with me much, but she didn't ask me to leave either. Sometimes we'd watch television together or read magazines side by side. Several times entire visits passed in total silence. But she always let me rub her. My fingers on her skin was our way of communicating.

"You'll be going to court in two days," I told her when I visited her that afternoon.

"Why?"

"I'm trying to become your conservator." It was the first time I'd broached the subject, and I could tell she was confused. I quickly explained that I was seeking the right to be able to force medical treatment on her.

"But I'm in a hospital now," she said. "Why can't I come home after that?"

"Trina, we tried that before. You stopped taking your medication and got sick again."

"But I wouldn't do that this time. I swear," she added.

I didn't say anything.

"I'm calm now. I won't run away again."

"Oh, Trina."

"I wouldn't. My thoughts aren't jumbled the way they were then. I can think clearly now. I just want to come home."

"I have to work; Frances is by herself, and I don't want to leave you alone."

"Where's Adriana?"

"She left."

"Why?"

"Adriana had some problems, Trina."

"Drugs."

I nodded.

"Did you fire her?"

"I told her she couldn't work for me until she got clean and sober again."

She was silent for a while. "I'll get better," she said.

Mental Health Court was way off my beaten path. Located near Cal State LA in a depressed industrial area, it was an hour away from Crenshaw in traffic. There was plenty of that. Cars were backed up on the 10E as Clyde and I made our way to the court. A hospital official would be bringing Trina. After we left the interstate, it took only five minutes before we were parking in the lot behind a square two-story building. The building overlooked an outdoor courtyard. There smokers congregated, puffing away the recesses as judges decided their fates. Inside, the waiting room was packed with LA's stepped-over. From time to time, people would drift off to courtroom 95A or 95B, where their fates might be handed over to relatives or the state. There was no talk of greenlighting or taking a meeting with the producers within the walls of Mental Health Court. Here the stories were mostly sad and unfilmable, with a tendency toward running way too long.

We saw Trina enter with a tall, heavyset man who took her arm, the escort from the hospital. Her hair was combed in a ponytail. She was wearing black pants and a white blouse, which, over the course of her stay at the hospital, had become too tight. Her lips were bright red, and her cheeks appeared rouged. When she saw Clyde and me, she turned her head. Clyde went over to her, but she wouldn't talk even to him. Later, I saw her go off with her court-appointed attorney, a good-looking, well-dressed Latino. How good was he? What was he saying to her?

We waited for about an hour before our names were called. When we finally went into the court, the judge had just granted conservatorship of an elderly man in the throes of Alzheimer's to his daughter.

When our case was announced, I could feel myself getting tense. Dr. Bellows, Trina's psychiatrist, underwent about fifteen minutes of testimony. I had agreed to pay him for his time, including travel to and from the court: $450. But he was organized and eloquent, and his testimony about both the extent and the history of Trina's illness lent a lot of weight to our petition. Clyde, of course, didn't know who he was until I told him.

After Dr. Bellows spoke, the judge addressed his questions to Trina. "Trina, do you know why you're here?" the judge asked.

"Yes."

"And why is that?"

"My mother wants to send me away."

"Trina, I think your parents feel that you need help. Do you know why?"

"I'm not crazy."

"No one said you were."

"Sometimes, things start speeding up in my mind, and then everything starts racing. I can't slow down, and sometimes I do bad things."

"Trina, would you be willing to let your parents take care of you and make decisions on your behalf?"

"I don't want to go away. My mother already took me away. She put me in this car with Brad and Bethany and Angelica, and they drove Angelica and me far away. I didn't want to go, and she made me. I'm eighteen. I'm an adult, but she made me."

Every muscle in my body froze. I couldn't feel my fingers. All I could do was stare at Judge Neulander, who was leaning forward, looking from Trina to me.

"They were going to lock us up," Trina said.

I stopped breathing.

The judge stared at me for what seemed like a year. He cleared his throat and then settled back in his seat. "Would you be willing to trust your parents with your welfare?"

She looked at Clyde and me for a long time. "I don't want to go away."

Judge Neulander leaned forward again. "Trina, I think you need help, dear. Your parents want to help you, and I'm going to let them. Conservatorship granted."

Clyde and I drove to a restaurant not far from the court. He seemed drained as he sat across from me. His face was haggard. I'd noticed his expression when Dr. Bellows was speaking. He looked as though he were watching a car crash. "You've really taken care of things," he said. "You were always good at taking care of everything. I'm sorry I left you hanging."

"I don't think you can help it."

He looked at me. "Yeah, you're right. I'm selfish, always have been. Smart, selfish, greedy. Always wanted a lot. Always wanted more, more, more. You put up with a lot."

"She's my child."

"I meant with me. Why the hell did I ever let you go?" Clyde said.

It was like kissing, the way he held my glance. The funny thing was, I could remember how Clyde kissed and how much I used to like it. When his eyes stayed on me, I remembered the rest, everything I'd been thinking about for years. I hadn't forgotten. I'd always wondered what it would be like to be with Clyde again. I'd always wondered, but I realized that I never really wanted to know. I looked away first, and the taste of him grew fainter. Maybe I could forgive him for steering his life away from mine, for reaching toward a sun that burned my spirit, for leaving me while I still loved him. "You let me go because you couldn't live with my grief."

He stared at me and didn't say anything. I felt myself smiling.

"I need you to pay for everything, Clyde, all the stuff not covered by the county and the insurance."

"All right."

THAT NIGHT I THOUGHT OF KISSES, THE ONES THAT lingered.

The phone rang just as I got into bed. The voice on the other end was raspy and thin. "I'm not going to disappear, Keri," my mother said. "I'm just going to keep calling."

"What do you want?"

"Is something wrong with Trina?"

"There was something wrong with me, Emma. My whole childhood was wrong."

"I was sick then. I'm in recovery now. If something is wrong, I'd like to help."

I sighed. "You can't help, Emma."

"Let me try. Please, tell me what's wrong."

I'll never know why I told her, only that once the words started coming they wouldn't stop.

After I finished speaking with my mother, I called Orlando. He answered on the first ring. I could tell he hadn't been sleeping. "I'd like you to come over," I said.

He handed me a bag of French fries as he walked through my door. The bag said Jerry's Deli. I got him a soda, and we sat in the kitchen. The fries were hot and crispy, with just enough salt. I put them into one bowl, as though they were chips. Our fingers touched as we reached for them. When the bowl was empty, Orlando leaned back in his chair. "I needed some space," he said.

"Why?"

"Because I had just found out that my son is gay, and I needed to sit with that by myself." His lip trembled, and he wiped his eyes. "I know what you're going to say: He's still PJ. I know that. But—"

"It wasn't what you were expecting."

We didn't say anything for a long while.

"You know, I was trying to give you some space too," Orlando said.

"Why?"

"Because I thought you needed it." He paused. "I saw the way Clyde was looking at you in Sacramento."

"What way was that?"

"The way a man looks at a woman when he realizes he made a mistake in letting her go."

"He did make a mistake."

"Did you?"

"Maybe. But that was a long time ago, Orlando. Clyde can't give me what I need now."

"What do you need?"

Somebody strong. Somebody who will be there. Somebody who'll stay. I couldn't say anything aloud. I was trembling too hard.

"Not some guy who's chasing the next sitcom, huh?"

Somebody who'll stay. Stay. Stay.

"Let me decide when the party's over. Don't try to fix my life. Fix yours."

So then we got quiet again. After a while we started talking about PJ and Jibari and Trina. We laughed about them, about nothing at all. Orlando said he was thinking about selling real estate. I told him I was getting back into massage. Then, without even taking a breath, he said he was up for an audition for a pilot. "With the producers," he said. I congratulated him, as I always do. And then I told him about talking with my mother and how strange that felt. He looked at me and smiled. Later we ran in the dark, with the wind on our faces. And we kept pace with each other.

32

THE HOSPITAL TRANSPORTED TRINA TO THE LIGHT HOUSE by ambulance. Clyde and I were waiting for her when she arrived. We had come early to fill out the paperwork that one of the admissions administrators gave us. We walked alongside the assistant who escorted Trina to her room, which was clean but cramped, with two single beds, two dressers, and two nightstands in a space as large as a prison cell. At least there was an adjoining bathroom, as opposed to one on the hall.

Trina's roommate, a Latina in her fifties or sixties, was lying in one of the beds. It was nearly three in the afternoon, and she was still in her pajamas. She opened her eyes and looked at us but didn't say anything. After a little while she turned to face the wall.

"I don't want to stay here," Trina whispered. "Please, please, please don't leave me here. I'll die in here." She grabbed Clyde's hand. "Daddy, why can't I stay with you?"

"Trina," I said, "you have to stay here for a while. You can come home once you get stable."

She began crying, encircling Clyde's waist with her arms. "Please don't leave me here. I don't belong here. I don't."

"You're going to be fine, Trina," the assistant said. He was a black man with an accent and a weary face.

Trina glared at him. He turned to us. "Maybe you folks might want to leave now. You can come visit tomorrow. She'll be fine."

What did *fine* mean? Did it mean she wouldn't scream in the hallway, try to scale the wall, or attempt to slit her wrist with a pilfered butter knife? Was *fine* just low-level survival at an institution forever, or did it mean eventual reentry into the world?

I was crying by the time I reached the car. Clyde's face was stoic. We didn't speak for the entire ride. When he dropped me off at the store, he drove off quickly.

My mother called that night. She had started calling me almost every day, usually around seven in the evening, LA time. We both tried not to bring up the past, but sometimes Emma would say something that would trigger a memory of her maternal betrayal and my pain, and I would lash out and then hang up on her. But tonight she'd called to find out about Trina.

"How did it go?" she asked.

I told her.

"You're doing the right thing. Sometimes you have to be hard. Trina needs for you to be hard right now."

"I don't know."

"Yes, you do know. This place will help her. It will give her structure, teach her to take the medication. The rest is up to her."

"I never thought her life would—"

"Things happen in life. You have to keep going. How is the other one doing? Your saleslady."

"Adriana? I haven't heard from her. I'm sure she's back on drugs."

"It sounds like it, from what you told me."

"How could she be clean for three years and then go back on drugs? I just don't get it."

"It's a struggle. Every day. You can't imagine it because you're not an addict, thank God. She might get clean again."

"Well, I hope so. Such a sweet girl."

"Meanwhile, you're shorthanded."

"I'm going to hire someone as soon as I have time to interview."

"Why not me?"

She spoke quietly, almost as though she were thinking aloud.

"No," I said, and got off the phone in a hurry.

But she asked me again. Every night when she called, she'd ask me if she could work for me. She wanted to help me, she said, to try to make up for all the bad times.

"Where would you stay?" I asked her one night after Trina had been at the Light House for nearly two months.

She didn't respond.

"She probably thought I'd invite her to live with me," I told Orlando later that night. We'd just finished eating. Since Trina had been institutionalized, we ate together every night. He'd practically moved in.

"Why wouldn't you?" he asked.

"I don't want her here," I said.

"Hold on, baby. Your mother can help you in the store, and she can help you with Trina."

"She just wants to stay here because she thinks I won't charge her anything. She's on a fixed income."

Orlando shrugged. "You can figure out the money later. You need her."

"No, I don't."

"Keri . . ."

"I thought you were going to be here."

"I'm here already, baby."

"You wouldn't mind if my mother stayed with us? Temporarily, I mean."

"If it doesn't work out, she can go back home."

I mulled over his words, then pushed them away.

Emma kept calling and asking if she could come. After a while I stopped saying no. But I couldn't say yes. Maybe she knew that.

One Saturday in November, two weeks before Trina was scheduled to leave the Light House, the door of As Good as New opened. It was early afternoon, and the shop was crowded. Frances and I were both with customers, and several women were waiting to be helped. I heard her before I saw her. "That's very nice; you look good in that. You need something to go with it." The voice could have belonged to anyone, somebody's girlfriend. But I excused myself and walked toward the voice. And there was Emma.

"Hi," she said.

"Hi." I was too shocked to be angry.

She moved toward me. I backed up and then stopped. "I took a chance," she said. She didn't have any bags with her. "I'm at a motel."

I nodded.

A woman was standing near her, peering at herself in an adjacent mirror. "Don't those pants fit perfectly!" Emma said. "She needs a top and a jacket, so she'll have an outfit."

"Over there," I said, pointing to some racks behind us.

"I'll be right back, honey," Emma told the woman. I watched her for a moment, collecting items.

"Keri."

"Oh, my God!" I said. I stopped and looked at the woman in front of me. Her face was just slightly fuller, and her hair was at least an inch long all over her scalp. "Rona! You look great!"

She smiled. "I'm getting well.

"Did you go to the reunion?"

"No. Next year, I'll go."

I took her hand and squeezed it, ran my fingers across her palm. There was strength in that resilient hand. "I'll go with you," I said.

I went back to my customer, but from time to time I glanced over at Rona and my mother. They were smiling, then laughing. At the register, Rona said she was buying more than she had planned.

Later, when there was a lull, I introduced Frances to Emma. "This is my—this is . . ."

Frances grabbed her in a big hug. "You don't have to tell me who this is. You look just like her."

"She's going to be working with us," I said.

My mother's eyes met mine. We'd escaped from a terrible land, thrown off our shackles, and crossed borders. What we acknowledged to each other in that swift, silent glance was that from now on it was all about and only about time—maddening, exhilarating time—passing, doing its job, setting us free.

33

"Don't be nervous, Mommy," Trina told me, right be-fore the play began. Outside, a February rain was soaking the ground. It was the kind of rain I liked, just hard enough to hear. It reminded me of Georgia.

We were standing behind the "stage" in the basement of Crenshaw Baptist Church, located two blocks away from the biggest liquor store in the city and only minutes from the highest-quality incense on the planet. The church had been home to the newest branch of the support group for about five months. The founders, Mattie, Gloria, and Milton, had enlisted me as an able-bodied volunteer as soon as Trina was placed in the Light House. Now the basement was filled with newly liberated black folks, free to seek help for and own up to loving people who had brain diseases.

The curtains were drawn. Standing behind them, we could hear the din the small audience was making, smell the commingled colognes in the air. There was a hubbub backstage as well, as performers old and young walked around, practicing their parts. There were other parents alongside me, some trying to soothe and calm down the adult children who were about to perform, others needing comfort themselves.

"Go sit outside," Trina said, effectively banishing me.

I gave her hair a pat.

Trina ducked her head. "Mommee!"

Fourteen again.

"Okay. Good-bye. Break a leg!"

"Go!"

The support group for "consumers," those suffering with bipolar disorder, schizophrenia, depression, or schizoaffective disorder, met on the first Friday of the month in the choir room. Unlike the group for family members, the one for consumers was "activities-based." Their meetings might consist of talking and sharing, but more often than not they involved going to a movie or to the mall. It was billed as a "life-skills enhancing" group. Writing and performing plays was one of their activities.

Trina had been practicing, that I knew. For weeks I'd pass her room and see her sitting in the middle of her bed, poring over the script, saying her lines with so much expression and intensity that I was alarmed, fearful that she was talking to people who weren't there, which, of course, she was. Only now it was a good thing. Another good thing.

THE FIRST FEW WEEKS AFTER SHE LEFT THE LIGHT HOUSE, being at home with Trina had been difficult, and I was glad Clyde was around. The institution had contained her; it hadn't, of course, cured her. Although the doctor at the facility had said she was quiet, when Trina returned home she began ranting at the least provocation. Sleeping through the night was a problem. But gradually her outbursts began to diminish. Mattie told me about a new psychiatrist, and I took Trina to see him. He stopped her old medications and introduced two new ones, slowly titrating the dosage until it reached optimal therapeutic level. By the six-week mark, she was sleeping through the night, she'd lost ten pounds, and her mood had improved. The longer she was on the new medication, the more compliant she became.

Trina was housebound in the beginning. But as the new meds kicked in, we began to go on brief outings. I took her to the grocery store and to get her hair done. We went shopping. Sometimes I brought her to the store and let her wait on customers for an hour or so.

Emma moved in with Orlando and me a few weeks after she

arrived. Sometimes, when I woke up, she'd be in the kitchen. I'd smell coffee and food. When Orlando and I went downstairs, everything would be ready: eggs, toast, grits, bacon, and juice. PJ had begun spending a lot of time with us. Sometimes I'd listen as Emma and PJ chatted. Both his grandmothers were dead. He was fascinated by this grandma-come-lately who'd suddenly taken root in his life.

By the time we brought Trina home, the gym had been transformed into a bedroom for PJ and Emma was ensconced in what had once been my office.

"Does everybody live here now?" Trina asked.

She was smiling.

"Yes," I said.

I didn't know how long Trina's smile would last. We were all embarking upon a grand experiment. Trina and Orlando had always gotten along, except when she was manic. She adored PJ but had never shared a house with him. As for Emma, she was completely unknown. All of us were in the midst of a major adjustment. We snapped at one another, fussed, stopped speaking, and said "I'm sorry" a lot. We laughed often and tried to be kind.

Once, when I was upstairs, I heard my mother talking with Trina. "How are you getting on?" she asked.

"I'm doing better, Grandma," Trina said.

"Sometimes it takes a while to get better. I was sick for a long time. Did your mother ever tell you that?"

"No."

"I'm an alcoholic, Trina. When I go out in the evenings, I'm going to my AA meetings. They keep me from drinking."

"I go to meetings too."

"I know."

"What do you do at your meetings?"

"Talk, mostly."

"Mine too. But you don't take medicine."

"Not for being an alcoholic. I take high-blood-pressure medicine. If I don't, I'll get sick."

"If I don't take my medication *I'll* get sick. There's something wrong with my brain."

Emma laughed. "Mine too."

· · ·

BETHANY WAS BACK IN TOWN TWO WEEKS AFTER I LEFT THE program, before my house was filled with people. My doorbell rang and there she was, blowing out the last bit of smoke from a cigarette she was stepping on. When I saw her standing at my door, it was like finding a war buddy, one you'd left behind in the trenches and never expected to see again. She handed me a bean pie.

"Let's party," she said.

We sat in my kitchen, eating pie and drinking wine and talking about our girls. Angelica was at the site and making slow progress, trying to learn how not to crave meth and pain and to be responsible for taking her medication. Trina, I told her, was coming along. She was still at the hospital then, and I was awaiting the court date.

"You're smiling," Bethany said.

"I feel happy. Our girls are alive. We're not in jail. We've got bean pie and wine. I'm not scared anymore. I feel strong."

"I feel fucking great," Bethany said.

THE NIGHT OF THE PLAY, I WORE THE GREEN PANTSUIT, THE one we couldn't sell. A silk flower covered the stain. Below it my heart beat fast. Orlando was sitting next to me and PJ was next to him. Bethany was on my other side. Frances and her new boyfriend, Mattie and Roger, and Gloria and Milton were seated in the same row. Marie, my patient and forgiving old friend, sat behind me. Emma was next to Bethany. Clyde, of course, was out of town. He'd sent flowers, enough to fill five vases. Orlando squeezed my hand.

Bethany leaned over toward me, just as the lights went down and the pianist began to play. She looked good. Her hair was loose, freshly cut and colored. It touched my face. "Honey," she whispered, "this is what they call a breather."

Long ago I sat on the top step with Ma Missy, watching my mother pass out on the living room floor from too much scotch. It was a bad time. Ma Missy held me close as I wriggled and writhed. She rocked me and hummed something that made me still, made me smile. Our song.

Maybe, after the devastation, what you're supposed to do is rebuild the space in your mind that's been blown away, but never fool yourself into thinking that it's stronger, that you've erected some impenetrable fortress that won't be hit again and again and again. Things fall down, people too. Crazy men wander the land, crashing and crumbling, and nobody gets a warning. There is always another swamp to cross. Passengers are both lost and found. Ol' Harriet learned that the hard way, the first time she retraced her path, erased her scent, outwitted the dogs, and followed the only star that lit the way, only to discover that when she got where she was going, new hounds were waiting. But there was that cool space on the bank of the murky water where she lay on fragrant moss, undisturbed for hours, and there was no barking, no sound of twigs snapping. A breather.

ACKNOWLEDGMENTS

I'd like to thank my editor, Phyllis Grann, for continuing to be my champion and for having faith in this project. You are the best in the industry, and I value your wisdom and guidance. As always, thank you, Lynn Nesbitt, for your expert handling of the business part of writing. To the members of my four-generational household: Mom, Ellis, Maia, and Elisha, your background noise helped to create the rhythm of this book. Ellis, you especially contribute such beautiful music to my life. Don't ever stop. And for all the faithful ones, courageous enough to believe that hard times can make way for good outcomes and even happy endings, may God bless you.

Bebe Moore Campbell is the author of three *New York Times* best sellers, *Brothers and Sisters, Singing in the Comeback Choir,* and *What You Owe Me,* a *Los Angeles Times* Book of the Year. Her novel *Your Blues Ain't Like Mine* won an NAACP Image Award. She is the author of several children's books, including *Sometimes My Mommy Gets Angry,* and has written a play, *Even with the Madness.* Her writing has appeared in *Essence, The New York Times Magazine,* and other publications, and her commentaries have been heard on National Public Radio. Ms. Campbell lives in Los Angeles with her husband, Ellis Gordon, Jr., and their family.

A NOTE ON THE TYPE

This book was set in Electra, a typeface designed by William Addison Dwiggins (1880-1956) for the Mergenthaler Linotype Company and first made available in 1935. Electra cannot be classified as either "modern" or "old style." It is not based on any historical model and hence does not echo any particular period or style of type design. It avoids the extreme contrast between thick and thin elements that marks most modern faces, and it is without eccentricities that catch the eye and interfere with reading. In general, Electra is a simple, readable typeface that attempts to give a feeling of fluidity, power, and speed.

Composed by Creative Graphics,
Allentown, Pennsylvania
Printed and bound by Berryville Graphics,
Berryville, Virginia
Designed by Virginia Tan